# War in the Void

■

"Steady..." Brim started to answer, but he was interrupted by a tremendous explosion outside as the old battleship fired off a ranging salvo at them. It missed, but the energy concussion nearly knocked *Defiant* on her beam ends. Loose equipment and debris cascaded along the deck again while startled crew members stifled screams on the voice circuits. Grinding his teeth, Brim steered closer to the transport. It would be hard for the battleship to fire without risking damage to its own ship. "How're you doing, Chief?" he asked.

"We're awfully close, Lieutenant," Barbousse answered through clenched teeth. "I can't miss at this distance, but you'll have to get out of here fast when I let 'em go, or we'll get caught in our own blast."

"I'm ready," Brim said tightly, "let 'em go."

"Aye, sir," Barbousse said; presently four torpedoes streaked past the starboard Hyperscreens, hurtling toward the transport from point-blank range.

"Nik!" Brim bellowed, "lemme have full EVERYTHING!"

GALACTIC CONVOY

Also by Bill Baldwin

*The Helmsman*

Published by
POPULAR LIBRARY

# GALACTIC CONVOY

## BY BILL BALDWIN

**POPULAR LIBRARY**

An Imprint of Warner Books, Inc.

A Warner Communications Company

POPULAR LIBRARY EDITION

Copyright © 1987 by Merl Baldwin
All rights reserved.

Popular Library®, the fanciful P design, and Questar® are
registered trademarks of Warner Books, Inc.

Cover illustration by John Berkey

Popular Library books are published by
Warner Books, Inc.
666 Fifth Avenue
New York, N.Y. 10103

W A Warner Communications Company

Printed in the United States of America

First Printing: December, 1987

10  9  8  7  6  5  4  3  2  1

# Chapter 1

# ELEANDOR-BESTIENNE

Wilf Brim pointed into the shimmering globular display and glared across the drafting console, angry now in spite of himself. "If Nik Ursis says a waveguide installed like that could short the Vertical Generators," he insisted to a determinedly unpliant Senior Engineer, "then a xaxtdamned waveguide installed like that could short the Vertical Generators. *Nobody* understands antigravity like Sodeskayan Bears, and you bloody well know it!"

"Bears or no Bears, I was not placed in my position of trust and authority to question Admiralty plans, Lieutenant," the engineer sniffed haughtily. He was a tall, aristocratic man whose expression was the perfect physical manifestation of bureaucratic arrogance, though his features themselves were indifferent to the point of banality. "I build starships strictly to specification," he said, "and I greatly resent the interruption of my busy day with complaints from flight crews. You may be certain your superiors will hear of this insubordination. Imagine, summoning a senior engineer—with wild tales of design flaws. Certainly you do not believe we meet production quotas by challenging Admiralty design teams, do you?"

"Voot's beard!" Brim exclaimed. "This has nothing to do with a challenge." He pointed to a drafting console. "Look for yourself—your design diagrams are just plain *wrong!* A hit anywhere near the KA'PPA tower could cripple *both* Vertical Gravity Generators—trip 'em out completely. And Verticals are the only things *I* know about that keep starships from falling out of the sky, at least when they're anywhere near something that's got gravity—like for instance the planet we're standing on."

Beside him, Ursis, a Great Sodeskayan Bear, frowned, shifted his peaked officer's cap between furry russet ears, and thrummed six tapered fingers on the console—clearly struggling with his own temper. Presently, he smiled, diamond fang stones gleaming in the bright lights of the quiet drafting room. "I thank you for your support, friend Wilf," he said in deep, carefully measured words, "but we have reasoned fruitlessly for more than twenty cycles, and I for one possess sufficient of this nonsense." With that, he gripped the massive drafting console and ripped it from its mountings in a cloud of sparks and acrid smoke. "Perhaps *now,* my good man," he said, turning to the startled engineer, "you will have an easier time shifting your mind from symbolic diagrams to reality, eh? In spite of what you might think, starships have no lifting devices such as wings, or the like—only Vertical Gravity Generators keep them up. They are of *critical* importance, yet these could be disabled by as little as a chance lightning strike on the KA'PPA tower." Before the civilian could recover, Ursis lifted him by his ornately embroidered lapels to a position no more than a milli-iral from his huge, wet nose. "When I replace you on your feet, Mr. Senior Engineer," he growled ominously, "you will locate a workable drafting display and carefully study what Lieutenant Brim and I have attempted to explain this afternoon. Do you understand?"

The man's face drained of color. "B-but the p-plans s-show..." he stammered, pointing to the darkened drafting console as if it were still a functioning instrument. All the bluster had suddenly gone from his voice.

"*Defiant* is the first warship of her class," Ursis stated firmly. "The imaginary machine pictured by your precious plans has never so much as lifted from the image of a globular display, much less cast off for deep space. There are *bound* to be errors. That is what you engineers are *for*—to catch mistakes before they hurt someone...." His laugh returned again, this time with a little of his normal humor. "It wouldn't be so good if one of your creations lost its Verticals and fell out of the sky, now would it? Someone could be hurt!"

The man only stared into the huge Bear's eyes, mesmerized.

"Well, civilian engineer?"

"N-no. . . ."

"No, what?"

"N-no . . . ah, I, ah, w-wouldn't want a starship t-to f-fall out of the sky. . . ."

"And what will you do to ensure this does not happen?"

"F-fix it—t-the waveguide so the Verticals are b-better insulated from energy strikes. . . ."

"Excellent," the Bear exclaimed, gently placing the engineer on his feet. "Your cooperation is most gratifying, civilian. I shall mention it favorably to my superiors. But," he added, "your equipment here is poor. Behold, Wilf, this very drafting display is not functional."

Brim could only nod as he fought the gale of laughter that threatened to overwhelm his control. "I'd noticed that," he choked.

"You should endeavor to find a workable instrument," Ursis advised the man seriously. *"Immediately.* Otherwise, by the time you order this waveguide to be reversed, it will be a difficult operation—every metacycle that passes sees new equipment installed in *Defiant's* already crowded machinery spaces. Eh?"

"Of *c-course*, Lieutenant," the engineer whispered as if he were badly out of breath. Suddenly, he turned and ran madly along the consoles until he disappeared through a door at the end of the room.

Ursis pursed his lips and frowned. "I only hope he really will *do* something about that waveguide," he said, "instead of just covering the mistake with a minor insulating job. Once the hull is buttoned up, there will be no way I can check." Then he smiled wryly and shook his head. "Groaning trees and growling wolves are all the same in a spring snowstorm, eh?"

"Huh?" Brim responded, looking up from the wreckage of the drafting table.

"An old saying from the Mother Planets," the Bear answered with a grimace, "and—it seems that I shall *never* learn to hold my temper," he observed. "Now we are probably *both* in trouble."

Brim shrugged. "A little, maybe. But it's at least possible now that something may be done to protect the Verticals. If we'd kept our mouths shut, nobody would even had looked. Besides," he chuckled as they boarded an elevator for the observation balcony, "I've dealt with bullies all my life. Once you scrape away their rank, as you did so well, they're all the same sort of cowards." He winked. "Now, if you want to talk about *real* trouble, imagine us fighting a dead ship after something like a lightning strike tripped the Verticals at low altitude—maybe during a landing. *Universe....*"

Nergol Triannic's all-consuming galactic conflict seemed terribly remote that day among the ancient starship yards of Eleandor-Bestienne. Outside a lofty Engineering Tower in the Orange-Eight district, cobalt skies and soft puffs of summer clouds ruled the late afternoon over Construction Complex 81-B. On an open balcony, a warm breeze rustled the blue Fleet Cape at Brim's neck and raised whitecaps out on Elsene Bay. It carried with it the clean fragrance of green vegetation —tempered by frequent whiffets of hot metal and fused logics from the frantic wartime construction below.

The object of Brim's attention—emerging from the waterfront clutter of bowing, swinging shipyard cranes—was the flattened teardrop shape of a half-finished starship hull that rested on a tangle of rusting construction stocks: I.F.S. *Defiant*, Imperial hull designator CL.921, and the first ship in a whole new class of light cruisers. As such, she was new in *many* ways—and subject to all the ills of each. The morning's waveguide incident was only one—albeit the most serious— of a hundred-odd irregularities and disorders uncovered since the starship's keel was laid. In spite of her great promise for the future, *Defiant* was starting life as a most troublesome ship....

While Brim mused, he overheard the voice of Lieutenant Xerxes O. Flynn joking with Ursis. Flynn was *Defiant*'s medical officer—the position he had previously filled aboard I.F.S. *Truculent*. He was short, fair, and balding, with a reddish face and a quick smile. "I say, Nikolai Yanuarievich," he said, "do you suppose yonder Principal Helmsman has become impatient to fly already? He shows up this time every day to watch them build our ship."

"Well, Doctor," observed the Bear, "either impatience guides his actions—or a well-known compulsion to single-handedly confound the League of Dark Stars. As we say on the Mother Planets, 'When the mountain dances with ice maidens, cold wind comes quietly at the hearth.'" He grinned suddenly. "One imagines anything is possible of persons who spend most waking hours flying a simulator—even Helmsmen."

Brim turned to grin at his old shipmates, fellow survivors of Regula Collingswood's battle-shattered destroyer I.F.S. *Truculent*. "You're both right," he asserted, "I *do* spend most of my time flying 'The Box.' But I am clearly not the only one impatient to get back into space—or the war. In fact, I personally know a certain Great Sodeskayan Bear who spends most of *his* time checking starship plans—and I'm sure he has the same thing in mind. Besides, it's rarely lonesome here on the balcony, as you both well know." He chuckled. "I understand people are starting to call it 'Point Defiant.'"

"Actually," Flynn admitted, "I might just prefer a battle zone if I had my choice—some place where I could occasionally contribute to the war effort by treating disorders more serious than meem hangovers." He shook his head. "That one task seems to occupy most of my duty time while we wait for those bloody civilians to build our ship."

Ursis laughed as he charged the bowl of his Zempa pipe with Hogge'poa. "You must never underestimate your contribution here, my dear Doctor," he asserted, tamping the weed with a professional countenance. "Hangovers are important on shipyard worlds like Eleandor-Bestienne. Especially since meem—and the drinking thereof—remains the principal diversion." He nodded sagely while he puffed a glow into the bowl of his pipe. "You will soon enough be up to your elbows in battle blood again."

Flynn nodded. "That's why I drink meem," he said wrinkling his nose as a cloud of smoke momentarily enveloped his face. "And they're my own hangovers, by the way."

While the two continued their salty banter in the lengthening shadows, Brim returned his attention to the stocks. For the thousandth time, he traced *Defiant*'s convexed upper deck as it gently arced from a pointed bow and peaked a regulation thirty irals from four Drive outlets in her ponderously rounded stern. Dramatically larger than old *Truculent*, her very size seemed to symbolize—dauntingly—the new responsibility Brim was about to shoulder as her Principal Helmsman. Abaft the forward mooring cupola, work gangs were energetically fishing heavy-gauge cable of some sort between two circular access hatches. Farther back, a pair of surveyors appeared to be checking the hull's loft lines against a fat book of blueprints. The ship's ebony hullmetal was everywhere marred by the bright blue of welding, and her upper decks were littered with cuttings, fastener cartridges, cables, and general sweepings. Apparently a great deal of the morning's construction effort had been expended preparing for installation of the two ventral turret assemblies. With the acrid smell of Hogge'poa burning his nostrils, Brim watched a heavy mounting ring glide slowly beneath the starboard beam, towed by one of the ubiquitous yellow shipyard locomotives. The two dorsal twin-mounts had been in place abaft the bridge for a week now; they required only installation of their long-barreled 152-mmi disruptors. The final turret, however, a single-mount 152 that would complete the ship's primary armament, was still marked by little more than a circular opening in the hullmetal directly forward of the skeletal bridge.

Presently, a fourth voice joined the others on the balcony. Elegant and polished, it belonged unmistakably to Commander Regula Collingswood, *Defiant*'s Captain and commanding officer. She was a statuesque woman, tall and well-shaped with a long, patrician nose, piercing hazel eyes, and soft chestnut hair that she wore in natural curls beneath her peaked uniform hat. An extraordinary commander of military warships, her appearance never for a moment let anyone forget she was also a woman, every milli-iral of her! She was known throughout Kabul Anak's fleets as a very dangerous adversary, and had lived with a price on her head for years. She seemed to enjoy the distinction. Brim saluted with the others.

"I rather expected I might find the three of you here," she

pronounced with a fatigued smile. "I too need tangible evidence that someday we shall find ourselves back in space. Especially since I presently spend most of my life staring at desiccated verbiage in a display." She grimaced at the portfolio under her arm. "*And* making peace with angry shipyard bosses," she added hotly, scowling first at Brim and then at Ursis. "What in the name of the Universe did you do to that poor engineer? His manager found him reduced to tears at a drafting display and mumbling nonsense about lightning strikes and Bears—*as well as Carescrians*, Wilf Ansor Brim."

Brim and Ursis began to speak at the same time, but Collingswood held up a perfectly manicured hand. "Don't bother, either of you. There was also the matter of the reversed waveguide that *they* installed—everybody in the yard was overjoyed that I declined to fuss to the Admiralty about *that* little blunder—a damned serious problem as I am given to understand."

"We, ah, did bring it to the engineer's attention," Brim stammered.

"Indeed," Ursis seconded, "one of the senior types initially found it difficult to separate his diagrams from the reality of hullmetal."

Collingswood closed one eye and wrinkled her nose. Then she nodded, pointing an accusing finger at the Bear. "Of course!" she exclaimed. "You helped him understand how to do it, didn't you? That probably explains the uprooted drafting table. We all sort of wondered about that bit of mayhem." She shook her head again, then chuckled. "At any rate, now that the two of you have finished dealing with recalcitrant civilians on your *own* side of the war, I trust you have saved a little violence to counter the promises of our opposites from the League as well."

Her voice trailed off. Everyone in the Fleet knew Emperor Nergol Triannic's boast of slavery and death—at best—for every Imperial Blue Cape who stood in the path of his plans to sack and subjugate the galaxy for his League of Dark Stars. And for eight grim years, the badly outnumbered Fleets of Emperor Greyffin IV had spoiled those plans out of all proportion to the meager resources at their disposal. Now, thanks to efforts like the one in the shipyard below, those fleets were growing larger—and more powerful. . . .

Sudden thunder boomed and crackled overhead as two pairs of starships plunged in formation from among the clouds. Brim identified them even before they entered the shipyard's landing pattern: Sinister-class light cruisers. At 315 irals overall, they were only a little smaller than *Defiant* and carried 150-mmi disruptors. Although they were known as handy ships with excellent habitability, experts considered that placement of blast deflectors near the aft deck house provided an ungainly appearance.

Ungainly-looking or not, these certainly could maintain formation. Perfectly synchronized, they banked into an abbreviated base leg, then rolled out on final, antigravity generators bellowing as they drew into line abreast and descended toward the bay. Cycles later, they were skimming the whitecaps, cooling fins whistling in the slipstream. Brim watched with professional judgment while their speed dropped and the ships gently unloaded mass onto the Verticals buried 'midships in their hulls. Each of the cruisers came to a hovering stop twenty irals or so above the thrashing footprint it pushed into the surface of the water, then turned smartly to taxi toward the wharves beyond the shipyard. Still in line abreast, they crossed between Brim and Eleandor-Bestienne's close-set trio of suns, now setting on the horizon. For an instant, every hull plate stood highlighted in the rippled path of blazing colors; then the starships continued on their way and disappeared into the forest of gantry cranes.

"Did that landfall meet with your professional approval, friend Wilf?" Ursis asked quietly, bringing Brim once more to reality.

He felt his cheeks burn. "They *all* look good to me, Nik," he admitted with a grin. "I won't be able to judge until I've had a bit of real experience landing a light cruiser." Then he laughed. "But from what I've been able to simulate in The Box, I'd allow we were watching some pretty competent helmsmanship."

"I suspect you'll find yourself at real controls sooner than you think, Wilf," Collingswood interrupted with a knowing smile. "Something big seems to be in the wind." She paused significantly to look each of them in the eye. "I have been informed that management here has specially stepped up *Defiant*'s completion schedule on direct orders of the Admiralty —even though the yard is already far beyond its rated capacity. That, and a few other hints I cannot share at this time, lead me to believe that we can expect a most difficult— and critical—assignment." She paused for a moment in thought, watching a destroyer stand out into the bay for take-off. As its running lights pierced the early-evening darkness, she turned again to her three senior officers. "And," she continued, "before the year is over, we may well help decide the outcome of the entire war. . . ."

Weary metacycles later, Brim's strenuous workday finally came to an end when he climbed gratefully from a simulator and signed out of the Training Operations Complex for the night. Under a mighty canopy of midgalactic star swarms, he waved off a hovering tram and made his way inland on foot, following a maze of streets winding circuitously through the shipyard complex. A damp bay breeze plastered the Fleet Cape to his side as he picked his way over glowing, multicolored tracks that crisscrossed the cracked and potholed pavements on the way to his temporary quarters. To either side, the shipyard's ear-splitting cacophony continued unabated from the daylight hours while shadowed forms of half-finished starships hovered under Karlsson lamps. Here and there hullmetal welding torches filled the sky with fountains of sparkling color, and high above it all the monstrous cranes swung and bowed to a rhythm all their own.

Brim smiled as the officers' quarters came into view from the top of a slight rise. His step quickened in spite of his deepening fatigue. Down there in his spartan room, a message would be waiting from halfway across the galaxy. Today was the day she customarily posted.

Casually returning salutes from sentries at either side of the doors, he strode across the lobby to the bank of lifts on the far wall. Cycles later, he entered the tiny cubicle that was his temporary home on Eleandor-Bestienne. As he hoped, the message indicator was flashing over his bunk: YOU-HAVE-NEW-MAIL. YOU-HAVE-NEW-MAIL. . . .

He closed the door and settled himself before the tiny desk that—along with its totally inadequate chair—constituted the only furniture in his tiny room. Instantly, a globular display materialized above the surface of the desk, then filled with a list of correspondence received since he last accessed his message queue. He smiled with pleasure, then selected the entry sourced "Margot Effer'wyck, Lt., I. F. @ Admiralty/Avalon 19-993.367."

A swirl of damp, golden curls and a flashing smile filled the display. Margot Effer'wyck was a princess in every respect. Tall and proud-looking, she was an ample young woman with oval face, full moist lips, sensually heavy eyelids, and the most endearing habit of frowning when she smiled. Her complexion was almost painfully fair and brushed with pink high in her cheeks. She had smallish breasts, a tiny waist for her size, and long, shapely legs. To Wilf Brim, she was the most beautiful woman who ever drew breath.

Discontent with nonproductive court life, she served on and off as an inordinately brave—and successful—young "operative" who risked her life on a number of clandestine assignments to Leaguer planets for Emperor Greyffin's Empire. Now—unwilling subject of that same emperor's protection—she still commanded a highly secret intelligence-gathering section at the Central Admiralty. But her days of life-threatening danger were now at an end. She was too politically valuable to risk.

In the background, Avalon's trees wore their brilliant autumn colors under a gray and lowering sky. When she spoke, her voice was soft and modulated:

"I have toiled sufficiently for the Empire today, dearest," she began. "Now I'm free to walk home instead of taking the limousine, so I can steal a few moments alone to compose." She smiled and looked into the sky, eyes slitted against a misting drizzle. "Avalon has not yet quite accommodated itself to the coming of winter. On the sidewalks, leaves are sodden and slippery, and the rain has just let up a little."

She closed her eyes and smiled wistfully. "'Red o'er the city peeks the setting star,'" she recited, "'The line of yellow light dies fast away / That crowned the eastern roofs; and chill and dun / Falls on the streets this brief autumnal day. . . .'"

Presently she brightened. "That's not really my autumn, Wilf," she said. "Not when I dream of you. Anshelm's *Ode to Autumn* I think is much more like it: 'Season of gold and misted grace, / Close bosom-friend of the life-granting sky; / Enveloping all with thy warming embrace, / Fruiting the vines that 'round my gardens lie....'" She shook her head slowly. "Oh, but how I miss the harvest of love you bring to my life. 'What gleaning half so sweet is / As still to reap thy kisses / Grown ripe in sowing? / And straight to be receiver / Of that which thou art giver, / Rich in bestowing?'"

Brim frowned. Who wrote that last poem? Compton?... Calpon?...*Campion!* That was who. Thomas Campion—a little-known ancient from a long-forgotten star system. Only the playful lyrics survived him and his whole civilization. He shook his head. "All passes. Art alone endures," as Margot often put it. Smiling wistfully, he recalled the archaic love of verse they shared—a nearly forgotten art form that brought them together for the first time in old *Truculent*'s wardroom. It seemed like a million years ago. Not many of *Truculent*'s crew survived her last battle off the planet of Lixor in the Ninety-first Province.

"Oh Wilf, I miss you so today," Margot continued. "Not a sad missing anymore, mind you—not like just after we've been together when there's real pain." A sudden swirl of wind rushed leaves past her face; she absently pushed a curl back in place. "But, after six months or so, you are the warmest spot in my heart. You are the part of me that petty politics can never reach—and the sanctuary to which I can always escape."

The rain began again, and she pulled her Fleet Cloak tighter about her neck. "I use many routes to walk home from the Agency," she continued, "short and not so short. Usually I take the one that crosses the old Broix River bridge. You've seen the district: narrow streets and tall, beautiful houses. Tonight, though, I've chosen the longer one that passes the Lordglen House. It always reminds me of you somehow— and the ball they gave for..." Her laugh sparkled like sudden starlight. "I forget now. That's how important *he* was. But you were there—and you never did have a chance to stay the night in that great house of state, did you, poor Wilf? I shall always hope sharing my bed for the first time was adequate recompense. . . ."

She blushed suddenly. "It's almost as if Gol'ridge wrote *Ristobel* about *me* that night—our night. Remember? 'Before my lover's gaze I bowed, / And slowly teased myself around; / Then drawing in my breath aloud, / With loving pleasure, I unbound / The coverings that concealed my breasts: / My silken gown and inner vests, / Dropt to my feet and full in view, / Behold! my bosom to pleasure you— / And legs and hips and secret place! / Oh come and fill me with thy grace! . . .'"

While the long message played, Brim marveled, as he did so often, that this young noblewoman—and quietly genuine war heroine—was actually in love with *him*. Of course, she was not entirely his in any sense—merely in love with him. Being a princess came with certain requirements, and Princess Margot Effer'wyck would soon enough pay her dues in a political marriage to (The Hon.) Rogan LaKarn, Baron of the Torond. Their wedding date—mandated by no less a personage than Emperor Greyffin IV himself—was to be set shortly.

And while Brim knew he could probably tolerate the marriage itself, he had long ago given up trying to make himself accept the fact that LaKarn would also share Margot's bed— even though he knew full well that no real love existed there. She was always careful that he understood where she stood on that point. In the privacy of her suite at the Embassy, she had concluded the message so erotically she left him sweating and short of breath. He fell asleep after his fifth replay. . . .

Next morning, as Chief Steward Grimsby, Collingswood's ancient family retainer, chauffeured the foursome to the stocks, Flynn sat bolt upright in his seat the moment *Defiant* came into view. "Who is *that?*" he exclaimed, pointing through the skimmer's windscreen, "and what in the Universe is he doing?" At the entrance, a huge, familiar figure was intently raising a great blue-and-gold banner onto a flagstaff newly attached to one of the gate uprights.

Brim recognized "who" in an instant, even though the man's broad back was turned from the road. "That's *Bar-*

*bousse!*" he exclaimed, hopping through the hatch before Grimsby could fully bring the vehicle to a stop.

"Lieutenant Brim," the huge rating bellowed, turning to salute with his free hand. He stood half an iral taller than Brim, was completely bald under his garrison cap, and might have weighed a quarter millstone—yet there was clearly not a measure of fat on his powerful body. He had gentle brown eyes that shone with intelligence and compassion, the nose of an eagle, and a jaw that must have stopped a thousand fists—clearly to the detriment of the fists. He had large hands and feet, yet he was perfectly proportioned in every respect. And he wore a huge, ear-to-ear grin. "*Defiant*'s a beauty, sir," he exclaimed, "every iral of 'er."

Collingswood followed Brim from the skimmer with Ursis and Flynn close on her heels. "Utrillo Barbousse," she whispered, shaking her head in helpless wonderment, "you weren't supposed to report for at least a week. I thought you were on leave. . . ."

"Aye, Captain," Barbousse admitted, saluting again, "that I was. But . . . Well . . . I sort of figured the four of you would have your hands full gettin' the new ship finished and all." He shrugged and blushed momentarily. "An' to tell the truth, I was gettin' tired of nothin' important to do, so . . ." He saluted Ursis and Flynn, then nodded toward the ship while he secured the flag halyards to a cleat on the flagpole. "I thought it wouldn't hurt if I pitched in signin' on the new crew."

Collingswood suddenly seemed to have something in her eye. She looked up at the great flowing pennant with its colorful depiction of a deadly Rhondell falcon—*Defiant*'s hallmark—then bit her lip for a moment before she spoke. "It's a most elegant banner, Barbousse," she said, "and we can certainly use your help with the crew."

Ursis kissed his fingertips and shook his great, furry head. "Utrillo, my friend," he interjected with a baleful eye, "this new banner will make such a fine impression on the entire shipyard that we shall have our hands full merely preventing other crews from signing on without orders."

Flynn frowned and stared at the great pennant flying lazily in the early-evening breeze. "How in the world did you manage to get your hands on . . ." His voice trailed off and he winced. "Ah, belay that, my friend," he said hurriedly.

"Aye, sir," Barbousse mumbled, busying himself with the flag halyards again.

Brim stifled a laugh as Collingswood suddenly scanned the empty sky as if expecting the arrival of an extremely important starship. No one who had ever shipped with Barbousse really wanted to know *how* the big rating acquired war-vanished luxury items like cases of fine old Logish Meem, and flagstaffs with custom pennants far in advance of launch ceremonies, only that he *could* and *did*—with satisfying regularity.

"Barbousse," Brim choked presently, "your banner is perfect—as is your timing."

"True," Ursis agreed, nodding his head gravely. "'Winter songbirds trill lustily from autumn treetops,' as we say—and with your arrival, Utrillo, comes my own personal feeling that this war may yet be won by our tired old Empire. . . ."

During the next few days, specialists among *Defiant*'s crew began to report aboard. For the most part, they were engineering technicians assigned to the big antigravity generators that lifted and propelled the ship at speeds below Sheldon's Great LightSpeed Constant. They went to work immediately on the two Admiralty CL-Standard-84 Verticals that would soon be needed when she was towed from the stocks for finishing.

One new lieutenant who was *not* assigned to the Engineering spaces appeared one morning at the simulators and reported directly to Brim. He was tall, redheaded, and barrel-chested—and he was *not* dressed in the blue cape of Emperor Greyffin's Galactic Fleet. Instead, he wore a light-gray tunic decorated by twelve golden frogs and a stiff crimson collar, dark knee breeches with crimson side stripes, and lightweight, knee-high boots.

He could also fly—with no help from machines. Midway between his shoulders, his tunic opened to accommodate a pillow-sized swelling common to his species known as a "tensil." This protrusion covered an outgrowth of his reflexive nervous system that automatically coordinated the complex motions of an enormous pair of auburn wings—really a second, specialized, set of arms—that arched upward like sandy cowls trailing long flight feathers in cascades that reached all the way to the floor.

He was an A'zurnian, dressed in the wonderfully old-fashioned regimentals of his home planet, the mild, lushly vegetated world on the edge of Galactic Sector 944. Entirely populated by flighted—determinedly peaceful—beings, A'zurn had been easily seized by League invaders early in the war. Less than a year previously, Brim distinguished himself in a daring raid to assist the very active A'zurnian resistance movement—and was subsequently decorated for his efforts by Crown Prince Leopold, leader of the Free A'zurnian government-in-exile at Avalon. There was something about the cut of *this* lieutenant's uniform that said "unusual." Especially his shiny, new Helmsman's insignia that fairly shouted of recent graduation from the Academy near Avalon. He had a wide forehead and narrow chin with a sharply chiseled nose. His huge eyes were those of a born hunter, and they sparkled with intelligence and compassion, as well as humor.

"Leading Torpedoman Barbousse suggested I report directly to you after I signed in," the young A'zurnian said in a strong, steady voice, saluting formally. "I am known as Aram of Nahshon, and I have wished to meet you since I learned that you personally freed my father on A'zurn."

"Your father?" Brim asked in astonishment.

"Yessir," the lieutenant said. "A man in a tricornered hat. You gave him your captured field piece—just before you boarded the launch for home. Do you remember?" he asked anxiously. "Torpedoman Barbousse did."

"Universe," Brim whispered. "Of course I remember—the nobleman."

Aram smiled. "Yes," he said. "First Earl of Xeres—and cousin to Crown Prince Leo who decorated you. The other A'zurnian in the field piece was Tharshish of Josias, our Prime Minister at one time. You and your men freed them both from the prison at the Research Center. It was by their personal petitions that you were awarded our Order of Cloudless Flight."

Brim ground his teeth as gruesome memories of the raid flooded back. The prisoners had all been horribly mangled—

wings cruelly snapped in half to prevent their escape. To the Leaguers, such treatment was quite normal—there was no conscious desire to inflict punishment. Pragmatism ruled their entire military establishment—especially the black-uniformed Controllers. Wingless prisoners simply required fewer guards than ones who could fly.

"Never for a moment pity them," Aram said gently, breaking the Carescrian's awful reverie. "Even though they are now flightless, they are still proud—and quite capable of considerable fight, as the Tyrant discovers each new day they are free."

Brim smiled and nodded his head. "Yes," he said quietly. "I understood that by looking into their eyes."

The A'zurnian lieutenant returned Brim's smile. "Thank you," he said simply. "Perhaps aboard *Defiant* I can somehow begin to repay my personal debt to you and Mr. Barbousse."

It took Brim a few moments to understand just what the young A'zurnian was talking about. Then he shut his eyes and shook his head. "No one owes anything to anybody," he stated firmly. "Barbousse and I were only doing our jobs as Imperial soldiers." He laughed. "Besides, if you have even half the guts of the other A'zurnians I met during that raid, then we'll all feel xaxtdamned lucky to have you aboard. We've got one hell of a war on our hands—all of us." With that, he motioned *Defiant*'s new Helmsman Second Class into the simulator room. "Now, let's introduce you to this new ship of ours. . . ."

On the stocks, *Defiant* herself gained a somewhat more finished appearance amid the coils of wire, hullmetal plates, cables, ducting, hoses, rumbling generators, and other detritus that littered the construction site. Within two weeks, the officers' quarters were more or less completed, and Brim moved aboard—marveling that his fortunes had so improved that he now required two traveling cases instead of the one that bobbed at his heels when he first passed through the gates of the Eorean Complex on Gimmas Haefdon, fresh from the Academy.

While more systems were completed within the hull, each

succeeding day saw larger groups of crew members muster through Barbousse's makeshift office near the main hatch, and the ship began to take on some aspects of an operational Fleet unit.

In due course, *Defiant*'s hull and superstructure exteriors were finished, and the day arrived when the starship could be moved to an ordinary gravity pool for completion. According to hoary tradition, a small launching ceremony marked the occasion—sadly rushed by a mysterious construction speed-up that had suddenly affected the entire shipyard.

Brim and Ursis witnessed the late-afternoon proceedings from *Defiant*'s rain-soaked, half-finished bridge with the ship's two CL-Standard-84 Vertical Gravity Generators rumbling steadily in the background. Barbousse's great banner snapped and fluttered in the strong wind from a temporary flagstaff at the bow. Overhead, a dreary sky was pregnant with lowering, scudding clouds—sure precursors of another in a constant parade of violent summer thunderstorms that had darkened most of the day and wrinkled the lead-toned bay with whitecaps.

"*Defiant* is certainly a much larger ship than was our little *Truculent*," the Bear observed, standing at the forward starboard corner of the bridge beside the only control console yet installed. He was holding on to his hat and motioning toward a pair of large, humpbacked tugs that had turned from the main waterway and were battling into the teeth of the wind toward the stocks. The powerful vessels rode atop streaming clouds of spray and foam as they ploughed contemptuously over the deep troughs. "I have often seen T-class destroyers moved with a single tug," Ursis observed with a grin, "but even incomplete, our *Defiant* requires at least two." He bent over the shoulder of Sublieutenant Alexi Radosni Provodnik to check the Vertical readouts personally. Provodnik, a new engineering officer fresh from Sodeskaya, was a much smaller Bear who had been assigned to *Defiant* only a short while. He had sharper, more pointed ears than most of his colleageus and smaller fangs—inlaid with two positively immense StarBlazes. The young Bear was clearly scion of an extraordinarily wealthy Sodeskayan family. He was also enthusiastic about anything that provided an opportunity to learn about starships, and had quickly become the darling of the whole crew.

Brim smiled as he leaned his elbows on a control ledge beneath empty frames for the ship's Hyperscreens—glasslike crystals that provided "normal" views of the outside at faster-than-light velocities. "From the feel of things in The Box, *Defiant* will be a lot bigger to fly, too," he observed with a chuckle. "Probably a lot like one of those tugs."

"If that is the case, friend Wilf," Ursis growled with a sparkle of humor in his eyes, "we shall *tow* Nergol Triannic to his doom. One fights with the weapons one finds at hand." His wink was punctuated by a lengthy rumble of approaching thunder.

Aft, at the beam ends of *Defiant*'s stern, teams of shipyard workers dressed in reflective clothing were already balancing themselves on the slippery hullmetal while they retracted protective covers from stout optical cleats set in the afterdeck end of the sheer strakes. By this time, the tugs had lumbered into position some two hundred irals out from the stocks and were hovering just clear of the tossing waves. Presently, thick hawser beams flashed from their huge optical bollards, contacted the cleats, and brightened as the tugs smoothly shifted into reverse, laying on the tension against *Defiant*, which was still fastened securely to the stocks.

To landward, a small crowd had gathered at a temporary platform near the bow—automatic umbrellas bobbed and hovered nervously in the gusty wind. Someone read a short speech that was totally unintelligible on the bridge. Then a brass band energetically yerked out a few off-key bars of Heroic Music from the Grat'mooz Sector—*that* came through all too well, at least to Brim's way of thinking.

"Hull 921," a voice rasped suddenly from a temporary COMM module fastened to a stringer by two oversized C-clamps, "contact Launch Operations on GTD zero five one. Good afternoon, sir."

"Hull 921 on GTD zero five one, and thank you," Brim answered, switching frequencies on the battered little box. "Hull 921 checking in from the stocks."

"Hull number 921, good day," a female voice answered promptly. "Verify readiness to melt the trennels, please."

"Hull 921, one moment," Brim answered. He looked at Ursis and raised his eyebrows. "OPS wants to know if we're ready to melt the fastenings to the stocks," he said.

The Bear bent to peer at the readouts again, frowned, then shook his head thoughtfully and spoke to Provodnik at the console. "Before the launch crew frees us from the stocks, Alexi Radosni," he said gently, "you may wish to balance the gain on the port-side Hartzel feedbacks. We want *Defiant* to ride an even keel from the very beginning, eh?"

"I think ve mayeh have problem, here, Nikolai Yanuarievich," the younger Bear said, passing delicate hands over an array of power controls. Immediately, a bank of indicators turned from yellow to steady green. "Is *third* time port generators have lost balance in last couple of cycles," he asserted; "I vas about to bring this to your attention." As he spoke, the indicators suddenly changed color again. "Ah, like that, sir," he added. "One of the feedback circuits seems to drop control data. Ten'stadt Fields there in X-Damper quadrant dump all the vay to minus sixtyeh-seven just before it happens."

Ursis bent and glowered at the readouts. "Hmm," he muttered. "I see what you mean." He frowned as he studied the flowing colors on the console readouts, then turned to Brim. "As you have probably gathered, Wilf," he said with a serious look on his face, "we have lost automatic balance of the port Verticals." He thought for a moment, staring out over the tossing gray water of the wind-swept sound. "Perhaps it would be wise to request a brief systems delay."

Brim nodded. "Hull 921," he announced after another, much louder, crack of thunder rattled to a conclusion in the distance. "Request five-cycle systems check, please."

There was a measurable pause before an answer came. "Hull 921: cleared for one five-cycle systems check," the woman's voice acknowledged with a slight edge. Brim understood that launch operations were meticulously timed, and delays of any kind could result in horribly tangled schedules. "Check in immediately when you complete, please," the controller added.

"Hull 921. Many thanks," Brim answered, then nodded to Ursis. "You've got five cycles, Nik," he said.

Ursis and Provodnik huddled for perhaps two cycles, conversing rapidly in Sodeskayan and exercising the controls. Presently the older Bear straightened and nodded to Brim. "It seems that we have serious problems indeed, my friend," he said, nodding his head gravely. "Probably Alexi and I can jury-rig a fix around the trouble in perhaps a metacycle. Would you inquire as to what that might do to the launch schedule?"

Brim nodded. "Hull 921. Requesting one-metacycle systems workaround," he said, but he was pretty sure of the answer before he started.

The controller's voice returned almost immediately. "Hull 921: sorry, that is a negative. Do you need to scrub your launching?"

"Hull 921. How long before you could schedule us again, please?"

"Hull 921," the controller answered after a slight pause, "estimate ten standard days before we have openings."

Brim looked at the Bear, who had been listening to the conversation. "What now, Nik?"

Ursis turned to Provodnik. "We could take the starboard generator off Automatic and run it ourselves, Alexi Radosni," he suggested. "Otherwise, we cause immediate cancellation of the launch—and put *Defiant* at least a week behind schedule." He stared the young Bear directly in his eye. "Do you think you can use the manual controls here to balance the generator with its mate to port? . . . If you feel any uncertainty at all, I should count it a privilege to take your place at the console—immediately."

Provodnik considered for only a moment. "I am sorelyeh tempted to claim that I can, Nikolai Yanuarievich," he said, sliding from his seat, "but that would be irresponsible. My sole experience with CL-Standard-84 generators is aboard this ship—and I arrived on Eleandor-Bestienne only ten days ago from the Mother Planets."

"Your honesty is appreciated, Alexi Radosni," Ursis replied pointedly, frowning up through a network of bare frames and stringers at the fast-approaching storm. "This is definitely no time for heroics of any kind." Then he pursed his lips and slid into the seat as the first drops of rain began to spatter the console. "Wilf," he said, "you will please to inform Operations that we shall be ready to proceed momentarily."

Brim nodded and touched the COMM. "This is Hull 921," he said, raising his voice to make it heard over the hiss of the rain. "Stand by for affirmative on launch decision."

"Hull 921: Much appreciated!" the woman's voice crackled from the COMM module. "Standing by. . . ."

"*Defiant* requires approximately one hundred ten on the Verticals," Ursis explained to the younger Sodeskayan as new color sequences began to cascade over the readouts. "So . . ." His hand hardly moved over the controls, but the generators changed pitch slightly and a number of indicators winked on the console. "Only the slightest lift while they melt the retaining trennels," he said, his voice now hardly audible over the drumming rain. He was all business now: a complete professional—totally consumed by his work. "Call out the vectors, Alexi Radosni—as they appear."

"One hundred ten in vertical," Provodnik repeated, staring at the readouts in rapt concentration. The rumble from 'midships increased noticeably as Ursis shifted a section of the control from green to a reddish orange. "And steady. . . ."

The elder Bear looked up momentarily and nodded to Brim. "We are now ready when Operations is, Wilf," he said.

"Hull 921. Prepared to detach immediately," Brim reported.

The woman's matter-of-fact reply came within a moment: "Hull 921: stand by." Her words were almost coincident with the actual firings of the trennels that held the ship to the stocks.

Bright flashes strobed in the stormy grayness from beneath the hull, accompanied by an ear-splitting volley of sharp reports that cascaded from the bow to the stern and rocked the ship like low-altitude turbulence. Clouds of acrid smoke swept the deck and burned Brim's nostrils while Ursis's hands moved surely over the gravity controls and lightning flashed from the lowering storm.

"One hundred fifteen in vertical . . ." Provodnik intoned. "One hundred twenty and steady. . . ."

The sound of the ship's Vertical generators rose almost negligibly and the deck swayed beneath Brim's feet. He looked out the Hyperscreen frame in surprise. *Defiant* was already halfway off the stocks and moving swiftly over the darkening shoreline in the wake of the two tugs. A sudden cacophony of air horns and sirens crashed through the teeming storm: *Defiant*'s welcome to the world. A small knot of dockyard technicians lining the quayside broke out in cheering—all ragged and spontaneous. Shipwrights from other stocks paused to wave their helmets as she passed. These men had built countless starships, both in war and in peace, and—the Universe willing—they would build countless more. Their cheers reflected fierce professional pride and sent a gesture of goodwill to the star sailors who would man this, the latest result of their craft. Brim felt his eyes fill for a moment—it was not the rain. . . .

Then all noise was abruptly swallowed in a stunning—deafening—strike of lightning on the high KA'PPA tower directly aft of the bridge. For a moment, the entire structure and its empty KA'PPA stubs blazed out like some skeletal beacon. Brim was knocked gasping to the deck by the concussion—and a tremendous thunderclap that instantly proceeded from it.

Nearly deafened by the violent discharge, he climbed shakily to his feet only to catch the rasping shriek of a runaway gravity generator. He'd heard that ugly sound a number of times before on failing Carescrian ore barges. They all sounded pretty much the same. It was the port Vertical this time—clearly its automatic damper had been blown out by the lightning strike, and the big generator was now spooling up to full power!

More blinding flashes of nearby lightning burned images of Ursis's grim visage in Brim's eyes as the Bear desperately fought *Defiant*'s controls. "Cap that machine, Alexi Radosni!" he roared to Provodnik as the deck canted up crazily to starboard, "NOW!" His words were nearly drowned by another cascade of crackling thunder. Eerie green light continued to flash from the empty KA'PPA masts and flickered along the network of open stringers above the bridge.

With no directional controls yet installed on the bridge, Brim could only hang on and watch helplessly while both deck crews aft slid across the streaming hullmetal in their protective suits, scrambling desperately for nonexistent handholds. One by one, the screaming men dropped over the metal precipice into the thrashing water beneath the ship. On the bridge, loose gear and small tools cascaded into heaps along the starboard bulkhead. Grabbing an open Hyperscreen housing, Brim hung on while the big starship tilted toward vertical, blanking the stormy sky with the darker mass of her own deck. *She was going over on her back!*

Suddenly through the driving downpour, he saw Provodnik scramble across the crazily canted deck of the bridge using empty console supports for footholds. In mere clicks, the young Bear grabbed a handle on the emergency power panel, twisted the door open, and—incredibly without losing his grip—pulled a main fuse block to the automatic controls. Instantly, the ear-splitting shriek died to an even rumble as the runaway generator spooled down to default power settings and *Defiant* slowly returned to an even keel. Aft, the ungainly tugs had been caught off guard and were completely unable to react at all, except for knots of crewmen that poured from the hatches, pointing with astonishment as the big ship settled back on an even keel.

Heart thumping wildly in his chest, Brim glanced forward toward the receding stocks just as ten broken bodies appeared in *Defiant*'s frothing wake: remains of the hapless work crews who were caught in the maelstrom of raging gravitrons beneath the ship. His skin crawled. Such absolute destructive potential was only one reason why powerful vessels like starships were rarely permitted to fly across land masses—at least at low altitudes. He shuddered in the chill air—had he grabbed at the Hyperscreen housing even a click later than he did, he might have fallen from the bridge and joined them himself....

A few irals away, Ursis and the younger Sodeskayan were again totally engrossed in the control console, each running one of the generators by hand. Apparently Provodnik had suddenly received a great dose of confidence in his ability at a console. Sudden necessity had a way of making that happen —Brim understood the process well. The very best of Carescrian ore barges he had once flown could supply three lifetimes' worth of sudden necessity—in a single trip!

Shaking his head, he realized for the first time that it was no longer raining.

The resulting inquest extended over nearly twenty-five interminable days, depriving Brim and Ursis of valuable metacycles they should have spent helping prepare *Defiant* for space. It was time that had to be made up from their own lives—but manpower was too short in those wartime years to permit substitutes at any job.

When the tribunal ended, however, all three officers present on the bridge were pronounced to be "without fault," and references to the incident were deleted immediately from their Admiralty records. Surprisingly, the official "culprit" in the shipyard report was not the lightning strike. Instead, sole blame was fixed on a defective signal mixer whose improperly synchronized feedback logic had slowly destroyed both automatic control mechanisms during the preceding weeks of intense system testing. But Brim and Ursis both noted a great deal of coincident work being done on the KA'PPA-tower insulation—and complete reisolation of the Vertical's waveguide system.

Neither the Carescrian nor his Sodeskayan friend mentioned anything about the waveguide work outside *Defiant*'s immediate flight crew, but Commander Collingswood subsequently messaged a number of highly classified reports to Vice Admiral Plutron—a close friend in the Admiralty—in case the trouble should surface at some later time. "It never hurts to have one's political homework promptly done," as she stated one morning in the wardroom. "You never know when a folder of well-placed reports might come in very handy."

Perhaps the only positive result of the tragedy was a totally revamped Vertical specification for the remainder of the Defiant-class ships. But the changes were far too late for *Defiant* herself—whose major systems were already on board and could only be retrofitted, not wholly replaced. Unfortunately, as Ursis often out it, "A whole year's worth of patches is often inferior to a five-minute design modification." In addition, *Defiant* herself was now widely known as a troubled ship, a reputation Brim suspected she would never fully escape.

And, of course, there was not much that could be done for

the men who were killed. *Defiant*'s crew joined the shipyard workers in a generous collection for their families, but a few things in that day and age were still beyond the capabilities of technology. . . .

With each new morning, the starship became more and more complete—inside and out—and crew members began to arrive in a steady stream. A new lieutenant commander reported aboard early one morning some two weeks following *Defiant*'s near disaster. He was middle-aged, handsome in a weather-beaten way, and looked as if he were clearly accustomed to command—although he had only a reserve commission. There was a certain agelessness to his face, framed by a gray beard and moustache, and even from a distance his gray eyes sparkled with the keen wisdom and humor of a longtime starsailor. One ring with an enormous StarBlaze graced his long fingers, and his new uniform, though casually worn, had clearly been fashioned for a prince—at a princely sum.

Brim was taking a fresh-air break when the man strode across the brow and stopped just short of the main entrance hatch. He leaned back to gaze up at the bridge for a moment, then shrugged in a sort of pained resignation. This ritual completed, he stopped to critically inspect Brim as if the latter had purposely presented himself there for just such an occasion. "They ca' me Baxter Oglethorp Calhoun," he said abruptly in a rich baritone. "I'm to be *Defiant*'s Executive Officer—an', Mr. Wilf Brim, with myself on board, ye are no mair the only Carescrian in the crew."

Brim felt his heart skip a beat—he'd spent years losing the same sort of thick Carescrian burr he'd just heard. "A *Carescrian*?" he stammered.

"Ay, chield, 'tis indeed a thing you'd better believe," Calhoun said with a grin, "even if ye *have* decided to forsake the old tongue. But don't get your hopes up for any 'down-home' commizzeratin'. 'Tis been so long since I ha' luiked upon that awful place, I hardly remember onything o't—except 'tis a good place to be *from*. Forever!"

"You'll get no arguments from me on that score, Number One," Brim vowed. "But how is it you happen to know *me*?"

"A better question is how might I ha' avoided it, mon," Calhoun declared. "Right noo, ye are the most famous Carescrian in the Empire—for which I am eternally grateful. The likes o' ye keeps the public eye off the likes o' me." He smiled with obvious satisfaction, then abruptly pushed his way past and continued on into the ship.

"I think I'm honored," Brim replied to the man's receding back. "What is it you normally do in peacetime?"

"I am no stranger to space, young mon," Calhoun muttered without even bothering to turn his head, "an' I may yet find my grave in it." He laughed. "For the nonce we'll say that I'm in what you'd call the salvage business—an' the less ye ask o't, the better. Understand?"

Brim started to reply, but by that time, Calhoun was busy at the sign-in desk, and Ursis was paging from the bridge. The young Carescrian chuckled as he made his way up a companionway two treads at a time. It looked as if *Defiant* was attracting a typical Collingswood gathering of miscellany. Somehow, he wasn't surprised—or disappointed—in the slightest.


*Defiant*'s crew ranged all the way from seasoned space veterans to raw new recruits—officers and ratings alike. And all voiced happy surprise at conditions aboard their new ship. The wardroom and spaceman's mess were constantly supplied with all sorts of normally unavailable food and potables—courtesy of the mysterious Barbousse. Already the ship was developing her own personality. Perhaps it was somewhat more clublike in pradigm than might be generally considered desirable throughout the Fleet. But then a very similar atmosphere had been—at least in Brim's opinion—largely responsible for old *Truculent*'s success before its near destruction while battling three NF-110s off Lixor in the Ninety-first Province with Brim at the controls.

"If anything," Ursis rumbled to Brim one afternoon as they relaxed in comfortable wardroom chairs, "friend Barbousse has become even more discerning since leaving old *Truculent*." He lifted a ruby goblet to the light. "Look at that color, Wilf. Such meem can only be described as 'glorious.'" In the background, a number of his countrymen were toasting each other heartily: "To ice, to snow, to Sodeskaya we go!..."

Brim's tastes were in no way so sophisticated as Ursis's. Before joining the Helmsman's Academy, he had experienced the pleasures of meem only twice in his life. "It certainly tastes 'glorious,' Nik," he said with a grin. "I guess I'll have to take your word on the color—I'm still kind of low on experience."

"Then you vouch for the taste," the Bear said, "and I shall vouch for the color."

"We have a bargain, Nik," Brim laughed. "Now, all we need is to find somebody who is interested in what we think."

"That," the Bear said with a thundering laugh, "may be more difficult than the vouching itself."

"Not so," grumped a deep female voice from a couch behind them. "I only signed on this afternoon. And I don't know anything about this wardroom at all—except *you*, Wilf Brim."

Surprised, Brim whirled around to confront a woman of average height with wide shoulders, narrow hips, long thin legs, narrow feet—and a perfectly awesome bust. Her face was almost totally round, with a button nose, intelligent eyes, short fuzzy hair, and a toothy smile. He felt his jaw drop. Nobody else in the Universe looked like *that*. "Professor—*Commander*—Wellington!" he exclaimed, scrambling to his feet. "I never missed a single one of your lectures at the Helmsman's Academy!" With a look of awe on his face, he placed a hand on Ursis's shoulder. "Commander Wellington, may I present Nikolai Yanuarievich Ursis, the finest Systems Officer in the Universe?"

"I am indeed honored, Commander Wellington," Ursis said, rising to his feet, then bowing deeply in the Sodeskayan manner. "And what place do you hold in *Defiant*'s crew?" he asked.

"My orders read 'Weapons Officer,'" Wellington declared, scratching her head. "But it all happened so quickly. A week ago, I didn't even own a battle suit; I am really a historian, you know. Then—zap!—I got the assignment by message, and here I am. My head's still spinning."

"Commander Wellington is probably *the* Universe's expert on antique weapons systems, Nik," Brim added.

Wellington laughed. "Just between you, me, and the bedpost," she said, placing her head conspiratorially beside her mouth, "I think they're getting a little desperate for crews."

"Say not so, good lady," Ursis said, eyes sparkling with good humor. "It would surprise no one if *Defiant* were to receive a battery or two of antique weapons."

"I thought of the possibility myself," Wellington quipped, "so I brought a few barrels of gunpowder with me in my kit. We may have a small problem with recoil in deep space, but . . ." She shrugged phlegmatically.

Ursis looked at Brim and grinned. "Nergol Triannic is in deep trouble now, my Carescrian friend," he said. "He might be able to fight radiation fires with N-rays, but how can he hope to counter cannonballs and grapeshot? You are clearly our secret weapon, Commander Wellington!"

"That's 'Dora,' please! I won't know who anybody's talking to."

"'Dora' it is, then," Ursis agreed. "Together, the three of us will blast the League of Dark Stars into spinning atoms."

"With a few deep-space recoil problems," Wellington piped in.

"Which it appears we shall soon toast with Logish Meem," Brim interjected as Grimsby magically appeared with a third filled goblet. "Probably not a half-bad idea, come to think of it," he mused as the ancient steward bowed and set the goblet before Wellington. "All problems dissolve eventually in this magic solvent."

"To ice, to snow, to Sodeskaya we go!" Ursis exclaimed. The three drained their meem in the fashion of Bears, then touched the goblets together upside down.

"Hear, hear!" Wellington replied with her eyes opened in surprise. She looked at the goblet. "By the Great Feathered Spirits of Higgins!" she exclaimed. "Where in the Universe did you find *this*? I haven't tasted anything like it since before the war started."

"We depend on a great deal of magic aboard this ship, Dora," Collingswood interrupted from the doorway. "When I discovered Glendora T. Wellington had volunteered for combat, I knew I'd found someone who could help sustain it. So I personally asked for you."

"Regula Collingswood!" Wellington squealed. "Well, I should have known."

The reunion lasted long into the hours of darkness. . . .

During the next weeks, Brim and Aram were joined in the simulators by Angeline Waldo, a Reserve Helmsman from the merchant service who decided she wanted a ship that could fight back, Galen Fritz, a veteran trooper-turned-Helmsman from the Bax cluster, and Ardelle Jennings, a junior Helmsman fresh from the Imperial Academy. Each, Brim found quickly, had a unique style at the helm.

Jennings, for example, flew absolutely by the book. She was so perfect it was almost annoying, and she left absolutely nothing to chance. Brim imagined that when she was at the controls, *Defiant* would leave a neat red pen tracing across space—exactly corresponding to the course she had laid out well in advance of their passage. He hoped she would be able to perform as efficiently in the heat of battle, where the best-laid plans could—and often did—change with each click.

On the other hand, Fritz and Waldo—both experienced Helmsmen—flew easily, almost casually. They were comfortable at the controls. Even during the most trying of circumstances the Master Simulators could throw at them, they remained calm and never "lost" the ship. Brim knew that Triannic's minions would quickly come up with more taxing challenges than any the civilian operators might conjure, but he expected that both would rise to the occasion. So long as the ship was capable of flight, they'd make sure her gunners accomplished their mission. And that was what the war—and *Defiant*—were all about.

Aside from that, Waldo had magnificent legs. . . .

It was Aram, however, that Brim found truly astonishing. Beneath his formal A'zurnian veneer, he was both technically astute and relaxed at the controls. And he could learn anything at any time, even after the many Sodeskayan meem bashes, when everybody—including himself—had toasted far more than was even remotely sensible. Not only that, he was absolutely unflappable in The Box. Even after sessions that left

Brim himself on the edge of taking a blast pike to the whole complex, Aram came through sweating but still firmly in control of every situation. The young Helmsman modestly explained that being naturally flighted made the act of piloting far easier for him, but Brim knew better. Aram was simply xaxtdamned good. . . .

Gradually over the ensuing weeks, sounds of construction subsided inside the ship, and her passages and companionways became less cluttered with loose wires, construction gear, and just plain dirt. Closed access hatches for the most part stayed closed as stores were packed away and secured for deep space. The smell of the ship changed, too: from dust, bonding chemicals, and drying paint to new carpeting, new electronics, hot food, and the unmistakable smell of polish— the universal element of every military starship that had ever been built.

During this time, the number of dockyard workers between decks and on the gangways also changed, thinning to a trickle as civilian contractors were replaced by ever-increasing numbers of the Blue Capes who would actually man the commissioned ship. And—much to the amazement of nearly everyone—the shipyard declared I.F.S. *Defiant* to be "officially" complete two days ahead of schedule.

The matter-of-fact announcement was delivered by one J. Leeland Blake, a tall, serious-looking builder's representative in the traditional stovepipe hat worn by all shipyard managers. He appeared during Collingswood's regular morning status meeting in *Defiant*'s shiny new wardroom.

"Following the successful resolution of Action Reports 11235 through 11781," Blake reported pretentiously, "Starship I.F.S. *Defiant* is hereby declared to be an operational vehicle and cleared for immediate flight trials. . . ." He frowned and cleared his throat while he peered into his display and adjusted a pair of wire-rimmed spectacles. "That, of course, specifically excludes Action Reports 791, 832, 5476, 9078, 9079, and 10517 through 11000," he added. "However, those have to do with interface modifications, and we agreed —I believe—to deal with them after *Defiant*'s trial. Am I correct, Captain Collingswood?"

Collingswood smiled noncommittally and checked her own display carefully. "That is correct, Mr. Blake," she said after a moment, then looked around the table at her senior officers. "You've heard the gentleman's words," she declared with a smile. "If any of you have disagreements, now is certainly an appropriate time to voice them. Nik, what of the systems? They've been troublesome since *Defiant* was on the stocks. Are you satisfied?"

Ursis scowled for a moment, then nodded thoughtfully. "*Defiant*'s systems are as thoroughly tested as we can make them, Captain," he said evenly. "In fact, Power and Propulsion appear to be virtually perfect." Then he held up a warning finger. "Admittedly, some electronic problems do persist," he added, "but nothing that appears serious—or schedule-threatening."

"Wad ye gi' her a full bill o' health noo, Nikolai?" Calhoun questioned, peering over his glasses.

Ursis nodded. "Yes," he said after some consideration. "Except perhaps for the starboard Vertical. That still functions somewhat on the rough side, thought it *has* been operating in a steady state for more than a week now." He shrugged philosophically. "I suppose I must admit that it is at least operational—although I do not fully trust it."

"There are no unresolved Action Reports on the Verticals, Lieutenant Ursis," the civilian replied defensively. "Both generators operate completely to specification, you know."

"Agreed," Ursis said dryly. "It is when I finally got to read the specifications themselves that I determined further complaints were useless." He crossed his legs and relaxed in the chair amid half-stifled guffaws and choked-back snickers. The builders had been less than gracious when asked for systems specifications. Most other crews were satisfied with user-operations and maintenance manuals.

"And you, Mr. Brim?" Collingswood interjected. "What have you to add on the subject?"

Brim grinned. "You've heard me grumble about our troublesome steering engines, Mr. Blake. But they've done well enough for a week now—and the new Chairman you downloaded is the best anywhere. The mods for parallel quantum/vector analysis seem to make a lot of difference in the way she keeps a course. At least that's the way she feels in The Box."

"I trust she'll come through at least as well during actual flight," Blake said proudly, regaining some of his good humor. "We've built some fine ships here over the past few hundred years—*Defiant* is one of the best, I am certain. . . ."

The meeting went on for more than an hour afterward, but in the end the pact was made. Collingswood signed the shipyard's Red Book, and *Defiant* was ready for commissioning.

The following morning just after dawn, everyone assembled outside the starship's main hatch while a polished brass nameplate was noisily fixed to a bulkhead with four old-fashioned rivets:

I.F.S. DEFIANT
JOB 29921
ELEANDOR-BESTIENNE YARD
19/51995.

In a simple ceremony, both Blake and Collingswood gave short speeches containing a number of necessary platitudes concerning the Emperor, home, hearth, and duty. Then a local beauty doused the bows with a bottle of Logish Meem, and—while Barbousse hoisted the Rhondell-falcon banner to the top of the KA'PPA tower—*Defiant* entered the Fleet lists as a "commissioned" vessel. Afterward, as the crew trooped back aboard to their stations (many first joining Collingswood when she stopped to polish the new plaque with her sleeve), a dockyard painting crew applied a Fleet Designator on both sides of her bow: "CL.921." I.F.S. *Defiant* was—at least officially—declared ready for flight.

Soon afterward taxi tests began, and the ship came through with a few minor snags, but surprisingly well considering her past record. Two weeks later, she slid for the first time into her own element: space. In spite of her size, she appeared to be handy and maneuverable, surprisingly light on her feet and astonishing in the way she could accelerate. Only the most powerful destroyers could outspeed her into Hyperspace, and in nearby taverns and meem halls, her crew was quick to crow her talents. She was still known as a "troublesome" ship, nothing would ever change that. But she was early on known as a happy ship, too. Probably that made much of the difference. . . .

Through the following days of space trials, *Defiant*'s crew took their first real steps toward becoming a team, capable— at least—of flying the big starship into deep space to run-in her four Admiralty CL-Standard 489.3G Drive crystals. At Hyperspeeds, she once more proved to be an extremely swift and nimble ship. Designed for a top velocity of no more than 32000 LightSpeed, on her final set of speed trials she actually sustained 36100. Afterward, it was widely rumored among the crew that Ursis and a number of other Bears—including old Borodov from I.F.S. *Truculent*, now stationed at the Admiralty in Avalon—had contrived to alter her N(112-B) Power Chambers at the time the waveguides were being reoriented, but Ursis vociferously denied any such Sodeskayan conspiracy.

Of course, nobody believed him.

After the last of the speed runs were recorded, Brim reversed course for Eleandor-Bestienne. There were last-minute modifications to be made following her first major excursion —and a number of discrepancies still required correction. Nevertheless, the ship appeared to be as ready as men could make her for actual service. It *almost* seemed as if she had outgrown her original propensity for trouble.

Almost . . .

# Chapter 2

# PREPARATION

*Defiant* had been slowed below Hyperspeed for more than a metacycle now and was cruising steadily toward Eleandor-Bestienne on her four lateral gravity generators alone. Inside the spacious bridge, only a few of her twenty-three consoles were occupied: Brim, Aram, Ursis, and Calhoun operated the ship while most of the other flight crew caught a few cycles' well-deserved rest. Ahead, the shipyard planet nearly filled the now-transparent Hyperscreens when Aram spoke up from the starboard Helmsman's seat: "I've just contacted Planetary Center for arrival information at Orange-Eight District, Wilf."

"Let's hear it," Brim replied, reluctantly interrupted in the midst of a particularly stimulating fantasy. Margot Effer'wyck was never very far from the surface of his mind.

"Weather twenty-six thousand irals: scattered; twenty-three thousand: thunderstorms; visibility five c'lenyts; temperature one zero one; dew point seven six; wind calm; atmospheric density two nine eight two; visual approaches in progress," Aram recited from memory.

"Very well," Brim said, shaking his head and grinning. The red-haired A'zurnian's ability to recall was absolutely prodigious. "Mr. Chairman," he said, "check us in with Planetary Center for arrival at eighty-one-B, Orange-Eight."

"Aye, Lieutenant," the Chairman answered. "Check in Planetary Center for Orange Region, District-Eight yards, Complex eighty-one-B."

Planetary Center responded presently from the surface.

"Fleet CL.921 cleared direct to North-eleven-E synchronous buoy, Region Orange. On arrival, continue descent to two five zero c'lenyts and decelerate to velocity two three zero zero."

"Fleet CL.921 acknowledges direct North-eleven-E arrival," Brim replied. "We are at two nine zero zero c'lenyts and two five zero zero velocity. Decelerating to velocity of two three zero zero." Then he turned to Ursis. "How do the Verticals look, Nik?" he asked.

"My readouts *appear* normal," the Bear replied from the corner console directly to Aram's right. "Both have been running in auto-modulation for nearly a metacycle now, but I am also prepared for switching to manual control—at any time."

"Thanks," Brim responded, bringing up the gravity pressure on both generators as he slowed the ship. "I'll hope you don't have to do anything like that."

"So will I," Ursis growled. After *Defiant*'s disastrous encounter with lightning on her first trip off the stocks, it was clear he meant it.

Less than half a metacycle after they surged past the North-eleven-E synchronous buoy, *Defiant* was well within the atmosphere and measuring altitude in irals rather than c'lenyts. Collingswood had taken her place at the commander's console directly behind Brim when Planetary Center came back on the COMM. "Fleet CL.921: descend and maintain flight level two four zero."

"Fleet CL.921 will continue descent to two four zero," Brim acknowledged. He carefully checked through the Hyperscreens for local traffic. The Center's controllers were good—but they were also brutally overworked, as was their equipment, and approaches to the great shipbuilding center were extremely busy during all watches. Disastrous collisions had occurred despite everything, and—as the saying went—it took only one of those to ruin your whole day.

"Probably it's time to call the hands to stations, Number One," he said over his shoulder to Calhoun; who sat beside Collingswood's position in the second row of consoles. "We'll be down in half a metacycle."

The older Carescrian nodded. "Mr. Chairman," he said, "I wad ca' t' all stations, if ye please."

"You are connected to the blower, Commander," the Chairman acknowledged presently.

Calhoun pulled a tiny whistle from a breast pocket and sounded a silvery note throughout the ship. "All hands t' stations for landing," he boomed. "All hands t' stations for landing, ahoy."

With a smile of satisfaction, Brim listened to alarms sounding from the decks below. In the intraship monitors, he could see people gathering at their flight stations from every quarter of the big ship. Landfall in a starship was always a busy time —often too much so.

To starboard, he followed the lights of a departing ship that crossed their path as she climbed out toward space. A look assured him that Aram had seen it, too. With a grin, he let *Defiant* plunge through the ship's churning gravity wake like a tram on a bad section of roadbed. "Morning, Dora," he said to a surprised Wellington while she took her seat at the corner console next to his. Behind him, he could hear the firing crews stumbling to their positions at weapons consoles along the port bulkhead.

He concentrated for a moment on the muted thunder of the four big lateral generators and the slightly higher-pitched rumble of the Verticals. A glance past Aram showed Ursis at his systems panel with an impassive look on his face. But the Bear's eyes never strayed from his readouts—especially the overhead sections where the two suspect Verticals were displayed. Something was not altogether right there; Brim knew it in his gut. But like his Sodeskayan friend, there was no way he could put his finger on anything specific. And Fleet repair policies ran on specifics. Otherwise, everybody would be so busy looking for things that *might* go wrong that they wouldn't have time to fight a war. . . .

During the next few moments, *Defiant* descended into broken clouds and Brim felt the first jarring of the turbulence below.

"Ooo!" Wellington exclaimed gleefully beside him. The weapons officer seemed to love rough air.

Chuckling to himself grimly, Brim guessed she might soon get enough to last her a lifetime—maybe even a bit more, judging from all the lightning flashes in the distance ahead.

"Wonder if they'd let us deviate around to the south of that weather we're making for," he mused aloud.

"Somebody up there just asked for the same thing and they wouldn't let her do it," Aram replied. "The Orange-Eight District controllers are working a pretty narrow corridor this afternoon."

"Fleet CL.921: descend and maintain one zero thousand irals, altimeter is two nine one, and suggest now a heading of two five zero—two five zero—to join the Orange-Eight zero one zero radial inbound."

Brim frowned as he estimated the intensity of the storm ahead. It was a big one, with a lot of lightning. "Fleet CL.921," he replied, "I'm looking at a big storm cell just starboard of two five zero. My energy detector says it's pretty active, and I'd rather go around it one way or another."

"Fleet CL.921: sorry, sir. I can't take you there—District Eight has a line of takeoffs to the south. But I've had about sixty starships go through that area, and they're reporting good rides—no problems."

"Well, lady, Fleet CL.921 is looking at another cell right now," Brim complained, "on the port side of that same heading, and it's active, too. You've got us bracketed."

"Fleet CL.921," the Center replied in a resigned voice, "take a heading of 270—when I can, I'll turn you into the Orange-Eight beacon. It'll be about the one one zero radial."

"Fleet CL.921," Brim sent, "many thanks."

"She must be going to turn us *before* we get to those storm cells," Aram observed.

"We'll want everybody down, then," Brim said over his shoulder to Calhoun.

"Aye, lad," Calhoun said. Instantly, chimes began to ring through the ship as the last duty hands raced for their seats.

"Lift augmenters at four," Brim directed.

"Lift augmenters at four," Aram replied. Noise level on the bridge increased as the Verticals spooled up to take the load.

"Atmospheric radiators out. . . ."

*Defiant* shuddered as finned cooling radiators pushed out from either side of her stern like stubby wings roaring in the slipstream.

"Atmospheric radiators out and...two green lights—they're locked," Aram reported presently.

"Fleet CL.921: proceed direct to intercept Orange-Eight beacon on the one one zero radial," the Center controller interrupted. "Cross the threshold at nine thousand altitude."

"All right," Brim replied, "Fleet CL.921 direct to Orange-Eight arrival; cross threshold at nine thousand and maintain altitude. Thank you, ma'am."

"Checklist: altimeters," Ursis warned from his seat beside Aram.

"Altimeters read nine one and nine two—within tolerances."

"Landing lights?"

"Check."

"The autopilot just disconnected," Aram reported as the big ship bounced and twisted through increasing turbulence.

"Check," Brim answered, glancing off to port. "Xaxt-damned glad we didn't have to go through either of *those* cells—look at the lightning, would you."

"Some of that ahead, too," Aram said calmly.

"Yeah," Brim said. "I thought I saw some." Outside, the clouds were closing in and the air was becoming increasingly rough. At his left, however, Wellington was still clearly having the time of her life.

"Fleet CL.921," the Center broke in, "turn ten degrees port, reduce speed to one eight zero."

"Fleet CL.921 acknowledges," Brim sent. "Crank in ten more on the lift augmenters, Aram—and start the landing checklist."

"Augmenters at fourteen," Aram reported. "Checklist: continuous high-energy flow to the gravs, Nik?"

"On," Ursis reported, "and locked."

"Navigation switches?"

"Switches set—and reset."

"Auto flight panels?..."

"Fleet CL.921," the Center controller broke in, "as soon as you have reduced your speed, descend to five thousand."

"Fleet CL.921 slowing to one ninety, going to five thousand," Brim acknowledged. "Did you say Auto flight panels, Aram?"

"Auto flight panels."

"Checked."

"Airspeed EPR bugs?"

"One thirty-nine and cross-checked," Brim answered, altering course slightly while a powerful downdraft caught the starboard deck and threw the big ship on her side.

"Speed brake controls?"

"Neutral," Brim answered after he rolled back onto an even keel. He frowned; it was looking bad ahead again. Aft, the atmospheric radiators were now trailing thick clouds of condensation in the damp air.

"Lotsa lightning," Aram commented, looking up from the checklist display panel. "ILS check. . . ."

"ILS is tuned and identified," Brim answered, continuing to monitor the storm ahead with growing concern. Bad enough flying through something like that at such low altitude, but with Verticals he didn't trust into the bargain . . . "This is Fleet CL.921," he transmitted to the Center. "We'd like to go around a buildup we have directly ahead of us. Can we turn to port a little bit and go on the other side of it?"

"Negative, CL.921—traffic separation regulations. Please maintain present course. Contact Complex eighty-one Tower on one one nine four."

Brim grimaced in disgust. "Here's your xaxtdamned regulations," he muttered to himself.

"Say again, CL.921?"

"CL.921 maintaining present course," Brim grumped in embarrassment. "Checking in to Complex eighty-one—and good day."

"Good day, sir."

"I think we're going to give *Defiant* a bath," Aram said, staring out the forward Hyperscreens.

"And how," Brim answered. "Just look at that storm." It was getting downright difficult keeping the big cruiser on course, much less maintaining any sort of accurate descent—and he still couldn't see the surface of the water. "Complex eighty-one Tower: Fleet CL.921 with you at five thousand," he said, shaking his head.

"Good day, Fleet CL.921," Complex eighty-one replied. "Reduce speed one seven zero and turn port two seven one."

"Fleet CL.921 going to two seven one at one seven zero," Brim answered. The clouds broke for a moment to starboard, and he spied a heavy cruiser steering a parallel path no more than three c'lenyts away. He smiled. No wonder they hadn't let him deviate!

"Fleet CL.921: turn port to two four zero, descend and maintain three thousand," Complex eighty-one broke in.

"CL.921 is two four zero out of five for three," Brim said, glancing across Aram's console to Ursis. The Bear was peering at him with a concerned expression on his face. "How're those Verticals?" the Carescrian asked, guessing what was bothering his friend.

Ursis shook his head. "I debated raising an alarm, Wilf," he said. "Your question has saved me the trouble of a decision." He pursed his lips. "Somewhere the spirit of Voot is at work today—in this most damned of all damned mechanisms, something is yet amiss; I know it is. But I cannot isolate where or what it is."

"Well, at least we're almost down," Collingswood interjected. "You've had bad feelings about those Verticals since *Defiant* came off the stocks. This time, we're going to get them cleared up to your satisfaction before we leave the ground again. The war can wait long enough to make this a reasonably safe ship."

Ursis grinned and shrugged his broad shoulders. "For all we know, Captain, she may well *be* safe," he said. "So far, it is only me who raises alarms."

Brim nodded as an icy surge of misapprehension coursed along his spine. Nikolai Yanuarievich Ursis was rarely bothered by problems that had no real existence. "*I'll* listen to your concerns, Nik," he said. "Any time. . . ."

"In that case," the Bear answered, "you will be ready to react if you lose one or both Verticals as they take the full load of the ship. It is my guess that if we are destined for a failure, it will occur then."

"I'll watch it," Brim promised as the cruiser bumped through another series of powerful updrafts. Then further conversation was interrupted from Complex 81.

"Fleet CL.921 is six c'lenyts from the marker," the controller reported. "Turn port heading one eight zero; join the localizer at or about two thousand three hundred; you are cleared for instrument landing vector one seven."

Brim could visualize that particular stretch of Elsene Bay. The vector was close enough to shore that you could see the construction cranes of Area B from the bridge. It didn't give him much room for error. "Fleet CL.921 acknowledges all that. Many thanks," he answered as he bent *Defiant* onto her new course.

Overspeed warning horns for the atmospheric radiators sounded five times in close succession due to violent oscillations in the roiling air.

"Wants to rip the radiators off," Aram observed calmly.

"Tell me about it," Brim grumbled as he struggled with the controls.

"Fleet CL.921: reduce your speed to one six zero, please."

"CL.921 will be glad to do that," Brim answered over the continuing noise of the radiator overspeed. "One six zero."

"One six zero," Aram repeated.

"Got the vector-one-seven glideslope and localizer," Brim reported presently. Then the warning horn sounded again, during another horrendous downdraft.

"The stuff is really moving in on us now," Aram said. "Look out ahead...."

"You look," Brim joked. "I'd rather keep my eyes shut." Beside him, Wellington was no longer smiling. She was now sitting bolt upright and staring silently out the Hyperscreens, her hands suddenly gripping the armrests until her knuckles were white.

"Fleet CL.921 eighty-one-B Tower here; you are cleared to land; vector two five right, wind from nine zero at three five, gusts to nine zero."

"Thank you, sir," Brim said, mentally cringing at the potential turbulence ahead. This was *not* the time for trouble with anything, especially the Verticals. "Let's do the prelanding check, Nik," he said over his shoulder to Ursis.

"Atmospheric radiators?" Ursis prompted.

"Locked: two green lights."

"Vertical settings?"

"Thirty-three, thirty-three."

"Normal operation," Ursis commented.

"Lightning coming out of that one," Aram interrupted calmly.

"Huh?" Brim asked, looking up from his glideslope indicator.

"Lightning," Aram repeated, "coming out of that cloud."

"Where?"

"Right ahead of us."

"Oh, thraggling WON-derful," Brim grouched.

"Faith, but ye sure get the gr'at landin' vectors, chield," Calhoun joked over his shoulder. "Did ye tell 'em ye war' a Carescrian, perhaps?"

"That's got to be it," Brim laughed over his shoulder as the storm cloud loomed in the forward Hyperscreens. There was no avoiding it now. "Here comes that wash-off you were talking about, Aram," he said. "Better call out the altitudes for me." Suddenly everything turned black outside as *Defiant* plunged into the storm cell. Immediately a torrent of rain and hail began to hammer the ship, filling the bridge with the roar of its impact—an angry, bewildering, sense-shattering cascade that seemed to obliterate every other noise in the Universe. The starship bumped and bucked as if she were alive. It was all Brim could do to maintain any sort of glidepath at all. He pulled back on the forward vector and increased the Verticals to maximum in preparation for setdown.

"Thirteen hundred irals," Aram intoned calmly.

Brim ground his teeth as he fought the storm with all his flying skill. At least the Verticals were running smoothly.

"Twelve hundred. . . .Eleven hundred. . . ."

At that instant, *Defiant*'s tall KA'PPA tower was struck almost simultaneously by three distinct bolts of lightning. Even inside the bridge, the sounds were deafening—like three tremendous explosions, each utterly echoless and flat in tone. Someone screamed in the rear consoles. Lamps pulsed, along with the local gravity, and every detail of the decks outside was lit with a blinding brilliance of white fire—muted only at the last moment by the protective Hyperscreens. In the midst of the chaos, the sound of the Verticals faded abruptly and the ship began to sink as if she had smashed into a solid obstruction.

"They've tripped out, Wilf!" Ursis yelled over the pandemonium. "The Verticals. . . . They're both *gone!*"

Suddenly they were tumbling sickeningly from the bottom of the storm, dropping like a brick toward the sea, which swept under them like a slate-colored torrent of wrinkled chaos—mountainous rollers and flying spume. With no Verticals to cushion the shock, *Defiant* would hit the water hard enough to smash her hull like an eggshell. From his right, Brim could hear Ursis and Provodnik frantically trying to restart the two generators.

"Six hundred. . . . Five hundred. . . . Four hundred. . . ." Aram intoned as if there were no particular emergency.

"HOOT! HOOT! PULL UP! PULL UP!" the Chairman shrieked with emergency inflection. "HOOT! HOOT! . . ."

Instinctively, Brim had been bringing the ship's bow up into a vertical position. Now he was ready to act. "Gimme everything you got on the Laterals, Nik," he yelled, baring his teeth with effort. *"Dump 'EM!"*

All four of the big generators suddenly erupted into violent overload as Ursis shorted the protective load limiters and dumped raw energy into every power chamber. But the big generators needed time to spool up to full power. . . . *Defiant*'s hull trembled like a leaf, groaning and creaking throughout each joint of her starframe. In the corner of his eye, Brim could see the great rollers of the churning sea below. The aft deck must now be nearing the surface. It was going to be close. . . .

"HOOT! HOOT! PULL UP! PULL UP! HOOT! HOOT! HOOT! . . ."

In the midst of the confusion, one of the great waves smashed into *Defiant*'s stern with a deafening rumble—clearly audible even above the mounting roar of the straining generators—and threatened to flip her over on her back like a rowboat. Heart in his mouth, Brim watched the horizon slide over the top of the Hyperscreens until—in a titanic upwelling of spray—the big cruiser's generators overcame her downward momentum and she began to rise hesitantly, straight up like one of the prehistoric chemical rockets.

"She feels it!" Calhoun yelled exultantly. "She feels it!"

Iral by painful iral by painful iral *Defiant* climbed away

from the raging ocean, still tossed this way and that by the tremendous winds overhead in the storm, but safe for the moment. . . .

"NIK, WHAT ABOUT THAT RESTART?" Brim yelled over the thunder of the straining generators. "We've got to get her down or head for space."

"One moment more, Wilf," Ursis rumbled back as the ship rocked violently in her vertical position. "Cold starting One," he said, almost to himself as his six-fingered hands ran surely over the controls. Suddenly, the rumble of the lateral generators was joined by the high-pitched whine of a single Vertical. "You can now start to ease her back into position," the Bear roared in triumph, "while we work on Number Two."

A few cycles later, Brim had *Defiant* back on an even keel and ploughing along under the clouds as if nothing out of the ordinary had happened at all—except for a hush that had suddenly come over the entire bridge. Aside from the generators, the only noise came from behind him as Collingswood and Calhoun frantically checked in with every duty section on the ship.

Presently, a hand touched his shoulder. "Well done, Wilf," Collingswood said from directly behind him. "We seem to have very little internal damage—after all that. Unfortunately," she added in a voice tense with anger, "it appears as if our *Defiant* is still quite susceptible to energy strikes."

Brim nodded. "It looks that way, Captain," he said.

"The backward waveguide, Nik?"

"I somehow doubt it, Captain," Ursis growled quietly. "They fixed that after the launch debacle—but it is related to that, or I miss my guess."

"Which is a thing you seldom do," she declared. "We shall this time insure *Defiant* is a lot more tolerant or we will not take her to war. I consider myself brave, but I am definitely not suicidal. . . ."

"Fleet CL.921: do you see landing vector two five right yet?"

"Fleet CL.921. As soon as we break out of this rain shower we will," Brim answered. "Yeah. . . . Now we've got it." Ahead, a solid ruby light flashed out of the gray distance. Sudden gusts of wind pushed him to port and the light began to separate into horizontal lines. As he corrected to starboard, the light shimmered into vertical lines. One last correction to port and it coalesced again.

"Fleet CL.921: arrival detector reports you had a problem out there," a female voice said from the Tower. She sounded a little bit like Margot, but without the latter's perfect modulation.

"Fleet CL.921 is under control and on final," Brim answered calmly.

"Thank you, sir."

Off to port, a forest of shipyard cranes slid by in the rain-streamed Hyperscreens. Brim glanced down at the bridge decking beneath his feet. It was littered with the paraphernalia people usually kept on their consoles: purses, eyeglasses, cvcesse' cups, a bottle of hand lotion, a box of tissues. They'd get it all sorted out in time. He remembered the pulsing gravity, but hadn't realized it was *that* strong—too busy to notice, probably. . . .

Only a hundred irals altitude now. He walked the steering engines, lining her up for flare-out and hover-down—then dropped the port deck against a stiff crosswind blowing from landward: the nose wandered a little toward the shore, but the big starship stayed on her original course like she was riding rails. Stable—the ruby landing vector ahead was still steady in the Hyperscreens. No wonder the shipyard was proud of *Defiant*—she was going to be a remarkable disruptor platform.

Now if she'd only learn to stay in the air. . . .

Time to bring her in. Brim checked his instruments: descent rate, speed, pitch. All on the button. The starship began to sink as he pulled back on the Verticals—this time on purpose. He eased off the steering engines; her bow swung back to line up perfectly with the ruby vector. He kept the deck slanted for the drift. . . . Nose up a little. . . . A little more. . . . He leveled the deck only an instant before gray cascades of water shot hundreds of irals into the air on either side of the hull and *Defiant* settled gently onto her gravity gradient.

They were down—in one piece, Barbousse's huge banner raised to the KA'PPA mast and snapping furiously in the wind.

The bridge suddenly erupted in wild jubilation. "Three cheers for Wilf Brim!"

"He got us through!"

"Hurray for Wilf!"

"To ice, to snow, to *Carescria* we go!..."

Brim felt his cheeks burn. "I was only trying to save my own skin," he protested, but nobody seemed to believe him.

"Fleet CL.921: if you can make that next high-speed turnoff, cross one seven right and proceed to gravity pool three one three."

"Fleet CL.921 copies," Brim answered over the continuing hullabaloo in the bridge. Leaning on the gravity brakes, he skidded the big ship around a turnoff marker bobbing wildly in the heavy swells, then rumbled across a long procession of flashing buoys. Landing lights of a heavy starship shone brightly at the distant landward end. "Crossing one seven right and proceeding to pool three on three three," he said. "Good afternoon."

"Good afternoon, sir."

As if it had been a routine landing....

Before the stormy afternoon was over, Collingswood had every civilian in the Complex running for cover. Literally hundreds of KA'PPA messages flashed instantaneously across the thousand-odd light years that separated Eleandor-Bestienne from the Imperial Admiralty on Avalon, and presently *Defiant* was populated by the highest managers in the region. Later—as soon as they could arrive—the top administrators on the planet joined their underlings cowering in the wardroom. And when Collingswood was finished, the civilians received personal orders from First Star Lord Sir Beorn Wyrood himself—via direct link with the Admiralty. Moreover, the orders were personally seconded by none other than Crown Prince Onrad, heir apparent to the Imperial throne at Avalon.

Both messages were short, to the point, and unmistakable. *Defiant* was to be put to rights immediately, at the highest priority possible. And this time, she was to be repaired *permanently*, or the Planetary General Manager and each member of his senior staff would be held individually—and personally—responsible. Progress reports were to be forwarded to the Admiralty every fifteen metacycles until the job was finished, and thoroughly tested.

With their positions—perhaps their lives, for all they knew —literally at stake, the shipyard managers caused absolute engineering miracles to be performed. Working around the clock for five solid days, technicians and engineers from all over the planet actually removed *Defiant*'s bridge and superstructure, then completely rebuilt her Verticals according to the new specifications created as a result of her initial accident. She was buttoned up on the morning and afternoon of the sixth day, then flown by an exclusively civilian crew, including the Planetary General Manager and his senior staff as passengers, through every thunderstorm that could be located in the entire northern hemisphere during the next week. After shrugging off at least one hundred fifty major lightning strikes in flight—and two more days of testing against an actual battery of disruptors—*Defiant* was once more declared safe.

Following three additional days of deep-space trials with Blue Capes at the controls, even Ursis seemed content with the ship and her systems, and Collingswood formally accepted the starship from the builders a second time. This time, the little wardroom ceremony was attended by none other than Reynard J. Eliott, the Planetary General Manager himself, who had lately been very much in evidence around *Defiant*'s gravity pool. From his tired eyes, it was clear that the man had not seen his palatial residence in the planet's other hemisphere since shortly after Collingswood invoked her powerful influence at the Admiralty. He was a small, buck-toothed civilian with a sallow complexion and the brisk air of one who is comfortable being important. His hair was carefully combed to cover a balding head, and he acted as if he were teetering between being annoyed on one hand and uneasy on the other.

Brim had never seen the man wear anything but expensive-looking business suits, and wondered if perhaps he had been born in one. Of course, he also carried the archaic, narrow-brimmed stovepipe hat of a shipyard manager. He might have been born with that, too, for all Brim knew. But then, it was doubtful that people at his exalted level often got that close to the shipyards they managed. . . . It was somehow satisfying to the Carescrian that the man's expensive shoes were this evening covered with the same construction dust as his own.

"Well, Commander," Eliott said loftily to Collingswood, "does the ship meet with everyone's approval this time?" Without waiting for an answer, he opened the Red Book and placed it on the table before her. "Box number 921, please— above your previous signature."

Collingswood made no move to acknowledge the book's presence. Instead, she glanced meaningfully at Brim, then at Ursis. "Well?" she said, placing her elbows on the table and steepling her fingers, "last chance, gentlemen."

Brim pursed his lips and nodded thoughtfully. At his personal insistence, he'd remained on board during the brutal disruptor testing—and had personally flown nearly all the deep-space trials. "I have no more problems, Captain," he said in a confident voice. "I'll fly her anywhere now."

Ursis narrowed his tired eyes. He, too, had been aboard during the disruptor testing. "At last I am satisfied with *Defiant*'s systems, Captain Collingswood," he declared with a wry smile. "It is high time we turn our energies once more toward combating the forces of Nergol Triannic."

At this juncture, Collingswood turned to the Book and applied her signature. Then she sat back and looked up at the General Manager. "Thank you for everything you've done," she said magnanimously. "You've been a great help. . . ."

For a moment, anger seemed to overtake the man's fear. Then he suddenly relaxed and nodded his head—clearly awed by this mere Commander whose ire could invoke the First Lord of the Admiralty *and* the Crown Prince.

"You are most welcome, Captain," he said evenly. He retrieved the Book and slipped it under his arm as if he were suddenly afraid she might change her mind. "I don't think the ship will disappoint you again."

"Shall we seal that with a goblet of meem?" Collingswood asked, nodding to Grimsby in the pantry nearby.

At first, Eliott shook his head, then brought himself up short and smiled the first genuine smile Brim had seen on his face. "Yes, I think I shall, Captain," he said. "I should be proud to drink to this gallant ship—and her extraordinary crew." After the usual toasts were offered, he raised his glass to Collingswood alone. "Not too late to wish *you* luck, too, Captain," he said.

Collingswood raised her glass to his silently. Brim knew her mind was already elsewhere. *Defiant* was under orders to depart in the morning for the Escort Training School on Menander-Garand, and in her own way she had already reduced this overblown civilian to a cipher. She was off to more important considerations than conquering nettlesome Planetary Managers.

The single-day flight to the training base passed without incident. Waldo and Aram flew *Defiant* to a flawless landfall —in flawless weather on a flawless evening, just as the huge binary-star system Menander was setting on the western horizon. After that, they all worked without letup for five solid weeks. The course was designed to harden new crews and accustom them to the conditions in which they would wage their part of the great intragalactic war. The entire ship's company, from Collingswood to the newest able starman, was under constant stress nearly every metacycle. If they were not out performing maneuvers, they were practicing disruptor drills, or running through Action Stations . . . or battling mock radiation fires, or landing the big ship with only part of her propulsion systems operational. And when they were not out in space, everyone attended cross-training classes about some part of the vessel that—before then—he or she had completely taken for granted. Thus, Brim learned a great deal about propulsion systems—firsthand. And Ursis flew a starship for the first time in his life—astonishingly well. One afternoon, Wellington and her weapons experts even found themselves in the Drive chamber, reorienting the sixteen primary tesla coils—a heavy job nobody ever wanted to do— but one without which *Defiant* might lose her ability to travel at Hyperspeeds. During their ordeal, every member of the ship's crew—including even-tempered Collingswood—was driven to the point of near-despair. They were tired beyond tiredness and deathly sick of the constant stress that sacked what little of their strength remained at the end of each watch. For the most part, however, each of them realized that this was the only chance they would ever get to become an integrated fighting team capable of surviving the savagery out in the convoy lanes—wherever they might be. And if the price of preparation was overwork to the point of pain, the other price—the one they might surely pay if they weren't prepared—was infinitely more expensive.

At first, they were not very effective as a crew. Individually, many were extraordinarily talented, but they had yet to form a coordinated team—and to experience the excellence that only synergy can produce. Little by little, however, they progressed. They smoothed off their rough edges and learned to work with each other. Moreover, it was a sort of progress that all could see, for the ship herself functioned better—on a daily basis. Soon, they were more often than not declared winners in the vicious hunter-killer games staged daily by professional "aggressor" crews aboard captured League warships.

Not only did they learn each other, they also learned the ship—all her little idiosyncrasies and quirks. And her strengths. Wellington was overjoyed at the disruptor batteries she had to work with. Perhaps her crew showed the most marked improvement, right from the beginning. Something about the woman's personality welded her weapons experts into effective teams first off. In only a few days, they were destroying targets even ships that had nearly completed the course could hardly track. And *Defiant* became known as a ship of marksmen—extraordinary marksmen. Before long, 152-mmi disruptors became known as "Wellingtons" throughout the huge training complex.

It was little enough time to prepare for what a few—like Collingswood—had known for some time now: that the war was about to enter a new and even deadlier phase. Brim learned about it one morning more than two-thirds of the way through the course when a scheduled maneuver was abruptly canceled for *Defiant's* officers and senior enlisted personnel. Half dead with fatigue, they were marched from their duty stations into huge skimmers and bussed overland to the central training complex.

There—in a most secret briefing—they learned that all was not well within the League of Dark Stars. Nergol Triannic, it seemed, had promised his nobles at the war's outset that mastery of the galaxy would be theirs in no more than two years. To that end, he sent his minion Kabul Anak on a bloody march of conquest across the stars that—at its zenith—reached out its claws for Avalon herself. However, since those first dark days, the rolling storm from the League had largely been stemmed—held to almost a deadlock as the Imperial commonwealth gathered itself into a war footing, then began to force Anak and his invaders to pay dearly for each star and planet, battle for each asteroid.

Now, more than eight years after the first savage attacks, Triannic found himself under intense pressure to make good his promise—however late. The League's most important ports were securely blockaded; the overall economy was almost totally stifled; and maintenance of his Controllers with their ever-burgeoning military empire was bleeding the economy white.

In a desperate attempt to accomplish his original covenant—and thus preserve his sovereignty— Triannic had ordered a sharp revision in strategy. The first inkling of this manifested itself when Anak's attacks became increasingly less frequent, then, in the last months, ceased almost entirely. Simultaneously, League shipyards nearly doubled their output—sacrificing whole cities for raw materials to feed the new building programs.

Working round the clock, Imperial intelligence gathering-and-analysis units had pieced together interlocking bits of information revealing Triannic's newest ploy. In one great throw of the conqueror's dice, he planned to send Kabul Anak and his new fleets on a direct attack at Avalon with an armada so powerful the Empire could not place sufficient counterforce in its path to save the capital before defenses crumbled and the government itself finally came under the League's collective thumb.

As a secondary objective, most of the Imperial squadrons would also be destroyed in the process, ground into space debris by concentrated fire from the most powerful starfleet in the known Universe.

A major complication in the League plan, however, was Avalon's location within the tempestuous galactic center. The five Home Planets and their triple star, Asterious, were surrounded by a nearly impregnable sphere of mighty asteroid shoals and blazing ramparts of drift, swarms of neutron stars, celestial debris, free atoms, and cosmic deserts—all of it swept by treacherous gravity storms and particle avalanches. Only one reasonable invasion path existed. This was an opening very much like the iris of an eye—with the great star harbor and military base of Hador-Haelic at its very center. A very powerful fleet would be required to force this passage, but such was precisely what Triannic—and his minion Admiral Kabul Anak—planned to bring about in the minimum time possible.

To that end, in heavily defended star harbors near the League capital of Tarrott, powerful battle groups were already assembling—under cover of great secrecy. Triannic had no idea that so much of his plan was already compromised. But now it was the Empire's task to fortify Hador-Haelic before the attack came. The one key item of information Avalon's forces lacked was when the attack might take place.

A great, historic clock was inexorably counting off cycles —and only the Leaguers knew how long it would run. But when Anak did choose to launch his great thrust, it was clear to Brim that *Defiant* would be on hand for the titanic struggle to contain it. And that was precisely where he wanted to be.

During the last hectic week of training, *Defiant* was pitted against a group of three captured League warships; this time she was cast in a role of an attacker. It was clear that the highly trained "aggressor" ships were ill-prepared to cope with the new light cruiser's surprising speed. And Collingswood used the ship's advantage brilliantly, forcing her "enemies" to fight by her own rules, attacking when they least expected it and never remaining in one locality long enough for them to use what would amount to their superior firepower. Unfortunately for the "aggressors," each time they did maneuver into a position to benefit from their combined disruptors, the wily Collingswood used her speed—plus Brim's extraordinary helmsmanship—to outmaneuver them, thus sustaining only minor "damage" to *Defiant* while Wellington scored sufficient "hits" to win the desperately fought mock combats.

At the end of the training period, the tired "aggressors" good-naturedly KA'PPAed a surrender.

"We give up," they messaged. "We'd rather fight Anak's people any day!"

Brim smiled to himself as a signal officer read off the message on the ship's blower. Tough as they'd made things seem, he well knew that *Defiant*'s real test would not occur until she faced actual combat. Nothing could quite simulate the real threat of death. . . .

Two days after the mock battles—and following a ceremonial flyby of the week's graduating ships for Rear Admiral (the Hon.) Nabonasser K. Comtist, Commander of the Escort School—*Defiant* and her crew were granted a short leave before reporting for convoy duty at Hador-Haelic. Brim had been half expecting this might happen, and had somehow found time—and energy—during the hectic curriculum to form his plans accordingly.

He got a civilian KA'PPA message off only cycles after *Defiant* was safely moored and he had personally secured her helm:

TO: MARGOT EFFER'WYCK, LT., I.F. @ ADMIRALTY/
AVALON 19-993.367

FROM: WILF A. BRIM, LT, I.F. @ MENANDER-GARAND
341.98-R31

*personal*:

MARGOT: FIVE DAYS' LEAVE AND A ROUND-TRIP HOP
TO AVALON ALLOW NEARLY A FULL DAY ON
AVALON! I.F.S. *ALBATRON* MAKES LANDFALL TWO
DAYS FROM NOW AT ZECHLEY FLEET BASE ON LAKE
MERSIN: NINE BELLS OF THE AFTERNOON WATCH. I
SHALL CONTACT AMBRIDGE, YOUR CHAUFFEUR AT
THE EFFER'IAN EMBASSY.
ETERNALLY—WILF

Afterward, he frantically packed a small traveling bag and —with Ursis and Provodnik driving an open skimmer at breakneck speed through the base—arrived at *Albatron*'s gravity pool while they were just about to collapse the brow. He was last aboard the little LK-91, a fast packet he had learned to fly at the Helmsman's Academy, squeezing through a half-closed hatch on his way to the cramped bridge. There, he traded places with the ship's regular pilot—a tall fellow with wispy moustaches, a great woolly head of hair, and a most relieved look on his face.

"Universe, Brim," the man said as he climbed nervously out of the Helmsman's seat, "I thought I was going to end up having to fly the Avalon run anyway. You don't believe in cutting things close or anything, do you?"

Brim laughed. "I'm here—and now you can go ahead and get married. What else matters?"

"I'll think of something by the time you get back, you rascal!" the man called as he galloped into the companionway to the main deck.

Moments later, Brim watched him run at full speed across the brow and into the arms of a dark, long-haired woman waiting outside a small skimmer near the brow portal. Then he occupied himself with the controls—too busy now for much of anything except making his own personal schedule to Avalon. He wasn't racing off to be married or anything like that—but he certainly had *related* thoughts at the back of his mind. . . .

The spaceways between Menander-Garand and Avalon were well within Avalon's sphere of influence, and the speedy little packet made her Hyperlight journey without incident, despite the great war that raged elsewhere in the galaxy. Brim smoothly made landfall and taxied to the military complex through a clear, sunlit winter afternoon, arriving at his assigned lakeside gravity pool three cycles before nine bells sounded in the bridge. He braked to a stop at precisely the same instant that a graceful black limousine skimmer slowed to a hover just outside the entrance to the brow, engulfing the bare trees in a cloud of blowing snow. Only in Avalon, he laughed to himself. The capital city was so full of limousines that many were actually used as delivery vehicles. This one would be picking up some important element of the ship's cargo, for there was certainly nobody of any particular importance aboard.

"Shut 'em off, Mack," he called over his shoulder to the Systems Engineer, then with the generators spooling down in the background, he braced himself for the switch to internal gravity. It was a transition that even in the best of circumstances made him staggeringly dizzy for a few moments—no matter how many times he went through it. And it happened at the precise moment he thought he spied a huge, green-liveried footman open the door of the limo for a strangely familiar figure bundled in a Fleet Cape—whose short blond curls in wanton disarray started his heart pounding all out of control. . . . He blinked his blurred eyes as the figure hurried through the portal and out over the brow. No one else in the entire Universe looked like that. "Margot!" he gasped, nearly tripping as he fought his way out of the helmsman's seat. "See you tomorrow," he called, grabbing his bag and plunging wildly into the companionway.

"Yeah," the engineer called after him. "If ya' don't break your xaxtdamned neck before that!"

As Brim ran toward the main hatch, he felt cold winter air rushing into the ship along the passageway. There was perfume in it! Special perfume. And then she was *there*, standing at the end of the brow with the most beautiful smile he had ever seen. All he wanted in the whole Universe—and he simply didn't have any words. But then, neither did she—which turned out to be all right anyway, because both their lips were abruptly too busy communicating in a much more Universal language than formal Avalonian.

Her arms were still tightly around him when he finally wrestled his breathing under control. Dockyard workers were pushing their way past into the starship when he guided her into a little alcove beside the hatch and out of the traffic. At that moment, not even direct orders from the Emperor himself would have made him interrupt this most magical interlude.

After a while, she half opened her eyes in the sleepy kind of way he knew—and loved—so well. He started to speak, but she placed a finger on his lips. "'Swiftly coursed o'er Space and Time /—Spirit of the Night,'" she recited in a breathless whisper. "'Out of the firmament sublime, / Where from the yet ungazed starlight, / Thou weavest dreams of joy and fear, / That make thee terrible and dear, /—Safe was thy flight.'"

Brim let the poetic lines of Laerites's "Ode to the Void," sweep over him from out of the past. "We shouldn't waste even a moment, Margot," he whispered. "This ship is due out again late tomorrow morning."

She grinned and rhythmically ground her torso into his. "You've got me off to a magnificent start already, Lieutenant Brim," she said a little breathlessly. "If it were warmer outside, I think I'd show you what I don't have on under this cape right here and now."

Brim laughed and squeezed her to him tighter, thrusting himself rhythmically against her. "Wouldn't I *love* that," he whispered in her ear.

"Oo-o," she giggled, as if she were suddenly out of breath. Her eyebrows arched and she smiled happily. "I'd hoped you might be off to that same kind of start." Her eyes suddenly sparkled. "The limousine has one-way glass, Wilf. Let's have Ambridge drive us to the embassy so we can do something about these hormones of ours. After that, perhaps we can love each other a little more rationally."

Taking a deep breath, Brim placed his hands at the small of her back and drew her even closer. "'Come let us twine together, you and I,'" he answered as she crouched slightly and opened herself to him, "'The moments we may love are far too few, / And helpless through Time's corridors we fly, / Embraced—you to I and I to you. . . .'" For a few moments afterward, he was too busy kissing to think of anything else except warm breath and wet, wet lips. Then, surreptitiously checking the hallway—which was empty—he backed her farther into the alcove and gently raised the hem of her cape to her waist. "Great Universe," he gasped while his knees began to tremble almost out of control.

"Would I try to deceive *you*, my love?" Margot asked, licking her lips and looking at him with what could only be described as a totally shameless smirk. "Or did you merely need reassurance that I am still a blonde? . . ." True to her royal word, in addition to a heated Fleet Cape, Her Royal Highness, The Princess Margot Effer'wyck, was wearing only boots. . . .

* * *

In the rapidly fading winter afternoon, neither Brim nor Margot found they would—or necessarily *could*—wait until they reached the embassy. Therefore, the surprise of the limousine's swerve and the grating shriek of collapsing metal came as a double shock.

"Voot's ear!" Margot spluttered, thrown spread-eagled to the floor of the limousine. "W-what was *that*?"

"I think we've had an accident," Brim said, still on the seat and shakily focusing his eyes through the cracked glass at an Army staff skimmer that appeared to have embedded itself in the limousine's engine compartment. A large crowd was gathering even as he spoke.

"Sweet, *thraggling* Universe," Margot exclaimed as she frantically struggled to retrieve her cape—it had somehow become jammed under a console—"where are we?"

"Mm-m," Brim grunted, discovering to his dismay how thoroughly trousers can become entangled with boots. "I don't know. It's a part of town I've never seen. Looks like some sort of ethnic sector, though. Everybody's got on weird colors."

Presently, Ambridge appeared outside in the glow of emergency lamps, frowning and stroking his chin as he inspected the damage. He was joined almost immediately by a short, rumpled Army captain with suspicious, rheumy eyes, a thick brown moustache, and a lantern jaw to rival any professional Corbut wrestler's. The officer had just raised an accusatory finger in Ambridge's direction when he was interrupted by a grating voice that absolutely set Brim's teeth on edge.

"I SAY! Can't you idiot civilians EVER learn to drive properly?"

Brim felt his eyebrows—and hackles—rise as a familiar figure swaggered into view outside. "Sweet, clotted crumbs of zorkfrew," he swore. "I *knew* I recognized that voice. It's thraggling *Hagbut*!" He shook his head as memories returned in a flood. General (the Hon.) Gastudgon Z' Hagbut, $X^{ce}$, N.B.E., Q.O.C., Imperial Expeditionary Forces (Combat) was the same small, intense-looking superpatriot of middling years under whose command he had served during The A'zurnian campaign. Red-faced and custom-tailored as always, Hagbut still spoke as if he disliked showing his teeth.

"*Hagbut*?" Margot demanded, attempting to comb her hair and apply makeup at the same time. "You mean *General* Hagbut?"

"I see you've already met him, too," Brim said dryly, watching the Captain and a number of gaily dressed onlookers muscle his clearly disabled vehicle to the opposite curb.

"I can't believe it!" Margot growled under her breath. "What perfectly horrible luck." She shook her head. "You were with him on A'zurn, weren't you?"

"Yeah," Brim acknowledged dismally, "bad luck then, too."

"I'll bet," Margot said, adjusting her service cap, "I have to work with that perfect stuffed shirt at least once a week." She peered glumly through the one-way glass. "I think I heard somebody say he's from the Ornwald region of the galaxy—and I'll bet we're in that section of town."

"YOU, in there!" Hagbut roared imperiously, pounding on the roof over Brim's head. "COME OUT OF THAT LIMOUSINE whoever you are!" Then he pointed to Ambridge as if the man were an especially dangerous adversary. "How DARE you exercise right-of-way over a General Officer of the Imperial Army?"

"B-but General," Ambridge protested. "The signal was clearly in the favor of my limousine. I was already started into the intersection when your staff car hit me."

"You had NO BUSINESS in that intersection when I was coming through," Hagbut interrupted. Then he pounded on the limousine again. "COME OUT OF THERE and face the consequences, you damned civilians!"

Brim glanced at Margot, who now seemed to be reasonably satisfied with her appearance. Her cheeks, however, had become flushed enough to be noticeable, even in the comparative darkness of the limousine. And her eyes were narrowed to slits. He had just reached for the door button when she placed a restraining hand firmly on his sleeve.

"Wait," she said between clenched lips, "this is *my* problem." With a dark look on her face, she climbed past him and opened the door herself. Ambridge was in the process of explaining again that the traffic signal was enabled for their direction when Hagbut interrupted him in midsentence.

"Here on Avalon, signals are of little concern to vehicles on IMPORTANT OFFICIAL BUSINESS," he blustered. "AND FURTHERMORE..." Abruptly, his voice trailed off while his jaw dropped. *"P-princess Effer'wyck,"* he gasped.

"You tell 'em, General," the Captain growled, still directing his anger—and his attention—entirely to Ambridge. "Damned civilians, anyway..."

"SHUT UP, Captain!"

"Huh?..."

"Princess Effer'wyck! What an *extreme* pleasure to see you here, YOUR HIGHNESS. How unfortunate of my clumsy aide to cause this accident...."

"I caused what?"

"Ah, good evening, General Hagbut," Margot answered coolly. "I believe that I heard you say Ambridge caused the accident?"

"Yeah, General, I ah..."

"Will you BE QUIET, Captain? You know perfectly well it was *your* fault."

"B-but, General, you was the one that was hungry. *I* didn't want to run the signal. They'd have kept our reservation at the restaurant...."

Hagbut's face turned a deep crimson, and he started to speak, but Ambridge—who had returned to the chauffeur's compartment—used that moment to spin up the limousine's traction engine. It failed to catch, however, and drifted to silence. Momentarily distracted, Hagbut glanced past Margot into the limousine. "BRIM!" he exclaimed in surprise. "What in the name of Kaehler are *you* doing in a limousine with a princess?"

"Good evening, General," Brim said, stepping to the pavement and saluting. "It is good to see you again, sir," he lied, raising his voice over a second unsuccessful attempt to start the limousine's traction engine.

"AH, YES," Hagbut crowed, clearly on the lookout for any distraction from the present situation. "I'm sure it *is*, young man!" He turned to Margot. "Last year," he said boastfully, "I not only helped further this young Carescrian's military career, but I—PERSONALLY—provided him with the tactical advice that enabled him to perform an OUTSTANDING mission and win an A'zurnian medal."

Brim gritted his teeth while Ambridge made a third unsuccessful attempt to start the limousine. Were the truth known, during the A'zurnian raid, he'd saved both Hagbut's career *and* his skinny neck. . . .

"I say, DIDN'T I?" Hagbut prompted, pulling on Brim's sleeve.

"It was a *fine* mission, General," the Carescrian replied.

"A 'fine' mission?" Hagbut exclaimed blusteringly. "Is that all you have to say about it? Why, thanks to *me*, it made you part of MY SUCCESS. Part of an IMPERIAL TRIUMPH!"

"Your Highness," Ambridge interrupted from the driver's seat. "I'm afraid the traction engine won't start. I have another car on its way from the Embassy, but the driver requires at least half a metacycle to drive here."

"MOST UNFORTUNATE," Hagbut boomed with a sudden look of concern. He frowned for a moment, then abruptly broke into a smile of sorts, one of the few Brim could remember. "With such a long time to wait, Princess," he said, shooting his cuffs grandly, "surely you will join me for supper. That way, your embassy driver need not hurry to pick you up—and I can enjoy your company whilst I endeavor to ATONE for the CLUMSINESS OF MY AIDE." He glared at his crestfallen companion while a gaggle of street urchins helped Ambridge push the Effer'ian limousine onto a side street.

Brim watched Margot's eyebrows rise—clearly, she hadn't expected anything like *this*. She opened her mouth. . . .

"Oh, come *on*, now, Your Highness," Hagbut interrupted, turning on all the charm he could muster. "As a native Ornwaldian, I know this section as if it were my home. We have an *excellent* dining establishment only A FEW STEPS from this VERY intersection: the Golden Cockerel; I dine there often. AND, I shall even EXTEND my invitation to Captain Quince—I believe you have met him, Your Highness—as well as Lieutenant Brim. The two of them can discuss, er, MILITARY matters and so forth whilst *we* speak on more

CULTURED subjects. Now, what do you say? In the interests on intra-Empirical relations . . ."

Margot turned to Brim with a frantic look in her eyes. "W-well . . ." she stammered.

It was the first time he could remember seeing her flustered. Of course, Hagbut could have no idea that she and a mere Carescrian planned to spend the evening making love. Most royalty considered that Carescrians were hardly sentient. . . . And then it hit him like a sack of rocks—if they joined Hagbut in a restaurant, *she'd be expected to take off her cloak!*

"Really, General," Margot imparted, color rising to her cheeks again. "It was only a minor accident—no one was hurt. Wilf and I can wait in the limousine until . . ."

"Nonsense, Your Highness," Hagbut countered. "I shall hear none of it. Quince caused you this inconvenience in MY service,"—he glared momentarily at the captain—"and I MUST make some restitution, at least."

"General," Margot articulated, unconsciously pulling her cloak closer around her neck, "I certainly appreciate your concern, but, please. None of this is necessary."

"It most CERTAINLY is," Hagbut protested, his glance flashing angrily to Brim. "OR," he continued, smiling sardonically, "should I report to the Intelligence Council that Your Highness is showing definite favoritism toward the Fleet?"

"How could you even say such a thing, General?" she protested. Brim could see that her hands were now balled into fists behind her back. Hagbut had scored a telling point.

"I jest, of course," Hagbut guffawed, clearly sniffing victory.

"Of course," Margot said sullenly.

"Well-l-l!" Hagbut crowed, moving quickly now. "That settles that, doesn't it?"

Panic flashed across Margot's eyes. She touched her throat for a moment, then took a deep gulp of air—like a diver facing a long descent. "I capitulate, General," she sighed presently. "Perhaps it *is* time we sat down together. Wilf, I believe there was something you planned to purchase on our way to the Embassy. Perhaps you ought to get that out of the way before you join us at the table?"

Brim frowned. "A purchase, Princess?" he asked.

Margot fixed him with an urgent expression in her eyes. "Yes," she said. "Remember? Size fourteen over point three thirty-nine."

*Size?* . . . Understanding suddenly dawned! "Er . . . yes," he stumbled. "*Yes*, the special purchase! What was the . . . ah, Duchess's . . . ah, size again, Princess?"

"Fourteen over point three thirty-nine," Margot repeated with a look of undiluted relief on her face.

"Thank you," Brim said, bowing with great deference. "I shall see to the matter immediately. General, a matter of great importance to the Effer'ian embassy."

Hagbut nodded—as usual, he hadn't been paying attention. "Well, don't be too long, m'boy," he advised, pulling Brim close to his face. "Oh, I know that you Carescrians don't frequent establishments like this one," he whispered in a fatherly tone. "Very high class and all that." His breath smelled as if he seldom brushed his teeth. "But don't let that drive you off. Simply follow *me* in your actions, and you will be quite acceptable. Quince!" he ordered, dismissing Brim like a street beggar. "Quick step ahead and secure a larger table for us, man. The name of HAGBUT is well known there!" With that, he deftly grasped Margot's elbow and marched her along the street like a prisoner.

Brim stood for a moment on the teeming sidewalk transfixed. *Now* what? He was prepared to handle any starship in the galaxy—or fight a hundred Leaguers single-handed—but *this* was a different kind of problem entirely! He started in the opposite direction, shaking his head in consternation. Displays of women's clothing were everywhere, in positively bewildering arrays of colors and styles! How did they choose anything to wear? From time out of mind, he'd worn nothing but uniforms—and there were too many versions of *them* for his liking. He chuckled to himself. Thank the Universe for uniforms. . . .

*Uniforms!*

Of course. He could certainly handle the purchase of a woman's uniform—especially since he knew the correct size formula! And it stood to reason that at least a few of the many dress shops would offer Fleet garb. . . . This time, he started off with a bit of assurance in his stride. . . .

After considerable walking and searching, however, it became clear that his newfound confidence was lamentably misplaced. Nowhere in the at least eleven billion display windows he had studied so far was there anything that looked even *remotely* like a Fleet uniform.

And there was precious little time to search any farther. He could imagine Margot's attempts to explain why she wanted to dine in her cape!

Close to something that felt a lot like panic, he stumbled reluctantly toward a large store whose windows displayed manikins that appeared to be about Margot's size and shape. However, except for a beautiful meem-colored gown she'd once worn to a ball, he'd only seen her in—and out of—her uniforms. He had absolutely no idea what she might choose for herself.

Inside, the sales floor was moderately crowded—all women—and every one of them was conspicuously ignoring his very *male* presence. Even Leaguers looked friendlier! Feeling his face burn with embarrassment, he picked his way to the sales console through a maze of little counters filled with silky-looking undergarments.

"Yes-s-s?" a woman said, glaring over her glasses. She was at least a head taller than Brim, with mean little eyes, mousy gray hair, and protruding teeth. She looked like a professional virgin.

"Ah," he stammered, "I need . . . um . . . a woman's outfit. . . ."

"For yourself?" the woman asked.

Brim ground his teeth. Whoever said that war was hell never tried shopping for women's garments! Swallowing a great lump in his throat, he pointed to a dress on a nearby manikin. "One of t-those," he stammered desperately. It was a tight-fitting bluish something that would at least go well with Margot's boots. And it also seemed as if it might be the proper shade for a blonde to wear, even though it certainly showed a lot of manikin. He shrugged to himself. If nothing else, it was clearly fashionable—he'd seen a lot of similar outfits on the street outside the store.

"*That* one?" the woman asked, her eyebrows raised in a surprised expression.

"That one," Brim said, trying to act as if he were even the slightest bit confident of his decision. He could feel sweat beading out on his forehead.

"Hmmph!" the woman muttered under her breath. "Well, it certainly takes all kinds."

By now, it seemed as if everyone in the store had stopped her shopping and was either looking at him in absolute repudiation or talking about him with a scowl on her face. Trying to stretch a collar that had somehow grown too tight, he gave the saleswoman Margot's size formula and his HoloID card. Then he stood by uncomfortably trying not to notice the lacy garments he usually glimpsed only in bedrooms.

The clerk required at least six standard months to complete his transaction, then another year or so to retrieve and wrap a blue outfit of the proper size. Finally—with a huge red box under his arm—he beat a hasty retreat back to the street, soaked with perspiration and embarrassed beyond belief. In comparison, *Defiant*'s launching had been a breeze!

Brim arrived puffing in the elegant rococo foyer of the Golden Cockerel after a much longer hike than he'd expected. Dance music wafted softly from the dining room while an abbreviated, crimson-uniformed major-domo bowed so deeply that the great feathered turban he wore nearly fell from his head.

"The Hagbut party," Brim said.

"Ah, yes—you must be their missing lieutenant," the little man purred. "General Hagbut awaits you in the dining room."

"First," Brim said, handing the man his package—with a sizable credit note on top—"Princess Effer'wyck will turn up here looking for this shortly after I am seated. Be sure that you deliver it into her hands *privately*. Is that understood?"

The major-domo pocketed the note as if it had never existed. "I shall *personally* see to it, Lieutenant," he said quietly, placing the package beneath a counter. Then he led Brim grandly through the foyer.

In the crowded, noisy dining room, Hagbut's table was located close to the tiny dance floor. Margot was seated rigidly upright at the General's right—and looking more than just a little distracted. At her fingertips, a barely sampled trio of meem, salad, and soup gave mute testimony to her discomfort—and lack of appetite. Brim could almost feel her look of relief when he took his seat and discreetly nodded toward the foyer. She excused herself within moments and disappeared through the arch.

"Harrumpf," Hagbut growled, rending a great chunk from his dinner roll. "The Princess claims she has a chill or something. Just like a woman. I suppose she isn't feeling well, is she?..."

"Ah, not entirely," Brim replied, "but she may pick up once she has something to eat."

"She sure hasn't eaten much so far," Quince observed with his mouth full. "Look at the good soup she's wastin'."

Brim tried a spoonful of his own—it was excellent although a bit cool by now. "Well," he added, "perhaps the main course will do it."

While they waited for Margot to return, Hagbut and Quince droned on without letup. The General was just hitting his stride in a noisy discourse on military discipline when he idly glanced toward the foyer, stopped in the middle of his sentence, then suddenly turned a chalky shade of white. "EGAD!" he exclaimed, his eyebrows hoisted to a state of caricature.

Simultaneously, the entire dining room lapsed into utter silence—except the orchestra. That was squelched a moment later by a stupendous crash when one of the waiters dropped his tray of dishes. Brim whirled in his chair just in time to see Margot stride regally across the floor in the blue dress with a look of triumph on her face.

She looked terrific! No wonder everyone in the dining room was staring.

Close in her wake scurried the major-domo—who for some reason had a positively distraught look on his thin face. He caught up just as she arrived at the table. "P-princess..." he stammered, clearing his throat nervously, "ah..."

Margot stopped behind her chair and looked down at him. "Well?" she asked imperiously.

"Um . . . your . . . um . . ." He nodded—apparently at her bosom. "Um . . . Your Highness's . . . um . . ." He nervously pinched the fleshy part of his hand. "Um . . . nothing, Your Highness."

"Then what, may I ask, are you waiting for? Help me into my chair," she commanded haughtily. "Clearly, none of my companions seems to remember his manners this evening."

On the instant, all four men scrambled in a comic attempt to reach her chair, but Margot slid into place by herself as if they hadn't moved. "Too late," she said, surreptitiously winking at Brim while the major-domo beat a hasty retreat back to the safety of his foyer. Moments later, their main course was served.

During the next few cycles, it rapidly became apparent that something had mysteriously inverted everyone's roles at the table. Now it was Hagbut and Quince who only picked at their food—silently. For the most part, they sat with their heads pulled in like turtles, staring uneasily at their plates as if they were unwilling to meet the eyes of others in the room.

Margot, on the other hand, was feasting as if she hadn't eaten for a week. Clad in her seductive blue dress, she was chattering ebulliently to everyone at the table. "Excellent fare, General!" she exclaimed happily. "And a wonderful choice of restaurant. I shall certainly return here again and again."

"Harrumpf. . . ."

"Why, General!" Margot said, peering at Hagbut's plate, "my stars, you have hardly touched your supper. And *you*, too, Captain Quince. Perhaps we should have new plates brought from the kitchen." She pushed her chair back. "I shall call the major-domo. . . ."

"Egad! Harrumpf. Ah, no, Princess," Hagbut stammered. "Indeed, that will not be necessary. Captain Quince and I *must* be leaving upon the moment." He rubbed his nose lightly.

"Ah, yeah," Quince affirmed, squirming in his seat. "P-pressin' matters an' all. You know." He nodded toward the foyer, where a tired-looking soldier with a driver's arm band leaned against the wall talking to Ambridge and another green-liveried embassy chauffeur.

"*General* Hagbut!" Margot asserted with a pout. "That cannot be! I am here, after all, at your invitation. Can these pressing matters be so important that you will not favor me with at least one dance set? Must I report to my Uncle Greyffin that you abandoned us after Captain Quince attacked my limousine?"

Hagbut's face turned a bright red again, and his eyes looked as if he had just been shot with a high-energy blaster. "D-dance set?..." he stammered.

Margot giggled. "Of course, General," she said, flaunting her bosom from the low-cut dress. "Certainly the great General Hagbut would not deny a poor princess the pleasure of dancing to such an elegant orchestra." She angled her head and fluttered her eyelashes. "I have often heard you tell my associates that you are a superb dancer." She turned to Brim with a look of victory in her eyes. "Lieutenant Brim," she ordered, "my chair, please!"

Perspiration beading his forehead, Hagbut got to his feet like someone facing a firing squad. His face had taken on a mottled effect: part angry crimson, part chalky white. "A-at your service, Princess," he said in a clipped, squeaky voice.

"Oh, thank you, General," Margot twittered, grabbing his arm and practically dragging him onto the dance floor. Brim had never before realized what a perfectly erotic walk she had. Of course, he'd never seen her in such a dress before, either—almost better than without one. . . .

It was clear that Quince had also noticed Margot's charming way of walking. He was sitting with his jaw hanging open and shaking his head in clear disapproval. "Universe," he whispered under his breath.

Brim frowned. "What seems to be the matter, Captain?" he demanded. "Both you and the General appear to be awfully upset over something."

"Xaxtdamned good and right we're upset," Quince sulked. "The very idea. I can sort of imagine a lowlife Carescrian like you thinkin' something like that's all right—but holy Gort, you'd expect a princess would have a little more pride."

Brim felt his face flush with anger. He considered the source, then shrugged it off—Carescrians could easily spend all their spare time dueling with dimbulbs like Quince. "I don't understand," he said evenly. "What does pride have to do with anything?"

"Huh?" Quince said, turning his full face toward Brim for the first time. "You sound like you really *don't* know what's goin' on."

"I wasn't aware that *anything* was going on, Captain," Brim said, "especially concerning the Princess. But if there is, I want to know about it—right now."

Quince frowned and nodded toward the dance floor, where Margot and Hagbut—who didn't look any too sure of himself—were moving to a complex, and quite energetic, version of the Zubian triple-hop. "Well, how about that whore's dress, for starters?" he asked resentfully.

"*Whore's* dress?"

"F'xaxt sake, yeah. Who else in this joint is dressed like one of them Ornwald prostitutes?"

Brim felt himself stiffen. He was about to grab the Captain by his lapels when a chilling thought hit him like a thunderbolt. "What's an *Ornwald* prostitute?" he asked, heart in his mouth. He was suddenly afraid he already knew the answer. . . .

The Captain made a face and shook his head. "Well, you sure must of seen a few of 'em on the street outside tonight. They're all over the place—lookin' just like the princess does. The Ornwald Bureau of Health makes the girls wear them blue dresses any time they're workin'—an' all the women's shops in the district has to carry 'em by law. Keeps the neighborhood nice an' clean." He shook his head sourly. "Still can't figure what a royal princess is doin' with one on, though—but it's sure steamed the General some. I mean, he's a *proud* man."

Brim felt his heart sink. Margot and Hagbut were now virtually alone on the dance floor—everybody was watching them and applauding. He squeezed his eyes shut in mortification. "Blue dresses like that are uniforms for prostitutes?" he asked, forcing the words through clenched teeth.

"Xaxtdamned right."

"Oh, thraggling WON-der-ful. . . ."

"Huh?"

"Nothing, Captain," Brim said. "Just clearing my throat."

After that, Quince began wolfing down the remains of his supper and only stopped when Hagbut hove into view, towed by a grinning, triumphant-looking Margot Effer'wyck. By now, the General looked as if he'd lost some vast territorial campaign. His eyes had taken on a gaunt, hunted look and his face was even redder than his epaulettes.

"My chair, General?" Margot asked, batting her eyelashes.

"Harrumpf . . . HAW!"

"Oh, thank you," Margot went on breathlessly. "You are indeed an excellent dancer. Why, I declare, simply everyone was admiring us out there, weren't they?"

"Ee-gad!"

"Um . . . General," Quince exclaimed rising suddenly from his seat with a worried look. "I'm gonna get him out of here," he said to Brim as he took Hagbut's arm. "He gets this way sometimes. . . ." With that, he led the tottering man out into the foyer.

Margot smiled a little ruefully, her cheeks still flushed with excitement. "I probably shouldn't have done that," she said, "but the old goat had it coming for such a long time."

Brim stiffened. "What do you mean?" he asked.

Margot giggled. "I mean, I shouldn't have upset the old fool so."

"You know *why* he was upset?" Brim asked. It was like waiting to be hit by a disruptor.

She smiled at him, then reached across the table to take his hand. "By the look on your face, I can tell that Quince let you know about the dress you bought."

"Great Universe," Brim exclaimed, "you must have been ready to kill me."

Margot laughed. "Well," she admitted with a grin, "I *was* upset for a few cycles. But then I thought, 'Why not?' With legs like mine, I was bound to look great—and what a wonderful way to get at a stuffed shirt like Hagbut—so I wore it."

Brim bit his lip. "Margot," he said, "I swear I had no idea, believe me. How can I ever begin to tell you how sorry I am? . . ."

She batted her eyelashes again. "Do I look as sexy as I think I do?" she asked, thrusting her bosom at him.

"Universe," Brim whispered, "like a zillion credits!" Abruptly, he felt her foot caressing his leg.

"Hey, starsailor," she whispered, nodding toward the foyer, "you lookin' for good time, huh? Weeth handsome stud like you, I do it for notheengs. . . ."

Within cycles, he and Margot were once again alone in the privacy of a limousine. But now they sat calmly, she sheltered by his arm with her blond curls in disarray on his shoulder.

"Bad luck," she whispered quietly.

Brim smiled. "We're together—I call that the best luck in the Universe."

She nestled deeper in his arm. "You know what I mean, Wilf," she said sadly. "We've lost a lot of time—and we didn't have very much to start with. You flew a long way to be with me for one night—and *oh*, how I wanted to make that worth your while. Every click."

"Well," Brim said, "you'd certainly made a fine start of it before the wreck—*Hogan's third eye*, but you're good at that."

She leaned over and kissed him on his cheek while they cruised past the great domed tower of Marva. "But we didn't get to finish before we crashed," she said reflectively, "and then I *had* to waste time dancing with that old fool Hagbut." She shrugged a little. "At least the whole mess makes it easier for me to say what I've got to say *sometime* tonight, Wilf."

Brim felt his heart catch. He knew what was coming, and tried to make it easier on her. "I guess you and LaKarn have finally set the date for your marriage," he stated, trying to sound as if the words didn't hurt.

Margot nodded and pursed her lips thoughtfully. "Yes," she said after a little while, "we have. There was simply no use postponing it. Greyffin IV put too much pressure on me."

Brim ground his teeth a moment as Ambridge stopped for a signal at the entrance to Courtland Plaza—he stared at the great Savoin gravity fountain without even seeing it. "When?" he whispered. He was afraid to look at her for fear he might lose what little emotional control he had.

"Soon, Wilf," Margot replied, her eyes filling with tears. "One month from tonight."

Brim squeezed her hand. "Don't cry," he whispered. "It's not the end of us—unless of course you want it to be that way."

She turned to him with a hurt look on her face. "Please, Wilf, don't *ever* say anything like that. I never loved before I met you—and there's no room left in my heart for anyone else. Besides," she added, "Rogan's so busy with his career, he doesn't have that much time for me."

"So long as I am never an anchor for you, Margot," Brim said.

She stared at the floor of the limousine for a moment, then took a deep breath and appeared to gather some reserve of strength around herself. "*That*," she said looking him directly in the eye, "is really what we must discuss tonight."

"My being an anchor?" Brim asked while a hollow of cold fear suddenly formed in the pit of his stomach. He'd always been afraid that . . .

"No," Margot answered. "*My* being an anchor—for *you*."

Brim frowned. "What?" he asked incredulously.

"We've been over it before, Wilf," she reminded him. "I simply can't ask you to live a celibate life, especially since I do *not* intend to discourage Rogan from—well, his rights as my husband. It wouldn't be fair—to him *or* to me. I couldn't live that way *either*." She pointed a finger at his chest and looked deep into his soul. "Wilf, dearest, face it. If we—our love—is to survive this marriage I am being forced into, *you* are going to have to share some other beds yourself. Otherwise, no matter how much you think you love me *now*, there will be lonely nights when your mind dwells on thoughts of me with him—like *that*—and it will poison your love for me just as surely as Avalon orbits the Asterious triad."

Brim started to protest. "I couldn't do anything like that," he said, but she gently closed his mouth with her fingers.

"Remember how tenuous our privacy was tonight—and I'm not even married yet," she whispered. "Then think about what difficulties the future may bring after . . ." Her voice trailed off. Suddenly she kissed him again, this time on the lips. "*Tomorrow* is time enough for reality, dearest," she said. "Tonight is ours to love—and I find that I have once again reverted to the generalized debauchery, venery, and lecherousness which seems to overtake me whenever I find myself within ten million c'lenyts of your person. Look," she said, pointing out the window, "the Boulevard of the Cosmos. We're almost there. Hold me, Wilf; *hold* me. . . ."

Shortly after that, the limousine arrived at the Effer'ian Embassy, where they made love until they lost their desperate struggle with exhaustion and fell asleep in each other's arms.

I.F.S. *Albatron* departed for Menander-Garand the next afternoon precisely on schedule. But the takeoff credit was recorded in the Cohelmsman's log book. Wilf Brim was asleep in the bridge long before the ship passed into Hyperspace.

# Chapter 3

# CONVOY DUTY

After more than a week at Hyperspeed, Convoy C'Y/98 was still battering its way through attacks so vicious that oldtime flight-crew veterans called it the worst trip in memory. Off-duty for the moment, Wilf Brim and Nik Ursis occupied two jump seats on the bridge, watching a brace of Hyperflares erupt around distant ranks of merchant ships in the van. Heavy flashes of disruptor fire followed immediately. Soon afterward, reverberating thunder from *Defiant*'s Drive rose in fullness and shook the bridge while Provodnik gated reserve combat energy to the cruiser's energy chambers—in case it was needed. . . .

"Here they come again," Jennings stated emotionlessly from the Helmsman's console.

"Too right," Collingswood agreed in tired resignation from her console—she *never* got to relax in a jump seat; there was only one captain. "I see the flares. . . ."

Brim took a deep breath and mentally cringed. He'd personally faced a lot of danger in his thirty years, but never anything like the last few days. Endless successions of assaults made him feel like a hoary veteran of the convoy lanes already—and it was only *Defiant*'s third escort mission. Was this the ninth attack—or the hundredth—since he'd gone off duty? He could feel tension mount rapidly as the crew waited for their inevitable dose of terror. Lately, Kabul Anak seemed to be committing every killer ship he could find in his frenzied quest to starve the Empire's key Fleet base at Hador-Haelic.

"Oh Universe, but they're t-taking their own sweet time getting here," a nervous voice stuttered from the rear of the bridge. "They must really be tearing things apart up ahead this time."

Brim recognized the high-pitched voice immediately. Tina Rasnovski was not only a first-trip midshipman, she was also the junior navigator of the crew. He couldn't blame her for the outburst. Tired as he was, he found himself almost desperate to get back to *Defiant*'s controls. At times like this, he needed to do something. *Anything*. The day-in, day-out passiveness of a navigating console would quickly drive him out of his mind, and he knew it.

"Thank your lucky stars we've been sharing their favors, lady," a sarcastic voice grated anonymously from the weapons area. "We might have them all to ourselves before you know it." Scanty laughter trickled from other points of the bridge, but it lacked real substance—like thin sunlight on a winter afternoon. Brim understood that, too. . . .

From experience, he also knew that complex, three-dimensional zigzag maneuvers—aligned on the galactic disk—would begin during the next few moments. He was just tightening his seat restraints in preparation when three blinding lights suddenly exploded from aft in a giant, convoy-straddling triangle of brilliance. One of the enemy scouts actually eclipsed its own Hyperflare for a heartbeat before it disappeared among the flowing stars. The blazing illuminators surged wildly forward along the convoy as they picked up speed, scalping the thin camouflage of darkness from nearby merchantmen, and tracing their outlines in the dazzling over-spectrum most visible to League target directors.

*Defiant*'s Hyperscreens darkened protectively on the instant, but not before a chorus of groans and curses escaped the bridge crew, now half-blinded in the streaming brilliance. Outside, more than three hundred irals of graceful armored deck and smoothly indexing disruptors appeared below in ghostly brilliance, disclosing radiation-blackened patches from hits already suffered since the convoy set out from the port of Harmon-21 nearly a quarter-galaxy distant.

"Stand by to begin zigzag pattern E-28 in five clicks," Calhoun intoned.

Brim shook his head grumpily. They didn't have a lot of choice—*Defiant* was presently "attached" to the convoy itself, and had been for the last three watches. At any given time, only a few of the escorts could be released to "independent" roving and attack. The majority were required to maintain position within the convoy, ensuring that the major defensive firepower remained among the merchantmen that were being protected.

Stars skidded abruptly toward low port as each ship in the large convoy executed the course change simultaneously. At the same instant, a great pulsing flareup toward the van marked another unarmed merchant ship that would never reach port. Brim clenched his fists in a paroxysm of angry helplessness. The Leaguer ships just kept attacking, no matter how many of them were destroyed—and the odds were clearly on their side. During the preceding year, 1,299 unarmed merchantmen—totaling forty-four million milstons—had been reduced to burned-out space wreckage, and their critical cargoes lost, at a cost to the Leaguers of only eighty-seven attack craft. The escorts could try to minimize the toll—but not even a squadron of battlecruisers could completely protect the slow-moving convoy: its overall speed was limited by the slowest members to only 12,000 LightSpeed.

As if triggered by Brim's dismal thoughts, every disruptor mounted by two "independent" escorts off to low port opened up at lengthening fingers of green light in the distant blackness: drive plumes of attack ships headed their way. On the far side of the bridge, he could see Wellington's gunlayers grimly setting up their disruptors, faces lighted from below by the flowing colors of the readouts.

"Just coming on the bearing now, Commander: Red 332, range 1778 . . ."

Another skidding turn by the convoy; this time the stars slid to high starboard. Still no command for independent action from COMCONVOY, the Escort Commander. Brim gritted his teeth with helplessness. He wanted something to be *done*. . . .

"Range 1650 . . ."

Suddenly one of the green traces in the distance welled into a huge pulsing light.

"A hit! Somebody got a hit! . . ."

"By the bleeding Universe—look at 'im *burn*!"

"*Still* comes the attack," Ursis intoned, breaking his grim silence as the attack ships—visible now as long-range NF-110s—steadied on course toward the two near escorts. One was I.F.S. *Obstinate*, easily recognizable by her squared-off silhouette: an old but long-legged O-class escort destroyer. Behind her moved the distinctive outline of a powerful CJ-class frigate, probably I.F.S. *Perillan*. "Bastards are out to get the escorts, this trip, eh?" the Bear asked.

Brim nodded mute agreement as others in the bridge began to shout ineffectual encouragement to the Imperial gunners—and still no release from COMCONVOY for *Defiant*. He watched in silence, reflexively angling his head as the cruiser slid into still another violent course change with the squadron.

Off to port *Obstinate* and *Perillan* flew as if tethered in line, turrets indexing smoothly and firing as if neither had just altered course at all. Abruptly, the leftmost NF-110 exploded in a molten burst of flame and wreckage. A moment later, debris struck the attack ship beside her. Immediately out of control, that ship pitched convulsively, launched her unprepared torpedoes far beyond the speeding destroyer, then exploded in a great flash of quivering brilliance. The deadly missiles themselves, however, described a wild spiral, then suddenly wobbled toward *Defiant* herself. . . .

Brim and the bridge crew watched in fatalistic silence as the confused swarm of torpedoes steadied on course. It looked to Brim as if each was individually targeted on his particular jump seat.

"There's time to take care of those, Alpern," Collingswood said sharply in the still bridge.

"Aye, Captain," the ECW Officer responded in a quiet voice. Abruptly, *Defiant* began to radiate with a glimmering web of bluish fire. Presently, a lustrous pseudopod formed to port, hesitated for a moment, then detached itself and shot up over the bridge, pulsing with a life all its own.

Immediately, the torpedo swarm pivoted and lit off after the decoy, eventually disappearing in a vivid fireball that nearly engulfed *Defiant* herself. Despite the cruiser's powerful built-in gravity, her bridge deck seemed to lift and shake until it threatened to shatter the Hyperscreens. Something heavy smashed into the starboard corner of the superstructure, cracking the corner Hyperscreen directly beside Provodnik's console, then battering itself along the deck until it disappeared into the wake.

And suddenly, they were in the clear again, flying on an even keel as if nothing out of the ordinary had happened.

"Voof!" Ursis commented with a phlegmatic shrug of his shoulder. "Close! As we say in the Mother Planets: 'Boulders and trees seldom rock a Bear's cradle willingly,' eh?"

"You bet, Nik," Brim replied with a tired grin. He was keeping his eyes on the remaining four NF-110s as they pressed home their assault on *Obstinate*, now weaving violently along her course and continuing her deadly fire with every disruptor that would train. At maximum distance, three of the Leaguers released their torpedoes, then stampeded out of range in a hail of disruptor fire from both escorts. The fourth, however, continued its run, boring in through an almost solid wall of concentrated energy. "*Obstinate*'s not using her decoy," Brim whispered.

"Ah, perhaps she waits for the last torpedo," the Bear suggested.

"She'll be too late in a few seconds," Waldo hissed from clenched teeth.

*Defiant* abruptly changed course again.

At the last possible moment, *Obstinate* launched her decoy. The three torpedoes visibly wavered as their logic systems debated between two tempting targets.

After an eternity in Brim's reckoning, they chose the decoy —which disappeared when all three missiles exploded harmlessly in the destroyer's throbbing wake.

"You ought to watch how *they* do it, Alpern," someone commented from the systems consoles. "It's a lot better when we can fly *around* the explosion, don't you think?"

"I'll take that under advisement," the ECW Officer grumped good-naturedly.

Ursis continued to watch, wiggling his long rumpled whiskers in perplexed interest. "Last ship continues on torpedo run, would you believe?" he said, scratching delicately below the band of his peaked hat. "A puzzlement. . . ."

"The torpedo must have hung up in her launcher," Brim said.

"Ah, that might be so!"

"Voot's beard, *Obstinate*, shoot!" Brim urged uselessly. So did a chorus of shouts from other parts of the bridge.

"Get him!"

"Fire, for xaxt's sake!"

At length, *Obstinate* did shoot, effectively concentrating her fire at short range and promptly reduced the bow and bridge of the fourth Leaguer to a fused, glowing mass of energy and radiation flame. In moments, the ship and her remaining torpedoes exploded in a giant, whirling fireball that engulfed both assailant and intended victim.

"Voof," Ursis ejaculated quietly. "It is all over now, Voot take it."

When *Obstinate* emerged from the fireball, cries of horror echoed everywhere among the consoles. Her bridge was completely gone, with a glowing section of the enemy's Drive chamber embedded in its place. The old destroyer slewed off as a solid mass of radiation flame suddenly vomited from her opened hull. She swiftly fell behind and was soon lost in the darkness, *Perillan* maneuvering wildly to avoid the glowing wreckage as she drove past to fill in the gap.

Following the next change of course, *Defiant* passed two more burning wrecks—cargo starships—as the remaining attackers lined up in the distance to start their next run. One of the cripples blew up a few moments later in a tremendous explosion, accompanied by flashes nearly as bright as the enemy flares.

"Poor bastards," Brim mused, more to himself than to anybody else, "they never even got a chance to fight back." Then he scratched his head in puzzlement. "Funny," he said to Ursis, "she looked like there wasn't that much wrong with her when we passed."

"Strange indeed," Ursis replied. "Almost as if there was another Leaguer out there we didn't notice."

"Looks like it's our turn next," Waldo interrupted.

"Perhaps," Ursis said, peering out a side Hyperscreen, "but I think not. 'Caves and ice grottoes hold neither winter nor spring,' as they say."

"Is true, Nikolai Yanuarievich," Provodnik agreed.

Brim raised his eyes to the Hyperscreens. As if by some visible sign, the remaining Leaguer starships were turning tail and losing themselves in the starry distance at high speed. Soon afterward, a whole squadron of heavy Drive plumes arrowed obliquely past the convoy and extended rapidly in the direction of the enemy ships. Indistinct in the dying light of the enemy flares, titanic silhouettes of cascading bridges, wide-shouldered hulls, and monstrous disruptor arrays proceeded the two thickest wakes.

"Did you see *those*?" Brim exclaimed in excitement. "Capital ships. . . ."

"Did I see?" Ursis repeated with a weary smile. "But how could I miss? Battlecruisers, one guesses—I had been expecting them. A little late for poor *Obstinate* and her crew, perhaps, but 'Old wolves often die alone beneath the trees,' as they say." Then he shrugged and shook his great furry head in sadness. "The war goes on," he rumbled to no one in particular, "and on and on and on. . . ."

Convoy C'Y/98 fetched the great star Hador within the next eighteen metacycles, making landfall at watery Haelic's sprawling Fleet base of Atalanta without further incident. Fleet battlecruisers appeared to have a dampening effect on the Leaguers' heroism.

At gravity pool 997/A/12, Wilf Brim stood atop *Defiant*'s bridge and shaded his eyes against the pitiless sunlight. Aft past her curving deck was the great expanse of gravity pools and serpentine canals that made up the Empire's ancient Fleet base at Atalanta. Beyond, the deep blue of Grand Harbor ended in a distant horizon of brown haze that supported a dome of pure, blistering light streaming from the star Hador, presently at its zenith.

To port, the three neighboring gravity pools had been reduced to a single oblong crater with a filthy lake of stagnant water and accumulated wreckage at its bottom. Frequent attacks from League raiders had turned many sections of the great naval base into charnel houses of concrete and twisted hullmetal. The hot wind smelled constantly of burned paint and scorched metal—no matter from what direction it blew.

Directly aft, a blackened, twisted KA'PPA mast protruded from the debris-strewn feeder canal: what was left of S.S. *Eu'lull* from the distant Rogell Cluster. On her last journey she'd carried a critical cargo of gravity generators for the ship-yard, and almost completed the voyage unscathed. Raiding Leaguers caught her only a few yards short of the gravity pool on which *Defiant* now rested.... Afterward, dockyard workers unloaded the desperately needed cargo from the bottom of the canal. Orange buoys now marked the extremes of the ship's torn hull.

It had been like that all the way in from the landing vector at Grand Harbor: wreck after burned-out wreck. S.S. *Indigo*, a goods ship from LORA'L-91 that crashed and broke her back across a generating station (the big machines were now running under temporary wooden sheds making a terrible racket, even in the middle of the busy afternoon); I.F.S. *Gallant*, a small escort that had fought her last battle on the surface—and lost; S.S. *Vicronn Enterprise*, an old Niolanian starship with a cargo of murderous disruptor flash chambers that threatened to destroy the whole harbor during the week she burned in the center channel of the main canal.

There were *too* many more....

*Defiant*, with her lustrous hullmetal, thundering auxiliary generators, and decks full of bustling activity, stood in vivid contrast to the areas of blasted, cratered desolation everywhere around her. On her port side, a frowning, angular Sodeskayan transport, S.S. *Pyech V. Bezapanost*, noisily readied for a return to space. The big ship's generous expanses of deck swarmed with a confusion of hurrying Bears in colorful native dress dogging down access hatches and stowing port-side gear even while final pallets of Drive crystals and gravity generators were lifted from her cargo holds.

Haelic's great Fleet base at Atalanta was miraculously still in full operation—but the price paid to maintain it had so far been utterly gigantic.

Forward, *Defiant*'s bow pointed inland across a further maze of canals toward weathered concrete walls and stone bastions that led upward in ever-distant terraces to the top of a great crag-capped hill. Every square iral of the slopes appeared to be totally covered by a most haphazard and fanciful collection of sunbaked structures—some with flat roofs, some with spires and minarets, others topped by gleaming domes, dazzling turrets, and colonnades of every conceivable shape and form. Surmounting this, the imposing Gradgroat-Norchelite monastery with its awesome, flame-shaped spire dominated everything below. Brim watched a tiny ferry lift in a cloud of dust from the ancient campus and claw its way upward toward one of the thirteen ancient forts still orbiting Haelic that The Order had constructed during a previous, paramilitary existence.

Atalanta: a most critical port, even before the Age of Star Flight when only seaborne ships from the planet's more important continents called at her already-crumbling stone jetties and piers. But while the planet's other land masses eventually lost their identities in the backwash of galactic events, militant Gradgroat-Norchelite monks changed the very course of galactic history. And insular little Atalanta became key to the very existence of an empire so large that the city's founders would have been without vocabulary—much less thoughts— to describe it. Now she was paying dearly for the Great Imperial Fleet base that crowded her polluted shores. Wherever Brim's eyes stopped, he could pick out flattened buildings, gaping roofs open to the sky, tumbled arches, and empty window frames in walls that stood without their fellows in the dusty sunlight.

Beside him on the bridgetop, a work crew had just completed adjustments to the N-ray splitter that fed five radiation dampers faired into the forward break of *Defiant*'s Hyperscreens like a row of old-fashioned searchlights. N-rays were Universally employed throughout the galaxy to fight radiation conflagrations—runaway cascades of pure, released energy —resulting from disruptor hits on hullmetal. These five dampers were designed to cover the forward dorsal deck and the single 152-mmi battery mounted directly below the bridge.

A yeoman—sweating in spite of his cooled battle suit— had just shut and dogged down the inspection door, and the crew was now eagerly clambering into the coolness of the bridge below. Brim followed and pulled the hatch closed— carefully dogging it down with the typical thoroughness of

Helmsmen everywhere. Air conditioning swept over him in a wave of luxury as he hurried down a companionway to the wardroom. He would be just in time for the Officer's introduction to the naval base and to the city of Atalanta that had grown up around it. It was planned that *Defiant* would remain at least a week in port, receiving critical, last-cycle modifications KA'PPAed in from Eleandor-Bestienne—and repairing some light damage sustained during the convoy run.

The briefer—a lanky, sun-browned Embassy staffer dressed in white-linen mufti with an old-fashioned sun helmet —was clearly a long-time civilian veteran of Imperial Station Atalanta. It was also clear that she was making her presentation for at least the ten thousandth time. Middle-aged and somehow desiccated with permanently squinting eyes, her mouth was rimmed with the thin, colorless lips of a habitual nag. She had just launched into her presentation when Brim quietly stepped through the hatch and hiked himself to the top of a nearby table. . . .

The woman described Atalanta as essentially a small, provincial center—in spite of its great age and size. She characterized its permanent citizens as brave, tenacious almost to a fault, and extremely proud of their unique and ancient heritage—as they had been since the dawn of recorded history. For the most part, they were also reverent—many openly worshiped with the Gradgroat-Norchelites—pragmatic, and extremely proud of their personal accomplishments. Numerous expatriates—educated and trained in far-flung learning institutions all over the galaxy—had eventually returned to the city of their birth and joined highly respected professional guilds—cadres of local talent without which the huge Fleet base would quickly cease to exist.

And although the heart of the city's economy *was* the Fleet base, a host of other activities went on in support of other pursuits. For example, the last of the famous Mitchell Trophy races had been flown out of Atalanta just before the war started. And, along less technical lines, a surprising number of farmers eked out livelihoods on neighboring hillsides, along with shepherds, an occasional vintner bottling e'lande, an extraordinarily potent form of meem, and numerous other food producers. There was even a small fishing fleet, or there *had* been before many of the fragile wood-and-varnish boats had been destroyed in the raids.

A number of the local spacecraft—called "Zuzzuous" and peculiar to the planetary system around Hador—were still in service, although their numbers were dwindling nearly as fast as the little fishing boats. Brim remembered seeing a few on gravity pools in civilian areas of Grand Harbor as *Defiant* passed—brightly painted little vessels with broad bands of lavender, red, and bright yellow around their narrow, angular hulls. Passenger cabins were pierced by rows of arched windows, and their control bridges—traditionally white with green stripes—were perched high over the stern like miniature Nimidan Hallo Houses. The unique ships could not exceed LightSpeed, and were most normally employed as interplanetary ferries.

For all its picturesque history, the town had been under almost constant attack for nearly a standard year now—fourteen *seasonals*, as Atalantian natives reckoned time—except when Imperial capital ships were in the area, as they presently were.

The devastating raids were likely to occur at any hour of the day, and were almost totally unpredictable. Because *Defiant* was scheduled for an extended stay, the woman from the Embassy went into lavish detail as to how one might identify shelters in various sections of the city: large green holoposters with white umbrellas appearing to float "inside" over animated directional arrows throughout Atalanta and her suburbs. Shelters themselves, however, were often uniquely marked in different sections of the city: some with icons of the Archangel Marvin—from the Kreejkl pantheon, Brim remembered, wondering how he had managed to store that particular element of trivia—some displaying holographs of the Emperor Greyffin IV, others using the grim visage of Nergol Triannic. During alerts, all were required to energize a strobing lavender beacon—at least until the raiders were actually sighted. And anyone out on the streets after that deserved whatever he got.

At the end of the woman's long briefing, Brim found himself with a real desire to see more of the ancient city and its fascinating people. He resolved to do some exploring before *Defiant* departed the port.

Hador was nearly at its blinding zenith when Calhoun and Brim met Rabelais T. Gastongay, *Defiant*'s dockyard representative, on a jetty near the ship's gravity pool. "At your service," the man said, raising his hand, palm open, in traditional Haelician greeting. He was young and muscular with a great wide chin and a beard that resembled a rick of sun-dried hay. His spotless but worn trousers had a tiny waist—all out of proportion to his massive chest—and his smile beamed with the sunlight of Hador itself. "We've received quite a list of items the Admiralty wants 'corrected' on your *Defiant* here," he said.

"I can imagine," the older Carescrian responded smoothly, returning the same Haelician salute as if he'd visited the old port a thousand times. "How many of those 'corrections' luik like they might actually be important, would ye say, noo?"

Gastongay laughed and peered up at the ship as she tested her moorings in the hot afternoon breeze. "Hard for me to make calls like those, Number One," he said, frowning. "I don't have to fly on her. But we'll be glad to do whatever makes you people feel right about your ship."

Calhoun turned to Brim. "Well, laddie," he said, "if anybody has the feel of the ship, it's a Helmsman. What'll make her right for *you*?"

Brim grinned and handed a small plastic memosquare to Gastongay. "When we saw an advance copy of the Admiralty list," he said, "a few of us got together and wrote up our absolute 'has to be done' list. Like changing out the starboard power dynamos—the ones that overheated and shorted out power to the Navigation tables."

Gastongay wiped mock perspiration from his brow. "*That*," he said earnestly, "is the kind of list we pray for around here."

"I assume that ye included the change order for the new mop handles in Hamper K, Station J-eighty-one, Lieutenant Brim," Calhoun said sternly.

"To tell the truth, Cal, I did leave those out," Brim admitted, touching the bridge of his nose in mock anguish. "I thought I might substitute something like a request for a launch to replace the one that got carried overboard when that torpedo part hit us. What do you think, Rab?"

"Well," Gastongay said, joining the spirit of their easy banter, "I've spent enough time in the Fleet to appreciate the importance of the proper mop handles—but I think I'd probably put replacing that launch a mite higher on my priority list." He frowned for a moment, scratching his head. "Unless, of course, you don't mind jumping a couple hundred c'lenyts between starships out there in intragalactic space. We get crews like that from time to time, you know."

"Not us," Calhoun said. "But sometimes young Brim here does try to land the ship with no Verticals. I'll bet that's almost as exciting. . . ." Abruptly, he focused his eyes between the two younger men toward a neighboring gravity pool and frowned. "Who," he said at some length, "is *that*?"

Gastongay glanced for a moment over his shoulder, then grinned. "That's Claudia," he responded with a chuckle. "She manages this division of the Yard—really something, isn't she?"

Curious, Brim also turned—and confronted a startlingly beautiful young woman whom the term "something" didn't even begin to describe. She was small and almost the perfect antithesis of Margot Effer'wyck. She wore her dark-brown hair almost to her waist in gently flowing waves that framed a countenance graced by wide-set brown eyes with long eyelashes, an almost, but not quite, pug nose, generous lips, and a strong chin. She was *gorgeous*! She also had an ample bust —neither emphasized nor obscured by the snug, fashionably short pelisse she wore that revealed a modest waist, perfect legs, and tiny feet in old-fashioned, high-heeled sandals. As she approached, she looked Brim directly in the face with the half-smile of a woman who is quite accustomed to having a sizable impact on men.

". . . may I present Lieutenants Calhoun and Brim?" Gastongay was saying when the younger Carescrian forced himself back to his senses. He half heard Calhoun respond with some magnificently gallant—meaningless—words. Then the laughing brown eyes were on him again.

"I, ah, didn't catch the name," he stammered helplessly as

he reached out to take the tiny warm hand she extended in standard Avalonian greeting.

"Claudia," the woman said squeezing his fingers in a perfect feminine handshake, "Claudia Valemont."

"I am honored, ma'am," Brim said, starting to regain his senses.

"I think it is I who am honored, Lieutenant," she demurred. "You *are* the famous Carescrian Helmsman, are you not?"

"I doubt if I am all that famous," Brim responded, feeling his face burn, "but I am a Carescrian. . . ."

"Even if he fails t' sound like ane," Calhoun teased.

Claudia smiled warmly. "We Haelicians usually can't recognize accents anyway, Commander Calhoun," she said in a soft voice that sounded like sunlight. "We hear every spaceborne dialect in the Galaxy—but never *listen* for them." She then turned toward *Defiant* with a professional eye. "So that's the new class of light cruiser," she remarked with a suddenly professional air. "Fine lines for such a large ship. Rumor claims she's fast, too."

"Very fast, m'lady," Calhoun answered.

"But she needs a new launch," Gastongay interjected.

"I noticed that," Claudia said, frowning. "According to the drawings, she should have two of them abaft the bridge. I only see one—and the dented area of scorch. How did that happen, Lieutenant Brim?"

"We got a bit too close to some jettisoned torpedoes," Brim explained. "When they went off, part of one hit us."

Claudia squinted up at the sunlight. "Yes," she said. "I can see the path it took. The Hyperscreens are cracked there above the large dent where the damage starts."

"Where do you suppose we are going to find another launch for these people?" Gastongay asked. "I don't remember any coming in with the spares."

"If one did," Claudia said, "I'd personally *kill* the person who shipped it. We need that kind of room for important goods—like more spares." Then she laughed. "But we do indeed have a launch here. Remember, Rab?"

Gastongay frowned and cocked his head. "From one of the wrecks, maybe?"

"We probably would find a few launches if we searched the

wrecks," she agreed. "But I wouldn't want to vouch for the condition they're in." Her eyes sparkled in the sunlight as she smiled. "No, the one I'm thinking about came in for I.F.S. *Intractable* almost a year ago. Remember it now?"

Gastongay shut his eyes and grinned. "Oh, *that* one?" he said with a guffaw.

"That one," she said, sighting over her thumb toward *Defiant*. "I'll bet a bottle of e'lande it'll fit right there when we get those dents out. She's got a bit of room on her boat deck."

Gastongay scanned *Defiant*'s boat deck, too. "Yeah," he agreed, wrinkling his nose. "You're right; it probably *will* fit, but . . ."

"But what?" Brim broke in warily.

"Well," Claudia laughed, "it is sort of an unusual launch."

"Actually, more what you might call an attack launch," Gastongay added with a smile.

"An attack launch?" Calhoun demanded. Then he shut his eyes and snapped his fingers. "Of course—I.F.S. *Intractable*, the attack transport! In fact, she was headed here when she hit that space mine, wasn't she?"

"That's the one," Claudia acknowledged. "They originally built her to capture the orbital citadels at Lazenwold. She wasn't very big, but she could carry four hundred fully armed space troops—I saw her the one time she made landfall here."

"But an armed launch?" Calhoun asked. "What would she need something like that for? If I remember right, she carried a few 125-mmi disruptors herself."

"That's right," Gastongay interjected. "But she also had all that hullmetal freeboard." He laughed. "She showed up on detectors like the Desterro Monument in Avalon—flame sculpture and all. Boffins at the Admiralty built the launch to make up for it. They designed her to barge into the vicinity of the forts without being recognized, then cause enough confusion and damage to let the mother ship land her troops."

"A single launch can do all that?" Brim asked incredulously.

"Not just any single launch," Claudia assured him. "This one's got a pair of experimental spin-gravs that can take her to .95 LightSpeed in less than fifteen cycles, if I remember correctly. And, I think, she mounts a 75-mmi disruptor, too."

"Spin-gravs?" Brim gasped. "With power plants like those, it's no wonder they expected to generate some confusion." He shook his head. "You say she's still here at the Atalanta Base?"

"I passed her only yesterday in one of the deep warehouses," Claudia said. "That's why I remembered. We kept her ready for combat months after *Intractable* got herself blown up—figuring the Admiralty would need it for the replacement they built. But I guess plans changed, because a couple of months ago they sent *Queen Elidean* to take the citadels out completely. And after that, the launch sort of lost its mission."

"We've tried to give her away a couple of times since then," Gastongay admitted. "But we've had no takers so far."

"What's wrong with her?" Brim asked.

"Well, she only holds about ten passengers," Claudia admitted.

"I heard that she's also a real handful to control," Gastongay added, pointedly looking Brim in the eye. "You know that Abner Klisnikov—the last Mitchell Trophy winner—was chief Helmsman on *Intractable*. He volunteered to fly the mission himself, and the launch was built to his personal specifications. From what I understand, he could fly anything."

"Abner Klisnikov," Brim repeated, shaking his head reverently, "the famous racer. I'd been told he was killed, but they never said where. . . . I think I've simulated every mission he recorded."

"So?" Claudia asked. "Do you think you could handle a launch built for his hands?"

"Probably," Brim said. "I don't expect to run trophy races or attack any forts with it—at least not soon."

"A sensible answer," Claudia replied. Her brown eyes met Brim's for only a moment—but flashed a clear message of interest before glancing away toward *Defiant* once more. "And she *is* the only launch we've got in flying shape at the base. We could probably fix one up for you from a wreck, of course, but it would take some time. . . ."

"What do you think, Wilf?" Calhoun interjected. "If you are half the Helmsman they say you are, we've got ourselves a new launch."

"But it'll only carry ten passengers," Brim protested. "Do you think the Captain will want it?"

Calhoun laughed. "If I know anything about Collingswood," he said, "she'll agree a launch that carries ten is a lot better than an empty spot on the boat deck that carries naught."

"Can I show it to you, Lieutenant Brim?" Claudia asked, nodding toward a battered, sun-bleached skimmer with a canvas top that was hovering nearby. "I happen to be on my way to that warehouse right now."

Calhoun winked at Brim and grinned. "I think ye ought to go nab a luik," he said. "Especially if this lovely lass is willing to take ye there. I can probably finish up with Mr. Gastongay here without any mair help."

Brim turned to Claudia. Whatever else she might be, she certainly was lovely. "At your service, ma'am," he said, squinting in the sunlight. "I'd *love* to see a launch like that."

Not half a metacycle later, Brim found himself shivering in the chill dry air of a warehouse five hundred irals beneath the lowest streets of Atalanta. Beside him, Claudia calmly piloted her little skimmer through the trackless maze of ancient stone tunnels and storerooms as if she traveled them every day—which, on reflection, she probably did. At every turn, their headlights picked out bewildering collections of every spare part imaginable: crated interrupters, gravitron compensators, wave shunts, dynamos, telsa coils, amplifiers, generators, multipliers, Drive oscillators, resonance waveguides, Deighton modulators, the billion and one items necessary to maintain a sizable fleet aloft and in fighting trim.

Atalanta's substantial accumulation of goods was mute testimony that convoys did work, even though Brim was certain that its cost was far beyond mere credit accounting. Clearly, for every milston of equipment delivered, at least two more had been destroyed by League raiders. And unfortunately, he estimated, it would take only a single major battle to empty the great store rooms again in very short order.

At the fifth level, Claudia abruptly turned left and headed the little skimmer back along a shadowed avenue of palletized J-type crystal synchronizers that led—eventually—to the entrance of a darkened, virtually empty room. Stopping for a moment, Claudia switched out her headlights and grinned at Brim in the glow of the instruments. "I have a feeling, Lieutenant," she said, thumbing a small controller at her side, "that you will find this immensely interesting."

She was correct. Brim suddenly caught his breath when the lights switched on. "Voot's left ear! . . ." he gasped, blinking his eyes in the harsh brightness. At the far end of a vast, but otherwise empty, stone chamber rested one of the truly startling auxiliary vessels he had ever set eyes upon. Claudia brought the skimmer to a halt just under its snub-nosed prow.

Resting on a wooden shipping dolly and covered by a layer of fine, whitish dust, the graceful little spaceship was no more than forty irals long, with remarkably clean lines and a relative lack of angles anywhere. Wordlessly, Brim jumped to the pavement and walked around its slim ovoid hull, marveling at the flowing, compact design that looked almost as if it was originally created for high-speed work within an atmosphere of some sort. Two great teardrop nacelles—as gracefully streamlined as the hull itself—clearly contained the ship's spin-grav generators. These were slung from the outer ends of wide, bladelike sponsons attached at the widest point of the hull perhaps eight irals aft of the prow. The rounded tips of the nacelles came even with the launch's stubby nosecap.

A tiny glassed-in bridge placed the Helmsman and Coxswain side by side over the leading edge of the sponsons. The forward location would certainly provide a splendid view through the V-shaped windscreens on landing, Brim surmised. But as the top of the bridge was faired almost flush with the rise in the fuselage aft, he silently predicted it would also be troublesome during a stern attack. Of course, if Claudia were correct in her claims about the little ship's power plants, that threat might well be minimized.

Abaft and below the flight bridge, five small portholes on each side of the hull fixed the position of double passenger seats. A quartet of .303 blasters protruded through the nose just above the distinctive barrel of a Brentanno MK-8, 75-mmi antitank disruptor in a pivot housing. Brim was not simply impressed, he was astounded. The deceptively graceful hull was clearly capacious enough to house such weapons under the flight bridge floor alone. . . .

"Should I assume you like her, Lieutenant?" Claudia broke in, almost startling Brim from his reverie.

"You may," he chuckled. "And, by the bye, my real name is not 'Lieutenant,' *Donna* Valemont," he added, using the Haelician polite form of address he'd learned at the briefing.

"All right," she said, smiling more with her eyes than anything else, "I shall call you Wilf if you will call me Claudia. A deal?"

"A done deal," Brim said with a grin.

"'Done' deal?"

"Happily agreed on," Brim explained, trying to concentrate on her existence as a highly placed professional. Her quiet, almost casual air of competence made this easy to do, but the occasional hints of nipples pressing through her close-fitting pelisse made it difficult to forget that she was also an extremely sensuous woman. Somehow, in Claudia Valemont, neither intruded on the other—both were there in easy view because she wanted things that way. It was becoming abundantly clear to Wilf Brim that he was in the presence of an extraordinary woman. With no little sense of culpability, he conceded that he would like to know a lot more about her. . . .

On the cramped flight bridge, Brim seated himself at the Helmsman's console and studied the array of instruments— amazingly well placed. The little ship was a work of art. He located the generator controls, steering gear, collective, navigation instruments, lights, trim, IFF detonators, fire extinguishers, flight-path scanners—all where they ought to be and easily grouped for natural interfacing.

After a few moments, Claudia joined him in the stale air of the powered-off spaceship. Climbing through the tiny starboard hatch, she inadvertently revealed a leg nearly all the way to the stunning whiteness of her inner thigh. Brim tried not to stare as she quickly rearranged her skirt, but a familiar stirring began in his loins and continued while she took her place at the console beside him. After a few cycles of rubbing shoulders while he pointed out the firing controls on the coxswain's console, he knew he would require a few moments' cooling off before he could stand outside the flight bridge again. His jumpsuit was also reasonably form-fitting—especially where it would show. . . .

Altogether, two full metacycles passed as if they were no more than a few elapsed clicks. All too soon, Brim found himself back under the blazing sun, and Claudia was dropping him off at *Defiant*'s brow. "You think you can fly her, then?" she asked as she braked the skimmer to a halt.

"I don't suppose I'll really know until I've tried her out," he answered truthfully. "But I certainly want to give it a try. When could you have her delivered?"

"Soon," she said, looking him in the eye. "But I shan't promise when."

"You'll be around to check when she arrives?" he blurted out as he stepped to the pavement. He certainly hadn't planned to say anything like that—and truth to tell, he felt a little guilty about the whole thing. After all, he'd never even mentioned Margot. . . .

"Perhaps," she said, revving the little grav. Then she smiled and smoothed her long hair. "I shall try to stop by. But if I can't, and *Defiant* leaves before I see you again, good luck with her, Wilf. Consider that you owe me a drink someday when you're back in town." Then, before he could answer, she was gone in a rush of heated afternoon air.

As he watched the skimmer disappear along the dusty road, a feeling of loneliness suddenly descended on him—and didn't go away even when he subsequently resumed his duties.

The next morning before work was scheduled to begin on the Hyperscreens, Brim was up early running checks on *Defiant*'s homing apparatus when Ursis stuck his head through the bridge hatch.

"Wilf," the Bear called, "Captain Collingswood finds herself 'invited' to a surprise briefing at headquarters immediately. We are expected as well, it seems."

"We got briefed yesterday, didn't we?" Brim asked with a frown, entering a PAUSE command at the console.

"Concerning the city and the base, yes," Ursis said. "Today's, however, carries a high security classification—so I think it will be something new."

"Another lecture on social diseases, I suppose."

The Bear grinned while he replaced his Zempa pipe in its pouch. "Possibly," he allowed. "But it matters little in light of the fact that our attendance is required. Commanding officers, Executive Officers, Principal Helmsmen, Principal Systems Officers, Principal Weapons Officers, and selected civilians," he recited, counting each category on each of his six fingers.

"Voot's beard." Brim laughed. "I was going to get some useful work done this morning."

"Fleet Regulations forbid useful work when in port," Ursis stated flatly. "Had you forgotten? After all, 'Blue snow brings cheer to the young hearts of red meer cabbages,' as we say."

"Yeah," Brim said, keying in a TEST EXIT and returning the console to the system.

"Will there be anything else?" the Chairman asked.

"Not today," Brim said. "Admiralty rules, I guess."

"It does," the Chairman acknowledged as Brim and Ursis passed through the companionway. "It certainly does. . . ."

The briefing took place in the sprawling stone headquarters complex at the edge of the Grand Canal. Brim followed Collingswood into an airless auditorium that reeked of new upholstery, fresh paint, and floor polish. It was nearly filled with ranking Fleet officers and civilians, many of the latter wearing the stovepipe hats of shipyard managers. Brim smiled. He'd never before seen the unusual headgear look as if they belonged. However, worn with the traditional Haelician dress of air-conditioned frock coats and vests with straight, tubular trousers and varnished boots—all in somber tones—they seemed quite natural. A singular place, Haelic, Brim considered as he peered about the hall.

Just as the house lights began to dim, his gaze met a familiar pair of brown eyes glancing at him: Claudia, bewitchingly dressed in a severe dark business suit and talking to a handsome redheaded Commodore. Grinning, he waved, and was rewarded with a soft smile and a wink. The Commodore turned and nodded in a cordial—if disinterested—manner. Then the room faded to complete darkness except for a beam of light at the podium, and they took their seats.

Into this stark illumination stepped a pudgy civilian dressed in a formal suit who introduced himself casually as Y. Adolphus Fillmore. His brooding eyes were deeply set in his head; he had a huge double chin; and his mustache looked like two straw brooms joined—where their handles ought to be—by a bulbous nose. He was also missing one of his front teeth. Fillmore might have made a comic figure there at the podium, except that his name was known everywhere—he was one of the most famous starship designers in the known Universe.

"Today, ladies and gentlemen," he began, setting a tall stovepipe hat beside his notes, "I have been sent to tell you about 'benders' and what we know of them."

Brim frowned while a rustle of surprised conversation abruptly swept the room. Benders were the stuff of runaway imaginations and science fiction: starships that could render themselves invisible by literally bending all electromagnetic waves of the spectrum around their hulls without otherwise altering their path. The technique required a data system so capable that it could track particles at the subatomic level, processing—in real time—terabits of information for every square milli-iral of hull surface. Such a system, for a ship even the size of an escort vessel, required unheard-of computing capacity and dynamic energy that might easily power a full-sized battleship.

The briefer waited for silence, then continued on in his placid manner. "I am aware of the tenuous makeup of my material, let me assure you," he said with a tired smile. "Unfortunately, it is tenuous only because it is not we, the Imperial Allies, who have developed such a ship. I should have many more details to present, were such the case. . . . Oh, we secretly built a couple of prototype benders ourselves some fifty years ago. Total experiments," he added quickly. "I pursued all the research notes during our initial analysis of the evidence. Interesting reading; however, nothing much came of the project. It took nearly all the ship's on-board power just to get them into 'spectral' mode." He grimaced and bit his lip. "The facts lead us to believe, however, that the bloody Leaguers have not only developed a truly practical warship of the type but have now put it into production."

During the next two metacycles, Fillmore carefully reviewed the Admiralty's facts, which were overwhelming.

But, like the Admiralty, he could produce no physical evidence—not so much as a hologram. In practice, the Leaguers seemed to be using their new ships as scavengers, attacking crippled vessels that dropped out of convoys. It was numerically predictable how many of these crippled ships should eventually reach their destinations in spite of their damage, and there were people to keep track of such data. When the numbers began to seriously dwindle, the search for a cause began—and ended with one inescapable conclusion.

The benders themselves were thought to be relatively small, no more than 250 irals in length with a beam of perhaps 25 irals and some 1200 milstons displacement. They were also pictured as armed with only one or two disruptors—almost certainly the standard 91-mmi's used on most smaller Leaguer starships—and five or six League-standard 533-mmi torpedo tubes. In all probability, the ships would be slow and clumsy when in spectral mode, but with the tremendous energy of the data processors available for their horizontal generators, they were assumed to be as capable of a good turn of speed as normal, visible starships. Additionally, they were rumored to be fitted with outlet filters that all but eliminated Drive plumes—at the price of considerable Hyperspeed performance.

At length, the lecturer exhausted his accumulation of Admiralty data and the briefing was over. Attendees were urged to keep a careful watch for the new ships, both from the ground —it was thought that benders might find limited action as attack craft—and in space during convoy duty. They represented a dangerous new capability for the League, and could spell critical trouble for the beleaguered Imperial Fleets that had only recently won themselves a breathing spell from the first insane rush of the war.

On his way from the auditorium, Brim searched the crowd for Claudia, but only located her in the sweltering courtyard as the redheaded Commodore ushered her into a sleek gray limousine skimmer. The two sped away in a cloud of blowing dust before Brim had a chance to even pay his respects.

The Carescrian smiled wryly to himself as he joined Wellington on her way across the dusty stones to the gravity-pool bus. In a way, finding Claudia with the handsome Commodore was almost a relief. There had been strong chemistry between himself and his beautiful host while they toured the warehouse together; he had no doubt about that. The discovery that she might well belong to someone else negated all the thorny questions concerning his feelings about her—they simply ceased to exist. And with Margot's marriage to LaKarn scheduled to take place only weeks hence, it would be very easy for him to become involved in something he might not easily shut down in the future. He shoved his hands into his pockets and concentrated on the Gunnery Officer's endless chatter. "Yeah," he agreed with a grin, "if I were building a bender, I'd certainly want a 155-mmi deck gun, too."

That evening, Brim joined most of *Defiant*'s officers at a huge wardroom party hosted aboard I.F.S. *Intrasigent*, a heavy cruiser on a gravity pool in another sector of the base. He arrived quite late, after completing the long test sequence interrupted by the morning's briefing. As he walked across the brow from the tram stop, his face was caressed by fresh, late-evening sea breezes heavy with smells of salt, iodine, seaweed—and vast c'lenyts of free, open ocean.

"Take the third hatch to your right down the main companionway, sir," a rating said after examining Brim's ID. "You'll find the wardroom there."

"Thanks," Brim said with a nod. Instead, he continued some distance along the shadowed main deck to stand alone in the peaceful darkness beside a disruptor turret, looking out across Grand Harbor toward the open water beyond. Perhaps half a c'lenyt away, a floating beacon blinked twice . . . then twice again . . . then twice again. . . . Over the horizon, distant lightning flashed through a necklace of suddenly golden clouds. Muted sounds of laughter and music reached his ears from below—along with the lapping of water on the nearby breakwater. He felt himself relax while the soft darkness enfolded him like a cool, velvet cloak. No simulators or checkout routines in his immediate future—at least not for the next couple of metacycles. He smiled. He had plenty of time to join the party below. In wartime, one took solitude wherever —and whenever—one found it.

He peered into the blazing firmament: galactic center was

nearly overhead at this hour. There.... *That* bright cluster would be the Golden Triad of Asterious—any Helmsman worth his salt could find it. And somewhere nearby, dimmed by light from the great streaming stars, would be Avalon—and Margot.

His mind's eye conjured her face for him, the frowning smile and perpetually sleepy eyes. He could almost feel her arms around his neck—smell the perfume she wore. He took a deep breath and shut his eyes in the darkness....

Abruptly, a giggle intruded on his reverie. He opened his eyes. A tall man in some sort of military uniform and a heavy-set woman were walking arm-in-arm toward him in the darkness—and it took only a single glance to know what they had in mind. To his horror, they stopped just as they came abreast of his position while the woman threw back her head to drain a large goblet and toss it over the side, giggling as it bobbed on the blue glow of the gravity pool some fifty c'lenyts below. Then she hiked her skirt momentarily to slide something down over her ankles.

In the shadows, Brim felt his face burn with embarrassment when this time the man drew her skirt up—this time all the way past her waist. Even in the darkness, her fat thighs were startlingly white. He caught his breath. If he tried to leave, they'd think he was spying on them—and if he didn't, it was almost certain he would end up doing precisely that.

He ground his teeth as the man lowered his trousers; then the two wrapped each other in a writhing embrace against the bridge superstructure—arms and legs. In near panic, he squeezed his eyes shut and tried to concentrate on *Defiant's* instrument panels, reviewing each readout and switch in his mind....

For a while, his ploy worked—even when the moaning began. The woman's little squeal, however, defeated him at last. When he blinked his eyes open, they were together on their knees and ... Brim almost fainted from sheer mortification.

But now, at least, their backs were toward him.

Knees shaking wildly with embarrassment, he tiptoed quickly past, stealing from shadow to shadow until the happy groans had long since faded into the darkness and he regained his proper companionway. He waited at the hatch for a few moments while he got control of his breathing. Then, shaking his head, he made his way below decks into a clamorous atmosphere of Hogge'poa, perfume, sweat, liqueurs, and—of course—polish. His heart was still pounding. The night out there was for lovers, not dreamers. And tonight he clearly belonged to the latter. . . .

Moments later, armed with a huge goblet of reasonably mellow Longish Meem, he pushed through the noisy, jostling crowd to where Ursis, Waldo, and Aram were in agitated conversation with Calhoun.

"I don' understand," Waldo was saying, slurring her words a little in her attempt to be heard above the surrounding hubbub. "You always tell me that you're in th' 'reclamation' business. Yet you go 'round making everybody else think you spend most of the time in space." She hiccupped with an embarrassed little smile. "Just how do you square all that, Cal?"

"Yeah," Aram piped in, "what is it you reclaim, anyway? Knowing the little I do about you, I can't imagine it's souls. Maybe you run a tug, or something? . . ." Suddenly he raised his eyebrows. "You weren't captain of a salvage ship, were you? One of your own, maybe?"

Calhoun suddenly looked a little uncomfortable, but continued to smile as unconsciously he placed his arm around Waldo's waist, much to the latter's apparent satisfaction. "Perhaps 'salvage' is a better term, noo," he admitted, gesturing modestly with a free hand—and ignoring the question of ownership completely.

"Space salvage?" the Bear remarked, holding a slim, tapered finger in the air, "but I have heard of such operations, would you believe?" He smiled thoughtfully while he sipped his meem. "Perhaps," he continued after a moment, "in peacetime, our Executive Officer cleverly makes his living by what one might call 'presalvage' operations." He smiled and looked Calhoun in the eye. "Is this not a possibility, my Carescrian friend?"

For a milliclick, Calhoun glanced coldly at Brim, then looked Ursis directly in the face and narrowed his eyes. "I am sure ye are about to define this term 'presalvage' ye use," he said, drawing Waldo protectively closer to his side—clearly a special relationship had formed between the two. Brim felt a tinge of wistful jealousy. She had *such* beautiful legs. . . .

Ursis stood his ground and calmly returned the man's steely gaze. "Normally," he explained, "one salvages a starship *after* it is disabled; only the most creative operators salvage them beforehand." He shrugged phlegmatically. "Clearly, dark caves whistle happy songs when a moon hides behind the clouds."

"Huh?" Waldo asked.

Abruptly, Calhoun's face reverted to a cynical smile. "One makes his living as the Universe permits, my friend," he stated quietly.

"I understand," Ursis replied, looking the man directly in the eye.

Calhoun nodded. "You know, Ursis, I actually think I believe you." Then he clicked his heels in a most formal manner. "Gentlemen," he said, "my compliments." Turning next to Waldo, he drew her even closer to his side. "I shall endeavor to explain everything later this evening, my dear," he said, and quickly guided her off toward the companionway.

"Nik, do you think he might *really* have been a space pirate?" the young A'zurnian Helmsman queried when the two were out of earshot.

"One draws one's own conclusions," Ursis replied in his most impassive manner.

"He certainly *said* he was no stranger to space," Brim added with a grin. "But what he actually did out there is anybody's guess."

"Yeah," Aram agreed, laughing. "Well, whatever it was, I'll bet he was good at it."

"That," Brim said, "is a bet I wouldn't take in a thousand standard years."

"Nor I," Ursis added with a toothy grin. "And mark these words, my friends: his expertise—whatever it turns out to be—will someday serve us well. Winning wars often requires thinking that is, shall we say, 'unconventional'?"

Brim was about to comment further when his gaze met a familiar pair of brown eyes—the same that he'd encountered earlier at the morning briefing. Claudia! Tonight she wore a white sweater that showed her ample bust to its best advantage and a skirt sufficiently short to reveal the slim legs and tiny feet that had so set him on edge in the flight bridge of the attack launch. This time, she was in conversation with a circle of civilians. He smiled and mouthed a silent "Hello" across the room. It was certainly too noisy for any other means of communication.

The Haelician returned his smile and winked, holding his gaze with her own as if she'd been waiting for him to arrive. And her red-haired Commodore was nowhere in sight.

Brim quickly took leave of his shipmates and pushed off again through the crowd, stopping at the pantry for two fresh goblets of meem. As he made his way across the floor, she said something to her friends, then navigated the rest of the way to meet him. "Thought you might need a refill," he said, trying not to stare. If anything, she was even more beautiful than he recalled.

"What?" she called out above the clamor.

"A refill," Brim fairly shouted, handing her one of the goblets. "I thought you might like a fresh drink."

"How thoughtful," Claudia said, bending directly to his ear. "Especially since I know your launch hasn't been delivered to *Defiant*. I thank you, Lieutenant."

Brim frowned and ignored the launch—he'd never have found time for it anyway. "Was that 'lieutenant' you just called me?" he asked with a grin.

Claudia nodded her head while she swirled her drink around its goblet in a most expert manner.

"I thought we were on a first-name basis," he protested with a raised eyebrow.

"Oh, we are," she said, looking him directly in the face. "I simply wanted to assure myself that you felt that way here. Long ago I learned the hard way that some of your Fleet colleagues dislike hearing their first names used in public— especially by a local."

"You haven't met many Carescrians then, have you?" Brim barked, just saving his meem from destruction when a tipsy commander stumbled into him.

"Not yet," Claudia shouted, nimbly avoiding a similar fate from his bleary-eyed companion. "And come to think of it,

I'll bet you haven't encountered many Haelicians, either, have you?"

"No," Brim admitted, "I haven't—but then, I only arrived a little more than two days ago."

"True," Claudia said as two more couples jostled past on their way to the pantry. Bumped for a third time in as many clicks, she narrowed her eyes for a moment, then grinned—her teeth perfect against generous ruby lips. "You know," she shouted, "instead of standing here being trampled, we could do something about both our predicaments—and this worse-than-damned noise."

Brim frowned. "What did you have in mind?" he growled, fending off a gesticulating dockyard manager at his back.

"Well," Claudia said, talking directly into his ear, "one of my favorite places just happens to be in a nearby section of town. And unless you really enjoy this noise and jostling," she said, "I'll bet I could have us there in no time at all."

Without a second thought, Brim stepped forward, grinned, and offered Claudia his arm. "Ma'am," he shouted, "I am at your service—immediately."

They left their goblets on a cluttered table at the companionway. . . .

The hoarse growl of Claudia's open-air skimmer reverberated from low concrete abutments on either side of the bridge deck as they glided over the famous stone arches of the Harbor Causeway and onto the mainland. Claudia herself chattered like a tour guide, pointing through the scarred, sun-discolored windshield at each street and lamppost as if it represented something very special—which clearly it did in her mind, at least. Her skirt had slipped well past her knees as she worked the control pedals in high heels, and Brim found himself hard-pressed to keep his eyes where she directed.

On the mainland side of the bridge, the Grand Canal was fronted with unending rows of monolithic government warehouses and office complexes—interrupted here and there by mountains of fire-blackened debris. The great, flat-faced buildings lined each barren street with the boring sureness of state-regulated architecture everywhere. Crowded sidewalks and furious night-shift activity in thousands of lighted win dows gave proof that the big base worked on a round-the-clock basis. Brim knew it had done so since long before Nergol Triannic's Great War began.

In the Government Section, Claudia found little of historical interest to point out, and drove considerably faster along the wide thoroughfares until the faceless buildings grew smaller and began to thin. As the skimmer sped inland toward City Mount, the office precincts gave way to light industrial complexes, and finally to ancient bedroom neighborhoods built of stone, brick, and mortar. Then, just short of the final canal bridge, they skirted the port's gaudy pleasure district. Claudia hurried through this section, too, ignoring the garishly painted nude men and women who shouted from brightly lighted storefronts to advertise their services. Brim found himself shivering as they sped along the crowded boulevards. Long ago, he had known places like these firsthand. He had no desire to return. Ever.

Presently, they bumped over the last steep canal bridge, slowed, and turned through a wooden gate in a massive stone wall, entering the ancient Rocotzian section of Atalanta. According to Claudia, the name derived from the shape of the wall itself, which traced the uniquely suggestive outlines of a male rocotzio bud.

Centuries in the past—long after such walls retained only symbolic meaning—Omot warriors overran Hador's entire planetary system, enslaving the whole civilization there for nearly three hundred years. Only when the warlike Gradgroat-Norchelite priests led an uprising—assisted by the newly confederated Galactic Empire—were the conquerors overthrown and ultimately slain to a man. The last Omotian was captured almost seventy years after the main forces capitulated—and beheaded on the spot.

During subsequent, unsettled years, the Gradgroat-Norchelite order constructed their great hilltop monastery and thirteen orbital forts to repel one last invasion, but the great space disruptors they installed never fired again. And during hundreds of intervening decades, the monster weapons fell into disuse as The Order assumed a more peaceful mission in the galaxy. Nevertheless, the Gradygroats, as they were by now Universally nicknamed, continued to maintain the orbital forts just as if the reliquaries still housed first-line weapons systems. Indeed, most Gradgroat-Norchelite friars and priests firmly persisted in their belief that their antediluvian—and by now unworkable—space cannon would yet be used to save the empire. But as the years passed, the term Gradygroat entered almost every dialect of Avalonian as a synonym for "ridiculous." Brim smiled as he watched Claudia tell the ancient stories. It was fairly clear she was a believer, too—although he doubted she would ever admit that to him! . . .

At night, The Section appeared to be a haphazard proliferation of tall stone buildings with intricately carved walls, dimly lighted arched windows, and balconies jammed with people taking the night air. Claudia piloted her skimmer smoothly through the maze of narrow streets, filled by men and women wearing bright-colored clothing with tasseled, pillbox hats. Children carried flowers as they trailed their elders along the crowded sidewalks. Here and there, robed Gradgroat-Norchelite priests chanted blessings to all passersby who would bow their heads. And at one corner, a great silvery egg-shaped Norchelite chapel rose sheer before them, its polished metal walls splendidly reflecting the vivid green light of Haelic's mid-evening moons. Glowing characters over the doors spelled The Order's curious motto: "In destruction is resurrection; the path of power lies through truth."

Often, the skimmer's headlights reflected pairs of greenish-yellow eyes in darkened alcoves: sable rothcats, a unique breed of felines imported during an earlier age to combat plagues of rodents and giant moths that once infested the city. The rothcats did half their job, and to this day consumed most of the giant moths as soon as they hatched. But *Felis Rothbartis* stubbornly ignored rodents of all forms. Haelic was still searching for a better mousetrap. . . .

Countless shops—often the merest slits in walls—lined the streets, enjoying a thriving business at this late, but comfortably cool, hour. All too often, however, huge gaps appeared in the buildings where ruined masonry and plaster cascaded into the streets—legacies from the League of Dark Stars. Claudia passed these without comment, but Brim could feel the dark anger that blazed within her. Leaguers would be better off if they didn't capture this target, he thought.

In a tiny street full of colorfully dressed people who stared at Brim's uniform as if he didn't quite belong, Claudia expertly wedged the little skimmer into a tiny opening along a curb and switched off the grav. "We're here," she said with a smile of pleasure.

Brim looked around him at the bustling shops, people, and animals. Smells of every kind assaulted his nostrils: spices, animals, hot metal from the skimmer, street dust, Claudia's perfume, cooking oil, even the stones themselves seemed to have a particular odor. An exciting place, he thought. Every inch of wall space was covered by elaborate bas-relief: battle scenes, statues of Norchelite saints, intricate scrollwork, ancient-looking starships, dragons, chilling alien forms—designs of every shape and texture. "Lead on, my trusty guide," he said with a grin, "for I am hopelessly lost."

"I *heard* that you Helmsmen are pretty dependent on navigators," Claudia teased, invoking a rivalry much older than spaceflight itself, "but I had no idea how much."

"Show me a Fleet navigator who could find his way in—or out—of here on his first trip, and I'll eat my battle suit," Brim remonstrated. "Unless he's a Haelician, of course. You people are clearly born with some sort of crazy navigational system; otherwise, nobody could ever go *anywhere*."

"You've guessed our secret!" Claudia exclaimed, dramatically raising her eyebrows. "And mine homes in on taverns, too—like this one." She indicated a narrow arched doorway, framed with exquisite wooden filigree and outlined in lacelike metal scrollwork. Above it was a colorful sign.

"'Nesterio's' something or other," Brim read aloud, peering at the carved letters. The rest was in Haelician.

"'Rocotzian Cabaret,'" Claudia translated for him. "'Spirits and Meem'—I assume that *is* what we've come for."

Brim cupped her elbow as they descended a steep staircase. "Doesn't matter what language the label's written in," he said, "just what's in the bottle." Then he laughed. "I must sound like a Sodeskayan," he said. "That's an old Carescrian saying."

Claudia smiled into his face. "I could *understand* it," she said. "There's a difference, you know."

"Yeah," Brim chuckled. "We Carescrians never were much for mystery."

In a dimly lit alcove at the bottom of the staircase, they were confronted by a muscular, heavily bearded man in crimson tights with long pointed shoes that curled into coils at the tips. He wore an embroidered blue tunic with shiny brass buttons in two rows extending from a high lace collar to a short skirt of brightly woven patterns. A broad, elaborately jeweled leather belt draped over his hips, placing a silver dagger in easy reach of his right hand. For a moment, his glance moved sidelong over Brim's uniform; then he narrowed his eyes and peered into Claudia's face. Only when she raised her hand in the traditional greeting did he bow and open the door. "This way, my beautiful friend," he said, his face brightening into a friendly smile, "and Lieutenant," he added graciously, "please feel that our poor tavern is always your home when you again find yourself in The Section."

Brim bowed. "I am deeply honored," he said, very much aware that Claudia's presence alone granted his singular welcome.

Inside, the room itself was long, narrow, and crowded. Lighted by dim oil lamps that hung from a high stone ceiling, it looked every bit as incredibly old as it probably was. The walls were of whitewashed plaster whose smoke-browned surfaces were relieved here and there by inset wooden beams painted bright green and lavishly decorated by colorful primitive designs. From the small corner stage, a trio of musicians created sinuous melodies that blended and separated, sometimes harmonically, sometimes discordantly, in what even the unsophisticated ear of Wilf Brim understood must be a unique, totally authentic Haelician mellifluousness. The air was thick with mu'occo smoke, a mildly narcotic—some claimed aphrodisiac—leaf the natives had smoked during moments of relaxation since time immemorial.

They were shown to a booth so narrow that Brim had no choice but to occupy a seat opposite his beautiful companion —a disappointment, somehow, but there was no help for it. Across the aisle, he recognized the Base's civilian manager— with *two* attractive women. He smiled to himself. He might be no more than a lieutenant, but Claudia Valemont was with *him*, and she was more stunningly beautiful than either of the manager's companions.

"Like it?" she asked.

"I love it," Brim responded as he relaxed in the surprisingly comfortable wooden bench. "And I want you to know I feel considerably privileged to be here."

"I suppose it's not a part of the City many 'outsiders' see," Claudia agreed.

"I sort of got that idea from your friend at the door," Brim replied.

Claudia smiled. "Nesterio is an old acquaintance," she explained, a soft blush rising momentarily to her cheeks. "He . . . ah . . . protects me."

"With muscles like that, I assume he can do quite a thorough job," Brim commented with a grin.

"Yes," Claudia said quietly, lowering her eyes to the table. "A childhood friend—and much more. Almost two years ago, he pulled me from the rubble of the building where I lived at the time. I'd been trapped for nearly a day before he dug me out with his bare hands. . . ." She laughed grimly. "Now, he seems to feel a responsibility for my continued safety. And Universe knows I shall never discourage him."

"By the beard," Brim said quietly. "I had no idea you'd been . . ."

"The scars don't normally show," she said. "But I no longer worry about bringing children into this Universe of war, either."

Brim could find no adequate response. Years ago, his own tiny sister died screaming in his arms after the very first of Kabul Anak's vicious raids on helpless Carescria—a raid that cost him everyone else in his immediate family, as well. Somehow, now was not the time to share his experience. Besides, he'd personally come through the raids without so much as a scratch. . . .

Presently, a shapely red-haired waitress in a white, floor-length skirt and bright green surcoat with huge, puffy sleeves took their orders: native e'lande for Claudia and meem for Brim. After that, she seemed to relax. Brim was stunned when she suddenly rummaged through her purse and produced a tiny silver case containing six of the slim, golden mu'occo "cigarettes," as they were called.

"I don't suppose you'd like one," she said.

"I wouldn't know," Brim responded with fascination. "I only heard about them during the initial Embassy briefing. Are they like Hogge'poa?"

"May the Gods grant us everlasting protection from Hogge'poa." She laughed. "But, yes, Wilf, they're pretty much like Hogge'poa—except for the smell. And if you haven't tried them yourself, then I shall smoke for both of us—at least tonight."

Brim smiled as the drinks arrived. "Sounds like a good idea," he said evenly. She didn't seem to be laughing at him. Carescrians were very sensitive to that. "I have a feeling there's a lot I can learn about Haelicians."

"We're people, basically," she said, sipping the clear liquid in her long-stemmed flute. "Love us, we love; hurt us, we fight. We're a pretty tough lot, I guess. . . ."

"You'd have to be," Brim said. "I know what raids are like when you can't fight back." Then he looked her directly in the eye. "Tell me more about the war, here," he asked, "from the civilian side."

Claudia frowned at him for a moment, then raised her eyebrows. "Why would you want to know?" she asked quietly.

"I guess war's been pretty fortunate for me, so far," Brim admitted. "'The business of barbarians,' as some forgotten emperor named it. Seems to me that I have an obligation to find out what it really means."

Claudia raised an eyebrow in disbelief. "I didn't expect that kind of honesty," she said after long moments of silence. "But I'll give as good as I've gotten, by Zamp. And perhaps you'll help me understand what it's really like on the warships I service." Then she lit her cigarette with a tiny golden match.

Through a second round of drinks they talked about the endless combat that penetrated nearly every part of their galaxy—and Claudia seemed as fascinated by his views as he was by hers. Both agreed that armed conflict was hardest on noncombatants: helpless civilians who happened to be in the way of the rolling, insane juggernaut military minds had long ago named "war."

After third and fourth rounds of drinks—and a second ciga-rette—their conversation returned to the raids on Atalanta, and finally to the one that nearly killed Claudia.

"I suppose it wasn't a total loss," she joked wryly. "After they sealed me up, I've never had to worry about, shall we say, the 'aftereffects' of a good romp."

Brim smiled at her good-natured frankness. "In other words, blood flows pure in your veins, unsullied by preven-tive chemicals," he said.

"By those chemicals, at least," she said. "But the plumbing they removed used to provide *other* chemicals that had a lot to do with my makeup as a woman." She took a last draught from her cigarette, then crushed it out in a tiny shower of perfumed sparks. "I've always been kind of wild—even my first time. Voot's hairy beard, Wilf," she laughed quietly, "he was hung like a gratzhorse. And I took him on gladly! It hurt about as much as it felt wonderful."

Brim laughed at her, remembering his own fumbling initia-tion—appropriately enough, in the hold of a starship.

"Well," she continued, "I'd been in the hospital about two weeks when it suddenly dawned on me that the wildness was all gone! Wilf, I didn't give a damn for that good stuff any-more. And I panicked—right there in the healing machine. They'd taken everything out to save my life, and I wasn't sure at that moment I wanted to be bothered with what they'd left me. . . ." She squeezed her eyes shut for a moment. "Luckily," she continued after a time, "as long as I let them slip a loz-enge into my arm now and then, I still get my urges, so . . ." All at once, she looked Brim in the eye and shook her head. "Sorry," she said with an embarrassed little smile. "I shouldn't get carried away like I do. Especially in front of someone who I understand was pretty badly wounded on his first tour of duty."

Brim reached across the table and took her hand. "I also survived." he said quietly. "And I didn't lose any plumb-ing."

"Wilf Brim," she declared with a grin, "I had no doubt about that at all."

He was about to press on with that encouraging line of

conversation when suddenly she stared at her timepiece. "By the beard!" she exclaimed, "do you know what time it is?"

Taken aback, Brim glanced at his own timepiece—in utter surprise. The civilian manager and his two women had long since disappeared, and dawn was only short metacycles away.

"Universe, how *could* I?" Claudia muttered as she rummaged in her purse. "Wilf, I've got to get you back to the base right away, or I shall *never* get to bed."

Brim almost commented on that, then thought better of it. Clearly, the mood of romance evaporated as soon as it met the air. "I suppose I could call a cab," he suggested.

Claudia laughed. "That would be a terrible thing for me to do to you—especially when it was *my* idea to come here in the first place." She squeezed his hand. "No, Lieutenant Wilf Brim, I shall take you directly back to your ship in my skimmer. But this time, I shall use a much more direct route."

True to her word, Claudia arrived at the entrance to *Defiant*'s gravity pool within twenty cycles of her departure from Nesterio's. As she drew to a rattling halt, Brim shook his head. "I didn't think this could go so fast," he said, only a little in jest. "Was it entered in the Mitchell Cup race?"

"Someday, I may even tell you about those races," she said with a soft smile. "But it won't be tonight." Abruptly, she grabbed his cheeks in her hands and deposited a wet kiss directly on his lips, then she sat back in her seat, and revved the grav. "Good morning, Lieutenant," she said firmly. "I simply must be on my way home—now."

Reluctantly, Brim stepped to the pavement. "Will I see you again?" he asked.

"If you like," she answered noncommittally, then smiled gently once more. "Thank you for a wonderful evening, Wilf," she added. "It was one I won't soon forget, believe me." A moment later—before Brim could think of anything else to detain her—she was gone.

He watched the taillights of her little skimmer until they disappeared on the far side of the Harbor Causeway. Then, trudging over the brow in the relative quietness of Haelic's early-morning watch, he showed his pass to the guard and made his solitary way to his cabin.

# Chapter 4

# ATALANTA

Late the next evening—after the new launch and its cradle were securely installed on *Defiant*'s boat deck—Brim checked the assignments roster and found himself completely free of duty during the next full watch sequence. Nothing of that nature had happened since Menander-Garand, and then he'd had a chance to see Margot. He shrugged. This time, he had only one day—and no way to get himself back to Avalon even if he did have more time.

Hands in his pockets, he wandered aimlessly in and out of the nearly empty wardroom, along a corridor past his solitary cabin, and finally through *Defiant*'s main hatch into the cooling glow of a summer evening. Hador was in the process of turning the sky a dozen glorious hues of red and orange while it set behind Atalanta's City Mount Hill. As he made his way forward along the main deck, *Defiant*'s ebony hullmetal took on its own reddish hue and transformed the great starship into a dreamlike landscape of glowing, streamlined forms and deep shadows. Then, even before he reached the starship's bows, these brilliant colors rapidly faded to magentas, and finally to lavenders as lights began to flash and flicker in the city beyond. He turned for a moment to face *Defiant*'s superstructure, now a deep-purple form against the still-blue sky. Pinpoints of colored light glowed and flickered from the navigating bridge—his eyes could pick out movement there, but details no longer penetrated the oncoming darkness.

Returning his gaze to the city once more, he could sense the first stirrings of an evening land breeze on his cheek. It carried the peculiar fragrance of age, masonry, dust, and a touch of growing things from the fields beyond. Narrowing his eyes, he thought he could recognize the Rocotzian section where he had spent the previous evening; of course, he couldn't be sure. Atop City Mount, the monstrous Gradgroat-Norchelite monastery was now a multitude of lights, surmounted by its glowing golden spire. His breath caught as he let the nighttime beauty surge over him. Atalanta was relatively safe from attack so long as Vice Admiral Zorn Hober and his 12th Battlecruiser Squadron were in residence. Tomorrow, however, he knew the powerful squadron was scheduled back into space. After that the city lights would not go on again until the 12th—or some comparable protection—was once again in residence at the base.

He shook his head. War! How good it was to him—and how utterly horrible to nearly everyone else. For a Carescrian, it was easy to forget that the Universe contained an almost infinite variety of realities—and that those having anything to do with poor, impoverished Carescria were nearly incomprehensible anywhere else. Suddenly, a wave of fatigue swept over him. Another long day, and no doubt about it.

Hands still in his pockets, he retraced his steps along a now darkened main deck to the main hatch, and from there to his cabin. His last conscious thought was a promise that he would spend the next day learning a little about the city and its people—on foot, the way a Carescrian would, not aboard a tour bus. If Atalanta could produce someone like Claudia Valemont, then it was well worth a proper effort. . . .

For the second morning in a row, Brim was roused out of his bunk early—this time by the ship's siren and a blaring call for "Action Stations" from the message frame on the back of his door. Jumping blindly into a battle suit, he fought his way through the orderly confusion in the corridors and companionways to his station on the bridge.

Ursis had arrived there no more than a metacycle or two before him, but the Bear already had power to *Defiant*'s gravity generators. By the time Brim slipped into the left-hand Helmsman's console, the ship was ready to taxi, although he was unsure whether or not *he* was. Ruefully, he recalled the old adage: "Sound sleep is the sleep you're in when you get wakened," or something like that. He was living proof.

No more than a c'lenyt to starboard, two large merchant ships were burning fiercely on their gravity pools. And even as he watched, a series of distant explosions erupted halfway up City Mount Hill. Lights were going out in huge patches all over the city. Nearby, along the darkened canal-side roadways, speeding emergency vehicles were weaving desperately through lines of personnel carriers rushing crews to their respective ships.

But strangely—to Brim, at least—no bolts of defensive firing arced through the dark sky anywhere. And for that matter, the source of the destruction was not obvious, either. Normally, you could see a disruptor go off. He raised an eyebrow. . . . Through the confusion of voices on the bridge, behind him he could hear Collingswood and Calhoun in busy conversation with the Port Authority. "Mr. Chairman," he said as a sleep-rumpled Waldo hurried into the Cohelmsman's console beside him, "put me in contact with the tower, please."

"A moment, Lieutenant Brim," the Chairman's voice intoned a few moments later. "All tower channels are presently in use."

Suddenly, Brim felt a hand on his shoulder. He jumped.

"Sorry to startle ye, laddie," Calhoun said softly, "but the alert's been canceled. You'll probably want to call off the Chairman," he added.

Brim frowned and turned in his seat. "Canceled?" he asked incredulously. Giant flames were even now leaping thousands of feet in the air from the stricken section of Atalanta. "I don't understand. . . ."

"Operations calls it a case of coordinated sabotage," Calhoun replied, "both here and in the city. There's no' an enemy ship anywhere in the remote vicinity of Hador. They've verified it with every scout and picket ship out there."

Baffled, the younger Carescrian shook his head and turned back to his console. "I won't need that tower channel, Mr. Chairman," he said. "Cancel the request."

"Aye, Lieutenant," the Chairman intoned. "Your request is canceled."

Suddenly, Brim turned back to Calhoun. "Sabotage, my foot!" he exclaimed. "I'll bet that was a bender."

Calhoun's eyebrows rose for a moment; then he glanced at Collingswood in the next console. "Makes some sense, doesn't it, Regula?"

Brim turned even farther in his seat to note the Captain's reaction.

Collingswood frowned for a moment. "Well," she said, "the possibility *had* entered my mind." Then she nodded thoughtfully. "There is one thing, however," she added, looking Brim directly in the face. "Nobody reported energy beams during the 'attack.' And unless the Leaguers have also invented a new type of disruptor, someone somewhere should have seen energy beams, don't you think?"

Brim could only nod agreement. "Aye, Captain," he admitted. "Someone should have."

"That is not to say I absolutely believe the sabotage story, either," Collingswood added, getting up from her console. "For the time being, however, I am more inclined that way—especially since I cannot think of anything I can do about the incident." She smiled. "At any rate, I still have a few metacycles of sleep coming, and I do not intend to lose any more of them than necessary. So, if you gentlemen will excuse me . . ."

Brim grinned. "Good night, Captain," he said.

"Good night, Captain," Calhoun echoed, "and good night to *you*, laddie," he said, standing at his own console. "The Skipper's got a fine idea if I have ever heard of one."

Moments later, Brim was almost alone on the bridge. "Good night, Waldo," he said as the lovely young Helmsman made off toward the rear of the bridge. He smiled to himself. He'd never even had time to say hello.

Quitting his own console, he walked over to where Ursis was shutting down the starship's power systems again. "Quickest flight we ever made," he said, placing a hand on the Bear's shoulder.

"Is true," Ursis growled, throwing the main breaker and shutting off the console's instrumentation. He grinned a toothy grin as he stood. "And speaking of truth," he continued, "I could not avoid overhearing your bender theory."

"You think it might be benders, too?" Brim asked on their way to the rear of the bridge.

"I do," Ursis said, ushering Brim into the companionway before him, "in spite of the lack of evidence. . . ."

Brim shook his head vigorously. "Unfortunately, I can't figure out what kind of weapons they're using. Collingswood's right—there's no disruptor I know of that doesn't leave a very visible path of ionization."

"That is also true, my impatient friend," the Bear said with a smile. "However, the other morning is the first time you or I even *heard* of benders. Real ones, anyway." He nodded his head as they stopped at his cabin. "This is a puzzle—to be sorted out in its own good time. Someone will eventually accomplish it. Perhaps even us. In the meanwhile, we do our best, which includes sleeping whenever possible. . . ."

"Good night, Nik," Brim said. "And thanks for the support."

"Good night, Wilf, for whatever remains of your bedtime. We shall perhaps discuss this further tonight over a glass of meem, eh?"

Brim smiled. "Nik, you've got yourself a bargain," he said as he started down the hall again toward his own cabin. But now he was wide awake. By the time he had his door open, he knew that going to bed now would be little more than a waste of time—especially since he planned to explore part of a large city. After changing into a summer uniform, he closed and locked his cabin again, then headed for the entry port. A bit early, perhaps, but he was ready to go. . . .

Hador was still only a glow on the lightward horizon when Brim signed out for local leave and stepped into the fresh sea air beyond *Defiant*'s main hatch. In the distance, Atalanta's huge fires had burned to a dull glow, and the two stricken merchantmen were little more than twisted skeletons collapsed into their ruined gravity pools.

Yet for all its recent chaos, the base appeared to have returned to normal almost immediately following the emergency. Brim nodded to himself as he caught a local tram for the base's main civilian terminal—the little vehicle was no more than a few cycles late. A hush passed over the passengers when they passed the two freshly burned out gravity pools—still smoking and littered with emergency vehicles. But as the tram bounced along its route through the huge starship base, it was filled and emptied a number of times by energetic-looking workmen who joked and talked among themselves as if this were simply another night shift. Haelacians *were* tough—he'd learned that in a hurry. And it looked as if Kabul Anak would discover the same thing himself, soon enough. According to top-secret situation reports, the Leaguer admiral had recently transferred his flag to his new super battleship *Rengas*. The attack wasn't far off now; Brim could feel it in his bones.

When he arrived at the base terminal, the end of the night shift was still more than two metacycles away, and both buildings were nearly deserted. Out in the tram shed, only two large interurban coaches hovered in the maze of shallow stone alleyways the vehicles used for a roadbed.

They were tall, old-fashioned-looking conveyances: Brim guessed as much as twelve irals in height, eight to ten wide, and perhaps seventy in length overall. Floating on two flat gravity packs near either rounded end, the floors of the big machines hovered approximately chest high. Forward, three-pane windscreens extended from slightly arched roofs halfway to the floor. Lines of similarly sized windows ran the length of each coach, the top third of each glazed with green stained glass. Powerful-looking headlamps were mounted below the center windscreen panels, directly over each car's number in brass Avalonian digits. The passenger entrance was a set of double doors amidships equipped with a retractable step. Open hatches forward and aft had only a short ladder; they were clearly for the crew. Car 312 bore three orange stripes painted across the center of its arched roof; car 309 had a single blue stripe. Aside from this, however, the trams appeared to be nearly identical except for signs at their turnstiles proclaiming "Monastery" and "Loop 12."

Brim frowned. It was reasonably clear that the former would arrive eventually at the top of Atalanta's hill at the Gradgroat-Norchelite Monastery. But what was a Loop 12? He rubbed his chin for a moment, then prudently decided on the monastery. If the mazelike Rocotzian section of town were any indication, he would be much wiser spending his time in bonafide tourist attractions until he was fortunate enough to attract another native escort.

He peered around the nearly deserted car shed; it smelled of stale food, stale sweat, stale mu'occo smoke, and the sharp stench of ozone from the humming, hovering trams. He guessed the last odor would easily reach unpleasant concentrations when the alleys were filled with coaches.

A green-uniformed worker dozed behind the ticket counter, but above his head hung a colorful map of the city. It was also marked with symbols that—wonder of wonders!—matched signs on all the turnstiles. On closer inspection, Brim discovered that Loop 12 was a route that circled the center section of the hill through a veritable maze of narrow side streets: a great place to become lost, he concluded quickly. Nodding to himself, he gently woke the ticket agent, purchased a round-trip ticket on the Monastery circuit, and made his way to tram number 312.

Inside, the empty coach smelled of hot oil, upholstery, and ozone; it was comfortably set up with four rows of carpet-covered bucket seats and a center aisle. It was also spotlessly clean. Brim took a window seat near the front where he could see out the windscreens as well. Then he sat back to wait.

During the next few cycles, he was joined by a number of workmen leaving early for one reason or another—mostly accidents. One limped on board with a fresh patch over her eye, two burly men in stevedore's overalls arrived with bandages around their heads, and a tall, angry-looking woman struggled up the stairs and into a seat despite the great cast that covered her right leg all the way to her knee. She was followed by a brace of grimy, tired-looking Gradgroat-Norchelite priests who smelled strongly of smoke. Brim quickly guessed where they came from. There would be a lot of work for priests at the two burned-out gravity pools. Wreckage such as he'd seen would allow for few survivors. . . .

At length the crew arrived: conductor and motorman dressed in dark green tunic and trousers, white shirts with green bow ties, shiny black boots, and orange-beaked pillbox hats decorated by a device that looked like a wheel pierced by a golden lightning bolt. Shortly thereafter, bells sounded officiously, doors rattled closed, and the floor vibrated beneath Brim's feet while ancient gravity packs ground into ponderous action, moving car 312 out of the station and onto a main alleyway heading inland. As the big, top-hampered coach picked up speed, she began a rhythmic swaying motion that, coupled with the monotonous throb of her packs, had a soothing effect all its own.

Relaxing in his seat, Brim squinted at the window itself. It was a tall affair with polished wooden frames and brass hardware that allowed the bottom to be raised past its green stained-glass partner above—hadn't they heard of environmental control? The transparent bottom pane even boasted beveled glass! Outside, they were now crossing a bridge that paralleled the seven moss-covered stone arches of the Harbor Causeway—he remembered that bridge from his evening with Claudia.

For a moment, her oval face and soft-looking brown hair filled his mind's eye—he imagined the musky fragrance of her perfume teasing his nose. Somehow, she had been popping in and out of his mind a great deal since that night—much more than she should have. Truth to tell, he felt more than a little guilty about being attracted so strongly to her—especially when he was pledged to someone else.

Then he shrugged. Right or wrong, that was the way things were. For the next precious metacycles, he intended to relax and enjoy his precious leave. Tomorrow was time enough to moralize. . . .

Car 312's gravity packs increased to a throbbing pulse beneath the floor as the alleyway began to climb City Mount Hill, and they entered a confusion of three- and four-story structures built mostly of whitewashed stone and mortar. By the early-morning light, Brim could see tiny gardens crowded into every possible nook and cranny, dappled with flowers that splashed the waking cityscape with a million dabs of color. These buildings were so close to the street that their balconies nearly touched overhead. The net effect was almost tunnel-like as the big car clawed its way up the steep grade. In places, the dusty alleyway actually doubled as a narrow street of sorts that they were obliged to share with dogs, barnyard animals, priests, fishermen, storekeepers, stonemasons, rothcats, dockyard workers, occasional Blue Capes, and droves of men and women in colorful native dress. None moved out of the way until the last possible moment, when the conductor applied the car's shrieking, ear-piercing whistle—which he was obliged to do almost every few irals.

All too often, they thundered past burned-out, roofless buildings—abandoned and left gaping at the sky. Many of the side streets Brim could see were filled with piles of tumbled brick and stone—clearly impassable for the duration of the war. Sometimes, whole blocks had been gutted, with narrow paths cleared through the rubble to uncover the alleyways. The motorman sped through these pursued by billowing specters of gray dust. They made Brim shiver. No glory here, only the remains of fragile homes, crushed and broken by the wild, blind lashings of wartime insanity. He shook his head. Somehow, sights like this never seemed to register with the leaders. Usually, he supposed, *their* homes were well protected. . . .

In due course, the car crossed a stone bridge over a deep ravine. Brim glimpsed the distant harbor far below. Admiral Hober and his battlecruisers were just putting out to space: *Iaith Galad*, *Oedden*, and *Benwell*, great hovering shapes on the placid morning waters.

Even while he watched, *Benwell* began her takeoff run at the head of a towering cloud of water vapor. In spite of himself, he felt shivers of thrill race along his back while the interurban's windows rattled in the rolling thunder. Battlecruisers were the stuff of dreams for him. Especially *Benwell*—built as replacement for *Nimue*, on which the legendary Star Admiral Merlin Emrys had disappeared more than five years ago. Like every young man in the Empire—even in Carescria—he had worshiped Emrys and the great ebony battlecruiser that ghosted in and out of harbors all over the galaxy, showing the colors—and power—of Greyffin IV's Galactic Empire. Their loss had been devastating at the time. Now, both man and ship were only half-remembered entries in a casualty list that would have seemed unbelievable at the time. But they would always hold a special place in his heart.

At length, the car thrummed across two intricately filigreed metal trestles, glided through a long, pillared colonnade, and came to rest on a spacious plaza planted with ancient, ocher-colored trees and paved with complex patterns of reddish-gold paving stones. On one side it fronted a colossal saffron granite crag at least two hundred irals in height and half a c'lenyt in circumference. A spectacular staircase and balustrade—sculpted from the granite itself—wound through a dozen switchbacks to the monastery above. It was occupied by black-garbed priests with high orange collars, Friars and Sisters in their long crimson gowns, novices wearing short robes of rough cloth, and an occasional, brightly outfitted layperson.

Opposite this stairway, the plaza was bounded by another ornate balustrade, also of saffron granite, but interspersed by graceful, flower-filled urns twice as tall as a man. From here, Brim got a spectacular view of the harbor and the great Imperial base thousands of irals below. He could feel the morning sea breeze on his face, cool and fresh at this altitude. He picked out *Defiant* on her gravity pool and grinned to himself. He'd seldom had a chance to see her at such a distance. "Graceful" was the word that came to his mind first. She was a beautiful ship, long and lean as she hovered—impatiently, as it seemed—to break the bonds that kept her from her own element.

With a whole day on his hands, he relaxed a few extra cycles at the balustrade, looking down at the many-hued roofs of Atalanta. Behind him, he heard the coach's doors rattle shut; presently it ground its way out of the plaza. Somehow its departure severed a symbolic tie with the war, and he suddenly felt freed—no matter how temporarily—from the death and destruction that swirled through the galaxy. He took a deep breath while a feeling of peace swept over him in the quiet, breeze-swept plaza.

Fifty irals to his right, another staircase—this built into the steep hillside—connected with the streets below. Like its opposite, it also carried considerable traffic. High overhead, a colorful little Gradygroat Zuzzuou lifted from the monastery and crackled up into the morning sky. As the archaic little spaceship banked steeply over the harbor, Brim saw that it was filled to capacity. He shook his head and smiled. A whole spaceship of Gradygroats flying out to service weapons systems that generations of Admiralty scholars dismissed as mere artifacts—unworthy of further study. He laughed to himself. Talk about wasting manpower! Yet the forts held a certain fascination for him. Silently, he promised himself that if he ever had more than a single day on leave, he would try to fly out and see one for himself. Then he laughed. Fat thraggling chance of extended leave in a place like Atalanta. . . .

At length, he turned and made his way through the dusk-blue tree shadows—boots clicking among gently dancing puddles of golden sunlight—until at length he came to the foot of the great staircase. He followed a trio of Friars onto the marble treads, and quickly discovered that Gradgroat-Norchelite clerics set a rapid pace on the way up. He laughed to himself as he found himself breathing deeper and deeper. Clearly, the staircase was a daily occurrence for them—and considerably longer than *Defiant*'s longest companionway.

He paused at a landing near the top while he caught his breath. From this high angle, he could see car 312 with its three orange stripes following a twisted route back down the hill. He idly watched the streets he would follow were he walking to intercept its course. An easy route, he discovered to his surprise. The hilltop was so steep that the heavy car required numerous switchbacks to negotiate the slope, and although it had clearly traveled a long way since leaving the plaza, its actual distance from the monastery was little more than an easy c'lenyt's walk from the lower staircase. He even strongly considered making the walk himself once he completed his visit to the monastery. When he reached the top a few cycles later, however, all thoughts concerning possible walks—or anything else, for that matter—were swept away by the mind-boggling structure looming before him.

Blazing in Hador's afternoon brilliance like a golden icon, the monastery's colossal, flame-shaped spire stood at least a thousand irals higher than the two massive, disk-shaped tiers that formed its base. The bottom story was nearly a quarter again as large as the top, and both were surrounded by lofty alabaster colonnades formed of pointed arches and graceful columns that were easily more than a hundred irals high at their apex. A second grove of gigantic ocher trees surrounded the sprawling campus, shading what appeared to be veritable c'lenyts of quiet paths dotted by rushing fountains and quiet glens.

Before Brim's nearly unbelieving eyes, a wide avenue lead across the first-story colonnade and into a pair of massive, ebony doors that themselves were at least sixty irals high. At present, both were open to a darkened space beyond. The Carescrian shook his head. Never—anywhere—had he encountered such an extraordinary structure. Greyffin IV's palace in Avalon actually paled in comparison.

Above the massive door frame was a carved motto written in Xantos, the archaic Universal script that even Carescrian youngsters were required to learn:

IN DESTRUCTION IS RESURRECTION;
THE PATH OF POWER LEADS THROUGH TRUTH

Brim chuckled as he stepped across the threshold into a darkened anteroom—Gradygroats made about as much sense as Sodeskayan Bears when it came to mottoes. When his eyes accustomed themselves to the darkness, he pushed open a second, inner door, and . . .

Unconsciously, he caught his breath. Sensible or not, the great circular commons room they had constructed was in many ways as impressive as the whole monastery.

From a stupendous balcony formed by the monastery's second tier, men's voices intoned one of the Gradgroat-Norchelite anthems—ancient words and music that stirred the hearts of believers and nonbelievers alike:

"Oh Universal Force of Truth,
That guards the homeland of our youth,
That bidd'st the mighty cosmos deep
Thine own appointed limits keep:
Oh hear us when we cry for Grace
For those at peril far in space. . . ."

Brim followed no particular religion—by any stretch of the imagination—but he nonetheless found himself lifted on a cresting surge of emotion. He'd loved the hymn as a child who dreamed of the stars. Now that he'd found them, the words were still never far beneath his personal veneer.

Before him like some preposterous crystal plain, the lens-shaped floor was dotted here and there by figures of men and women who appeared to be diminished—somehow, *humbled* was a better word—by sheer, unmitigated magnitude. On further inspection, he discovered that the surface actually comprised three concentric circles. Spaced equally around the outer ring, three inlaid sets of Xantos symbols faced the center of the room and spelled "Destruction" in shining gold metal. The middle ring contained three sets of gold inlaid symbols for "Resurrection," also facing the center. And the unmarked inner ring served to frame a large, central cone of gleaming gold-colored metal studded with irregular patterns of what appeared to be a thousand or more multicolored gems. The symbol group for "Truth" was deeply engraved three times into a polished band of clear metal around its base.

Overhead, soaring high above the balcony, a monumental dome modeled the nighttime firmament over Atalanta with Hador blazing forth through a lenslike aperture that seemed to hover in the center of the sky surrounded by the word "Power," in Xantos letters. Brim frowned as he stared up into this artificial starscape. Something peculiar about it. . . . He snapped his fingers. Of course. The dome itself was unquestionably constructed of some translucent material, and whatever the Gradygroats were using to model Hador shone from considerable distance *behind* its surface! He smiled. Clever, that. A shimmering beam of focused brilliance plummeted straight from the "hovering" lens to shatter on the jeweled cone in the center of the floor; its light then mirrored back to the dome in a thousand separate reflections to form the stars. Brim nodded in admiration as he studied the cone. Each of its seemingly scattered jewels had actually been placed with exquisite care! He wondered what sort of artificial flare the Gradygroats had placed behind the dome to shine like that one did.

Interestingly enough—at least to Brim—the tower itself was almost fourteen hundred irals high, but the inner dome above his head extended no more than three hundred irals into it. Rather disappointing, when he came to think about it. Idly, he wondered what the Gradygroats did with the remainder of the space—he certainly remembered seeing no windows in the tower, at least from the outside.

On the surrounding wall, scores of inset display-window tableaux depicted the long, varied history of The Order. Brim promised himself ample time to digest these—especially ones depicting the thirteen orbital forts and their mighty disruptors. Wouldn't Wellington love this, he thought as he continued his fascinated inspection of the commons room.

During the next metacycles, Brim availed himself of everything the monastery had to offer: its great circle of tableaux, the library with the rare collection of Primitives, the museum, the art gallery, and the gloriously wooded parks. Each was fascinating in its own way, and to his surprise, neither the Friars nor the Sisters he met attempted to proselytize him or, so far as he could see, any of the other visitors, although there *were* only himself and perhaps four or five families on a holiday. Wartime, he supposed, severely limited the tourist trade. At length, he deposited a generous—at least for a Carescrian—donation at one of the intricately carved alms boxes, then strode down the top staircase to the coach plaza. He had most of the long afternoon still before him. Warm breezes carried the voices of the choir from the monastery:

> "Far-called, our starfleets melt away;
>      Dominions and our pow'r depart;
> Lo, all our fame of yesterday
>      Without The Motto, leaves the heart—
>      From Truth the path of Power leads yet,
>      Lest we forget—lest we forget! . . ."

Leaning his elbows on the balustrade, he peered down at the roofs of the city again. An afternoon sea breeze was still surprisingly cool on his face, and the sky was now dotted by ranks of flat-bottomed, fair-weather clouds. He watched one of the big coaches glide into the alleyways, exchange passengers, then growl on its way again, disappearing at length among the giant trees. Once again, he gazed into the distance at *Defiant*, then at his timepiece. Impulsively, he vowed he would present himself at the sign-in desk no more than a milliclick before he absolutely had to. Then, with a smile of determination on his face, he started down the staircase toward town. . . .

By the time he reached the bottom, he was glad enough to enter the narrow streets and their protection from Hador's burning rays. The sky was only a slit now between the white stucco buildings that hovered protectively over him and the other pedestrians with whom he shared the shadowed byway. As in the Rocotzian Section—wherever *that* was from here! —most of the buildings were decorated by jutting balconies, colorful coats of arms, and sinuous, bas-relief carvings depicting every subject the mind could conjure, plus a few that Brim's, at least, could not. Birds chirped everywhere, flying constantly in and out of holes in the walls that seemed to be specially provided for this particular use. Occasional rothcats sauntered into the streets to brush against his legs. Curious animals. And as always, his nose was alternately pleasured and repelled by the million and one odors that inhabited the dusty air.

He passed a great, heavyset man with a bulbous nose, red ears, and huge hands that delicately weeded a tiny garden where the afternoon sun managed to linger for a few extra metacycles. He found himself returning the Haelacian's polite palm-open greeting as if he'd been doing it all his life. Something comfortable about Atalanta—and the Atalantans. Farther down the street, a crew manhandled a long, red cable from an opening in the pavement. He was now into an area of shops, and the street had became crowded with people carrying gaily colored baskets of groceries. Odors from the stores and open stalls reminded him that he was both hungry and thirsty himself. Smiling, he had just chosen a promising, cool-looking tavern when a strident bellow abruptly split the air, rattling windows and scattering flocks of birds from their high shelters. He paused as the noise continued, assaulting his ears from all directions as it reverberated from the walls of the narrow street. Somehow, it had an urgent timbre. What was it? . . .

A moment later, he was nearly bowled over by frightened-looking people as they rushed past him from the tavern. A thin, gray-haired woman with a cook's pointed hat and a forgotten towel thrown over her shoulder looked up as she pushed past. "Come on, Blue Cape," she screeched as she started down the street. "Haven't you heard the sirens before?"

Sirens! Brim's heart jumped—the battlecruisers had taken off early that morning. Clearly, their departure was all the Leaguers were waiting for. Forgetting his empty stomach, he joined the stream of people running headlong downhill, hoping against hope that they were heading toward a shelter and not simply fleeing blindly in panic.

A terrific barrage of disruptor fire suddenly flashed overhead, bathing the street in strobes of blinding green light. Pealing thunder blasted his eardrums and raised clouds of dust from the streets. Brim recalled the briefer's words, "Take shelter at the first warning." Well, he was trying to do that—and so, it seemed, was everybody else on the street!

At one of the parks that dotted the city, he elbowed his way from the streaming river of people and stopped to scan the skies. He was just in time to see *Defiant* hurtle overhead in an almost vertical bank, scaffolding and construction equipment cascading into her wake as the big ship added her firepower to the defense of the city. He wondered who was at the controls. In spite of the danger around him, his heart leaped with both pride and sorrow. *Universe*, how he wished he were with her!

Then, even before the cruiser was out of sight, explosions began to rock the earth. Tremendous geysers of flame, dirty black smoke, and debris shot high above the housetops. In the street, people began to scream and run for any cover they could find, cowering under trees and in doorways. Dogs barked madly between the disruptor bursts while panicked Atalantans ran wildly out of their houses and then back in again. At the far end of the park, an old woman flung herself blindly into a stone wall screaming one of the Norchelite chants Brim had heard only a short time ago at the monastery. He ran to help her, but before he could catch up she disappeared into the street again.

Ignoring his own safety, Brim scanned the skies for some

trace of attackers. There. . . . In the distance at great altitude, he could just make out three squadrons of starships streaking in from the polar regions on an arrogantly straight run over the base. On the moment, *Defiant*'s grim silhouette sliced down among them from the clouds, powerful disruptors flashing and strobing like an avenging storm. Instantly, two of the Leaguers disappeared in roiling fireballs that hung in the sky dripping flame and debris while the other ships scattered in every direction. A third attacker trailed sudden flame and smoke, then broke at the center, its two halves tumbling through the air trailing wisps of smoke like spent holiday fireworks. Clearly, the Leaguers hadn't counted on the presence of a new light cruiser—or had badly underestimated the power of her disruptors.

Abruptly, more explosions rocked the ground nearby. Startled, Brim scanned the skies for their source, but failed to spot even a single starship in the vicinity. And he considered himself an expert spotter—although, he acknowledged, *all* Helmsmen considered themselves expert spotters. Moreover, starships weren't exactly the smallest machines one might look for, either. He frowned. All the explosions going on around him had to come from *somewhere*!

By now, he was clearly trapped in the open park. Reacting at the last possible moment to his own precarious situation, he flattened himself in the grass near a tree—sheer milliclicks before two stunning explosions shook the earth and collapsed a house across the street in an angry wave of fierce heat and choking dust. The violent blasts sent a blizzard of deadly stone splinters whizzing in all directions as the tall building collapsed with a hideous, grinding crash.

He could still hear bone-crushing detonations from the direction of the base, but where in Gratz's name were the Leaguers who had been tearing up the scenery where *he* was? He crawled away from the trees to get a better look, but the adjacent sky still looked empty and quite blameless.

Then suddenly, a muzzy area materialized for only a moment as it streaked directly overhead toward the foot of the hill. Brim could hardly credit his eyes when the indistinct specter suddenly defined itself into a pair of doors that opened into thin air itself. And even as the apparition disappeared beyond Atalanta's rooftops, a succession of tear-shaped objects dropped from its mysterious "opening." Moments later, the park heaved spasmodically as a whole succession of new explosions raised geysers of smoke and flame a few blocks away.

Impulsively, Brim grimaced and snapped his fingers. So *that* was what benders looked like! And how they attacked. No wonder Collingswood hadn't seen energy beams during the predawn raid. The damage had been caused by *bombs*! Old-fashioned, aerial bombs. . . . He shook his head. Outdated they might be, but he couldn't think of a single defense against them, either. He squeezed his eyes shut while another cascading series of explosions tossed the ground violently and covered him with a veritable shower of leaves and branches. A dead dog came looping through the air to leave a bloody smear on the pavement nearby. He nearly cried out in helpless frustration as superheated air from still another blast singed the hair on the back of his neck like a great torch, then ground his teeth in anger as a second deduction formed in his head. The *bastard* Leaguers! They were using their conventional strike on the harbor as a cover for the benders that were carrying out the real raid—a terror attack on the Atalantian civilians, without whom the Imperial base would cease to operate.

As he lay helplessly amid the Leaguers' frenzy of destruction, familiar thunder again filled the air, drowning out other noises of the attack. A moment later, *Defiant* appeared overhead, riding parallel to one of the Leaguer attack ships. Suddenly, the cruiser's starboard side erupted in a glowing mist of green flame as she loosed a whole broadside of 152-mmi disruptors. Her opponent, a powerful NF-110 destroyer, abruptly stopped flying as if it had been smashed by a giant mallet. An instant later the Leaguer starship exploded in a brilliant eruption of yellow and green flame that flashed blindingly from every seam. Shortly thereafter, it disappeared in a large puff of gray cloud as *Defiant* thundered steadily out of sight over the trees.

The mind-numbing local explosions continued for at least another ten cycles before Atalanta's battered cityscape fell quiet again—except for the still-frenzied barking of neighborhood dogs and an angry cacophony from the trees as Haelic's birds returned to the remains of their nests. Presently, sirens sounded, and soon afterward people gradually began to reappear in the debris-fouled streets—along with racing emergency vehicles of every size and shape.

Stunned by the violence, Brim shakily started off downhill to report what he'd seen, but now it seemed as if he had entered a different city—in a different Universe. Bloody corpses lay everywhere in grotesque attitudes that only the dead can assume. A smashed child's hand still gripped the leash of a whimpering puppy. Gritting his teeth, Brim waved a swarm of flies from the tiny, dead face. Then he released the frightened animal—which immediately scurried off to its doom in the blazing shell of a nearby house.

Farther along the smoke-filled street, he encountered the shattered ruins of a large apartment building that had collapsed into the street. Nearby, a silent crowd watched rescue workers desperately sifting through the rubble. Medics were just carrying a young woman—mauled over every part of her body—to a sidewalk depository when Brim passed on the street. He stopped in his tracks as the stricken woman looked up at him with terror-filled eyes and opened the bloody gash that remained of her mouth as if she wanted to speak. Totally consumed with pity, he knelt and took her hand. "Say it," he whispered. "I won't leave you—I'll listen. . . ." But before she could utter a word, her mouth overflowed with blood. For a moment, her eyes became large as saucers. Then suddenly they lost their focus and her hand went limp. Moments later, the air filled with the telltale odor of feces.

Flies were beginning to cover the corpse even as Brim numbly resumed his way down the hill again, tears blinding his eyes.

Later, as he crossed the intersection where he once planned to board the coach, he gasped and shook his head in dismay. No more than a few irals back along the alleyway, a firefighting unit had just extinguished the charred remains of an interurban car. Rescue workers were now sifting through the twisted wreckage for survivors—but it was clear to Brim they were wasting their time. Not much remained of the big vehicle except a blackened fragment of one end that mounted a large, broken headlight and the brass numerals "312." He squeezed his eyes closed. Had he been perhaps half a metacycle earlier finishing his tour of the monastery...

Two c'lenyts or so farther on down the hill, the destruction mysteriously ceased—as if the Leaguers had purposely targeted only specific portions of the town. Brim shook his head in disgust. He was far beyond any attempt to justify the Leaguers' strategy, especially their attacks on random civilian targets.

Presently, he was able to flag down a passing Fleet vehicle and hitched a ride all the way to the Government Sector at the bottom of the hill, where he called in a hurried report of his sightings. From there, he continued on foot; if memory served him, he was only six c'lenyts or so from the base.

He had walked no more than a thousand irals, however, when he came upon another charred and battered area of fresh destruction, this one among a number of private homes and storefronts that clearly predated the surrounding government structures by at least a hundred years. As he hurried through the rubble, he could see no buildings at all that had escaped at least some damage. Rescue workers were everywhere shouting at each other and scurrying through the rubble like insects whose hive has been disturbed. The whole area reeked of smoke and the sickening, sweetish odor of burned flesh.

Suddenly, he felt his hackles rise when he thought he recognized one of the vehicles parked just off the main thoroughfare—a familiar sun-bleached skimmer with a frayed canvas top... Claudia's? He stopped in his tracks to peer inside with a growing concern.

There it was! Her red leather briefcase—and on the floor, the menu from Nesterio's Cabaret. He bit his lip. Was she one of the casualties? Heart in his mouth, he found himself running toward the smoking rubble nearest the spot where she'd parked.

And then he spied her with two other women in the wreckage of a nearby house, struggling to lift a heavy wooden beam. "Claudia!" he called impulsively as he picked his way through the crumbled wreckage.

Still struggling with the beam, she could turn her head only slightly. "Wilf," she grunted through her effort, "thank the Universe.... Help us move this beam—quickly!"

Without another thought, Brim grasped the heavy timber, and the four of them forced it through a layer of fallen stone until it could be moved freely. Then, nearly choking on the dust they had raised, they dragged it to one side and braced it against a great chunk of fallen masonry. Instantly, the three women returned to the shallow trench they had created and began to dig frantically until a low moan issued from a bloody face still half covered with brick dust and debris. The man had clearly been trapped when the ancient timber fell across his chest. Brim pitched in with his bare hands as if he had purposely arrived to join in the rescue effort.

When the victim was safely turned over to a tired-looking ambulance crew, Brim found himself looking at Claudia in an altogether new light. She was a great deal changed since their evening in Nesterio's Cabaret. Now, her long chestnut hair could most charitably be described as disheveled. Her dust-covered face was streaked with sweat, and her tunic and trousers were seriously burned in a number of most unfashionable places. She appeared to be wearing a pair of cast-off boots that were at least a hundred sizes too large for her feet, and she was covered with thick clots of drying blood— enough that it couldn't be her own, or she'd long ago have joined the nearby pile of corpses that waited for identification.

She also appeared to be looking at *him*. "Well," she said in a tired voice, "it looks as if you got caught in it, too." She frowned for a moment. "I thought I saw *Defiant* take off . . ." she said.

"You did," Brim said, finally catching his breath. "I wasn't on her."

Suddenly she seemed concerned. "Why?" she asked. "I mean, I thought you were Principal Helmsman. . . ."

Brim smiled, somehow pleased by her concern. "I am *still*, so far as I know," he explained as rescue workers carried another live victim to a waiting ambulance. "But I was also on leave this morning—near the monastery, exploring this beautiful city of yours."

Instantly he wished he had never opened his mouth, for Claudia's face capitulated to a look of despair. Tears slowly formed in the corners of her eyes, and she looked away in embarrassment. "It lost a lot of its beauty this morning," she choked.

"I'm terribly sorry," he mumbled, touching her arm. He wanted in the worst way to draw her to his shoulder, but a crowd began to call from the street.

"Come on," a man called. "We've found more of them!"

"Children!" another voice yelled. "Hurry."

"Now!" shouted another. "We've got to get them out of there!"

"Can you stay and help?" Claudia asked with a desperate look on her face. "Universe knows we need everyone we can get."

Brim nodded. *Defiant* was still out, probably chasing the remnants of the attacking fleet. "I'll stay," he said, rolling up the sleeves of his already ruined tunic, "as long as I possibly can."

During the next metacycles, Brim lost all track of time as he and Claudia helped rescue five children—two of whom died before they could be lifted into an ambulance—and eight retired starsailors. The children had been trapped as they waited for their transportation to school; the old starsailors were residents of a complex specially set aside for elderly residents of the district.

Toward morning—while he and the other rescuers combed the wreckage a second time looking for victims they might have missed in the early panic—Brim heard the approaching rumble of heavy gravity generators. Presently, *Defiant* thundered in from landward, turned, and projecting great white beams from her landing lights, sank smoothly toward a touchdown out on the bay. Moments later, he felt a hand on his arm. It was Claudia. "That was *Defiant*, wasn't it?" she asked wearily.

"She was," Brim said. "And I suppose it means that I shall have to leave here almost immediately. I still have quite a few c'lenyts to walk."

Claudia smiled—beautiful in spite of the dust and dried blood. "I think we are *both* finished here for tonight," she said. She pointed to a large tram that had just pulled up to a nearby curb. "A fresh crew of rescue volunteers from the day shift," she explained. "They'll take over for us now—although I don't know how many more they can save."

Brim smiled and looked her in the face. "They have to *try*, though," he said gently. "If they save even one more person, it'll be worth their while."

"And if they don't?"

"Still worth while," Brim said resolutely.

Claudia looked him full in the eye. "Quite a thought for a bloodthirsty warrior like Wilf Brim," she said quietly while the shouts of the fresh rescuers echoed in the rubble around her. Then she gently touched his cheek. "How did you get here?" she asked.

"I walked—actually I ran," Brim said. "Transportation got a little behind schedule up there by the monastery."

"They got the section below the tram stop, didn't they?" she asked.

"Yeah," Brim said. "Pretty thoroughly. I was there."

"And you walked all the way from there?"

"No," Brim said with a smile. "I hitched a ride to some government buildings about a c'lenyt from here."

"What would you think about hitching another ride tonight?" she asked.

Brim gently grasped her arms and drew her closer.

She moved against him easily, then looked into his eyes meaningfully. "How about settling for a ride to *Defiant* tonight?" she asked. "I don't think I'm up to anything more strenuous—and I doubt if you are either, Mr. Brim."

"I should be most glad for a ride to *Defiant*, or *anywhere* for that matter—as long as I ride with you," he answered, surprising himself with the truth of what he had just said. He felt a rush of guilt as Margot's face passed his mind's eye.

Claudia smiled as she planted a peck of a kiss on his lips.

Brim grinned. "At some time later, however, we might . . ."

"Some time later," she said as she led him toward her skimmer, "will be time enough to talk about some later time. . . ."

Less than fifteen cycles following that, they were once again in the delivery lot before *Defiant*'s gravity pool. In the half-light of false dawn, Brim looked deeply into Claudia's tired eyes. She was totally disheveled by now, yet her natural beauty remained unquenchable. "One more kiss?" he asked. "You know that *Defiant* leaves again tomorrow, and I don't know when I'll be back. . . ."

Suddenly she was in his arms, with her mouth, wet and open, covering his. He held her that way for a long moment before she pushed him firmly away.

"As I said before, Lieutenant Brim," she murmured, "some time later will be time enough for us to plan some later time."

Brim nodded stepped to the ground and saluted. "Here's to then," he said.

Claudia blew him another kiss as she turned the little skimmer around and glided out of the lot.

Then she was gone, and Brim found himself again standing in a great deal of confusion as he watched the taillights of her skimmer fade into the distance. He shook his head. Perhaps it was best to stay confused about this most beautiful woman— and let Lady Fate chart his course. Claudia Valemont might very well spell trouble, but, as he had lately discovered, he definitely had no desire to end things, either. Time, he discovered, would tell. . . .

Early the next morning, he made detailed reports of his bender sightings to a number of surprisingly high-ranking— and *very* attentive—Fleet Intelligence officers. Then, two metacycles into the Midday watch, he piloted *Defiant* back into space on another convoy run. War and the Admiralty's tight provisioning schedule for Hador permitted little time to catch one's breath at all.

# Chapter 5

# THE BENDER

EMERGENCY PRIORITY: SHIPS APPROACHING CONVOY DIVISION TWO FROM SECTOR GREEN NADIR AT HIGH SPEED; CONSIDER HOSTILE UNLESS OTHERWISE NOTIFIED. INDEPENDENT UNITS STAND BY TO REPEL. The Leaguers were making a run on the convoy from dead astern and below. Dressed in his battle suit, Brim smiled grimly as the familiar litany flashed in his KA'PPA display. This time, *Defiant* was a designated "independent," cruising in the gap between the two widely separated convoy divisions to the left front of Division Two in its blue sector. And even though he was limited to operating in a specific zone, he could at least do *something* when the attackers caught up to him. He listened impatiently for Collingswood's voice directly behind him. . . .

"You may call action stations, Number One," she intoned calmly to Calhoun.

"Aye, Captain," the older Carescrian answered. He'd clearly been waiting for the order too, for he immediately began to issue commands throughout the ship.

Brim gritted his teeth. *Come on,* he thought. . . .

Finally, amid the clamor of alarms sounding below and a confusion of boots pounding on hullmetal decks, Brim felt a hand on his shoulder.

"Targets of opportunity when they reach our zone, Wilf," Collingswood declared. "Go to it."

"Aye, Captain," a relieved Brim answered over his shoulder. Then peering across Cohelmsman Galen Fritz, he nodded to Uris at the systems console. "Combat energy, Nik," he said.

"Combat energy," Ursis repeated, moving his six-fingered hands surely among an orderly confusion of systems controls. Immediately, the sound of *Defiant*'s four DDB-19.A7 Drive crystals began to intensify. Aft, their greenish wake took on a brighter glow as the accelerating ship shrugged off more and more L-units of relativistic mass.

Brim winked at Wellington, then glanced at his intraship display reflecting Provodnik and his team of Crystal Tenders stoking the cruiser's eight antimatter power chambers. He shifted to the sick bay and Flynn's last-cycle preparations there, then to the interior of each major turret. Everything and everyone appeared to be ready. In the last few months, actual combat experience had fine-tuned *Defiant* and her crew into a spectacularly efficient fighting unit. Brim smiled. Somehow, he wasn't surprised. "I'll take the helm now, Mr. Chairman," he said, placing his hands over the controls.

"Aye, Lieutenant Brim," *Defiant*'s Chairman intoned over the mounting roar of the crystals. "Steering vector is null and amidships—you now have the helm."

Outside, Brim watched *Defiant*'s disruptors training balefully back and forth as he turned in toward the convoy. Light from a nearby star swarm lit her decks for a moment as she hurtled past at nearly twenty-five thousand LightSpeed.

In total, Convoy J18/9 extended more than fifteen c'lenyts from the van of Division One to the rear of Division Two. Each division was a full c'lenyt wide, nearly two deep, and contained fifty merchant starships escorted by thirty-odd warships. The latter ranged in size from the convoy flagship, I.F.S. *Heroic*, a heavy cruiser of the Hostile Class, through two light cruisers and a number of destroyers, to a small trawler squadron.

The other light cruiser was I.F.S. *Perilous*, one of the three Petulant-class light cruisers from which *Defiant*'s design was derived. Like all Petulants, she was fast and reliable with eight 155-mmi disruptors in four twin-mounts. But she was also virtually unarmored. Brim had always appreciated the thick, 75- to 120-mmi armor that protected *Defiant*'s inner chamber and bridge.

Nine of the twenty-two destroyers attached to Convoy J18/9 were T-class ships like old *Truculent*. Tough scrappers all—and worth their weight in firepower when it came to a fight. The others were a mixed bag of newer K- and N-class ships.

All in all, Brim considered that *Defiant* was in powerful company. Yet losses among the merchant starships had begun the first day out and continued to mount despite everyone's best efforts. It was a tough war—and no doubt about it. . . .

Far astern, Brim could now see the attackers through *Defiant*'s aft Hyperscreens: fifteen speeding traces of green grouped into three elements and closing rapidly. He recognized the hard-edged silhouettes immediately against a star swarm—and COMCONVOY could forget about any recall notice. These were Leaguers, all right: fast, maneuverable Gorn-Hoff 380A-8s with big rapid-firing 137-mmi disruptors that could crumple a merchant ship's hull by a hit anywhere near the Drive-chamber structures.

With at least half the escorts protecting Division One, *Defiant* and the remaining Imperial ships would soon be considerably outnumbered—as usual. Wars that extended over the better part of a galaxy left only so many ships to go around on either side. He shrugged to himself and checked his instruments while he slightly increased his rate of turn. The Leaguers had started their war with vastly superior numbers of warships, and the convoy runs to Hador-Haelic were a good indication that the Empire had a long way to go before it caught up in that department.

Brim peered out over the plodding merchant ships as *Defiant* streaked toward the constantly zigzagging convoy: a long, cylindrical formation of ten "wheels," each made up of four merchantmen surrounding a fifth. The "rims" rotated around their "axis" ship with slow and majestic precision, randomly changing speeds and direction. He could only imagine what it must be like in the unarmed cargo ships as the crews watched impotently for another wave of deadly attack ships.

The Gorn-Hoffs were growing bigger every cycle as they approached the convoy. At this distance, Brim could make out their four turrets mounted on outriggers in a crosslike arrangement. Each mounted two rapid-firing Schwanndor 137-mmi disruptors. His mind's eye recalled the captured performance tables he'd seen about them at Menander-Garand:

## AN AVERAGE 500-IRAL MERCHANTMAN CAN BE DESTROYED WITH:

| Certainty Percentage | Shots at distance (c'lenyts) | | |
|---|---|---|---|
| | 0.5 | 1.0 | 1.5 |
| 50 | 40 | 104 | 308 |
| 95 | 76 | 203 | 650 |

And with the recovery rate of the new Schwanndor disruptors, it didn't take very long to get off a lot of discharges—especially with four turrets. Gorn-Hoff 380A-8s were powerful destroyers, and Brim had early on learned to respect their devastating capabilities.

He eased up on his turn as the enemy ships approached. Combat at Hyperlight velocities was a different sort of thing than fighting below the speed of light. For one thing, you couldn't go head to head. No computer in the known Universe could react fast enough to fire a disruptor at those closing speeds. Too, before you could turn around, your quarry had traveled a long distance away. Hyperlight tactics consisted almost entirely of speed control, stern chases, parallel fighting, and occasional dodging off at narrow angles—all generally in a forward direction.

Abruptly, the rear zone of Division Two was bathed in the painful glare of Hyperflares. Only clicks later, disruptors flashed—from both sides—and space itself heaved into a wild confusion of pulsing explosions. Simultaneously, massive blasts glared among attackers and attacked alike.

"Got one of the bastards," somebody cheered from the jump seats. "First shot, too! . . ."

"For the price of I.F.S. *Gallant*," another voice snapped. "That was *two* explosions out there."

Brim glanced aft for a moment to see the little trawler veer out of line—blazing from bow to stern—then fall rapidly behind and explode in a wink of reddish-orange flame in the distance. Scant clicks afterward, another searing flash of light came from behind.

"Oh, Sweet Gratz!" someone gasped. "Look at that! They got another merchant ship already!"

"Universe, lookit 'im burn."

"But he isn't pulling out of line, either."

"A miracle. . . ."

"Come *on*, fella, get those fires out. . . ."

Then a Hyperflare blazed into life so close to *Defiant* that the bridge filled with gasps of terror. Brim could see the little scout ship speeding out ahead from beneath *Defiant's* bow.

"Bandit at red nadir just coming on the bearing," one of Wellington's gunlayers said slowly. "Range 189.7, and opening. . . ."

"I see 'im down there!" someone shouted. "Get the bastard Leaguer before he gets away!"

"Yeah, blast 'im!"

"Hold your fire, Dora," Collingswood cautioned in a quiet voice. "We're after bigger game than a scout."

"Aye, Captain," Wellington answered. Outside, *Defiant's* disruptors continued to sweep back and forth.

Off to starboard, Brim's eye caught a series of flashes. He looked up from the instruments to see hits landing aboard a familiar silhouette: S. S. *Wakefield*, the elderly starship in which he'd traveled from Carescria to Avalon on his way to the Helmsman's Academy. He'd eagerly learned everything he could about the graceful old liner during the week she took to make the trip—a surprisingly short time, considering her advanced age. By the harsh glare of the Hyperflares, the finish of her hullmetal was in the same state of disrepair that it had been eight years ago, but she was still moving along easily with the rest of the newer ships—as she had done when she once set a trans-something record. Brim couldn't remember what it was, but the gallant old ship had evidently been a first-rate liner in her day.

Now, she bucked and shuddered as bright flashes of hit walked forward along her decks—with devastating results. Huge chunks of hullmetal plate tumbled away into her wake along with her port-side launches and a number of big E-containers that she carried as deck cargo.

Suddenly, the flashes concentrated on her unarmored bridge, which immediately disintegrated in a cloud of debris and glittering Hyperscreen shards. Moments later, the whole forward end of her deckhouse welled up in a great fountain of sparks and radiation—at the same moment that *Defiant*'s deck kicked from the salvo discharge of her own big 155s. A great light throbbed momentarily somewhere below and aft; then the hits on old *Wakefield* abruptly stopped.

"Got the bastard!" Wellington cheered from the console beside Brim. Her single, brilliantly placed salvo, however, was too late for old *Wakefield*. Bright green tongues of radiation flame were now vomiting from at least ten glowing holes in her side. Brim gritted his teeth—her whole interior must be burning—far too much for her ancient N-ray system to contain. Presently, the steady glow from her Drive crystals began to waver, and with great dignity she slowly rolled to one side, pulling up and out of her position in the wheel. Now clearly out of control, the old ship began to fall behind, her Drive guttering like a dying campfire. Suddenly, she pitched over with a violent motion, skidded to starboard, then broke just behind where her bridge had been, bursting into a brilliant green fog of crystal energy and shredded hullmetal that collapsed in upon itself and quickly disappeared astern as if it had never existed.

Brim swallowed the lump that had formed mysteriously in his throat. Old *Wakefield* hadn't been much of a starship as modern liners went, but she'd probably weathered more galactic storms than any other vessel in service—and she had a special meaning, so far as he was concerned. It was, as he had thought so many times before, a *tough* xaxtdamned war.

Off to port, another of the Gorn-Hoffs was boring in on a small, twin-crystal freighter: one of the slowest in the convoy. "Bandit to purple nadir," Wellington cautioned.

"Got a three-eighty coming on bearing," acknowledged one of the gunlayers. "*Big* deflection," he added.

Brim skidded slightly to port. "Better?" he asked.

"Tough shot in any case," Wellington answered through her teeth. Then, into her communicator: "Watch out, he's swerving!" Shortly afterward, the deck bucked three times in rapid succession as five of *Defiant*'s big 155s fired.

"Missed the bastard!" a gunlayer growled in disgust.

"Get the next one," Wellington said, "and don't get suckered into any more shots you can't make."

"Aye, Commander. . . ."

Moments later, they were lining up for a try at another attacker when Brim swiveled in his seat and shouted, "Don't shoot!" On the instant, *Defiant*'s Hyperscreens darkened when a familiar triangular shape angled past, completely eclipsing their intended field of fire. "Half speed, Nik!" he added hurriedly as *Defiant* began bumping violently through the starship's bled-off relativistic mass. The console clock pulsed rapidly from slow to fast and back again.

"Universe!" Wellington exploded angrily. "What is it that miserable zukeed is trying to prove? We thraggling near blew him to Rosfrew!"

"He's firing," someone yelled angrily, "at *our* target!"

"Voot's beard," one of the firing crew grumped, "if I'd known he was going to do that, I'd have blasted him, too!"

Brim nodded in angry agreement. He'd recognized the ship, all right. I.F.S. *Terrible*, a T-class destroyer commanded by Jason Davenport, son of the Hon. Commodore Sir Hugh Davenport, now commander of the Nineteenth Heavy Cruiser squadron. Davenport had long ago made himself—and his prejudices—known to the upstart Carescrian Wilf Brim. It was clear that his son followed closely in his father's arrogant footsteps.

"There are plenty of targets to go around," Collingswood admonished in a quiet but firm voice. "The only thing important is to protect the merchant ships. Or had some of you forgotten?"

"Aye, Captain . . ." a number of voices grumped in chorus.

*Defiant* suddenly bucked as she took two glancing hits on her armored hull near B turret. Brim banked slightly, and five big 155-mmi's answered the challenge in a welter of return fire. The incoming rounds stopped abruptly.

Moments later, a terrific explosion to starboard pulsed the Hyperscreens. As they began to translate outside again, Brim could see that the big transport flying in hub position of number-four wheel had just exploded in a great ball of radiation fire and sparking Drive-crystal parts. The hub ship of wheel five ploughing along behind had to dodge violently to avoid the cloud of tumbling debris that remained.

Then, seemingly out of nowhere, a Gorn-Hoff flashed past high and off to port. She was clearly after something up ahead and too much concentrated on her intended target to notice *Defiant*—presently throttled back to an easy cruise and leaving only minimal glow in her wake. Once the Leaguer was completely past, Brim called up full speed, and—as usual—Uris was ready with maximum thrust. Instantly, the light cruiser's wake turned brilliant green and she took off like a frightened Corconian Gogen'shoat, passing nearby merchantmen as if they were at rest.

"Let's get that one," Wellington ordered quietly as Brim turned into the enemy's wake. "All disruptors prepare to engage red eighties apex."

"Red eighties apex it is, ma'am," one of the gunlayers responded. "He's just coming on the bearing. . . ."

"Watch 'im, he's veering to nadir," another warned.

Brim adjusted course accordingly, and *Defiant* soon began to bob in the 380's wake while unshielded clocks all over the ship cycled slow and fast, slow and fast, slow and fast. . . . He took a moment to check his proximity instruments and scan the surrounding skies for another enemy craft. It required only moments of carelessness to find one's self in real trouble—as the Leaguers in front of him were about to discover. . . .

"Back off to about eighty-five percent, Nik," he ordered suddenly—*Defiant* was getting just a bit too close to the fleeing enemy ship. His lips silently mouthed a word of thanks to Margot Effer'wyck, who, more than a year ago—as a behind-the-lines operative—had captured the secret tables that Leaguers used to set their proximity-warning systems. It was because of her bravery that he knew Gorn-Hoff 380A-A8s could be approached to within 1.75 c'lenyts before their Leaguer Helmsmen received any kind of warning. He listened to the gunnery crews setting up their disruptors—all bow shots, straight ahead with minimum deflection. He let her fall off a few points.

"Target bearing red four five, range three thousand. . . ."

"Very well," Wellington said. "Set your wave charges to one-fifty-three, K-force to three hundred—just to give our friend something to wake him up."

"Aye, Commander Wellington, charges one-fifty-three, K-force at three hundred."

Brim glanced ahead to a large crippled merchantman, on fire in two places moving out of its place in wheel two and starting to fall behind the convoy. That's where the Gorn-Hoff had been heading. He imagined what the Leaguer Helmsman must be thinking: a fat, easy target, ripe for the taking. He laughed grimly as he checked *Defiant*'s proximity indicator again. He was about to change that perception—permanently, if he could.

The Gorn-Hoff veered slightly, setting up for the final kill. Brim let the helm fall off a few points more, then deftly pulled up just outside the Leaguer's zone of proximity. Still they hadn't spotted him! Warily, he checked his own proximity indicator, then peered around *Defiant*'s general vicinity with his own eyes. He wasn't about to fall victim to the same mistake.

"Disruptors are ready when you are," Wellington said finally.

"Ready," Brim answered. "Stand by on the bridge for maximum acceleration."

"Standing by," Calhoun acknowledged.

"Maximum energy is available," Ursis said.

"Combat velocity," Brim ordered.

"Combat velocity," Ursis grunted, moving *Defiant*'s thrust controls into OVERLOAD. Suddenly, the light cruiser surged ahead with a vengeance.

Brim could imagine the consternation in store ahead when the 380's alarms began to sound. With the head of speed he'd built up by the time he crossed the threshold, it would be far too late for the Leaguers to react.

"Bearing red. Range twenty eight hundred and closing."

In moments, *Defiant* was well within the 380's zone of proximity and bearing down on her stern like a blazing wraith. Brim fought the controls as powerful mass waves from the enemy's Drive threw his bow in all different directions and sent the console clock into wild oscillations.

"Twenty four hundred and closing."

Suddenly, the 380's Drive outlets exploded in brilliant emerald plumes, but the Leaguers were far too late to save themselves. *Defiant* was now bellowing down on them so rapidly that Brim had to order a speed decrease to keep from running up her stern.

"Steady. . ." the gunlayer said.

Brim forced himself to check the proximity indicator once more. All clear. Now he focused his concentration on the Leaguer. Any moment . . .

"Two thousand and closing. . . ."

"Shoot!"

*Defiant*'s deck bucked violently as all nine of her powerful 155s split the darkness in a single blast of raw light and primal energy that rumbled through her starframe like a great, rolling peal of thunder. Clouds of angry, glittering radiation streamed into her racing wake. Wellington and her crews simply couldn't miss.

Instantly, the Leaguer's starboard side erupted in a roiling cloud of fiery destruction. Her starboard turret and its mounting pedestal flew off into the wake in a shower of hullmetal plates and ice particles from within the ship.

"Sweet Almighty!" someone gasped. "Look at that!"

"Properly nailed the bastard!" People were cheering all over the bridge.

The Gorn-Hoff staggered crazily for a moment, then steadied and skidded off to starboard with Brim following close on its tail. Moments later, its three remaining turrets began to index around.

"Watch those!" someone shrieked, but Wellington's gun crews were more than ready. This time, a welter of independent shots thundered out from *Defiant*'s disruptors and exploded along the Gorn-Hoff's starboard side, reducing the ship's vertical gun pedestal to a ragged skeleton and spinning its turret like a child's toy—the disruptors swinging lifelessly. The devastating salvos also ignited a big radiation fire midway along her hull and threw the ship violently off course— just in time to spoil the aim of her two remaining turrets, which discharged spasmodically off to port nadir.

"Going to need the gravity brakes, Nik," Brim warned through clenched teeth.

"Gravity brakes are energized, Wilf Ansor," Ursis reported calmly.

Brim smiled as two green indicators began to glow in the otherwise darkened portion of the antigravity control panels. His hand moved to the landing controls. . . .

Suddenly, the Gorn-Hoff skidded into a steep bank, then slowed as if she had smashed into a great Sodeskayan ice wall. It was the Leaguer's normal evasive tactic when things got out of hand, but both Brim and Ursis had been ready for it.

Instantly, the Carescrian slammed his own Drive back to idle and smashed the gravity brakes to full detent. *Defiant*'s bow pitched up while her spaceframe creaked and groaned in the massive deceleration, but she did not overshoot her target, and Wellington's heavy disruptors continued to blast away at their target with devastating accuracy. In the next moments, the Leaguers were able to hit *Defiant* twice, tearing away an unoccupied docking cupola on the starboard bow and scoring a direct—but ineffective—hit on the massively armored A-turret directly beneath the bridge. Soon afterward, however, both enemy turrets fell silent as the blazing radiation fire amidships evidently severed their energy sources. Clicks later, their Drive cut in again, but now the destroyer's acceleration was diminished, and Brim had no trouble keeping *Defiant*'s big disruptors within range. He drew closer and slid out to one side of the fleeing starship. From about eight hundred irals, Wellington sent a long burst into one of its Drive outlets. Pieces of crystal modulators flew out, along with a geyser of raw energy—and the ship began to stagger along a curving path.

Amid the maniacal thundering of the disruptors, Brim once again scanned the void around him and checked the proximity indicator—all clear. Ahead, the Leaguer was visibly slowing. After taking another devastating salvo, one of her atmospheric radiators slowly deployed about halfway before grinding to a halt as radiation flames began to pour from the open doors. Brim could only imagine the fiery horror inside the other ship, which must by now have become a roaring furnace.

Suddenly, a hatch tumbled away into the wake, followed by two shimmering lifeglobes. As the dying ship bunted out of control, the first 'globe soared free and was quickly swallowed up in the distant void. The second, however, was not so lucky. In the fraction of a click in which it followed the first, the Gorn-Hoff lurched drunkenly, catching the lifeglobe on the lip of its escape hatch. Instead of falling freely into the stricken ship's wake, it hammered along the riddled hull and smashed into the half-deployed atmospheric radiator where it exploded in a glittering fog of frozen atmosphere punctuated by at least twenty figures—arms and legs thrashing—that spun and whirled past *Defiant*'s bridge like children's toys. One exploded in a red mist near the bow mooring-bollards; another bequeathed Brim the instantaneous memory of wide-eyed fear encased in a battle helmet before it collided with the Hyperscreens directly above his console and disintegrated into a frozen red smear overhead. The Carescrian would carry that terrified visage with him to the end of his life.

Now the enemy ship began to skid off course, presenting a broadside target to Wellington's disruptor crews as Brim pulled out to one side. This time, they fired at extremely close range, directly into the 'midships radiation fire that appeared to be centered in the heavy structures around the ship's primary energy retorts. Instantly, a tremendous explosion lighted the void. Debris flew everywhere. Brim could pick out individual pieces with stark clarity—like a complete control console that flashed by from somewhere, trailing at least fifty irals of cabling. For a moment, the ship's blown-out viewports gleamed like rows of fiery eyes. Then, everything erupted into a solid wall of flame—accompanied by tremendous shock waves of raw energy as her entire Drive system vented directly into space.

After that there was nothing, and *Defiant* found herself alone in the void—the convoy was now only a pattern of green lines in the starry darkness at least thirty c'lenyts ahead and to starboard. "Well done, Defiants," Collingswood shouted emotionally. *"Well done!"*

Brim grinned as he turned back toward the distant merchant ships—he knew Collingswood meant it.

Then, not a cycle afterward, COMCONVOY terminated

the alert, and *Defiant*'s tour as an independent was over for another three watches.

With a surge of almost physical relief, Brim turned the helm over to Jennings and Waldo, then joined Ursis in a jump seat at the rear of the bridge, too keyed up to leave the bridge just yet. "Bad," he said through clenched teeth.

The Bear nodded quietly. "Bad..." he repeated, shaking his great, furry head. No other words were required.

As *Defiant* returned to her position at the van of the division, the great wheel formations of starships were again stationary except for their forward velocity. Brim could now see the results of the last savage raid firsthand. Many of the merchantmen had sustained terrific damage. One had lost—at the very least—an entire Drive crystal in some hellish explosion that ripped open her port side from bridge to stern. Somehow, she was still keeping station, ploughing along on her remaining two crystals. Another in the next wheel had no bridge but was being steered from some alternate helm. Brim shook his head as *Defiant* passed. At close range, he could see that the blast had nearly cut the big ship in half. With her hull in that sort of condition, she'd have to be unloaded in orbit—if she made it to port at all. After that, they'd scrap her, and it was clear that she was almost brand new. He winced: everywhere he looked, he could see guttering Drive plumes, glowing radiation fires only just under N-ray control, hulls and decks shining with ice from leaking environmentals, and the garish blue of temporary pressure patches.

Ursis nodded soberly out the Hyperscreens toward the merchant ships, then turned to Brim. "Out there, Wilf Ansor," he brooded, "are the *real* heroes of this war. To fight from behind the disruptors of a warship is something anyone can do. One can always count on lucky shooting to save him from disaster —or heavy armor plate at the least. But to face a Gorn-Hoff with only the black void and a thin sheet of hullmetal separating you from those Schwanndor 137s—and *then* to stay in formation—that is the kind of bravery we Sodeskayans record in the Great Books."

Brim found himself speechless with emotion. He took a deep breath, ground his teeth, and nodded agreement. After that, the two comrades sat silently and stared into the dark void while Waldo completed their return to the cruising station.

Less than a day later, as Brim sipped a hurried goblet of meem in the wardroom with Fritz and Aram, a buzzer sounded quietly from the tabletop, and a message board over Grimsby's pantry began to flash: LTS. WILF BRIM AND NIKOLAI URSIS TO THE BRIDGE IMMEDIATELY. LTS. WILF BRIM AND NI-KOLAI URSIS TO THE BRIDGE IMMEDIATELY....

Brim raised an eyebrow. "In case I don't come back," he said with a mock-serious look of apprehension, "you two know where to start looking." Then he hurried to the bridge. He beat Ursis by only a moment, and the two Blue Capes trooped onto the bridge at double time. There, they found Collingswood and Calhoun sitting in the jump-seat area that often doubled as an ad-hoc conference room. Outside, *Defiant* was rapidly overhauling a huge star shoal that appeared to extend ahead all the way into infinity.

"Number One and I have a little challenge for you," Collingswood said without looking up from a display screen. "Sit down, quickly, both of you. There is precious little time to act."

Brim and Ursis quickly turned two seats around and seated themselves, frowning.

"Baxter," Collingswood continued, still engrossed in the display screen, "since this all started with you . . ."

"Aye, Captain," Calhoun said, sitting forward in his seat and frowning. He paused a moment as if gathering his thoughts, then looked first at Ursis and then at Brim. "Well, lads," he started, "just before the change in watch, we received a routine message concernin' S.S. *Providential*, a big Vergonian cargo liner in Convoy J18/7 that passed thro' this same area three days ago wi' a load o' antimatter power supplies." He looked at Ursis. "I imagine *you* understand how critical that cargo is to Haelic, don't you?"

Ursis nodded gravely.

"Thought so," Calhoun continued. "Well, the ship took three direct hits during ane o' the attacks and was soon burnin' out o' control amidships—in the machinery space between holds eight and nine." He peered ahead through the Hyperscreens and shook his head angrily. "Worthless civilians," he growled. "First thing off, they simply pulled her out o' the convoy, dampened the Drive, and then abandoned ship."

A deep chuckle rumbled from Ursis's chest. "Whether or not I approve of what they did," he said, "I certainly know *why* they did it. Were the ship in perfect condition, her cargo makes her a colossal flying bomb—with the radiation fire providing a surefire fuse."

"I understand," Calhoun said. "But that is not the entire story."

"Somehow, I thought that might be the case," Brim interjected.

"Clever of you," Collingswood said, looking up from her console with a smile. "Go on, Baxter."

"To make it short," Calhoun said, "the fires burned themselves out within a few metacycles—an' apparently did so wi'out affectin' the ship's ability to fly or to KA'PPA her position on a regular basis, just as if she war' still in commission. Evidently, the xaxtdamned Vergonians war' so much in a hurry that the only thing they bothered to shut down was the Drive itself."

"And the Vergonians themselves?" Ursis asked. "Why didn't they return to their ship?"

"They couldn't," Calhoun said grimly. "Only a single escape capsule remained flyable after the attack—an' unfortunately, it had sustained hidden battle damage. Every survivor suffocated when the atmospherics blew out shortly after it separated from *Providential*. Ane o' the convoy trawlers, little I.F.S. *Marigold*, provided them a decent 'burial' into deep space."

Brim nodded. The traditional spaceman's send-off: propelled forever into the Universe by a funerary ion rocket. Every warship carried a supply—in case.

"*Providential*'s cargo, however," Collingswood said, picking up the thread of the story, "is considered to be so crucial to the war effort that Convoy Office at the Admiralty has ordered a major effort to salvage the ship. And, unfortunately, COMCONVOY has afforded us the honor of making the first try."

"Fly her all the way to Hador-Haelic, Captain?" Brim asked.

"If she can be flown, yes," Collingswood answered, "but that is the easy part. What must be done *first* is to see if the ship can be powered away from a huge star that captured her approximately eleven cycles after she slowed to Hypospeed. 'Zebulon Mu' is the official name, and unless something is done soon, *Providential* will fall into it. That's where you two come into the picture," she said, looking at Brim and Ursis in turn, "as if you hadn't guessed."

The two Blue Capes glanced at each other and smiled. "Aye, Captain," they said in resigned unison.

"I sort of thought so," Collingswood chuckled. "Well, as we approach the Zebulon cluster in approximately—" she checked her timepiece "—thirty-one cycles, the two of you and anyone else you want to place at extremely high personal risk will depart *Defiant* in our ridiculous 'attack' launch, land on what remains of S.S. *Providential*, and subsequently attempt to fly her away from the gas giant before she crashes. From what little I have been able to gather from the Admiralty, you will have no more than five metacycles to bring the whole thing off."

"Does anyone at the Admiralty have technical data on the ship, Captain?" Ursis asked. "The system controls, perhaps? Or the Helmsman's console?"

"That sort of information is what I have been gathering here on the bridge," Collingswood answered, pointing to the jump seat's display. "It's not much, but I suppose it will serve better than nothing at all. I'm having HoloCards made up right now. . . ." Then she suddenly grimaced and shook her head. "Look, you two," she said abruptly. "You are clearly the best Helmsman and System Officer on this ship—and as such ought to be immune from such a mission. I'm certain you both know that. However, you are also the only two people who have even a ghost of a chance of returning alive—much less salvaging that ship and her critical cargo. This mission is so difficult and dangerous that my assigning any other team would make it a suicide run." She shook her head sourly. "I suppose you'll take Barbousse?" she asked.

"Miracles are a lot easier when you've got help from some-body like Utrillo Barbousse," Brim observed.

Ursis nodded solemn agreement.

Collingswood smiled. "I'm ahead of you on that, then," she said. "I've already ordered 'Coxswain Barbousse' to prepare the launch."

Brim grinned. It was no surprise. Collingswood was that sort of perceptive leader. "Thank you, Captain," he said, then glanced at his timepiece. "And if there are no further orders, we had better be on our way."

"Do you have anything to add, Number One?" Collings-wood asked.

"I think that aboot covers it," Calhoun answered. "We'll hae your systems HoloCards delivered to the launch in the next few cycles. But, Mr. Brim," he added with a slight wince, "ye'll find the flight-control information as slim as a Gabrolean beggar."

Brim smiled. It figured; intelligence libraries usually were a lot more interested in describing systems than telling how to use them. He shrugged. "Once Nik gets it started, I'll fly it," he asserted, winking at the Bear.

"On your way, then," Collingswood said in a businesslike manner. "Our launch window for Zebulon Mu is less than fifteen cycles' duration."

"Aye, Captain..." Brim and Ursis chorused and started aft.

"Oh, and.... Wilf, Nikolai..."

"Captain?" Wilf asked, stopping just short of the compan-ionway.

Collingswood blushed and hesitantly raised her hand. "We all know there's no such thing as luck," she said, "but just in case..."

"Thank you, Captain," Brim said, saluting indoors in spite of regulations. Ursis followed suit. Then they clambered down the companionway, pulling their battle-suit helmets over their heads and running flat-out for the boat deck.

Within cycles, they had crawled through the twin boarding tubes—Ursis with the HoloCards to the passenger compart-ment, Brim into the flight bridge.

"G'afternoon, Lieutenant," Barbousse said. He had both spin-gravs ticking over already.

"Good afternoon, yourself," Brim answered, scanning his console readouts while he wriggled into his seat restraints. Each rev indicator was hovering steadily at 2400 and the coolant had already reached operating temperature. Outside—with no Hyperscreens to translate the confusion of photons at greater-than-light speeds—fantastic patterns of color were all the view that he would have until the launch "glided" to just below LightSpeed and normal vision. "Looks like you've got everything ready to go," he said, trimming up the flight controls. "Xaxtdamned good job, too."

"Thank ye, sir," Barbousse said, blushing proudly.

Brim grinned at the big rating's obvious pleasure—he'd pretty much learned to fly the same way himself—without benefit of formal training. He touched an intraship circuit to the passenger cabin. "All right down there, Nik?"

"'S'all right," the Bear answered, waving a thumbs-up hello to Barbousse. "But whoever claimed this toy cabin could seat ten was definitely not counting Bear noses." He was straddling two seats.

"You ready to go?" Brim asked.

"I am ready, Wilf Ansor . . ." the Bear said, folding his arms and relaxing as much as he could, strapped as he was in the cramped space.

Switching the display to *Defiant*'s bridge, Brim spooled up the spin-gravs, balancing both out at just under 9500 sp's for a smoother deceleration to Hypolight velocity. "Requesting permission to cast off into Hyperspace," he said, downloading their latest position relative to Zebulon Mu into the launch's autohelm.

"Permission granted," Calhoun answered. "You may cast off when ready."

Brim nodded, then touched a control on the right side of his console. Presently, noises of straining motors sounded through the davit attachments. Wild patterns in the windscreen whirled and changed more rapidly as the launch moved out from behind the protection of *Defiant*'s superstructure and into the ship's photon slipstream. Brim's mind raced back to his tour of blockade duty and the day he cast off in one of old *Trucu-*

*lent*'s launches to capture his first Leaguer ship. He smiled to himself. Even below LightSpeed, those operations had been ticklish. The davits were controlled from the destroyer's bridge, and often coordination between the launch and launcher was not the best. Ivan Kalisnakov's specially built cradle allowed him to control everything himself.

When the motors fell silent, Calhoun nodded in the display. "You are now clear of the ship," he said.

"Casting off," Brim said.

"Good luck, you young pup," Calhoun said quietly. Then the display went blank as all connection was broken with *Defiant*. Shortly afterward, Brim nearly lost his meem with the onset of weightlessness, but he managed—for at least the ten billionth time—to force his protesting stomach into angry submission. He shook his head and laughed at this most embarrassing of his manifold weaknesses. Local gravity was a wonderful thing—and one of the best reasons he could think of for rarely leaving large starships unless they were on the ground.

After nearly half a metacycle, the frenzied patterns in the Hyperscreens began to disintegrate, then erupted into an angry crimson fabric of sparks that coalesced finally into a normal starscape as the launch slowed through Sheldon's Great Constant and passed the Daya-Peraf transition. Brim's LightSpeed indicator read precisely 0.99 when mighty Zebulon Mu filled the windscreens with a streaming brilliance that seemed to light the entire Universe. Presently, he switched off the autohelm and took the controls himself. "Anything like a cargo ship registering on the proximity scanner?" he asked.

"Nothing, Lieutenant," Barbousse answered, squinting into a display at the top center of his console.

"I'll continue on around until something shows up," the Carescrian said, steering the launch around the huge star. Even traveling at nearly LightSpeed, it took nearly five cycles to locate the merchant ship.

"I've located her, Lieutenant," Barbousse reported tensely. "But she surely doesn't have much altitude anymore."

"How bad off is she?" Brim asked, altering course toward the stricken merchantman.

Barbousse pursed his lips for a moment, then shook his head. "Probably," he said, "we won't have much time before she's too far into the star's gravity envelope to fly her out."

"And," Ursis added from the display, "we don't want to be within a standard light year of here if that cargo of power supplies goes up in the photosphere. The resulting flare will melt whole planets."

Brim grimaced. "I'll keep that in mind, Nik," he promised as they bored down into the brilliance. "Believe me!"

S.S. *Providential* was typical of the big Vergonian merchantmen constructed back during the Twenties. She had a long, black hull shaped like a spindle with a sharp bow and rounded stern. A blunt, single-unit deckhouse in corrugated white hullmetal began just aft of her short foredeck and straddled the hull nearly all the way to her stern. Forward, the structure was approximately five levels in height and surmounted by a control bridge that extended beyond the limits of the deckhouse to both port and starboard like short, thick fins. According to Ursis's HoloCards, the ship was 407 irals in length, 44 irals at maximum horizontal beam, and displaced 34,351 milstons empty. She was powered by two arcane Grandoffler triple-phisotron Drive units—anyone could see that by the three focusing rings mounted aft of each Drive outlet. She also had the dubious distinction of being the largest ship in Imperial service with twin-Drives of the type.

Up close, it was clear that *Providential*'s fires were extinguished, at least externally. "With a quenching system like that, sir," Barbousse said in an awestruck voice, "radiation fires simply couldn't burn very long. Just *look* at those big N-ray emitters—all over the hull. And they're still on—every one of them!"

"Doesn't say much for the crew," Brim observed.

Ursis grinned from the display. "Easy for *you* to say, Wilf Brim." He laughed. "But not everyone gets his start in a Carescrian ore barge, either. Terror is only a relative thing."

Brim chuckled wryly. "I guess you've got a point," he admitted, but he still didn't approve of abandoning a ship until it was about to self-destruct.

For the next ten cycles, they inspected the starship's exterior from every angle, peering carefully at each of the three ragged, stove-in holes where the ship had been hit. "All right," Brim said, when they reached the big ship's stern, "what's the verdict? Shall we set down on her for a closer inspection?"

Ursis nodded. "I can see little risk in that," he said.

"Aye, sir," Barbousse agreed. "How about inside that open cargo hatch over there in the deckhouse—right under the bridge? It'll save us a lot of radiation from the gas giant."

"Good idea," Brim agreed, and maneuvered along the hull to a hovering position over the foredeck in front of the cargo ship's main deckhouse. Switching on the launch's powerful landing lights, he pointed the nose of the ship into the yawning hatch.

"Looks like lot of big crates on oversized pallets, sir," Barbousse observed. "About the right size for antimatter power supplies, I'd judge."

Brim nodded agreement. The huge, octahedroid crates were secured to the deck on either side of an aisle that Brim guessed might be slightly wider than one of the pallets themselves. He frowned—was it wide enough for the launch?

"Going to be close, sir," Barbousse observed.

"Yeah," Brim said, nodding agreement, "xaxtdamned close." But no closer in many respects than he'd been quite used to only a few years previously. Ore barges weren't allocated wide berths on Carescria—expensive structures like that decreased profitability of the mines. And both barges and Helmsmen were considered to be expendable commodities— a routine business expense. Presently, he narrowed his eyes, took one last look at the antigravs, then nodded. "She'll fit," he declared.

"Probably," Ursis growled from the passenger compartment, "you will want to avoid bumping those crates too vigorously."

Brim nodded and concentrated on easing the launch through the doors. "I'll watch it," he said.

"We have about two point seven metacycles, Lieutenant," Barbousse announced, peering into a display. "Gravity's gettin' worse every moment."

Brim nodded, totally concentrating all his mental resources on the controls as he maneuvered carefully into the opening. . . .

Suddenly, Barbousse spoke up. "Lieutenant Ursis, if you would check our clearance to port, I can monitor starboard."

"Good idea," Ursis rumbled, looking up from the display. "I would say we have perhaps an iral of clearance here."

"And at least two on this side, Lieutenant," Barbousse added.

Brim eased slightly to starboard, hardly daring to touch the controls.

"Better now on this side," Ursis reported.

"You still have an iral and a half over here, Lieutenant," Barbousse said.

Brim nodded. "Thanks," he mumbled, then cautiously applied a slight forward thrust vector to the spin-gravs. The launch crept slowly between the towering crates, its landing lights transforming the dark interior of the hold into a two-dimensional cartoon. When the nacelles were centered on the second crate in from the hatch, Brim let the little craft settle gently to the deck. It was like parking a skimmer in a narrow alley between two large, windowless buildings. "All right, everybody," he announced, taking the first breath he could remember for at least a half metacycle, "helmets on—this is as far as she goes." He pulled the spin-gravs back to idle, enabled the gravity brakes, and set up the control panel for a quick getaway. Then he wriggled out of his seat restraints and followed Barbousse to the cargo deck. While the big rating closed the hatches, Brim placed a glove on Ursis's broad shoulder. "Do those HoloCards show any sort of route to the bridge, Nik?" he asked.

Ursis grinned through the visor of his battle suit. "I think so," his voice announced hollowly in Brim's helmet. He looked around as if taking his bearings from the light of the open hatch, then pointed the handlight directly overhead. "Six levels up," he said.

"Won-der-ful," Brim said. "Anything more specific than that?

"Well," the Bear chuckled, "there are indications of a crew lift directly over . . . that way." He pointed to the starboard wall of the hold. "I suggest we try that first."

"Lead on," Brim said, motioning Barbousse to follow. "If

we end up lost, we can at least blame you while we burn up in the star. It'll be a lot more satisfaction that way."

"Not to worry, Wilf Ansor," the Bear said, starting out between the huge pallets at a rolling gate. "Science has proved that a person can survive almost anything—except death, of course."

"Are you comforted?" Brim asked, turning to Barbousse in the near darkness behind him.

"Absolutely, Lieutenant Ursis," Barbousse said with a grin. "Everything comforts me."

"See?" Ursis growled.

"Hmmpf. . . ."

After passing their third building-sized crate, they came to the starboard bulkhead: a solid wall of seamless hullmetal nearly fifty irals high. Ursis consulted the HoloCards for a moment. "To the right," he said presently. "Make sure I don't miss the lift."

"How about that red sign ahead, beggin the gentlemen's pardon?" Barbousse piped up. "It's little more than a glow."

"I see it now. . . ." Brim said, squinting at the red light ahead. "What *does* it say?"

"'Crew Lift,' in Vergonian," Ursis translated presently. "And as dim as it appears to be, I am reasonably certain that the ship's emergency power supply is beginning to dissipate." He began to move along the wall even faster, rolling from side to side in the surprisingly agile manner of Bears in a hurry. "We shall have to reach the bridge directly," he said, "before the ship closes itself down to protect its logic systems. Undoing that sort of situation takes a whole crew—and more metacycles than remain to our use."

At last, they arrived at the dim red light and the heavy-looking hatch it marked. Ursis immediately turned four stout levers to C'OTT ("Open" in Vergonian, Brim surmised), then tugged on the latch mechanism—nearly pulling himself from his feet. The door remained firmly in place.

"What's the matter?" Brim asked.

"I don't know," Ursis grunted, testing the levers and pulling on the latch mechanism again. Still the panel remained in place. "By the rancid, garbage-clotted beard of Voot himself," he swore sharply, "I think the xaxtdamned thing is *locked!*"

He tugged once more, then shook his head. "Perhaps I am doing something wrong. You should check my work, Wilf Ansor."

Brim took the Bear's place before the hatch. He first inspected the levers—each one was loose and in an open position—then he placed both hands on the latch mechanism and pulled. The latch moved freely, but the door remained immovable, still clearly secured. "Sweet thraggling Universe," he said through clenched teeth. "Now what?"

"May I have a try at it?" Barbousse asked.

"Absolutely," Brim said in a disgusted voice. "We might as well *all* have a go."

"Thank you, sir," Barbousse said, stepping before the hatch. "If the Lieutenants will stand back a few paces . . ." he added presently, and unslung a heavy blast truncheon from his back. "I think *this* will take care of the inner lock."

"Where'd you get that?" Brim asked with arched eyebrows.

"Oh, I picked it up on m' way to the launch," Barbousse said, aiming the powerful weapon at the latch mechanism. "I stowed it in the cabin—thought it might come in handy, like." Then he turned his head to one side. "Watch the eyes, now," he warned. Instantly the hold was bathed in a fulgurating green brilliance and the whole latch side of the door dissolved in a shower of sparks and molten metal that splashed harmlessly off their battle suits but incinerated the Imperial comet at Brim's left breast. "There," Barbousse said presently, kicking the glowing remains of the door aside with his boot.

"You surely have a way with locks," Brim commented in an awed voice.

"Clearly, precision work," Ursis added.

"Thank you, Lieutenants," the big rating said, slinging the truncheon over his back and leading the way into a small alcove with a circular door at the far side. Beside the door was a vertical row of seven sensors labeled with Vergonian symbols. "I suppose this lighted one is where we are," he said, pointing to the bottom sensor.

Ursis frowned and silently peered at each symbol in turn, beginning from the top. "Yes," he said momentarily, "and the top one reads 'Control Bridge,' roughly translated."

Barbousse mashed the top button. . . .

It took what seemed like a year for the car to finally arrive —and a great deal longer than that for it to spiral its way to the top. But at last—nearly thirty-five cycles after Brim landed the launch—the three Defiants stood on *Providential*'s bridge. Not much time remained at all.

Brim had only begun work at the Helmsman's console when Barbousse once more interrupted his concentration.

"Um, I hate to bother you gentlemen," the big rating began hesitantly.

Brim turned in his recliner; Barbousse never interrupted unless he had something galaxy-shaking to say. "What?" he asked with a grin.

"Well, sir," Barbousse said, holding three of the HoloCards in his hand like a talisman. "Beggin' the Lieutenants' pardons, but—as I mentioned before—m' calculations say that we have somethin' less than a metacycle before we've got to be underway." He shrugged uncomfortably. "Um, otherwise, at the rate we're fallin', those two crazy triple-phisotron Drive units—the 'Grandofflers'—won't be able to push this rust-bucket out of the gravity sphere anymore. Those popping n' creaking noises you hear every once in a while are the hull plates beginnin' to work from the stress."

"Voof," Ursis exclaimed, "I too have heard those noises." He shut his eyes and pinched the bridge of his great muzzle. "It gives us something less than twenty cycles after a failure on this ship to fly away in the launch before it too is no longer able to escape the star. We must indeed hurry." Immediately, he returned to his instruments.

"Thanks, friend," Brim said, throwing the big rating a quick salute.

Barbousse reddened through his visor. "Wasn't nothin', Lieutenant," he mumbled.

"Garbage," Brim said with a grin, turning back to his console, where he quickly lost himself studying the archaic flight instruments. He devoutly thanked the Universe that starship controls all pretty much operated the same sort of steering mechanisms. First he located the autopilot master switch—it was off, which accounted for the ship's perilously low altitude. Before he switched it on, however, he had to establish the settings it would be expected to hold. Rapidly, he reset the roll, pitch, and yaw controls at neutral, then forced the artificial horizon to realign itself with the galactic disk. Turning to the left console, he mentally calculated a spherical course to permit the ship's escape with a minimum expenditure of energy, then registered the parameters—by thumbwheels!—in the heading window. At last—after an especially bothersome groan from the ship's hull—he located all four trim wheels and noted their relative positions. Clearly, they had been set by the crew to offset latent gyroscopic torque generated by the hulking Grandoffler Drives—why anybody had ever built such contraptions! . . . Then, settling back in the recliner, he checked the entire array of instruments and nodded to himself. He was about to inform Ursis that the helm was ready for flight when Barbousse's deep voice again broke the silence of the bridge. But this time there was an edge to the man's voice that he'd never heard before.

"I think there's somethin' wrong with m' bloody eyes," Barbousse gasped. "Sweet thraggling Universe. It's all wobbly outside. . . ."

Brim looked up to see the big rating staring out the starboard Hyperscreens with a positively awestruck look on his face. "What's the matter? . . ." he began, but stopped in midsentence when at the same time Ursis half rose from his console and began peering out the Hyperscreen, too—also with an amazed look on his face.

"My vision is likewise wobbly," the Bear exclaimed presently, blinking rapidly and shaking his head. "What *is* that out there?"

Frowning with concern, Brim rose from his recliner and quickly joined the others beside a starboard console. He required only one glance through the Hyperscreens. "By the beard!" he swore, rubbing his eyes. "I can't look directly at it, either. . . ." Outside, perhaps three hundred irals off the starboard boat deck, was the shimmering, half-seen ghost of a small starship—and for some reason, his eyes refused to focus on it properly. He shook his head and peered into the emptiness beyond the bow. All the stars in the shoal appeared in sharp focus. Yet when he tried to look at the ship off to port, it seemed to be ephemeral. Some of the brighter constellations were actually shining through its hull! As if it were from another dimension. His heart thumped with sudden apprehension. Perhaps the crazy fiction writers weren't so far off after all! Or . . . "Do you suppose we're looking at a *bender*?" he whispered.

Ursis smote his forehead. "I vould bet on it!" he exclaimed. "And somewhere this ship is clearly radiating something that it cannot bend!"

"Do you suppose *they* know that?" Brim asked sharply.

The Bear shook his head and smiled sardonically. "No . . ." he said slowly. "I believe that they do not. And . . . *look*, they are drawing closer."

"If only we knew what it was that they cannot bend," Brim said over a whole chorus of creaking hull plates.

"Whatever it is," Ursis rumbled, "we must at least notify the Fleet that something of the sort exists." He turned to Barbousse. "Utrillo," he ordered, "see if you can prepare the KA'PPA set for use. I was about to restore the ship's main power when you spotted this apparition. I shall finish the work immediately."

"Aye, Lieutenant," Barbousse said, moving slowly off to the communications console. The big star was now making itself felt through the ship's weakened local gravity.

Amid a nearly continuous dissonance of sepulchral groans and clamor from the overstressed hull, Brim continued to watch the little ship as it slowly approached *Providential*'s starboard rail.

"Stand by to switch power from storage cells to the normal reactor," Ursis warned.

"Ready, sir," Barbousse answered.

Suddenly—at the exact tick the whirring consoles went silent on the bridge—the little ship disappeared completely, then rematerialized a moment later in the same position when the consoles resumed operation. Now, however, the bender was considerably more visible, with only the brightest stars shining through its ghostly hull. Suddenly, Brim felt at least a milston lighter in the ship's revitalized local gravity. "What'd you just do?" he asked.

"Restored primary power to the mains," Ursis said hurriedly, then turned to Barbousse. "Utrillo, see if you can get a message off to—"

"Hold off a moment, Nik," Brim interrupted, pointing out the Hyperscreens at the bender. "I think whatever else you did to the mains, you also put the bender back into...what do they call it when the ship's invisible?"

"'Spectral mode,'" Ursis said, frowning out at the little ship and shaking his head. "But it is still perfectly visible, Wilf Ansor. See for yourself."

"I know full well what it looks like *now*, you stubborn Sodeskayan," Brim answered hotly, "but it wasn't that way a cycle ago when you momentarily shut off power to everything. Remember, I was *looking*...."

Ursis held up a hand of supplication. "I do not doubt your word, friend. Believe me. During the moment of switchover, *everything* on board the ship lost power—including whatever we've got on board that is transmitting those radiations the bender can't bend."

"Speaking of which," Brim added, pointing over his shoulder with a thumb, "the Leaguer is a lot more visible now, for some reason."

"So it is," Ursis agreed. "Therefore, our mysterious radiating source must also be getting more power." He shook his head in frustration. "What in the filthy name of David L. Voot do you suppose it could be?"

"I wonder, gentlemen," Barbousse interjected, looking up from a large utility console at the rear of the bridge, "if it might be the N-rays this ship is sprayin' all over the Universe? I've been checking around, and those Vergonians shut most everythin' else down cold, like..."

Brim looked at Ursis and shrugged ignorance.

"The N-ray projectors are still emitting?" Ursis asked.

"Aye, sir," Barbousse said, "at least accordin' to these five switches they are. The diagram here shows the mains are wide open."

"You may have found it, then," the Bear answered, getting to his feet. "Switch them off—all of them—and we'll have a look through the Hyperscreens."

"Aye, sir," Barbousse answered. Presently, a series of sharp clicks sounded from the rear of the bridge. "How's that?" the big rating asked.

Brim peered at the enemy ship just in time to see it go completely invisible again. "It's *gone!*" he exclaimed in amazement.

"By the ice lizard's toe!" Ursis said. "So it is, Utrillo. Turn them on again."

Barbousse switched the N-ray mains on again, and the ship immediately reappeared.

"Switch them off again."

"Aye, sir."

"Aha! On again, please."

"Aye, sir."

"And off again."

"Aye, sir."

"Barbousse figured it out!" Brim cheered. "Look, the bender's disappeared again."

"That seems so," Ursis said, nodding his head thoughtfully. "It seems that the damned Leaguers have not tested their new vehicle thoroughly." A rumbling chuckle escaped his lips. "It makes sense when I think about it, too. N-rays are nothing but highly compressed beams of photons that act by swamping electron energy that must be present to sustain the uncollapse of an electro-collapsite like hullmetal. Imagine what happens when such a highly packed beam hits a bender."

Brim frowned. "I guess it saturates the bender, too, doesn't it?"

"Correct, my furless friend," Ursis said. "The bender simply cannot retransmit so many quantums at one time—and some of them reflect." He peered through the Hyperscreens. "Ah-ha—see: he has now *reappeared* again." He turned to Barbousse at the utility console and waited until a particularly noisy creaking spent itself somewhere in the decking beneath his feet. "Perhaps we should stop the testing now, my friend," he suggested, "before something gives us away."

"I didn't do anything that time, Lieutenant Ursis," Barbousse protested. "The N-ray mains are still closed."

"Then she's come out of spectral mode on her own," Brim stated through clenched teeth. "Probably looking us over to see if we're worth finishing off." Grimly, he peered through the Hyperscreens and listened to the hull breaking up below. The bender was small—perhaps 115 irals in length. And narrow: no more than ten irals in diameter—little more than three times the height of a man. An awkward-looking control bridge jutted vertically from the hull almost dead amidships. It was topped by a stubby KA'PPA antenna. A row of small Hyperscreen panels extended around its forward curve like a toothy smile. Aft, the tower returned to the hull in two steps, each surmounted by an ugly-looking disruptor. Brim easily identified the top one as a rapid-firing 37-mmi Tupfer-Schwandl. The lower weapon was much larger: probably one of the long-nosed Schneidler 98s he'd run up against on A'zurn—he'd never seen one up close. At either side of the hull, obese nacelles welled outward like great, swollen tumors. These clearly housed the Drive components; each ended some twenty irals abaft the control bridge in finned reverser rings.

And every square milli-iral of the ship's surface (including gratings in front of the Hyperscreens) was covered by a fine pattern of tiny, rectangular logic units—literally millions of them. Steady waves of feeble ruby light flowed over these from the bow to the stern in regularly timed sequences.

As Brim watched, the ship began to swivel around until it pointed directly at the cargo ship's hull amidships. Suddenly, there was movement on the port side of its narrow, knifelike bow plate as one of two rectangular doors opened inward. Moments later, the ship began to glide backward until it was perhaps half a c'lenyt distant.

"She's going to put a torpedo into us even before this blasted hull collapses in on itself," Brim muttered through clenched teeth. "And there's no way we can get down to the launch in time to do anything about it." Then he shook his head and pounded a fist on the Hyperscreen ledge. "Barbousse," he shouted. "Get that KA'PPA going *now*. Maybe we can still do the Leaguers a little damage. . . ."

"Ave, sir," Barbousse said, jumping for the communications console. Moments later, when Brim arrived at the rear of the bridge, the KA'PPA gear was already humming while Ursis furiously hammered a two-fingered description of the Leaguer ship into its buffers.

"Get ready to send this," the Bear warned. "I may be about to meet my esteemed ancestors, but until then I still have the fastest two fingers in the galaxy."

"The Leaguers'll see our KA'PPA rings go out for sure, Lieutenant," Barbousse warned. KA'PPA transmissions—the only known technique of nearly instantaneous communication at galactic distances—began as a series of glimmering rings that expanded from the antenna like waves from a pebble tossed into a calm pond. In the darkness of outer space, they were hard to miss.

"So they see," Ursis said, shrugging phlegmatically. "They will send their torpedo one way or another. But with the special cargo we have below, at least we shall have the satisfaction of knowing that the Leaguers will go up with us. . . ." He rapidly keyed another few symbols, then turned to Barbousse. "Ready to send," he said.

"Aye, sir," Barbousse responded, reaching for the transmission key.

"Wait!" Brim exclaimed suddenly. "I think they're shutting the torpedo doors."

"Sweet thraggling crag wolves," Ursis roared, seizing Barbousse's arm at the last possible click. "Now what?"

"I don't know," Brim said, his heart thumping as if it were about to burst through his chest. "But they're now closed completely."

"Hmm," Ursis rumbled thoughtfully. "I wonder . . ."

"What?"

"Perhaps our friends in the Leaguer ship have now calculated how soon *Providential* will crash into the gas giant behind us."

"Voot's beard! I'll bet that's it," Brim exclaimed. "So far as they're concerned, we're not worth a torpedo. Old Zebulon Mu down there will soon reduce us to subatomics free of charge."

"Which, of course, it *will*," Ursis said, looking at his timepiece. "We don't have much more than a half metacycle before the Leaguers will be quite correct." He turned to Barbousse. "From the sounds of the hull, perhaps you should retain that KA'PPA buffer I entered. We may yet need it. . . ."

"Aye, sir," Barbousse agreed.

"He's on his way back again," Brim warned from the Hyperscreens.

"Excellent," Ursis said. "Perhaps he will tire of looking at us soon and leave. We dare not move the ship while he is still in the vicinity—otherwise, he will decide to use those torpedoes quickly."

While Brim watched, the bender pulled in close to starboard, then made a quick circuit of the ship and ended up once more alongside—this time no more than sixty irals from the bridge wing. Now he could clearly see the rows of protective devices lining the enemy's hull. Each was rectangular in shape and divided into six quadrants with a tiny ruby light that pulsed at the intersection of the dividers. And on the bridge—behind the protective grid—he could see men shading their eyes and looking through the Hyperscreens. They were pointing at *him*. "We've been spotted!" he warned.

Ursis sauntered up and joined Brim at the Hyperscreens. "Indeed?" he said, peering out at the other ship. He snorted. "Not only have they spotted us, they are laughing at our plight—perhaps by now they have heard the hull creaking with their own ears."

"Sweet Universe!" Brim swore. "They *are* laughing, the bastards! The absolute bastards!" Then he snapped his fingers. "But it also means that they missed the launch on their flyby inspection!"

"Apparently so," Ursis said calmly. "One hopes, however, that they don't remain to watch us burn."

"Something like that could ruin the whole afternoon," Brim grumbled, nodding his head.

"Friend Barbousse," Ursis said while the deck vibrated under their boots, "switch on the N-ray mains. I have an idea."

"N-ray mains are on, Lieutenant," Barbousse reported presently.

"Thank you," the Bear said, turning to Brim. "Now, Wilf Ansor, you and I are going to wave at them as if we expect to be saved. Are you ready?"

Brim raised his eyebrows. "You mean you want me to *wave* to those bastards? What if they actually decide to help us?"

"Judging from the size of their starship," Ursis shouted

over a renewed attack of cracking and groaning, "I'd be willing to bet a Sodeskayan dascha they simply don't have enough room on board."

"You've got a point," Brim conceded. "All right, come on, Utrillo, let's all wave. . . ."

In the next few moments, the three comrades desperately waved their arms and pointed at the roiling photosphere of Zebulon Mu only a few thousand c'lenyts below them. They couldn't have been more clear if they'd been able to call for help in the Leaguer's native language of Vertrucht. And the Leaguers continued to laugh. . . .

At length, the ugly little ship went spectral again—although she still remained quite visible in the powerful illumination of *Providential*'s N-ray systems.

Brim and Ursis stopped waving immediately. "Do you suppose he knows we can still see him?" Brim asked rhetorically.

"I doubt it," Ursis answered. "But that is probably of small consequence to them. I am sure that they also think that our KA'PPA system is nonoperational. Otherwise, we would have sent a warning message by now—which they could have seen going out. Is this not so?"

Brim grinned. "Sounds right to me," he answered, turning back to the Hyperscreens in time to see the little ship accelerate away and quickly discorporate into true spectral mode as it outran the effect of *Providential*'s N-ray system. "She's gone," he said in a sudden wave of relief.

Ursis was out of the COMM console in a matter of clicks. "Send the KA'PPA immediately, friend Barbousse," he rumbled as he strode hurriedly to the systems console. "We have so far only avoided one of the dangers facing us," he added, raising a titular index finger next to his ear. "Now we must remove ourselves from the menace of this xaxtdamned star before we become the infinitesimal kernel of a large stellar flare."

"The antigrav systems are now ready for flight," Ursis rumbled only cycles after returning to his console. "Wilf, you may power up your flight controls at any time."

"She's ready to move," Brim replied, throwing all the flight switches with one sweep of his hand. Suddenly, the deck began to throb under his feet with a reassuringly steady beat as the generators coupled to their mains. He switched on the autopilot, and with renewed creaking and groaning the abused hull of the merchantman obediently oriented itself to the galactic disk. Moments later, steering engines struggled to align the ship along a vector that would produce Brim's desired course while countering the savage gravity outside. "All right, Nik, slow ahead both. . . ."

"Slow ahead both."

The ship began a cacophony of protesting creaks and groans, often vibrating so badly that Brim could hardly see the instruments before him. Aft, however, a haze of green streaming away against the glare from the star boded well for the state of the propulsion gear. "Looks like we're moving," Brim whispered, half afraid to speak. "Quarter speed ahead, both."

"Quarter speed ahead, both."

Soon, the ship began to steady on course and the vibrations settled considerably. "She's balancing," Brim said with a happy grin. "Listen—the hull's not creaking so badly. Let's have half speed ahead and see if we can't make some distance."

"Half speed ahead," Ursis said. Even he sounded happy for once.

Shortly thereafter, Brim was able to order full speed ahead, and within the next half metacycle, they switched to Hyperlight Drive and a heading for Hador-Haelic. It had been a long day indeed. . . .

# Chapter 6

# THE D-SHIP

On the third day out from Zebulon Mu, Brim eased S.S. *Providential* into a parking orbit some two hundred c'lenyts above the surface of Haelic, then watched Ursis and Barbousse shut off most of her systems. He had orders to leave the once-derelict cargo liner in orbit so she could be inspected for structural damage before anyone attempted a landfall. Her critical cargo of antimatter power supplies was much too valuable and potentially destructive to risk in a hull that might not make it all the way down in one piece. . . .

Later, as he lined up the attack launch on a landing vector over Atalanta, he listened to his two comrades trading details over the intercom about an N-ray generator they'd dreamed up—once that could focus its output in the manner of a searchlight instead of a radiation extinguisher. They planned to build a prototype from spare parts available nearly anywhere in the field. He was tempted to interject his own thoughts concerning Randall amplifiers and automatic focusing logic when a woman's voice interrupted from the console.

"Fleet Launch 325: wind out of three five zero at one one: vector two zero five to G-pool nine eight; you are cleared to land."

"Fleet Launch 325, wind three five zero at fifteen; vector three zero five—thank you, ma'am," he called out, easing off power for his final let-down to the base. The Gradgroat-Norchelite monastery and its high golden spire glided past under the port nacelle, and from somewhere in the recesses of his mind he dredged up the mysterious Gradygroat motto: "In destruction is resurrection; the path of power leads through truth." He shook his head. Whatever meaning the words once might have possessed was certainly lost on him now.

He smiled to himself when *Defiant*'s graceful lines defined themselves ahead in the distance—almost lost against the massive silhouettes of two battlecruisers moored nearby. Collingswood's latest warship was rapidly gaining a reputation as one of the most handsome vessels in the Fleet.

Through the side Hyperscreen he spied a colorful maze of little streets and alleys below, enclosed by a rambling wall. Claudia lived in a section like that. He glanced at the panel clock—she'd be going home about this time, too. Absently, he wondered how she planned to spend her evening, but quickly put that sort of dangerous speculation from his mind. Fascinating as she might be—and he had to admit that she was definitely fascinating—her evenings were none of his business. Shaking his head, he trimmed the ship to neutral, then energized the Collective. "All right, everybody," he announced, "strap in. I'm about to set her down."

"Aye, sir," Barbousse replied from right-hand console.

"You are maybe planning for a rough landfall, Wilf Ansor?" Ursis teased over the intraship.

"Only in the passenger compartment," Brim countered. "Barousse and I don't have a thing to worry about up here in the bridge."

"Smart-aleck Helmsmen . . ."

Brim grinned as he switched both spin-gravs into vertical mode. From here on in, momentum from his descent would provide all the forward speed required. "We'll need the coolant radiators set to DENSE ATMOSPHERE," he warned as he checked his instruments.

"Aye, sir," Barbousse answered, adjusting the radiator flap switches at the top of his console. From either side of the flight bridge, powerful electric motors whined and the noise of the slipstream quieted considerably.

Brim banked a few degrees to port for the crosswind and eased the Collective until he established a glidepath—then held it steady all the way past City Mount Hill and out across the inland portion of the Fleet base. Just short of *Defiant*'s gravity pool, he simultaneously pulled the nose up and raised the Collective. Scant moments later—with vibration from the thundering spin-gravs pounding the soles of his boots—the launch glided to a stop, then settled gently onto her cradle.

"Smo-o-o-oth, Lieutenant," Barbousse commented, reaching up to switch off power to the COMM systems.

"Nothing to it," Brim said modestly—but he was a little pleased with himself, too.

Outside, four yellow-suited ground handlers in blue skull-caps and protective gloves were now at work securing the launch to its special cradle while a shapely blond ensign flounced out across the boat deck toward them. She was dressed in the tight, jet-black coveralls of the Imperial Intelligence Services.

Brim frowned to himself. "Looks like we won't have long to wait for our debriefing," he remarked, watching SAFE indicators light on the tie-down panel.

"Could be worse—beggin' the Lieutenant's pardon," Barbousse said as he eyed the ensign appreciatively. "They *might* have sent somebody that looks like Y. Adolphus Fillmore."

"You have a point there, friend," Brim chuckled. "You definitely have a point."

Moments later, the blonde pulled open both hatches. "We have a staff car in the parking lot, Lieutenant," she said, smiling up into the flight bridge. "I'm afraid all three of you are under strict quarantine until we've had a long chat."

Ursis chuckled from the door of the passenger compartment. "'Snow caves and lightning often mean warm friends,' as they say on the Mother Planets," he growled gently. "No doubt the Intelligence mavens are most anxious to discuss N-rays."

"*Most* anxious, you big smartie," the woman affirmed with a grin. Ursis was a large Bear by anybody's reckoning: one who could clearly kill a man with a single swipe of his hand. Yet he seldom invoked a sense of fear in anyone—unless he wanted to.

"Never heard of such interest in fire-fighting gear," Brim commented laconically. While he finished shutting down the launch's systems, he couldn't help ogling the blond officer. She was a good-looking woman: amply built with a creamy complexion and curly hair. From the launch's little flight bridge, she might even be taken for Margot. As if anybody could be taken for Margot. He grinned in sudden anticipation. At least two messages from Avalon would be waiting. It had been a long convoy. Then he grimaced. It also promised to be a long debriefing session before he got a look at those messages. Wearily, he climbed through the hatch and followed the Ensign toward a companionway. First came the war...

True to Brim's predictions, the Intelligence people required a lot of time before they were convinced that no more information could be extracted from the three Blue Capes, either as a group or individually. When he was finally free to return to *Defiant*—in an early watch of the morning—he learned that his two comrades had been released more than a metacycle previously.

Outside, it was darkest night, and—of course—the message center was closed. He shrugged phlegmatically. Margot's messages would keep for one more evening, but the delay was still a disappointment. As he waited at the tram stop—Intelligence provided no limousines on the way back!—City Mount Hill was a mass of lights, despite a permanent alert status at the base. Clearly, he mused, Atalantans placed great faith in the two battlecruisers moored nearby. With the advent of benders, however, he doubted their blind faith was still justified; at least until the Fleet learned more about N-rays.

Of course, most civilians didn't yet know about benders, either....

He took a deep draught of fresh night air. The breeze was from landward and carried with it smells of foliage, polluted canals, dust, the distant city... Once more, his mind turned to Claudia. She was part of that city—and somehow she was on his mind a lot more than she should be....

At last, he flagged down a tram, and within twenty cycles *Defiant* hove into view through the windscreen. Beyond loomed the mighty shapes of two Greyffin IV–class battle cruisers: *Gwìr Neithwr* and *Princess Sherraine*, now that he had a chance to look. He smiled wryly to himself. No Carescrian Helmsmen aboard *those* proud beauties, he'd wager. Capital ships were still an unchallenged bastion of the privileged. Oh, he'd visited a few of them. But once on board, his hosts always firmly gave him to understand—with great finesse, of course—that he was there only to look. The patronizing treatment he received on those magnificent ships still bothered him—made him feel cheap. For the thousandth time he shrugged aside the ugly harridan of resentment. All things would eventually change in the face of this war—as would ancient prejudices against people like Carescrians. The people of Greyffin IV's Empire needed every assistance they could get these days—from anyone who could help. And sooner or later, they would also have to ante up. He smiled to himself. He'd already had tremendous boosts from patrician officers like Regula Collingswood and Nik Ursis—as well as First Star Lord Beorn Wyrood. When the war was finally over, he trusted that these same patricians would make sure that justice was done. . . .

Within the metacycle, he'd signed back aboard *Defiant* and treated himself to a long, luxurious shower. Soon afterward, he was comfortably situated in his own bunk again. Perhaps, he thought as he dropped off to sleep, the controls of a battlecruiser weren't *that* far from his grasp. Like everything else in the Universe, all one needed was a bit of talent, a lot of hard work, and a measure of good luck—the last at exactly the proper time. . . .

Even though he was free during most of the following watch cycle, Brim roused himself early and downloaded his mail only moments after the message center opened. He eagerly watched as header after header scrolled through his display, but among the usual solicitations for Academy class gifts, announcements, advertisements from uniform makers, and the like, only one was sourced "Margot Effer'wyck, Lt., I.F. @ Admiralty/Avalon." And it had been sent nearly a week ago. . . . Frowning, he opened it to the globular display. When Margot's face filled the screen, her eyes were tired and she looked . . . defeated, somehow.

"Wilf," she began softly. "I am just beginning to understand how dearly I love you—now that I must totally exclude you from my life for a time." She suddenly sniffed and wiped her nose—which had taken on a definitely red hue against her otherwise creamy white skin. She shook her head. "I shall not make a third attempt to record these words without tears. That seems to be impossible today." She paused again while she wiped her nose. . . .

Brim almost stopped the message before she could speak again; he could guess what was coming.

"With my marriage to Rogan only weeks away, dearest," she continued presently, "I can no longer continue our correspondence—at least until such time as I can somehow regain a semblance of my personal privacy." She shook her head angrily now. "My life is no longer my own," she said with a wry grimace. "Royalty pays dearly for its privileges, Wilf, and privacy is part of that price. I can no more compose a love message—especially the kind you expect, my spoiled lover —than I can fly a starship. I am reduced to finishing this in a secure conference room at work—during the brief interim between an audience with my future mother-in-law, the Grand Duchess, and a meeting with broadcast representatives who will tell me how to act at my own wedding." She laughed softly. "But then, it's not really much of a wedding, my darling, is it? Not when the bride is totally in love with you. . . ."

A chime rang, and she reached out past Brim's field of view. "Yes, I'm coming," she snapped angrily. "But I require another few moments to finish what I am doing, and you *will* wait. Do you understand?" She grimaced as she returned her gaze to the display. "I must go, *now*," she said hurriedly. "I have no idea when you will next hear from me, but the time will certainly be measured in months; perhaps even *years*." Her lip trembled for a moment. "Meanwhile, dearest, please remember I love you—and *only* you." The chime sounded insistently. "That can *never* change, no matter what you may see or think you see." Then she shook her head. "Good-bye for now, Wilf—may the Universe watch over you and keep you safe until I am once more in your arms." Moments later, with chimes again ringing harshly in the background, the display went dark. . . .

Numbly, Brim shut down his message system, then spent the remainder of his daylight wandering aimlessly through the huge Fleet base on foot without really seeing or caring for anything around him. To the end of his years, he could recall only muzzy, unconnected scenes from that dismal expedition into nowhere. When he finally did return to *Defiant* during the late afternoon, he buried himself in work until the last watch was over—afraid to occupy his mind with anything more sensitive than the business of being a Helmsman. . . .

The following morning, Brim returned to the bridge early and—except for brief visits by Aram and and Fritz Galen— toiled without serious interruption through the better part of the next three watches. Finally, rumblings from his stomach served as reminder that he hadn't eaten since the previous morning. Shaking his head, he looked up to discover sunset streaming through the Hyperscreens to paint the deserted consoles in shades of deep shadow and glowing amber—just as *Defiant*'s Chairman interrupted the stillness. "Lieutenant Brim?" the voice inquired.

"Yes, Mr. Chairman?"

"Captain Collingswood requests that you join Lieutenant Ursis and Torpedoman Barbousse in her cabin as soon as practical."

"Thank you, Mr. Chairman," Brim said, walking off toward the companionway. His stomach could wait.

Ursis and Barbousse were waiting for him in the corridor. As usual, soft music was drifting from Collingswood's partially open door. Brim smiled to himself. She never seemed to be without music if she could help it. It fit, somehow.

Barbousse knocked politely.

"Come in and sit down, gentlemen," the Captain called out. "Don't stand on ceremony."

Brim followed the others through the door and took a chair at a corner of her cluttered oak desk. Collingswood wore the same threadbare gray sweater she was wearing years ago the day he reported aboard old *Truculent*. It still looked just as elegant as it did then. He supposed that the elegance of old gray sweaters on people like Regula Collingswood had a lot to do with what they called "class."

"Thank you for coming at such short notice," she said, settling back in her chair and crossing her legs comfortably. "It was my intention to commend all three of you personally a long time before now, but the processes your interrogations set in motion the other night kept me rather more occupied than expected." She turned to materialize a globular display. "At least by now I have reviewed your testimony sufficiently that I not need to bother anyone for still another personal recap of his part of the mission. . . ." She frowned over her glasses at each of the Blue Capes in turn, then smiled and shook her head in apparent incredulity. "Rather," she said presently, "it is my guess that each of you will be much more interested in a KA'PPA message that I received early this afternoon from the Admiralty. I'm afraid my display here is the only one on board that can decipher the special code; it's why I have asked you to come to my cabin. We can talk once you finish."

Brim nodded, then began to read:

K140981KANCCK
[TOP SECRET NOFORN COURTLAND]
FM: ADMIRALTYCOMINT
TO: COLLINGSWOOD@CL.921:HAELIC
INFO: COMFLEETOPS
<<23MSAF8ASKMHVF-ASLK-SDOIFNQWMN/193B>>

1. TASKFORCE RESULTS:
SPECIAL TASKFORCE STB-12 COMPLETES PHASE ONE
OF LEAGUE BENDER STUDY BASED ON EYEWITNESS
REPORTS RECEIVED FROM LTS. BRIM / URSIS AND
CHIEF TORPEDOMAN UTRILLO BARBOUSSE (NOTE:
BARBOUSSE PROMOTION EFFECTIVE IMMEDIATELY;
DOCUMENTATION FOLLOWS UNDER SEPARATE
UNCLASSIFIED COVER.) ALL INFORMATION RECEIVED
CORRELATES ACCURATELY; IMPERIAL GRAPHIC
CENTER (IGC) PRESENTLY PREPARING DRAWINGS FOR
IMMEDIATE DISTRIBUTION THROUGH HYPERLIGHT
COURIER. PERFORMANCE DATA SIMULATION
SUGGESTS ADOLPHUS FILLMORE ESTIMATES 92
PERCENT CORRECT. ALL UNITS WILL USE THESE

ESTIMATES UNTIL FIRSTHAND LABORATORY
INFORMATION AVAILABLE (SEE 'SPECIAL REQUEST'
SECTION, BELOW).

2. CLASSIFIED PERSONNEL ACTIONS:
EXTRAORDINARY CITATIONS TO BE PLACED IN FILES
OF LTS. BRIM/ URSIS AND CHIEF TORPEDOMAN
UTRILLO BARBOUSSE COVERING HIGHLY
INTELLIGENT TEAM HANDLING OF THIS CRITICAL
SITUATION.

3. FOCUSING N-RAY PROJECTOR:
INITIAL LABORATORY TESTS/SIMULATIONS SUGGEST
URSIS/BARBOUSSE N-RAY PROJECTOR COMPLETELY
WORKABLE. EXTENDED SIMULATION INDICATES
SOME REWORK OF RANDALL AMPLIFIERS NECESSARY
FOR MAXIMUM EFFICIENCY. WILL ENSURE
PROJECTORS CAN BE MANUFACTURED IN THE FIELD
FROM STANDARD PARTS. ALL UNITS MUST
CONSTRUCT THIS EQUIPMENT IMMEDIATELY ON
COMPLETION OF NOTICE.

4. SPECIAL REQUEST:
YOUR SPECIAL REQUEST UNDER ACTIVE
CONSIDERATION BY ADMIRALTY PROJECT BOARD.
WILL NOTIFY OF DECISION SOONEST.

[END TOP SECRET NOFORN COURTLAND}
HIGHEST PERSONAL REGARDS TO COLLINGSWOOD
BORODOV SENDS
1428021KANCCK

"First," Ursis remarked breaking the silence of the cabin, "it seems that congratulations are due our new Chief Torpedoman!"

"Yes!" Collingswood exclaimed with a grin. "What have you to say for yourself, Utrillo Barbousse?"

Barbousse sat for a moment, dumbfounded before he found his voice. Finally, he smiled and looked about the room with color rising to his cheeks. "I don't know *what* to say, Captain," he answered simply. "I am almost as much surprised as I am honored."

"You certainly earned that promotion, Utrillo," Collingswood said.

"Indeed," Brim added, forcing himself out of his depression. "Don't forget who discovered the N-ray mains were still emitting."

Barbousse was visibly uncomfortable now. "I-it's good to know t-they liked our plans for the N-ray searchlight. . . ." he stammered, rigid with embarrassment.

"Ah, yes," Ursis deflected energetically in a good-natured attempt to relieve the man's discomposure. "Approved by an Admiralty task force, no less. And chaired by my old boss Borodov, would you believe?" He grinned. "*Truculent*, it seems, remains in all our lives, does it not?"

"So she does," Brim reflected, his mind drifting helplessly to the wardroom party at which he met Margot Effer'wyck. "So she does." Then he fought himself to a draw and glanced at Collingswood. "Were you possibly thinking of letting us in on that 'special request' of yours, Captain?"

Collingswood smiled. "I thought you would find that last part intriguing," she said, changing the contents of the display. "This is the message I sent that prompted it." She took off her glasses and began to clean them carefully with a dainty white handkerchief. "KA'PPA's text-only limitations permit no flowery niceties," she added, "so I shall ask that you forgive the wording—and the content. Nothing personal, of course. It's just that I simply don't trust my *own* eyesight, either."

Brim frowned, wondering what she meant by that. Then he began to read again. . . .

K092106KGLNNV

[TOP SECRET NOFORN COURTLAND]

FM: COLLINGSWOOD@CL.921:HAELIC

TO: BORODOV@ADMIRALTY:COMINT
INFO: COMFLEETOPS
<<3QM5BFNCYA98PW+EBKJ.VDFG98/Q2W3947M>>

1. PERSONAL REVIEW LEADS TO CONCLUSION THAT
PRESENT BENDER DATA SET TOO SPECULATIVE
DESPITE HIGH RELIABILITY OF PERSONNEL
INVOLVED. I QUESTION ACCURACY OF INFORMATION
COLLECTED UNDER EXTREME, LIFE-THREATENING
PRESSURE.

2. EXEC. OFFICER CALHOUN SUGGESTS OUTFITTING
DECOY SHIP TO CAPTURE ACTUAL BENDER NOW
THAT N-RAY MAKES ACTIVE SIGHTINGS POSSIBLE:
ARMAMENT HIDDEN UNTIL BENDER APPROACHES
FOR CLOSE ATTACK/INSPECTION.

3. SEVERAL SUITABLE SHIPS PRESENTLY AVAILABLE
AT ATALANTIAN BASE: S.S. BYRON, MOREAS, AROSA
SKY, PRIZE, VULCANA, AND VON STUBEN.

[END TOP SECRET NOFORN COURTLAND]
HIGHEST PERSONAL REGARDS TO BORODOV
COLLINGSWOOD SENDS
1016041KGLNNV

"All right," Collingswood asked at length, "what do you think?"

"I certainly have no problem with your doubts about memories Captain," Brim said truthfully. "I even *agree*, if that's what you want to know."

"About the D-ship, gentlemen. . . ."

"Yes, the D-ship," Ursis said. "Well, 'One must always kiss an ice maiden on the lips before he knows how cold her nose is,' as we often say on the Mother Planets. I assume this decoy ship you have in mind is to operate in the time-honored fashion?"

"It is, Nikolas," Collingswood answered, "if you refer to harmless-looking merchant vessels fitted with concealed armament. They've been used from time immemorial for luring pirates and privateers to close range where they can be identified and then destroyed."

"That fits my idea perfectly, Captain," the Bear declared.

"And yours, Wilf?"

Brim nodded. "That is my understanding also, Captain— although I've never seen one, so far as I can remember."

Collingswood smiled. "If you saw a *successful* D-ship, Wilf, you might not recognize it."

"You have a point, there, Captain," Brim admitted with a smile.

"Chief, are you following this?" Collingswood asked.

Barbousse reddened. "Um," he stammered, "well, Captain, I did put in a few cruises on *Voot's Mariah*, now that you mention it. We, um, decoyed quite a few pirates in the days before the war."

Collingswood's brows rose. "You served on *Voot's Mariah*?" she asked in astonishment. "Why, I've heard it said that she was the greatest D-ship of all time."

"We *were* pretty proud of her, ma'am."

"I can certainly believe that," she said slowly. "Then you must know all about D-ships."

"A little, Captain."

"Tell us about *Mariah*, Chief."

Barbousse looked around the cabin with embarrassment. "Well, Captain," he started. "T-there isn't really much to tell. Old *Mariah* started out as a star packet. . . . Solid little ship— built someplace in Godthaab, as I remember. . . . Um, maybe the big yard at Siddoth." He shrugged self-consciously. "She mounted three main disruptors—one in the bows, one in the stern, and one amidships." At this, he smiled and his eyes suddenly focused somewhere far in the past. "She had this little Varnhauser 1.88 up forward—rigged to look like a stowed cargo hoist. Haven't made disruptors like that for at least a hundred years now. But in the right hands, they could shoot the wings off a fly at ten c'lenyts."

"Those 'right' hands weren't *your* hands by any chance, were they, Utrillo?" Ursis asked with a grin.

Barbousse reddened. "Well," he stammered, "I don't mean to brag, Lieutenant Ursis . . ."

"Chief," Collingswood interrupted gently. "I doubt if you're *capable* of bragging. Now, what other armament did she carry?"

"Um," Barbousse hesitated, his face turning a bright crimson, "aft she carried a rapid-firing Keuffer 91-mmi twin mount. That was hidden under a collapsible deckhouse, but the crew could bring it to action in six clicks—wearing battle suits, too." He scratched his head for a moment. "An', yes . . . she carried a big 125 amidships under the shell of a launch." He laughed. "We had to be awfully accurate with the 125, though. It used so much energy that the ship's generators needed almost five cycles to recharge between firings."

"Would you go out in a D-ship again?" Collingswood asked. "It was a pretty hazardous duty, wasn't it?"

Barbousse nodded and smiled. "Aye, ma'am—to both your questions."

"Hmm," she said, glancing at Ursis, then Brim. "And you, gentlemen?"

Brim looked at the Bear. "Nik," he said, "I have this feeling that I am about to hear us volunteer for a number of dangerous missions," he said, grinning in spite of himself.

Ursis laughed. "Indeed, Wilf Ansor, I believe I am about to hear the same thing. Strange . . ."

"Only if I get Admiralty clearance for such a mission," Collingswood interjected with a laugh. "And a ship. Until then, you three and the D-ship's prospective skipper are at least relatively safe from my more perilous schemes."

"Her *skipper*?" Brim asked, suddenly curious.

"Of course," Ursis answered. "Your countryman, Baxter Oglethorp Calhoun, unless I miss my guess. . . ."

"How did *you* know that?" Collingswood exclaimed in amazement.

"Pure conjecture, Captain," Ursis said, grinning. "Commander Calhoun's background in the 'salvage' business made me feel that he might be, shall we say, *specially* qualified for such a job."

Collingswood looked at him for a long moment and nodded ever so slightly. "I see," she said, breaking into a knowing smile. "I see. . . ." Then, shaking her head and chuckling, she turned toward her work station in a clear sign of dismissal. "That will do for now, gentlemen," she said, peering at the old-fashioned timepiece on her wall. "I shall let all of you know as soon as I hear one way or another."

"Thank you, Captain," Brim said amid the scraping of chairs, then followed the other two into the corridor. "What was *that* all about, Nik?" he asked as he closed the door behind him.

Ursis chuckled, watching Barbousse hurry back to his N-ray prototype in the repair shop below. "Only a little wager I made one evening at a party," he explained, grinning until his fang gems sparkled in the overhead lights. "I predicted that Number One's previous occupation would one day prove to be highly valuable to *Defiant* and her mission," he said. "And I am about to be proven right."

Brim rubbed his chin and frowned. "I think Calhoun said he was in the 'salvage' business at one time, didn't he?"

"That is what I remember," the Bear answered.

Brim narrowed his eyes and frowned for a moment, then snapped his fingers. "Of course," he said, shaking his head. "How could I have missed it? *I'm* from Carescria, even. The polite word for 'piracy' there is '*pre*salvage.' "

Ursis shrugged. "Often what is closest to one's nose is actually most distant."

"Well, he certainly ought to know about D-ships, then," Brim declared.

Soon afterward, the two comrades parted company. Both had a great deal of work to do before Collingswood received the answer to her proposal. And with old Borodov on the Task Force, they were reasonably sure they knew what *that* would be.

K324976HJGCCK
[TOP SECRET NOFORN COURTLAND/CAMPBELL]
FM: ADMIRALTYCOMINT
TO: COLLINGSWOOD@CL.921:HAELIC

INFO: COMFLEETOPS

<<98RQWEIH92CNU98U4-QOW213HCPQ3CO-CMQ95C>>

1. SPECIAL REQUEST FOR 'D-SHIP' APPROVED UNDER
PROJECT CODE NAME 'CAMPBELL'.

2. FUND L-533 ESTABLISHED TO COVER 'CAMPBELL'
EXPENSES. INITIAL AMOUNT UNDER SEPARATE
UNCLASSIFIED COVER.

3. STARSHIP S.S. 'PRIZE' ASSIGNED AS LEAST LIKELY
TO COMPROMISE PROJECT PURPOSE.

4. CLAUDIA J. VALEMONT (MGR/CIV/FLEETOPS4)
ASSIGNED TEMPORARY DUTY BASE PROJECT OFFICER
FOR ALL MATERIAL, SUPPORT, AND CIVILIAN
SERVICES RQMTS.

5. INITIAL D-SHIP COMBAT CREW MUST SOURCE
FROM 'DEFIANT' CREW CONTINGENT.

6. COMFLEETOPS EXPECTS 'PRIZE' WILL BE READY
FOR ACTION WITHIN 40 STANDARD DAYS.

[END TOP SECRET NOFORN COURTLAND/CAMPBELL]
BEST OF LUCK TO COLLINGSWOOD
BORODOV SENDS
K325003HJGCCK

"Well," Collingswood said as she peered around her crowded cabin, "I wanted everyone to read it together, for it seems as if we shall have our project—even if it must be ready for action within forty days. All that remains is to get on with everything—while we maintain our primary mission as an escort vessel." She looked at the dark-haired figure sitting to her left. "Claudia," she asked, "you're a relative latecomer to the project, but I assume *some* of this makes sense, doesn't it?"

"Only in the broadest terms, Captain," the Atalantian Yard Manager admitted with a smile. "Dr. Borodov's office at the Admiralty sent a long message just as I was on my way over here, but I've yet to read it." She glanced at Calhoun. "If you hadn't sent Lieutenant Brim to meet me, I should be completely in the dark."

"Wilf will mak' sure ye ha' *all* the facts, my dear," Calhoun assured her. "Won't ye, Lieutenant?" he added with a knowing look.

"Count on it, sir," the younger Carescrian answered, feeling his cheeks burn. "I've promised to fill in the details while we drive over to inspect S.S. *Prize*. We're due at the salvage yard directly following this meeting." He looked around him. "Nik, Utrillo, you're coming with us?"

Ursis shook his head. "Not this time, Wilf," he said, "the Chief and I have test time in the radiation lab. . . . But you and Miss Valemont should begin learning everything about the ship immediately. With only forty days to work, we don't have a lot of time to lose."

"Agreed," Brim said, hoping the elation he felt about spending an unshared afternoon with Claudia didn't show up too much on his face—even if it also made him feel slightly guilty. "We'll start going over her this afternoon."

"All right, people," Collingswood said, holding up her hand. "I promised I should keep this meeting to an absolute minimum of wasted time—and I shall. *Defiant* is due out on patrol in precisely six days, so we Blue Capes must work with all deliberate speed—and a little more. Claudia will bear most of the refit burden here while we are off trying to discourage Gorn-Hoffs from the convoy lanes." She smiled and winked at the Haelacian. "We shall have another brief meeting again tomorrow morning at the top of the Morning watch to discuss today's progress—make it the wardroom this time, so we can breakfast together. Oh, and by the bye," she added, "because we do retain our primary mission as an escort ship, I shall employ other members of the crew only as their services become necessary—by leaving them behind if necessary. So, if the work force appears to be a bit short of Blue Capes at present, take heart. Things will improve as the project progresses. . . ."

Brim followed Claudia through the door, sheepishly aware of her powerful sensuality. He readily acknowledged that she was a true, hardworking professional in every sense of the word; ironically, it was her very professionalism that he found most attractive. He'd encountered lots of good-looking females around the galaxy. Very few of them, lamentably, had what it took to be very interesting out of bed as well as in. Taking a deep breath, he resolved he would maintain a professional relationship with her at all costs—for Margot, if for no other reason. "I'm making the assumption that you know where this *Prize* is moored," he said, guiding her into the companionway.

She grinned over her shoulder. "If you'll show me the way out of this maze you call a starship, I'll promise to find S.S. *Prize*. It seems to be the least I can do as Project Officer." She laughed a little self-consciously. "Perhaps after I get a chance to read that message from Dr. Borodov I can be a little more useful."

Brim abruptly stopped at the bottom of the steps and looked her in the eye, frowning. "You really don't remember the way out," he asked, "do you?"

Claudia glanced both ways along the long corridor and shook her head. "I was in so much of a hurry when I came that I didn't pay all that much attention," she admitted ruefully.

"Good," Brim said with an evil leer. "In that case, before I lead you to freedom you will also have to promise to chauffeur me wherever we go today—I don't have a staff car."

"Universe," Claudia swore in mock rage. "I just knew you'd take advantage of me the first chance you got!"

"Basically," Brim retorted, "we Fleet people are all without honor when it comes to walking halfway across a base the size of this one."

Claudia laid the back of her hand against her forehead. "All right, you cad," she said theatrically, "I shall drive, but oh, the shame of giving in so easily!"

Giggling like schoolchildren, they made their way to the brow. There was always so much to talk about when he was with this beautiful woman. It never failed to make him feel a little guilty—when he thought about it. . . .

Shortly before the turn of the watch, Claudia parked her skimmer and disappeared inside a dirty brick tower to inquire about the ship's location. Beyond stretched an ugly square c'lenyt of radiation-blackened clay and dead weeds where obsolete starships were stored until it was time to tow them to a breaker's yard. Brim had noticed the dull rows of ancient vessels from the air, parked side by side on the bare earth. No gravity pools graced the base salvage yard. Instead, old ships were propped up at wild angles by forests of rough wooden poles. Most were old C- and V-class destroyers, with a few angular Resolute-type monitors, but there were also whole rows of the graceful little ED-4 packet ships that were so popular in his grandfather's day. Interposed among these were a number of ancient-looking merchantmen of all possible shapes and sizes. Brim always found something melancholy about the area when he soared past it on takeoff or landing, but now—with time to contemplate the corroding old hulks from close range—it was downright depressing.

Claudia returned in a few moments carrying a voice recorder, two handlights, and a large electronic key—all of which she handed to Brim while she climbed back into the skimmer. "Row fifteen, slot thirty-one," she said, starting off toward the opening gate. "I've become pretty objective about most everything on this old base," she added, setting her jaw, "but I still find something perfectly obscene about the salvage yard." After that, she drove in silence.

As soon as they were inside the compound, Brim understood why. He could literally smell the dead starships: dried lubricants, reactors leaking coolants, long-fused logics, and occasionally the faint stench of decay—battle-damaged ships were often hopelessly soaked in blood. Everywhere he could see peeling paint, dented and patched hullmetal, yawning scuttles, weeds growing from recesses in the hulls, and empty Hyperscreen frames gaping sightlessly at a sky upon which they would never again embark. In the eerie silence of this grotesque boneyard, wind moaned around unkempt deck-houses, cycled loose hatches with creaking hinges, and rattled shards of metal on broken decks high overhead. Squealing little animals with naked tails and huge ragged ears scurried out of the skimmer's path in the weeds ahead. Brim shuddered in spite of himself. "I see what you mean," he said with an involuntary grimace.

A little apart and at the far end of row fifteen stood a lone civilian ED-4. The most widely used commercial vessels of a bygone era—and long afterward—ED-4s had the snub-nosed bow and elongated, teardrop hull that characterized a whole generation of starships. Their flight bridges with old-fashioned V-shaped Hyperscreens forward were faired smoothly into the top of their hulls, and large side ports gave them the frowning, raptorlike countenance that whole generations of children associated with the romance of starflight. Actually, the clean, streamlined shape reduced reentry temperatures to safe and comfortable levels for the metallurgy of the day.

This one looked as if she had so far been spared from most of the parts scavengers, although both her great teardrop nacelles were stripped of their Drives. The last SGR-1820 crystals had been produced years in the past, but an active market in spares made replacements relatively easy to obtain. And aside from her missing crystals, it was clear the old ship hadn't been around the salvage yard very long. Her hullmetal was even burnished to a reasonable sheen.

Propped up here on the ground, she rested with a kind of innate dignity, although every ED-4 that had ever been built —and there were a lot of them—possessed the unique sort of grace and beauty that even the best builders design only by accident. Though he'd never had the opportunity to fly one, Brim knew from long experience that her hull was exactly one-hundred-sixty irals in length and twenty-five irals in diameter. Not large as starships went, but perfect for nearly every light cargo job in a whole peacetime galaxy. Big liners carried the glamorous cargo between major ports, but at least a thousand times more commerce still traveled everywhere else in little ships like ED-4s. They'd caused a revolution in space when they were first introduced.

Claudia broke into his reverie. "We're here, Wilf," she said in a hushed voice, "or had you already noticed?"

"I'd noticed," Brim answered, eyeing the old-fashioned characters that spelled "Prize" just short of the old starship's bows. He spoke in the same hushed voice Claudia had used. There was something about this particular vessel that seemed to demand respect.

Presently, they walked over to the hull; closer up, her age showed—there were countless little dents on her bow from collisions with a billion-odd grains of space debris over the years. And up on the bridge, her big port-side Hyperscreen had been holed, probably when she was laid up. But antennas and atmosphere probes were still neatly in place beneath her chin, and someone had thoughtfully stuffed wadding in some of her larger intakes—as if on the odd chance that she *might* someday be called upon to fly again. . . . Claudia touched a button on the strange-looking key and a ground-level hatch dropped slowly outward, stopping before it was fully open because the old ship's teardrop hull rested in a nose-high attitude.

After a rapid walk-around, they climbed on board and made their way up the canted decks by handlight to the bridge. It was clear that no one had been on board for a considerable time. The air inside the vessel's corridors and companionways was dead—as stale as if it hadn't moved in centuries. It was definitely not, Brim noted, the sort of cozy darkness he would choose for a social evening with his lovely companion. He paused at the hatch to the bridge and looked for the old ship's nameplate; it was just inside. He rubbed away a coating of dust that appeared to have settled all over everything from the broken Hyperscreen.

S.S. PRIZE
SERIAL NO. 4
CLOVERFIELD
51783

"This is the number-four ship," Brim gasped under his breath. "They must have built ten thousand of them. She's—

let's see—two hundred twelve standard years old. Voot's beard, Claudia, someone must have *flown* her here, too."

Claudia nodded. "That's right, Wilf," she said. "I got a chance to read about her when she was delivered. Quite a ship, our old *Prize*."

"I want to hear," Brim said, brushing dust from the old-fashioned Helmsman's console. There were even levers and digital readouts!

"Well, for one thing," Claudia related, unconsciously leaning back against a navigation console until her nipples protruded distinctly through her coveralls, "*Prize* was a real celebrity in her day."

Brim desperately struggled to keep his eyes locked to her face. He set his jaw and ground his teeth as he settled himself in the Helmsman's recliner, then felt his cheeks burn as he remembered—too late—the covering of dust. . . .

"A lot of famous people stood right here on this very bridge, Wilf," Claudia continued, quickly stifling a smile. "Would you believe that she carried Cortez Desterro to Avalon after his discovery of the Edrington Tetrad? Or that August Thackary Paladin himself flew her from Vornhold to Throon a few months after his circumnavigation of the galaxy?" Her eyes lit with an inner excitement. "She even won some sort of trophy—for helping open the Eoreadian sector. She was *special*. And then, for the longest time she just disappeared: no log entries or anything. But we know she was in use almost constantly, recording time on her automatic spaceframe counters. Voot only knows where she wandered all those years. She was seen in at least a dozen dominions—and served Universe knows what purposes." Claudia shook her head. "The Xervellos Cluster—she was registered there for nearly eighteen years, you know—is *still* knee-deep in the slave trade, and . . ." she threw up her hands, "who knows what else?"

While she spoke, Brim found himself frowning up at her in the dim light that streamed in through the dirt-caked Hyperscreens—and his fascination this time had nothing to do with her tight coveralls or anything like them. Here was a Claudia he hadn't really expected to meet: someone who loved starships the way *he* did. "You know a lot about the old girl, don't you?" he asked. "Especially for somebody who isn't on a flight crew."

She smiled wistfully and looked out through the old V-shaped Hyperscreens. "You don't necessarily have to be a Helmsman to love starships, Wilf Brim," she said. "We all make do the best we can with what gifts the Universe provides us—I just happen to be better at yard management than piloting."

Brim felt his face burn. "Sorry," he said.

She held up her hand palm first. "It's all right," she said, turning her head just slightly. "You're no different than the other thousand or so Helmsmen I've encountered." Then she softened. "And now, Lieutenant Brim," she continued with a smile, "it is high time we get to the job at hand. Captain Collingswood will expect some sort of report about this old starship—other than the list of celebrities she once carried. And I have an appointment for tonight that I do not expect to miss. All right?..."

Brim felt a sudden rush of emotion that felt a lot like jealousy. He squelched that quickly enough. He had no claim on this woman, even if he was strongly attracted to her.... "All right," he agreed, hoping she hadn't noticed his hesitation. "We might as well start here on the bridge."

For almost three metacycles, the two recorded a reasonably careful inspection of the old ship and her general condition. The bridge was missing a few consoles, but Claudia was pretty sure those would be available on some of the other ED-4s in the Salvage Yard. And although most of the passenger and cargo decks below had been completely stripped out, the ship would certainly never serve as a transport again, so this was no great loss either. Moreover, her Laterals and single Vertical appeared to have been untouched since the day she was last shut down. The most important news, though, was that she seemed solid as the day she was built—*very* solid. Only warships were constructed with that sort of strength anymore.

They returned to *Defiant* in the early evening—during the shift-break commuter rush. Claudia was clearly anxious to be on her way, so Brim took the recorder with him as he stepped from her skimmer. "I'll do the editing for us this evening," he said with what he hoped was a convincing smile.

"I really appreciate that," she said with a hurried smile. "I'll try to join you in the wardroom a little early tomorrow to go over it before the meeting." Moments later, she was off in a whirling cloud of dusty sand, skillfully darting nimbly through the heavy traffic like a destroyer among a fleet of battleships.

After she had driven out of sight, Brim jammed his hands in his pockets and made his way to the wardroom, where he knew Ursis and Flynn would be sipping meem prior to supper. He shook his head; somehow, every time he parted company with Claudia Valemont, he got the same empty, lonely feeling in the pit of his stomach. As he stopped at Grimsby's pantry for his own split of meem, he took a deep breath and frowned. He was getting far too involved with the lovely Atalantian. It was high time he simply put her out of his mind—which he attempted by joining his two friends at their table a few moments later.

It didn't work. . . .

Later that evening, after he finished editing their recorded voice report, his fitful sleep was constantly troubled by visions of someone—whose face he never was able to see—rutting noisily with the beautiful Atalantian on the bunk beside him. It made for a very long and very lonely night.

The following morning, Claudia showed up only a few moments before the meeting began, whispering an embarrassed apology for sleeping later than she had planned. Her bloodshot eyes looked as tired as Brim felt—and try as he might to convince himself otherwise, he knew in his heart of hearts that his dream had been all too accurate.

Using a number of her local contacts, Claudia soon located a huge, dilapidated warehouse in Atalanta's ancient waterfront district that was perfect for *Defiant*'s new enterprise. The weathered brick building featured both an ample wharf on a main canal and an indoor gravity pool that, once properly refurbished, could accommodate an ED-4. Collingswood immediately leased the building for "Payless Starmotive Salvage" through the local Intelligence field office. By common

consent, Barbousse won a fine old bottle of Logish Meem for
the name that only just edged out Brim's "Imperial Rigging
and Refurbishment." As soon as the lease was official, Ursis
and a crew of systems specialists from *Defiant* moved in to
repair the decrepit gravity pool. They were supplied with parts
trucked in from Fleet-base stores aboard civilian skimmers
hastily painted with the logo "Apex Starship Supply." Finally,
the new "businessmen" contracted for *Prize* to be towed from
the Salvage Yard by a commercial salvaging firm. It was a
tired crew that watched from their pier while a tug from Atalanta All-Watch Towing and Salvage maneuvered *Prize* up the
big ramp in the seawall. They had been at work for only five
standard days—thirty-five remained—but the Blue Capes
were due out for convoy duty the next morning. War had a
way of getting in the way of everything.

Little more than a week later, Brim found himself back in
one of the building's loft offices poring over a set of system
diagrams. He now had a bandage around his head and a severely burned left arm whose replacement skin was still quite
tender. *Defiant* had suffered serious damage during her latest
convoy and would be out of commission for at least a week.
After making landfall with only the starboard Lateral in operation, he had turned her over to the shipwrights, then headed
directly for the Payless warehouse.

Below him, centered in littered disorder on the main floor,
*Prize* floated on her newly renovated gravity pool amid the
shattering discord of power cutters and hullmetal forming
tools. The smoky air was alive with odors of fusing metal,
Hyperscreen sealant, hot lubricants, and the usual toasted
logics. Crews of brightly dressed "Atalantian locals" busily
worked on her hull from hovering power scaffolds. Thick
bundles of glowing cables ran from every open port to rows of
kaleidoscopic checkout consoles manned by an improbable
assortment of "waterfront toughs." The old ship's waist
hatches had been enlarged considerably, and already the
snouts of powerful 122-mmi twin-mounts protruded from the
openings. Near the bow and stern, still-crated 90-mmi rapid-
firing antitank disruptors lay on the stained brick flooring
waiting to be installed behind removable caps.

While Brim studied the diagrams, a movement outside caught his eye. Peering through the filthy windows, he watched a hugh flatbed barge lumber around the corner of the canal, its powerful gravity engines shaking the floor beneath his feet. The only cargo on her decks consisted of two heavy looking crates, each stenciled SGR-1820 HYPERDRIVE CRYSTAL (REMANUFACTURED). As the cumbersome vehicle warped onto the Payless wharf, a suspiciously professional group of "civilian" dockworkers secured the great, awkward vessel, and a shapely woman dressed in worn coveralls advertising "Ace Salvage and Parts" climbed to the dock. The latter made her way into the work area and continued across the floor to a steep metal staircase that led to his loft. Even with her long hair in a bun, it could only be Claudia.

"Wilf," she exclaimed over the construction noise as she stepped from the staircase, "then it *was Defiant* I saw landing earlier this afternoon." She frowned and glanced at his dressings. "I heard she took a couple of hits this time. How badly were you hurt?"

Brim nodded. "I'm all right," he said grimly. "I just happened to be down with Ursis when the Leaguers took out our starboard Lateral. We both got a little singed—but nobody was killed." Then he frowned. "They do say she'll take a whole week to fix, though."

She smiled and shook her head. "Just so long as you didn't get killed," she said. "And keep in mind, Mr. Wilf Impatience, that *Defiant's* the first of her type," she added defensively. "Whoever heads up her repair crew will literally write the manual for everything they accomplish. Second time's always easier."

"I understand," Brim said. "But I think everybody in the Fleet expects that you people can perform magic on a regular basis. You know. . ." He gestured toward *Prize* below.

She stood beside him on the rail and nodded happily. "Not bad for less than three weeks' magic, is it?"

"You must be killing yourselves," Brim observed.

Claudia laughed. "It's a lot safer than having the Leaguers try to do it for you," she said as a hullmetal trimmer began a long, noisy cut.

"Huh?"

"I SAID . . ." Then she put her mouth close to Brim's ear. "Let's go out on the Wharf," she said. "It's quieter there. . . ."

Brim nodded, then followed her down the long flight of stairs and across the bricks to a rear door. Outside, the air was still thick with acrid smells of burning rubble—an all-clear from Atalanta's latest raid had sounded only metacycles earlier. Compared to the confusion inside, however, the bustling wharf was like a haven of repose. "How do you stand it in there?" he asked.

"These," she said, pulling earplugs from her coveralls. "Otherwise, I'd be deaf." Then she grinned. "The *Intransigent* party wasn't quite *that* noisy, Wilf Brim," she said, suddenly serious, "but it did get us an evening away from all of this for a while."

Brim felt his heart leap. "Didn't it, though?" he agreed. "Maybe we ought to do something like that again. Soon. . . ."

"I sort of hoped you might take the hint," she admitted, her brown eyes sparkling.

Brim grinned. "My pleasure," he said. "But I think *you'd* better say when—I'm the one with a flexible schedule."

"All right," she said, "let's see . . ." She frowned for a moment. "Not tonight, that's for certain. Everyone in The Section is going to watch Princess Effer'wyck's wedding—the BroadcastPac came in on your convoy, you know."

Brim nodded, grinding his teeth. He didn't need to be reminded about that. "Yeah," he answered grimly. "I suppose I'll watch in the wardroom. . . ."

"What's the matter with the royal wedding?" Claudia challenged defensively. "You sound as if you don't approve."

Brim smothered a bitter laugh. "Oh . . . nothing like that," he lied, avoiding her eyes. "It's just that, ah, I probably have duty tonight, myself." He shrugged uncomfortably.

"Well, I hope you don't have to miss it," she said, raising her eyebrows. "From what I've heard about the preparations, Avalon hasn't put on a spectacle like it since before the war. And Universe knows we Imperials can stand a little something beautiful in our lives these days."

"I imagine *this* Imperial might survive . . ." he grumbled.

Abruptly her face became serious and she touched his

cheek. "I'm sorry," she whispered gently. "I guess things look a lot different when one has nearly gotten himself vaporized."

Unconsciously, Brim took her hand—it was small and warm in his. "Let's see if we can schedule that evening together," he temporized.

Claudia nodded—without removing her hand from his. "I guess it's not going to be for the rest of *this* week, either," she said presently. "About a year ago, I signed up to chair an Operations seminar. It starts tomorrow afternoon and runs through the rest of the next thirty watches. There's simply no way I can get out of it."

"How about the evenings?" Brim guiltily heard himself ask.

Claudia laughed. "That's when the seminar is, Wilf," she answered. "*Nothing* changes my day schedule—especially with this crazy Payless Project your skipper has me on. *Prize* has to be finished in a little more than three weeks, you know."

Brim nodded. "Just my luck," he said, forcing a smile. "When you get to your office, you'll learn that *Defiant* is due out at the end of the week."

"I had a feeling it might be something like that," she answered with a frown. "I guess that does it for this trip." Then she brightened. "But I haven't any more seminars scheduled for a month—and you *will* be back."

"You bet I'll be back," Brim said. "Especially if I have something special to look forward to—like another evening with you."

"Come on, Claudia!" someone interrupted from the barge. "Let's get this rustbucket on the road. She's due back in two metacycles—and you have to sign the release papers."

Claudia grimaced. "I'm afraid I've got to return the barge, Wilf," she said.

"Yeah," Brim mumbled, mesmerized by her brown eyes.

"Hmm, . . .perhaps you'd better let go of my hand before I turn around and everyone can see," she whispered.

"Voot's beard," Brim said, feeling his cheeks burn. "I'm, ah . . ." He cleared his throat. "Ah . . . sorry."

The man in the barge was waving again. "Hey, Claudia. We need to go!"

"Don't be sorry," Claudia said with a little smile. "I thought

it was nice." Then she turned and hurried onto the deck of the
barge. Moments later, the huge vehicle lumbered out into the
stream. Just before it disappeared around a bend of the canal,
Claudia looked back and waved.

Brim could feel the warmth all the way back to *Defiant*. . . .

That evening, after he ran out of excuses for being anywhere else, Brim trudged reluctantly to *Defiant*'s wardroom
—determined to sit out Margot's wedding ceremony as if it
were nothing more than an interesting spectacle. Every officer
who could spare as much as a half metacycle was already
there, staring raptly at a huge three-dimensional monitor Provodnik rigged for the occasion in the center of the room. By
the time he purchased a bottle of meem at Grimsby's pantry,
he could see that most of the interminable prewedding rituals
had already been broadcast and the main event was about to
begin. He took a seat near the door between Ursis and Calhoun, then poured himself a deep draught of meem and braced
himself for the worst.

It didn't work. . . .

His first glimpse of Margot in the monitor was like a searing tongue of flame—and there was no protection from love.
She was so beautiful in her wedding gown that everyone in
the wardroom gasped.

"By Voot himself—isn't she a picture!"

"Oh, look at the gown! And she's wearing the Stone of the
Empire."

"Yeah. She *is*, isn't she?"

Brim remembered the huge StarBlaze pendant—she'd
worn it the first night they'd shared her bed. . . . His mind
raced back, filling for a moment with delightful recollections.
Then abruptly he tried to imagine what she might be doing
now—at that very instant! The BroadcastPac had been com-
piled days ago. He shook his head. He knew what *he'd* be
doing in the same circumstances. . . . He took another healthy
swig of meem.

Then he felt a hand squeeze his arm. "You are a brave man,
Wilf Ansor," Ursis said in a quiet voice, "and also a fool. Is
this pride of yours worth all the pain it brings?"

Brim shut his eyes. "I don't know what you mean," he whispered, then took another great draught of meem.

"The way I see it," Ursis continued, "whether or not you *care* how I see things—is that you are suffering because you don't want people to know how melancholy you are about watching Margot Effer'wyck marry someone else."

Brim opened his eyes and frowned. "Whatever gave you an idea like that?" he bristled.

Ursis smiled sadly and shook his head. "Only Chief Barbousse and I know about your, shall we say, 'friendship' with Her Highness. We were the ones returning with you from the Typro mission—in the captured scout ship—when Princess Effer'wyck extended your invitation to Avalon. Remember?"

"Yeah," Brim whispered, clenching his teeth as he watched Baron Rogan LaKarn—impossibly handsome and bemedaled —put his arm around that gorgeous waist. . . .

"Accordingly," Ursis concluded through the side of his mouth, "I am the only one in this room who could possibly know what you are trying to hide—and you have already failed to hoodwink me." He puffed thoughtfully on his Zempa pipe. "Or am I wrong, friend Wilf Ansor? Can it be true that you *want* to watch this 'friend' of yours marry Rogan LaKarn?"

"Xaxtdamned Bears," Brim grumped under his breath. He poured himself another generous draught of meem, but abruptly set the goblet on the table, nodding to himself. There was no way he could drink this kind of sadness away. After a few moments, he looked over at his Sodeskayan friend. "If anyone needs me, Nik, I'll be in the simulators." With that, he corked the meem bottle, set it in front of Calhoun, then slipped out into the hallway.

He never did see the actual wedding.

Signing out of the ship for a three-day "recuperative" leave —he had *six* days coming to him because of his wound—he made straight for the simulator building. There, he configured one of the older flight-bridge simulators as an ED-4—he was again amazed by the levers and gaugelike instrument readouts that materialized—then buried himself in practice for two solid days at the old-fashioned console.

When at last he returned to *Defiant*—in the early-morning

darkness before the change in the watch—he had become an expert ED-4 Helmsman, by simulator standards, if nothing else. Stopping at the deserted wardroom, he checked out a bottle of meem from the ever-present Grimsby, then made his way to his cabin. There, he drank himself into insensibility at his desk and slept the clock around.

The following morning, he awoke—miraculously—in his bunk. Even more miraculously, his clothes were hanging fresh and clean in his closet. Precisely one metacycle later, he reported on the bridge for duty—still somewhat numb, but once again in total control of himself and his Universe. And though he had his suspicions, he never did attempt to discover who was responsible for tucking him in his bunk and cleaning his clothes. Some favors were best left unthanked. . . .

Atalanta's reconstruction of *Prize* continued unswervingly. *Defiant* flew her next convoy mission without sustaining so much as a scratch in battle damage. Then suddenly the forty days was over. Throughout the hectic rebuilding program, Brim and Claudia had encountered each other often, but only by chance in passing when they could find a few moments to exchange greetings—and a wistful "one of these days! . . ."

At the same time, the war's pace had picked up considerably. Not only did attacks on Atalanta increase in violence and frequency, but Intelligence reports indicated that Nergol Triannic's preparations for The Great Assault were now almost complete. In fact, Cloud Fleet units were beginning to embark even before rework on *Prize* was complete. The first to sortie was Vice Admiral Liat-Modal's 91$^{st}$ Troop Transport group that departed the League's capital planet of Tarrott. Immediately, he set course for what the Admiralty expected would prove to be a main assembly point where the formidable old starsailor could await further orders before setting off for the actual battles. His carefully shadowed armada included fifteen troop carriers, nineteen transport vessels and supply ships, auxiliary warships, and escort vessels—nearly one hundred in total. The transports carried a landing force of more than ninety thousand specially equipped shock troops, a third of whom were said to be Controllers, for the occupation of Haelic—and then Avalon. These were under the command of Marshal Ogen z'Kassierii—known as "The Butcher of Rennigal" for his bloody occupation of that star system early in the war.

Subsequent to Liat-Modal's departure, Imperial Fleet units began to arrive in Atalanta with astonishing regularity. The 19th, 43rd, and 61st Destroyer Flotillas were followed by the 3rd Battlecruiser Squadron and then both divisions of the powerful 4th Battle Squadron. After this, all Leaguer raids came to an abrupt halt.

On the convoy lanes, however, a different story had begun. The new benders were now making their unseen presence felt acutely, and there were few defenses against them. It was imperative that a bender be captured immediately, and *Prize* constituted the best Imperial hope for that.

A little after dawn on the thirty-ninth day—following the tumultuous arrival of Admiral Penda's 1st Battle Squadron at the already crowded base—Collingswood traveled to the Payless warehouse with Calhoun in tow. Brim, Ursis, and Barbousse had been at work there for the last week, toiling the clock around with Claudia and her civilian shipwrights. I.F.S. *Prize* was almost ready to fly.

"Well, Claudia," the Captain said with a pleased smile, "the old girl looks *most* impressive."

"Thanks, Captain," Claudia responded wearily. "Except for a launch, she's ready to fly again. Isn't she, Wilf?"

Brim nodded. "We've got Barbousse out beating the bushes for something about the same size as our attack launch. But little ones like that are hard to find anymore."

Collingswood frowned. "Am I to understand that *Prize* might be held up because you can't find a launch for her?" she asked.

Claudia frowned. "I'm afraid that's right, Captain," she admitted. "We can't get an Admiralty sign-off without one—and we need that before they'll even let the tower clear her for takeoff."

"Fleet regulations," Brim explained, shaking his head grumpily. "We can't take her up without a launch, even though I don't particularly need one. ED-4s are so maneuverable that most Helmsmen use the launch chamber for extra payload." He shook his head angrily. "I've argued the point for a week now with some stupid clerk in the xaxtdamned Admiralty. Wouldn't be surprised if her name was Voot."

"Specifically, the woman quotes Fleet Ordinance Regulations Number ED-2/3/4.998.12p, A and B," Ursis rumbled. "Series AGN-32, to be exact."

Chuckling, Collingswood stepped over one last checkout cable and entered the old starship. "Well," she said, "I believe I have an answer to your problems—at least until we can get the Admiralty to redesignate old *Prize* as some sort of special-mark ED-4 that *doesn't* carry a launch." She looked at Brim. "I shall lend you back *Defiant*'s attack launch. Since we took delivery, the little ship *has* served mostly as a private space yacht. That is correct, isn't it, Wilf?"

"Aye, Captain."

"That takes care of that," she said, symbolically dusting her hands. "Now come show me the rest of the ship. . . ." Collingswood had a way of solving problems like that.

Inside, *Prize* little resembled the abandoned hulk she had been only forty days beforehand in the salvage yard. Every interior surface had either been shined or coated with standard Fleet Gray #619 (INTERIOR). Forward, her tiny flight bridge was unaltered except for the addition of new, more powerful communications gear and standard Fleet KA'PPA COMM panels between the two Helmsman's consoles.

Outside, however, she was a different story. Not a hull plate had been refinished. With exception of a new Hyper-screen panel, every stain and dent the old ship brought with her from the Salvage Yard was intact. One had to look closely indeed to discover the tremendously enlarged waist hatches for her 122-mmi twin-mounts. These could, of course, have been normal enough modifications during an ED-4's many years of hard duty all over a galaxy. ED buffs—and they *did* exist in considerable numbers—might also have noticed a slightly enlarged KA'PPA antenna in its streamlined housing under her chin—or the beautifully machined hatches in her bow and stern behind which the 90-mmi antitank disruptors were mounted. Brim had been most unhappy about the latter. They were simply done too well for a ship her age. But by the time he discovered them, every one of the shipwrights had fallen hopelessly in love with the graceful old ship, so he'd simply let it drop.

The most noticeable features were rather outsized dorsal and ventral anticollision beacons mounted amidships. *Prize* looked as if she belonged to someone who—at one time or another—had experienced a very close call and was making sure it didn't happen again. In reality, the "beacons" were focusing N-ray generators, disguised to the degree that they even included large, strobing beacons as part of each assembly. Brim did approve of the way each was constructed of stained hullmetal to match the rest of her hull. After they were mounted, the pair looked as if they might have been installed at the factory.

While Claudia showed Collingswood around the warehouse, Calhoun called Ursis and Barbousse together with Brim just outside the gangway. "Is auld *Prize* really ready to fly, noo, gentlemen?" he asked, looking forward around the gentle curve of the hull. "You've had scarce forty days to ge' her in order." Suddenly he turned and nodded to Brim. "Wha' do ye think, laddie?"

Brim frowned for a moment. "I guess I'm ready to take her up, Cal," he replied. "Just as soon as we move her to the harbor." Then he grinned and held up his index finger. "But only if Nik also agrees that she's ready to go."

"All right, Nik, how aboot ye?"

The Bear shrugged. "She tests out as if she's ready to fly, Number One," he said. "But I won't have anything better than test data to go on until we get her into space and the systems go under some sort of load."

"Ye're willin' to fly under such circumstances, tho'?" Calhoun asked.

"With Brim at the controls, of course," Ursis replied with a shrug.

"An' ye, Chief?"

Barbousse grinned. "I'll go just about anywhere with these two gentlemen," he said.

Calhoun laughed while the building trembled to the thunder of more heavy starships arriving in formation. "Probably I'm crazy," he continued when he could be heard again, "but if the three o' ye are willing to bet your necks in that auld bird, I guess I am, too. How many mair innocents maun we risk gettin' this gr'at auld bucket of bolts off the water?"

"Well," Brim answered, scratching his head, "I'll need a backup Helmsman, for certain. I've had Ardelle Jennings in the ED-4 simulators since we got back from patrol. She's good enough technically for long cruises, but she needs a lot more experience improvising." He nodded for a moment, then raised his eyebrows. "That way," he added, "I can also put Galen Fritz in *Defiant*'s left seat for a while—with Aram and Angelene to back him up."

Calhoun nodded. "Sound like guid choices to me, Wilf. How aboot you, Nik?"

Ursis chose Alvin Gambler, one of the younger systems officers, as his backup—a human, no less—after which Barbousse named a small crew of quartermasters, signalmen, and disruptor crews.

"You'll be in charge o' the ratings, Chief," Calhoun directed.

"Aye, sir," Barbousse answered as if he'd been in charge all his life. Brim smiled—there was a lot more to Utrillo Barbousse than met the eye. A *lot* more. . . .

"A'right, gentlemen," Calhoun said with a smile. "I wu'ld suggest that ye round up your crews immediately. We are goin' to move this ship to the harbor right after sundown—an' be on our way into space afore dawn. Any questions?"

"No questions," Brim answered in unison with the others. He grinned when Collingswood and Claudia returned to the gangway. He could tell by the look on the latter's face that she knew, too. She winked surreptitiously. Tonight was the night they had plans to finally get together.

"Claudia tells me that she thinks she can have *Prize* provisioned by sundown, Cal," she said. "How about your crew?"

"They'll be ready, Captain," Calhoun answered. "All they need now is thy orders."

Collingswood smiled. "They have them, then," she declared. "Go to it, gentlemen. Our civilian friends have worked miracles with old *Prize*, here. Now it's our turn. Bring us back a bender! . . ."

Brim met Claudia on his way to the street door. She'd clearly been waiting for him.

"One of these days," she said with a wistful grin.

"One of these days," Brim affirmed, touching her hand as he passed. Clicks later, he settled into the old taxi they used for transportation, Barbousse gunned the grav, and they were off for *Defiant*.

Later that evening with the sweet rumble of two ancient Galaxy 10-320-B1C gravity generators in his ears, Brim squeezed between Ursis at the systems console and Calhoun in the commander's seat, then settled himself behind the controls of the ED-4. "All set?" he asked, turning to Jennings at the right-hand Helmsman's console.

"Just like the simulators, Wilf," Jennings assured him. "Nothing to it."

"How about you, Nik?" he asked.

The Bear looked up from his instruments for a moment with a pleased grin on his face. "Just *listen* to old Galaxy's purring down there—like a couple of extra-large rothcats. She's ready to go."

Brim swiveled in his seat. "On your command, Cal," he said.

The older Carescrian glanced at his timepiece and nodded. "Let's be on our way, laddie," he said.

"Aye, sir," Brim answered, scanning the ancient control panel. He took a last look at the 'tween-decks monitors, then activated a ground link. "Stand by to move ship," he ordered. Below, someone in the sizeable throng waved, and moments later the huge ramp door began to slide up into the ceiling.

"The door is open," a voice announced presently from the control panel. "At your orders. . . ."

"Wheel is amidships; trim is neutral. Ready to proceed, sir," Jennings announced—all professional Helmsman's Academy now.

"Hands to stations," Brim ordered over the ship's intraship. "Special duty starmen prepare for departure." From the open door at the rear of the bridge, he could hear alarms and the sound of running feet as space hands made last-moment adjustments to spare gear and focused the ship's gravity fenders. Powerful electric motors whirred and the deck began to pulse gently beneath his boots as Ursis raised the ship a few irals to clear the pool. Outside, ground crews were running here and there, singling up mooring beams and umbilicals from poolside.

Brim swallowed hard and braced himself. "Switching to internal gravity," he warned. Moments later, a wave of nausea swept over him as *Prize* dipped momentarily, then regained her hover. He blinked his watering eyes clear and took a long, deep breath. "Cast off, fore and aft," he ordered into the ground link.

Simultaneously, all mooring beams winked out and a ground technician yanked the last umbilical, expertly catching the long cable in three looping coils before its plug end could touch the brick floor.

Brim slid the Hyperscreen panel open beside him. Then, half leaning out of the opening, he carefully backed *Prize* out of the warehouse—only just negotiating the narrow doorway and the sides of the ramp as he eased the old starship into the chilly night. Swinging her stern around to parallel the stream, he drew abreast of the spray-swept Payless pier at the same moment that a familiar long-haired figure stepped into the glow of a Karlsson lamp and peered out toward him.

With a free hand, Brim waved through the Hyperscreen frame while he cycled the generators to FORWARD.

Claudia must have been able to see him; she waved back.

"Friend of yours?" Calhoun chuckled quietly.

"You might say," Brim answered noncommittally. A moment later, *Prize* began to pick up speed and headed into the main canal. Just before she nosed into the first turn, he leaned out the Hyperscreen frame and peered back toward the Payless wharf—barely in time to see the figure under the Karlsson lamp throw him a kiss. Then she and Payless both disappeared behind another dreary warehouse. . . .

Presently, the canal emptied into Grand Harbor and Brim set up a high-speed taxi toward the takeoff vector. A stiff hibernal breeze was now blowing through his still-open Hyperscreen frame, filling the bridge with smells of the sea. Brim soaked up the sensations of the old ship: her generators vibrating his boots, the distant splashing of her gravity footprint twenty-five irals below the hull. Presently, a voice interrupted from the COMM console. "S.S. *Prize*: Atalanta Tower.

Taxi into position and hold nineteen right, traffic landing two five left."

"Position and hold nineteen right, S.S. *Prize*," Brim answered, sliding the Hyperscreen panel shut and activating the seal. Claudia's distant figure blowing a kiss appeared momentarily before his mind's eye, but the pretakeoff checklist kept him too busy to dwell on such thoughts—appealing as they were.

Within moments, a ruby light appeared in the distance and blinked three times. "S.S. *Prize* cleared for takeoff," sounded from the COMM console.

"S.S. *Prize*," Brim acknowledged, advancing the power levers to MAXIMUM TAKEOFF. He grinned as the old starship began to speed over the water. "One of these days, Claudia," he whispered to himself. "One of these days." Somehow, there never seemed to be time for anything but war. . . .

# Chapter 7

# I.F.S. *PRIZE*

Within days, *Prize* settled on station, audaciously cruising the main trade routes to and from Haelic in an ironic attempt to counter an entirely new technology with one of the oldest ruses known to warfare. And true to Ursis's conjecture, Calhoun accepted the challenge as if he had been dealing with D-ships all his life.

The elder Carescrian did everything he could think of to get into contact with a bender. Each day, a special bureau in the Admiralty collated all reports that even suggested bender activity, then KA'PPAed the lot in a specially coded message to *Prize*. Calhoun personally plotted each of these "sightings" in case the Leaguers might be employing any sort of "system" with their new ships. But except that they sometimes worked in pairs, it seemed clear that—during this early period of their deployment, at least—each bender captain was free to devise his own system.

Frequently the old ship traveled under markings of neutral civilizations such as Lixor, Vornardian, or Rhodor—a strategy requiring much preparation that was often carried out under the most difficult circumstances imaginable. Nationality markings had to be removed—then reapplied—often while the ship was at Hyperspeed. This necessitated use of special, highly caustic chemical coatings applied in the absence of all but the most basic safety techniques. In addition, both nacelles usually required some sort of special modification. At minimum, the port of registry had to be changed on her nameplates with painfully correct language translations, and the KA'PPA antenna was constantly returned, just a hair off either way, to give the ship disparate transmission signatures. They even removed her Reynolds Pivot Marks—required by intragalactic legislation to visibly indicate the hull's pivot point. Most neutral "tramp" transports didn't bother with such niceties.

At first, the Admiralty theorized that benders might well be forced to navigate by internal gyros, especially in spectral mode, and would therefore be forced to reaffirm their positions with considerable frequency. Accordingly, Calhoun concentrated his initial efforts off some of the larger, more well-known navigational beacons at intersections of major trade routes. He tried schemes such as dampening off both Drive and generator systems, then drifting as if the old ship were out of control or disabled. And, indeed, *Prize*'s powerful KA'PPA receiver did intercept two benders talking to each other—one of them even sounded as if it were fairly close. In the end, however, no contact was made.

On another occasion, they thought to encourage a bender attack by making clear KA'PPA signals to their "owners" in Haelic: HAVE BEEN DELAYED BY GRAVITY STORM; AM NOW AT GT*21/-18:154; EXPECT TO ARRIVE PAYLESS WHARF HAELIC 2ND WATCH THREE DAYS.

By prearrangement, they were answered from Payless Starmotive with: MESSAGE RECEIVED, YOUR VALUABLE CARGO ANTICIPATED THROUGHOUT CITY.

The ruse failed utterly; perhaps, as Ursis conjectured, benders didn't monitor all possible frequencies.

*Prize* finally flushed her first quarry by broadcasting another series of distress messages on the intergalactic emergency frequency. This time, she reported a sham failure in the ship's navigational system and requested a position verification. Brim and Jennings had the D-ship running well below LightSpeed just off a powerful binary star. As a third interval of messages flashed out from their KA'PPA tower, Brim heard Barbousse report a target bearing from directly aft. The

Chief's voice brought instantaneous silence to the bridge. "It's a bender, Commander Calhoun," he said from the intercom. "I've cycled the N-ray searchlight three times now, and every time he's disappeared."

"Very well, Chief," Calhoun acknowledged. "Keep him in sight." A moment later, alarms sounded throughout the ship, and presently the aft gun crew could be heard muttering over the intercom.

"Target bearing Green ninety-eight, Apex ninety-five, range one hundred ten percent and steady...."

"Slow her a mite, Wilf," Calhoun suggested. "Let's see if we can't lure them a wee bit closer."

Brim nodded and retarded *Prize*'s speed a few notches.

"Target bearing Green ninety-seven, Apex ninety-eight, range one hundred six percent. Look lively now, she's closing...."

Brim carefully retarded the power levers again.

"Target bearing Green ninety-six, Apex ninety-seven, range... Uh-oh—wait: she's slowing." An unpronounceable Lhtrhian oath fouled the intercom for a moment, then, "Range one hundred ten percent... range one hundred thirteen percent... range one hundred fifteen and steady."

Brim bit his lip. He knew he'd caused the Leaguer captain to reduce speed by his own impatience; clearly the man had been closing with *Prize* through carelessness alone. "My fault," he muttered to nobody in particular.

"Patience, laddie," Calhoun said softly. "We'll gat him yet."

But in fact they didn't. The two ships cautiously toyed with each other for more than two metacycles before the bender apparently tired of their arduous game, reversing course and disappearing into the starry blackness before *Prize* could get off a single shot. During the entire episode, the Leaguers had never come within range of the 90-mmi antitank disruptors concealed behind *Prize*'s tail cone.

Afterward, Brim found it nearly impossible to put the episode from his mind—especially since he blamed himself for depriving the disruptor crew of their only chance to get off a shot. Two days later, he was still dwelling on his blunder as he sat with Calhoun, Ursis, and Barbousse in the ship's tiny canteen. "If we're all agreed that the Leaguers still don't know we can see them," he said, "then I fail to understand why neither of them would come any closer."

"For that matter, I wonder why they did'na take at least a couple of shots at us." Calhoun added with a frown.

"Possibly because we weren't in range of their disruptors," Ursis interjected. "They certainly weren't within range of ours."

"We were indeed close eneugh to launch a torpedo," Calhoun observed.

Ursis nodded, puffing thoughtfully on his Zempa pipe. "Unless the Leaguers had already used their entire supply on the supply lanes," he answered. "The convoys are certainly running at peak volume these days."

Barbousse abruptly scratched his head and nodded as if he had just reached a decision. "Beggin' the gentlemen's pardon," he said, "but I wonder if there's still a *third* factor to consider."

"What might that be, Chief?" Calhoun asked, peering over his glasses.

"Novice crews, Commander," Barbousse stated. "I've been watchin' the reports about those benders. An' I get the idea they haven't been operational for much more than a couple of months—at the most. Is that true?"

"That's the information I hae," Calhoun answered, looking at the other two Blue Capes. "Wilf? Nik? How aboot it?"

Both nodded accord.

"Well, sirs," Barbousse continued presently, "if that *is* true, then I'll estimate that there aren't more'n ten or fifteen bender crews in the whole League that have even finished their initial training cruises yet. An' most of *those* are probably research teams that don't normally fly combat missions at all. The ones we're running into right now are only trying out their space legs—on training missions, like."

Ursis snapped his fingers. "That makes abundant sense, Chief," he exclaimed. "Inexperienced crews could easily cause their own discovery—and the price of that would be far greater than any possible gain from destroying old *Prize* here or even S.S. *Providential*."

"Absolutely," Calhoun agreed with a nod. "If someone

opened fire at a ship and failed to cleanly destroy it with the first shot—or at least knock out its KA'PPA—then the resulting distress message might weel reveal the Leaguer's whole bender program afore they e'en develop a proper strategy."

Barbousse nodded. "I guess that's what's been going around in my head," he said

"Well, if it turns out that you've guessed right," Calhoun said following a few moments of thought, "and I hae a strong feeling that you have—then it also means that we aren't aboot to lure ane within shootin' distance, at least very easily. . . ."

"That may not matter," Brim interrupted with a frown. "Maybe we don't need to lure them any closer." He looked around the room. "The crazy attack launch Captain Collingswood gave us mounts a Brentanno 75-mmi with a whole array of .303 balsters. And with those spin-gravs, she'll out-accelerate just about anything in the galaxy. If we set things up right, we can probably move enough firepower into range before the Leaguers even realize what's going on."

Calhoun grinned. "Somehow, I suspected that you might hae something like that on your mind, laddie," he said. "But you'll be badly outgunned if that first bender the three of you spotted off Zebulon Mu is any sort o' standard configuration. Ane hit anywhere on your wee thin-skinned launch, and it's vaporized—along with *you*."

"I certainly can't deny that," Brim admitted grimly. "But we *would* have surprise on our side. As well as a green Leaguer crew." He looked at Barbousse. "What do you think, Chief? Would you be willing to try it?"

"I'm ready any time, Lieutenant," Barbousse assured him with a grin. "All we need is a bender."

Little more than a day later, with Jennings running the ship from the right-hand console, Brim restlessly scanned a long, bleak asteroid shoal off to starboard. It seemed to go on forever. After intercepting coded messages from what was clearly a Leaguer ship in their immediate vicinity, *Prize* had been operating for some metacycles now under the colors of neutral Vishu-Berniaga, exchanging faked distress messages on the intergalactic emergency frequency.

He listened to the smooth rumble of the old ship's generators, felt their steady vibrations through his feet. Somewhere behind him, feet scraped the deck and a hatch slammed shut. He checked the proximity warning—nothing. Outside, a few points off the bow, ruby and green beacons strobed from a distant asteroid promontory. Prudently swiveling his head, he peered around the vicinity with his own eyes: only stars—and the seemingly infinite shoal.

"Do you think we ought to start the crystals?" Jennings asked nervously from the right seat. "If that Leaguer message came from a regular warship, we may have to get out of here on an instant's notice."

Brim smiled and shook his head. "Wouldn't be much use," he said softly. "We aren't about to outrun any military starship launched in the last hundred years—except maybe a bender in spectral mode. And if it's one of those, we *want* to be caught. . . ." He studied the tail monitor—nothing there, either, save a receding cone of stars. "How's the gravity gradient out there?" he asked.

Jennings checked her course indicator, then turned to answer. But before she could utter a word, the ship's alarm sounded deafeningly and a lookout's voice crackled from the intercom.

"Unidentified starship bearing yellow nadir three at violet, blue-violet apex ten."

"Action stations!" Calhoun shouted into the blower. "Action stations!"

Brim looked up in time to watch a now-familiar shape turn sharply and pull into formation about five thousand irals off *Prize*'s port bow—well beyond the range of her disruptors. This bender, however, immediately trained both its powerful disruptors directly, it seemed, at his head. Gritting his teeth, he waited for the incredible shock of their first hits. . . .

A full metacycle later, however, the bender still hadn't fired a shot—nor had it come out of spectral mode. Brim had long since decided that he might survive the encounter after all and was now watching the enemy ship with a great deal of interest. He had attempted to close with the enemy ship a number of times since the original sighting, but no matter how subtly he handled his controls, the bender skittishly moved off in a like direction. If Barbousse's guess concerning neophyte crews were correct, this was still another Leaguer on a training mission.

"The bastard Leaguer Helmsmen are probably practicin' their covert hunting routines," Calhoun muttered in the tense silence of the bridge.

"If they stick to that and forget the disruptors, it's all right with me," Jennings declared.

"Unfortunately, we're here to *capture* them," Calhoun countered, "while they seem to be quite weel satisfied keepin' their distance. That means we've got to lure them within range."

"And then pop off a couple of bursts to disable their ship without vaporizing all the secrets aboard," Ursis put in, shaking his head gravely. "Chief, those firing teams have a tall order indeed."

Barbousse grinned. "They'll give it their best shot, beggin' the gentlemen's pardon."

Brim groaned. "I knew I should have volunteered for old Hagbut's ground forces," he said, shaking his head.

"You may actually *mean* that aefore we're through with this ane," Calhoun commented. "Those Leaguers over there luik like they're settlin' in for the winter. Mind you, they're in no particular hurry; they think they're invisible. An' since we hae no idea—yet—how fast that oddball ship can accelerate, we can't very well light out after them, either. It's been a long time since old *Prize* here has been known for fast getaways. It would be a damme shame to let the Leaguers know how well we can see their new ships—until we get at least a couple of reasonable shots off at them."

The next metacycles were a tremendous test of crew discipline. Jennings put the situation as well as any when she declared that she felt strange being used as "live bait."

Calhoun chuckled. "You're right," he agreed, pursing his lips, "and nothin' improves a fisherman's luck than fish that are in a bitin' mood." He thought for a moment. "What do you suppose we might do to make ourselves mair interestin' to our quarry over there?"

"Well," Jennings replied, "for starters, we could send a work crew out to 'repair' something on the hull—in those civilian space suits they packed for us."

"Good idea, lass," Calhoun said, nodding his head. He touched the intercom. "Chief Barbousse to the bridge—on the double!"

Less than twenty cycles later, the big rating—and a party of seven "Vishu-Berniaga civilians"—could be seen floating around the port Drive nacelle as they replaced one perfectly serviceable plasma generator assembly with another just like it. His "fumbling" team of professional Blue Capes took nearly two metacycles to accomplish a task that they could easily finish under normal circumstances in barely a quarter of the time.

At length, Calhoun ordered them to finish up and come back inside before the Leaguers became suspicious. "Only a team o' Personnel Officers could be so bumble-headed," he complained, shaking his head, "an' even Leaguers do na send those types out if they want anythin' important done."

After six full metacycles, the Leaguers still had made no overt actions—except for maneuvering to precisely match *Prize*'s purposely irregular course toward Atalanta, and remaining tantalizingly beyond the range of her disruptors. Finally, Brim could endure no longer. "Cal," he said, checking his timepiece, "how about the Chief and I going after the bastards in our launch?"

Calhoun frowned for a moment and shut his eyes. "For certain I ha'na come up with another approach that's half so promising," he said, "e'en though it's a mite maer dangerous than I like." He took off his glasses and polished them for a moment with great concentration. Then, shrugging more to himself than anyone else, he looked up and smiled grimly. "All right, laddie," he said, "give your helm over to Ardelle. I think the time has come that you and your friend the Chief ha' a go at it. Tell me wha' you plan to do—I know you've been thinkin' o't for days, noo."

"Aye, sir," Brim replied. "Ardelle, the helm is yours—ships is trimmed neutral."

As Jennings assumed the controls, Brim glanced at the bender paralleling their course and pursed his lips. "I haven't really done all that much planning, Cal," he admitted at length. "The Chief and I aren't going to have a lot of time for anything but the most basic dogfighting." He pursed his lips while he rang for

Barbousse to meet him at the launch. "As things seem to be right now, I think we'll have the starboard hatch opened first so the Leaguers can't see what we're doing, then I'll run up the launch's spin-gravs until she's just starting to overrun her gravity brakes. At that point, Barbousse'll give somebody a signal to swap the Imperial Comet for our Vishu-Berniaga colors and open the port hatch—*fast*. The way that launch of ours takes off, I don't think our Leaguers will have much chance to escape before we've at least popped a couple of volleys their way, even if they decide to come out of spectral mode."

Calhoun nodded. "Sounds good so far," he said. *"Then* what?"

"Well," Brim answered, "I don't know what kind of armor benders carry, but if we accomplish nothing else, any hits we score will sure raise Voot with those little logic units she has all over her hull."

"Aye," Calhoun agreen. "An' if the boffins are right in their guessin', she may be a wee easier to see afterward." He frowned for a moment, then nodded toward the bender. "But after you mak your first run, laddie—then what? Yon bender hae quite a sting from wha I can see."

Brim glanced across at the disruptors mounted on the enemy ship's control bridge. "After that first run, Cal, I don't have much in the way of plans. Possibilities become xaxt-damned near infinite at that point."

Calhoun nodded, then pointed an accusing index finger directly at Brim's chest. "Aye, child," he said, "so they do. But they are precisely why you maun keep your mind's eye firmly on the purpose of your mission. Otherwise you are liable to lead with your chin and waste yourself—*plus* your ship." His gray eyes narrowed. "I ha' na' heard you speak o' anythin' luik a *mission* yet. That should ha' been the first thing you' told me aboot. You do ha' an overall goal in mind, do you na'?"

Brim frowned. "Of course I do, Cal," he objected. "We're supposed to capture a bender."

"Aye, right you are, laddie," Calhoun replied calmly. "But that wasn't the first thing on your mind, as I remember. Shootin' was." He shook his head sternly. "That sort of blind bravery ha' served you well in the past—and make no mistake, lad, it wull again in the future. But you maun be able to do mair than just shoot somethin' to pieces." He raised an eyebrow. "Today, you may cause only enough damage to deprive yon Leaguers of a means to escape. The *real* mission is to get a bender safely back to Atalanta an' the intelligence units waitin' there. After you finish with the Leaguers, the rest of us will bring *Prize* alongside their ship an' board it. I'll grant that burned, twisted wreckage wad be a lot easier for us to board—but it wull be neither interestin' nor useful to the Intelligence people. Do you understand?"

"But . . ."

Calhoun looked Brim directly in the eye. "I knew that you had all the details somewhere in the back of your mind, you stubborn chield. But it was na' *foremost*. An' in the entire Universe, nothin' is so important as your mission—*nothin'*. We have only time to do things right—very little has been set aside for mistakes. Do you understand, laddie?"

Brim nodded his head. "*Now* I understand," he answered. In fact, he did. . . .

"And the rest of ye?" Calhoun asked, looking from Jennings to Ursis. "The lesson was na' just for young Brim here."

"I understand, Cal."

"I, too, understand, Number One."

"Good," Calhoun said. "Noo, young Brim. Let me hear those plans of yours again. From the beginning, if you please."

Mind racing, Brim glanced quickly through the Hyperscreens. Outside, their bender was still keeping perfect formation. He nodded, then turned to Calhoun. "What I want to accomplish overall, Cal," he said, "is to keep that bender over there from escaping until you can land a boarding party from *Prize*—with minimum damage to any of the three ships. . . ."

"Aye, laddie—*that's* the stuff. Noo, how do you propose to go aboot such a thing?"

Brim closed his eyes, examining every detail he could conjure. Finally he nodded, looking Calhoun square in the face. "On our first run—right out of the hatch, so to speak," he said, "I'll have Barbousse concentrate his fire on their KA'PPA antenna. That'll stop them from warning their friends back home that benders may not bend quite everything. Next, I suppose we'll try to take out those disruptors behind the control bridge. After that, we'll concentrate on the Drive nacelles." He nodded. "My best guess says that the 'bending' mechanisms are located amidships, near the power supplies, so we'll keep away from there as much as possible. Then," he added with a shrug, "we'll try to get her to stop, or at least cut her power so she can be boarded. I don't think there'll be much trouble getting that idea over to them. Disruptors speak a pretty Universal language."

Calhoun chuckled grimly. "Ye hae a true point there, laddie," he said. "Noo, what can we do in old *Prize* to help you?"

"Well," Brim answered with a grin, "aside from boarding —if the Leaguers do start to move off, I'll expect you to follow as close on their tail as you can. *Prize* has the only N-ray searchlights. We never had time to mount one on the launch."

"Well done, young Brim," Calhoun said, glancing out at the bender, himself. "Now, I think, perhaps you are ready for your mission. Go to it, laddie."

Brim nodded and pursed his lips. "Thanks, Number One," he said. "I'll see what I can do."

Barbousse was directing a team of handlers at the launch when Brim arrived at a dead run. The chamber had already been evacuated, and everyone was wearing battle suits. "She's unstrapped, Lieutenant," Barbousse's voice crackled through Brim's headset. "I've got the main bus energized, an' the disruptors are all checked out."

Brim noted that the protective tip covers had been removed, and he grinned in spite of his haste. "Good work, Chief," he chuckled. "Let's be at it." With that, he hoisted himself through the hatch and settled into the Helmsman's console.

Scant clicks later, Barbousse took his place in the right-hand seat, then pulled the door closed—just as the *Prize*'s starboard hatch cover rolled into the open position. "Everybody's clear," he reported a few moments later.

Brim started the auxiliary power unit, then pressed the master switch and watched his instruments come alive. Next, he toggled the bright-orange energy-charge lever and gated the power impeller. Clicks later, the Grav panel read ENERGIZED.

"Plasma set," Barbousse reported.

"Stand by, then," Brim warned, switching the starter circuits to PORT, "here comes the port generator."

"Standing by port," Barbousse echoed.

Brim hit the START and energy boost in unison; instantly, the big spin-grav whined, its interrupter strobing. . . . One . . . two . . . three. . . . The strobing began to speed up, reflecting from the chamber walls with a dazzling fireworks display. Eight . . . nine . . . ten. . . . He mashed the ENABLE button—the spin-grav fired, then caught, shaking the launch's starframe with a steady rhythm while the interrupter became a bright blur and slid closed.

"Stand by starboard," Brim warned above the thunder of the idling spin-grav.

"Starboard," Barbousse echoed.

Brim switched the starter circuits, then hit START and energy boost. The starboard spin-grav whined, strobed . . . At the tenth flash of its interrupter, he mashed ENABLE; it fired, but suddenly flashes from its interrupter slackened and almost stopped. *More plasma!* Heart in his mouth, Brim worked the energy charge vigorously until the spin-grav started to fire again. This time, it caught—and ran. Brim moved the energy levers a fraction; the deck began to throb beneath his feet as the big generators synchronized and smoothed.

He nodded at Barbousse—who grinned and held his right thumb vertically in the Universal sign of total approval. "Stand by to switch insignia," he reminded the handlers in the control room. Then he lifted the little ship an iral or so above the deck and swiveled until her nosecap was a few irals short of *Prize*'s port hatch cover with her tail protruding from the starboard side. For a moment, Brim chuckled to himself, imagined that the old ship must appear as if she were calving. Then—standing on the gravity brakes for all he was worth—he eased the power levers forward.

Moments later—long before the levers were even halfway along their arc—the launch began to totter and stumble forward toward the closed hatch. Grinding his teeth as he pushed harder on the brakes, Brim glanced at Barbousse. "Those disruptors enabled?" he asked tersely.

"They will be, Lieutenant," the big rating assured him, "soon as we're out of the hatch."

Brim made a final check of his instruments—all normal; the launch was as ready as he could make her. . . . He nodded to himself, then bellowed into his voice pickup. "Open the port hatch," he ordered, *"NOW!"*

As the hatch began to rise, Brim tested his grip on the power levers. No room to slip up right now, he reminded himself. At the high power settings he planned to use, if both levers didn't go forward at *precisely* equal rates, the resulting asymmetrical thrust would whirl the touchy little launch around like a child's pinwheel—probably overstressing its spaceframe, and certainly killing both himself and the chief.

"Halfway raised, Lieutenant."

"Check halfway." The launch was bucking against its gravity brakes like something alive.

"Sixty percent raised. . . ."

"Check sixty." He glanced at the door. A few more irals should clear their flight bridge. He could see the bender in the distance now. He knew they were watching closely, and wondered what they thought of this.

"Seventy. . ."

That was it. "Hang on, Chief!" Brim cried, his heart thudding in his chest. During the next moment, he shoved his power levers all the way forward to the stop at MAXIMUM, then clenched his teeth. The big spin-gravs spooled up swiftly until they sounded like two bull Gynnets in rutting season, shaking the launch's spaceframe wildly and vibrating the deck until it became difficult to keep his feet on the pedals. When Brim was certain the brakes would no longer hold, he lifted his feet and suddenly found himself and the Chief hurtling through space like projectiles from an old-fashioned chemical cannon.

"Disruptors energized, Lieutenant," Barbousse shouted a moment later, peering intently into the ranging display. "I'm givin' 'em all three rings on the sight to make sure!"

Ahead, the bender expanded in the windscreens like some shadowy insect of unbelievable dimensions and abhorrence. Close up, its surface was laced by a hideous network of gray tubes in various thicknesses—and the whole shrouded in glimmering, florid scales. In spite of himself, Brim felt an instinctive shudder start up his back. There was something obscene about benders—something that affected his most primitive emotions; he felt an insane urge to smash it.

Following what seemed like an eternity, the seventy-five began to fire. Within clicks, the 303s were also clattering beneath the deck. A string of glittering flashes appeared at the bender's Drive nacelle, where a number of the "scales" flew off in her wake. "Chief!" Brim cried over the discord and confusion, "get the KA'PPA tower first! We're almost past him."

"Aye sir," Barbousse shouted. "Soon as I can—I'm sort of calibratin' on the fly, so ta' speak!"

Immediately, the flashes began to "walk" up the hull, but it was nearly too late. The Leaguers had begun slowly turning away from them now, presenting a smaller target with each passing click. Abruptly—while Brim reflexively held his breath in anticipation—they flashed over the bender's control bridge. His last image was of a disintegrating KA'PPA tower, and two wicked-looking disruptors ponderously indexing around toward him.

"Good shot, Chief!" he cried jubilantly, hauling the launch around for a second strafing run. Then his heart suddenly leaped into his mouth. All he could see was the never-ending panorama of stars and the old ED-4 hurtling along toward them in the distance.

The bender was gone!

Voot's hairy *ass*!" he shouted in dismay. "We've got to get back to *Prize*! She's got the only N-rays!" Icy fingers gripped his chest as he strained his eyes toward the distant starship. What if the old transport couldn't keep up? . . . Very close to something that felt a lot like panic, he measured her rate of approach, then breathed a long sigh of relief. She was bowling along like a Sodeskayan avalanche!

Suddenly, space astern came alive with a torrent of powerful explosions that followed the launch's track in an erratic but determined fusillade. "The bastards aren't accurate, but they're sure determined—beggin' the lieutenant's pardon," Barbousse observed grimly, looking over his shoulder as Brim rolled into an even steeper bank and tightened his turn. "If you could point the nose a bit more to port, sir—an' about plus five apex—I think I can get a shot at where those volleys seem ta' be comin' from."

Brim gladly obliged.

Instantly, the seventy-five began to thunder again—with disastrous results for the bender. By the fifth salvo, a bright sparkling of hits commenced in what appeared to be totally empty space. Abruptly, the Leaguer ship became visible by the light of a nearby star, then went spectral again.

"Good shot!" Brim shouted.

"We pranged 'em, all right, Lieutenant!" Barbousse shouted excitedly as he continued to fire the seventy-five with deadly accuracy. Moments later, the bender again cycled through visible to spectral—and then again as more and more hits continued to glitter in the distance. The Leaguers stopped firing abruptly —but Barbousse increased the rate of his lethal barrage. . . .

On the moment, Calhoun's admonition rang in Brim's ear: "Today, you may cause only enough damage to deprive yon Leaguers of a means to escape. The *real* mission is to get a bender safely back to Atalanta. . . ."

He was about to shout out an order when Barbousse stopped shooting on his own.

"It's gone," the Chief said with a frown of concern. "It's just plain *gone!*"

"What happened?" Brim asked, putting the launch back on course for *Prize* and its N-ray illumination.

"I don't know," Barbousse answered, staring off past Brim into the starry darkness. "All of a sudden, it stopped flying a predictable course—and I lost it." He looked across the console at Brim and grimaced. "It was just like somebody new took over at the controls."

His voice was cut off precipitously by a furious volley of disruptor fire—this time close enough to rock the launch violently. On its heels came a second barrage, even closer. Brim put the helm over and shoved the power levers all the way forward —*just* outrunning a third volley that would have burst in precisely the space they would next have occupied. "Somebody new just took over at the disruptors there, too!" he growled.

"Swing her back to vector blue, Lieutenant," Barbousse growled, peering into his display. "I'll stop the sons of grokfuls!"

"Not firing blind like that!" Brim groaned. "You might hit something vital and blast her to pieces." He shook his head desperately. "I've *got* to get us back into *Prize*'s N-ray beams so you can see what to fire at—straightaway!" Outside, another furious salvo tossed their launch on its side, the concussion blasting streamlined covers from their port nacelle and altering its thrust vector. Immediately out of control, the little spaceship pivoted viciously around its damaged spin-grav—less than a click before space once again erupted in an enormous discharge that smashed them sideways like a Vixlean shuttlecock, shattering the canopy in an avalanche of spinning crystal shards. Blinded for the moment by the flash, Brim sightlessly fought with the controls, desperately struggling to retrim the launch before her wild oscillations fractured the spaceframe.

"I see the bastards!" Barbousse suddenly yelled. "Try an' hold 'er, sir—right where she is!"

Brim bit his lips and sweat poured down his forehead as he strained to wrest control from the launch's runaway physics. With the port generator stuttering along at half power, he somehow willed the stars to stop sliding sideways until... There it was! Dead ahead and lighted by *Prize* as if it were high afternoon. The bender was coming about slowly, but directly bow on to them, her aft-facing disruptors masked by the tall control bridge.

On the instant, Barbousse opened fire again, and this time he needed no calibrations. At his first shots, the bender's control bridge erupted in a glittering shower of Hyperscreen crystals. Then the launch plunged diagonally *under* the hull. This time, however, Barbousse continued his withering fire on the other side. The top of the control bridge—and *both* its disruptors—were now visible in the bright starlight, protruding from starry emptiness above a jagged line where the bender's logic chips were no longer functional. Below this, numerous "holes" in the vastness of space revealed those areas the Chief had previously hit while firing blind.

Firing with the precision of a master surgeon, Barbousse next rendered both Leaguer disruptors inoperative with a well-placed inferno of radiation and shock. As Brim circled 'round for another firing run, the weapons could be seen dangling loosely from blackened mountings, their firing chambers glowing red hot and completely open to space. They would never fire again....

Peering over his control panels, Brim at last found time to search for *Prize*. He discovered her straightaway, now fairly bristling with her powerful disruptors, and vectoring in at top speed toward the bender from green zero. Unavoidably, she was *also* squarely in the path of a torpedo attack! Brim soon found he wasn't the only one who had grasped the opportunity for a devastating bow-on shot—the bender's torpedo doors were sliding open even as he glanced their way!

"She's gonna' fire a torpedo," Barbousse swore. "We can't stand back and let 'em do that, Lieutenant!"

"Put a shot past the bridge, Chief," Brim ordered grimly. "Then if they don't shut the doors, take out the whole bridge!"

"With pleasure, Lieutenant," Barbousse grunted through clenched teeth as he peered intently into the disruptor display, "but I hope he leaves 'em open, all the same!" Shortly, the seventy-five spoke once, and a tremendous, fulgurating explosion tore the fabric of space only irals from the bender's bridge. When the sparkling radiation cleared, every logic grating covering the Hyperscreens appeared to be gone, and at least three of the ten panels were now empty frames. "Oof," Barbousse muttered under his breath, "perhaps that was a *mite* too close. . . ."

Brim chuckled in spite of his anxiety. "I'll give them a count of five to react, Chief," he cautioned. "They may be a bit shaken up in there. One . . . two . . . three . . ." Precisely on the count of four, the bender's image became crystal clear as she came out of spectral mode. Moments later, a figure dressed in gray battle gear appeared at one of the blown-out Hyperscreens and placed its hands atop its head in a clear gesture of surrender. Simultaneously, both torpedo doors slid closed.

"Now what?" Brim asked with a shrug.

Barboussee shook his head. "I don't know, Lieutenant. D'you suppose they might try to scuttle her or somethin'?"

Brim tried to scratch his head, but the closed helmet of his battle suit got in the way. "I suppose that's a definite possibility, Chief," he said, hoping Barbousse had missed his little gaffe, "especially if they have Controllers aboard."

"Those dudes in the black uniforms with the TimeWeed habit, Lieutenant?"

"Yeah," Brim acknowledged. "It rots their minds—at least that part that has anything to do with ethics." He shook his head. "Unfortunately, it doesn't seem to interfere with much else. If that bender really *was* on a training mission, it's my guess that Controllers were doing the training."

"Maybe it was Controllers who took over the disruptors when they almost got us," Barbousse said.

"I wouldn't be a bit surprised," Brim speculated. "Those bastards are *good*—and wholly dedicated to Triannic's League. I'll wager there's one horrendous struggle going on inside that bender right now about surrendering. You'll want to keep our disruptors ready to fire just in case the wrong side wins."

Barbousse leered evilly. "Wouldn't I love that," he said, fingering the trigger mechanism of his seventy-five.

Only clicks later, the Blue Capes watched thirty-odd, gray-suited figures clamber through two deck hatches, dragging the limp forms of three others clad in jet black.

Brim had his answer when the first two stretched what appeared to be a white hammock between them and began to shake it vigorously in a clear message of surrender. "Smart move, *Hab'thalls*," Brim whispered in the Leaguers' native language of Vertrucht.

"What in the name of Voot?..." Barbousse interrupted, pointing suddenly to one of the black-suited figures that had regained its knees and was painfully crawling toward the rear hatch, unnoticed by the other Leaguers.

"Thanks, Chief—we'd probably better keep an eye on that one," Brim said, drawing his sidearm as the crawling figure reached the open hatch and pointed something small and heavy-looking through its aperture.

"It's a *blaster*!" Barbousse warned, reaching for his own side arm. "He's gonna scuttle her!"

Brim was quicker. Leaning from the shattered canopy of the launch, he fired two powerful bursts from his ancient side-action blaster, disintegrating the Controller's upper torso in a roiling pink spray that was highlighted by spinning fragments of helmet and other debris he chose not to identify. The Leaguer's blaster twirled off into space like a child's toy top. Forward, gray-suited crewmen clambered for cover behind any shelter they could locate, and the hammock wavers tripled their efforts to be noticed. Brim holstered his weapon and waved to the frightened Leaguers, then turned to Barbousse and winked. "Send to *Prize*," he ordered, "'One slightly damaged bender—under entirely new management!'"

Within a quarter metacycle, Jennings warped *Prize* smartly alongside the bender while Brim and Barbousse circled slowly in the launch, indexing their powerful seventy-five from stem to stern over the ever-organized Gray Leaguers, who had by now aligned themselves into two neat lines and were standing patiently with their hands on their heads.

Presently, hatches opened in the side of the ED-4 and a gangway slid across the void. At once, blue-suited boarding crews with high-amplitude blast pikes clambered to the opposite deck. They were led by two tall figures. One was slim and strode much in the manner of Calhoun, the other could only be Ursis. Both made directly for the open hatches, roughly pushing gray-suited prisoners out of the way as they ran. While salvage teams rigged stout optical bollards at the bender's bow, others followed Calhoun and Ursis below.

After a number of tension-filled cycles, two blue-suited figures appeared at empty Hyperscreen frames on the bridge and waved in the direction of the launch. At the same moment, Calhoun's voice boomed in Brim's ear from the short-range channel. "Damme guid work, you twa'," the elder Carescrian asserted. "An' young Brim: your mission is accomplished, indeed. Ursis informs me yon bender logic remains intact."

"Barbousse did all the shooting," Brim answered, clapping his grinning companion on the shoulder.

"'Tis guid," Calhoun replied. "We'll see that you both gat a wee credit." Below, on the bender's deck, Blue Capes were conducting the surviving Leaguers across *Prize*'s gangway to a specially constructed brig on the middle deck.

"Anybody left inside?" Brim asked.

"Dead meat only," Calhoun answered. "But twa' o' those wounded Controllers out on deck wull probably live." He laughed grimly. "No doubt, the Intelligence people wull luik forward to meetin' both."

"All six of them appear to have been on the bridge when you fired the shot that took out their Hyperscreens," Ursis interjected. "Three survived the blast, but each had serious wounds from crystal splinters. They say that the one you shot at the rear hatch was their captain—a *Provost*, no less."

"Ye both might *also* be interested to know that we found scuttlin' charges just inside that same hatch, too," Calhoun added. "So whichever of you zapp'd the bastard also guess'd well. He'd ha' taken everyone with him—includin' *yourselves* wi' a charge the likes o' that ane. . . ."

Soon after this conversation, Calhoun returned to *Prize* and sped off into a spherical patrol approximately one c'lenyt out from the bender. Brim and Barbousse were ordered to follow, limping along in their damaged launch as best they could manage. As Calhoun explained, "If Leaguer vessels do actually travel in pairs—an' this ane's mate closes in for a closer look, I don't want yon crazy-looking ship of yours to scare them off. Who knows, we might e'en add a second trophy to our spoils."

After an amazingly short stretch of time, *Prize* was relieved from her patrol duties by all three of the Greyffin IV–class battlecruisers: *Princess Sherraine, Gwir Neithwr*, and *Greyffin IV*. The mighty squadron of capital starships had clearly been lingering out of sight in the event that Calhoun's old ED-4 did—however serendipitously—land a catch. The real importance of the mission became clearer still when these three magnificent warships were joined by none other than *Diathom* from the Vice Admiral Plutron's Fifth Battle Squadron, one of the most powerful warships in the Fleet. After circling the ugly little bender a number of times, each of the great vessels ponderously lumbered out to form the corners of a huge square—twenty c'lenyts on a side—that no force less than a full battle fleet could threaten.

Significantly, each mounted a number of strategically located N-ray searchlights that—except for power and size—resembled quite closely those designed by Ursis and Barbousse.

As *Prize* coasted back alongside the bender and rerigged her gangway to its deck, still a fifth colossal vessel hove purposefully into view: S.S. *Gomper Throdorian*, an enormous transport hauler owned by IGL Starlines and "called up" to military service shortly after the beginning of hostilities. This angular starship—nearly 526 irals in length and 75 in breadth—reminded Brim of nothing so much as a huge brick that paid casual deference to atmospheric realities with a moderately rounded bow. She extended some twelve decks from keel to upper deck, and was surmounted by a veritable clutter of low deck houses, massive derricks, and scores of gantry cranes—with a massive, overhung bridge placed close enough to her bows that she actually took on a brooding visage. As was the case with many large cargo carriers of the day, her bows swung open when it was necessary to accommodate oversized cargo—such as a bender.

Brim shook his head as he parked the launch some hundred irals out from their kill. "Chief," he said wearily, "what do you say we put this poor old launch back aboard *Prize* now? I doubt if the Admiralty requires our little seventy-five anymore. They've got enough 408-mmi disruptors out there to start a new war."

Barbousse nodded. "Sounds like a good idea to me," he said with a broad grin, "but I think I'll settle for the war we've got. You get *too* many of them going on, and it might get difficult keepin' track of who's shootin' at ya."

Within the metacycle, two-hundred-year-old *Prize*—eminently successful D-ship, famed passenger liner, and one-time candidate for the breaker's yard—was on her way back to Atalanta flying Haelician colors. With PAYLESS STARMOTIVE neatly lettered on either flank, she was primed to embark on an entirely new career as a warship targeted against a whole new technology. Somehow, when Brim stopped to think about it, nothing seemed especially remarkable about the situation —especially when he considered the actual circumstances. War was always absurd—from its very origins. . . .

As Helic's disk filled the old-fashioned V-shaped Hyperscreens, Brim slowed *Prize* to approach speed and began his let-down to Atalanta. Liat-Modal's troop transports were now at their staging area, with the ground troops already engaged in "secret" maneuvers. Admiral Penda had taken official charge of the Hador-Haelic perimeter, and efforts to fortify Atalanta seemed to be racing toward an ultimate climax. He checked his instruments, then glanced at the clock. The port city was still at least a full half-day from the planet's light/

dark terminator. There was even a good chance Claudia might be waiting at Payless when he arrived. . . .

He was not disappointed. As soon as he taxied in from the main canal, he could easily pick her out among the others waving enthusiastic welcome from their blustery wharf—even through the spray-streaked Hyperscreens. Twenty cycles later, with *Prize* safely moored inside, he followed Ursis over the brow and onto the main floor. Claudia was waiting. The Bear stopped for his accustomed hug and kiss, then hurried off toward the iron staircase and a noisy celebration that was already well underway in the loft.

"Congratulations, hero," she whispered, pushing aside a luxurious strand of brown hair and taking his arm. "You should be *terribly* proud of yourself."

Brim smiled and looked into her brown eyes. "I guess I do feel pretty good about everything,'" he admitted, "but Barbousse did do all of the shooting."

"Except for the *last* shot," she corrected with a little wink, "the one that saved the whole mission." She grinned. "You see, I've heard the report already."

Brim felt his face burn. "Well . . ." he stumbled. Then he brightened. "Hmm,' he said, raising his index finger and grinning. "I'll bet there's one thing that you don't know, smart aleck."

"What's that?" she asked with mock impudence.

"Did you know that the mission has made *today* the 'one of these days' that we've been promising each other?" he asked.

"Oh, *Wilf*," she groaned suddenly, her happy smile turning to a grimace, "you've always arrived before on some, ah, preset convoy schedule . . . you know. This time—well, nobody had any idea when you'd be back, and . . ."

Brim squeezed his eyes shut in embarrassment. "I think I understand," he said sadly. "It wasn't very long ago that *I* didn't have any idea when we'd be back, either." Then he bit his lip. "I guess this isn't going to be *the* day, is it?"

Claudia's face reddened for a moment; then she smiled and pushed her hair over her shoulders. "Well," she said, looking down at the old brick floor of the warehouse, "I'd be lying to you if I said I didn't have plans for tonight. . . ." Then suddenly she frowned and peered directly into his face. "I *have* been looking forward to another night out with you, Wilf Brim—for a long time now," she declared with a determined shrug, "and . . . well, I suppose it wouldn't be the first time I've told a white lie."

Brim grimaced and held up his hand and started to protest. "Claudia . . ."

"No 'Claudias' about it, Mister Brim," she interrupted with a determined grin. "And since your *Defiant* is not due back until sometime tomorrow, I shall pick you up here by the street entrance at . . ." she glanced at her timepiece, "the beginning of Twilight watch. How about *that*?"

Brim chuckled and nodded happily. "Claudia, you lovely lady," he said, "I feel so honored that I'll be here, even if *Payless isn't*."

"Good," she said with a wink. "Now go on up to the party while I make a quick personal call. I'll join you in a very few cycles. . . ."

That evening, Claudia was as good as her word. Her little skimmer—looking even more battered than Brim remembered it—pulled up under the Payless Starmotive Salvage sign precisely as the Twilight watch began. A chill autumnal evening had just begun to hide the shabby streets in shades of dark mauve and shadow, and hints of coal and wood smoke hung in the still air. When she leaned over and opened the passenger door, she looked even more beautiful than Brim remembered. She was dressed in a bulky white sweater, dark woolen skirt, black stockings, and high boots. Silken tresses of brown hair framed her soft oval face like a graceful hood. "Need a ride, sailor?" she said, batting her long eyelashes in a mock display of sensual fireworks that—feigned or not—set Brim's blood to pounding in his ears.

"More than anything else I can think of," he answered, hoisting himself inside. For a long moment, he sat mutely staring at her. "By the very stars," he whispered at length, "you *are* beautiful, aren't you?"

Claudia pursed her lips in a pouting smile. "Flattery will get you nearly anywhere, *Mister* Brim," she said—he was dressed in mufti left over from the mission—"unless I happen to freeze to death before you stop letting all the heat out."

"Sorry," he said, slamming the door. "But I'm only a simple starsailor."

"*Only* a simple starsailor, eh? . . ."

"Honestly, I am—I don't even know where we're going."

Claudia's eyes sparkled. "Well," she said as she navigated through the twisted streets, "I had originally planned to dine in one of the more genteel City Mount cabarets tonight. But since you are *only* a simple starsailor, I suppose you'll probably be more comfortable in some place more casually comfortable—like my apartment. How does that sound?"

Brim sighed as he relaxed in the shabby seat. No Helmsman's recliner had ever seemed as comfortable. "I can think of nothing so incontestably elegant, madam," he answered, "or half so pleasing."

Claudia lived in an ancient, three-level dwelling that fronted the intersection of two cobblestone alleyways in her beloved Rocotzian section of Atalanta. By the glow of nearby streetlamps, the old building's walls appeared to be splendidly sculpted in bas-relief. Tiny trees—now winter-bare—were tastefully located in ornate balconies and on either side of an elaborately arched entrance. The surrounding streets—designed for transportation a thousand years gone—were crowded with a variety of parked vehicles that for a few moments threatened to force them a considerable distance away. However, just as Brim was preparing himself for a significant hike, she finessed the skimmer into an incredibly small opening between an arrogant-looking limousine and a dilapidated delivery vehicle less than a block from their door. He saluted this masterful Helmsmanship with loud applause. Then they picked their way over the uneven paving blocks, laughing and talking about every subject imaginable—except the war.

Her flat occupied all of the top floor, two double doors in its dusky, old-fashioned drawing room providing unobstructed views of the darkened harbor—now occasionally lighted by flashes of lightning from a storm out to sea. The ceilings were delicate trompe l'oeil scrolls connected to painted cameos framed in white and touched with gilt against backgrounds of pastel mauve, sapphire, and jade. The curtains, furniture, and carpets all blended into one exquisite—totally feminine—

whole. An ornate corner fireplace in dainty tiles blazed cheerily between the doors—its glow seemed to warm the whole of Brim's war-torn Universe. Velvety music wove patterns of incredible elegance through air spiced by wood smoke, perfume, and the yeasty odor of baking bread. "Like it?" she asked.

"I love it," Brim uttered quietly as he shed his coat. "It's beautiful—like its owner."

She smiled warmly and blew him a kiss. "I asked the caretaker to start the wood before we got here," she said, settling into the corner of a great plush couch that fronted the fire. "It seems his timing was perfect." She lit an aromatic mu'occo cigarette and indicated a wall cabinet between two ancient-looking oil paintings. "I have both e'lande and what my dealer assures me is some perfectly respectable Logish Meem over there. And, Mr. Brim, if you'll be so good as to pour, I shall patriotically start with e'lande."

"I admire that kind of patriotism," Brim declared with mock solemnity as he strode across the room. "Fortunately, the national Carescrian beverage is water, mostly polluted, so I enjoy considerable patriotic latitude." He opened an ornate door. In the glimmer of hovering GlowOrbs, a half-dozen shelves crowded by liqueur containers of every possible shape and hue surrounded three sides of a waist-high counter. This latter held a pair of crystal goblets, an ornate decanter of clear liquid that smelled like e'lande when he pulled the stopper, and a half-dozen flasks of elderly-looking Logish Meem. Choosing the latter for himself, he filled each of the goblets and carried them to the couch. "To the 'one of these days' that finally came true," he said, delivering the e'lande to her manicured hand, then touching the rim of her goblet with his.

"To tonight," she said, looking up at him. She saluted with her goblet and then sipped.

At that moment, she was so painfully sensuous that Brim felt himself losing control of his emotions. Taking both a deep breath and a long draught of meem, he stepped to the double doors and looked out at the scattering of lights that fronted the bay. While he stared, a luminous cascade burst into life far out on the water, lengthened, then accelerated across the darkness until it vaulted into the starry sky, echoes from its passage rattling the door's crystal panes as he stared in utter fascination. Eventually, its navigation lights disappeared among the stars, and then he felt her standing close beside him.

"You *do* love starflight, don't you?" she asked quietly.

"It's about all I know," he answered, looking into her brown eyes. Suddenly, as if someone else were in control, he set his goblet on a nearby table and drew her gently into his arms, the sensual fragrance of perfume heavy in his nostrils. She came with no hesitation, molding herself easily to his chest and searching his eyes, mouth open slightly and lips pouted. "May I kiss you?" he whispered.

"I think you'd better," she sighed in a low voice, then delicately placed her free arm around his neck and covered his mouth with hers. Her breath was an erotic blend of mu'occo and e'lande as she kneaded his lips gently.

Of a sudden, he found himself trembling like a raw fifteen-year-old boy. He tightened his embrace while he pressed her lips until he could feel her teeth against his. Her breathing began to shorten and her mouth opened wider. His breath shortened, too—considerably—while his heart began to pound against his chest.

Then the pressure on his neck ebbed and her lips withdrew as she took a deep breath. Her eyes opened and blinked slowly before she dropped her arm and leaned back in his embrace, nodding wide-eyed at the goblet of e'lande she was holding at a perilous angle. "Wilf Brim," she said with an embarrassed little smile, "if we keep that up, I am going to spill e'lande all over my carpet and . . ." She gestured with her free hand. "Well, you know—we haven't even had supper."

"One more," Brim begged.

"One more like that, and by the time I feel like cooking again, everything will be burned to a crisp."

Brim released her after a final embrace, and they retired to opposite ends of the couch to kick off their shoes and finish their drinks. There was still a whole Universe of interesting things to laugh and talk about, but now Brim could no longer force himself to take his eyes from her legs. Nor did she seem to be very committed to smoothing her skirt any farther toward her knees than the position at which it had originally come to rest when she sat in the deep cushions.

In due time, Brim refilled their goblets, then—at the insistent tone of a hidden timer—followed Claudia into the kitchen. Much of the tantalizing room was lined by carved wooden cupboards and pantries adorned with copper implements of every size and description. One end was dominated by a large black-metal stove, clearly operated by an old-fashioned flame mechanism. He smiled. Somehow, he was not a bit surprised, although the little he knew about this woman was closely related to starship technology and Hyperlight Drives.

Donning a ruffled apron and huge flowered mittens, Claudia opened the oven and removed two golden-brown loaves of bread that she set on a nearby counter to cool. They filled the air with a yeasty scent so agonizingly delicious that Brim found he could—to some degree—forget how tantalizingly provocative this naturally sensuous woman could be.

In short order, she prepared the remainder of their supper while Brim reposed like crowned royalty in a stout wooden chair, watching with the rapt fascination of the uninitiated. Truly, he had very little experience with such a cookery—or cook. After Kabul Anak's early raids, he had known only institutional cooking—when he could get even that. Now, he found himself totally absorbed in warmth and pungent, mouthwatering odors while he watched an extravagantly beautiful woman bustling in the most outlandish example of a kitchen that he could imagine. "Small Universe," he thought to himself.

Eventually—only just short of his commencing to gnaw on his chair—Claudia directed him to fill two fresh meem goblets at an exquisite glass table in still another softly lighted room. Then, with great bustle and fanfare, she fetched a steaming tureen of soup and served their plates beneath ornate silver hemispheres. Subsequently, considerable food, Logish Meem, and time disappeared before their conversation rallied to anywhere near its previous level.

Much later, after a thoroughly preposterous dessert—that Claudia admitted she had purchased—they retired to the couch and the fire for liqueurs. This time, Brim permitted no distance between them. He felt wonderfully full and just the slightest bit tipsy after their second bottle of Logish Meem. Beside him, Claudia relaxed on the cushions, drawing on a mu'occo cigarette in a long silver holder. Her cheeks had adopted a healthy blush as she stared into the fire and her skirt revealed significant expanses of black-stockinged leg above her knees. Without a word, Brim placed his arm around her shoulders.

Only after long moments did she turn to look up at him— studying his face with a grave expression in her brown eyes. Abruptly, she seemed to reach some conclusion, for she straightaway placed her liqueur on the end table and quashed out the half-finished mu'occo in a spicy puff of smoke. With a little half-smile, she next took the liqueur from his hand and set it beside her own, then leaned back in the crook of his arm and took a deep breath—her eyes fairly sparkling. "You are a very handsome and desirable man, Mr. Brim," she sighed. "When are you going to ask me for another kiss?"

Almost before he realized what he was doing, Brim affectionately pulled her close and covered her partially open mouth with his. This time, they began gently and tentatively, but when Brim found his lips again pressing wet inner membranes, his heart begin to hammer once more in his chest and he discovered his resolve evaporating before he'd gotten it fairly in use.

Suddenly, she threw both arms around his neck and squeezed almost desperately. After that, things became a lot less gentle and tentative.

"This could get out of hand," he mumbled shakily, opening his eyes for a moment.

"I know," she whispered, blinking once or twice. "I think it already has."

In spite of himself, Brim felt his hand slide to cup her breast. It was much larger than it appeared—delightfully heavy and firm as he gently fondled its sensual curve. . . . Then his breathing suddenly went all out of control, and he found himself fairly gasping for air.

"S-stop, Wilf," she murmured, pushing his wrist away, "not our first time, please."

"S-sorry. . ." he stuttered, struggling desperately with himself, but his passion continued to grow with each moment— and clearly, so did hers.

Once again, he cupped her breast, his heart now thundering in his ears like a runaway Drive.

Twisting her body slightly in his arms, she touched his wrist once more—and her hand lingered there for a moment. Then, with a smothered sigh she slowly drew her sweater up and out of the way. "What harm can it do," she whispered, her voice now urgent and out of breath. "You couldn't help knowing how much I've wanted you."

"Universe . . ." Brim whispered, feeling the incredibly soft nakedness of her skin warm his trembling hand. Moments after he started to gently finger her taut, swollen nipple, she thrust her tongue into his mouth with an animal urgency, and her hand dropped to his crotch. After a moment of fumbling, she gave a little gasp and grasped him even tighter. He was ready. . . .

Long after they completed their first—quite violent—coupling, Brim and Claudia clung to each other in trembling silence while coals from the fire snapped and spit in the fireplace. At last, he arose and threw another log on the fire. As she lay back on the rumpled cushions in the firelight, her moist body shone in a flickering study of soft shadows and rounded highlights.

Brim marveled silently as he feasted his eyes on the loveliness before him—had he purposely tried to discover Margot's opposite, he couldn't have made a better job of it. Where one's beauty was blond and ephemeral, the other's was luxuriously dark and hirsute. Margot's breasts were small and pointed with pink nipples while Claudia's were large and round, tipped by geat dark aureoles and generous paps. Margot herself was a large woman with truly sensual grandness; Claudia, on the other hand, was small and well proportioned, graced by just a touch of plumpness—precisely where it belonged. Both, however, were quite alike in one important element: when sufficiently aroused they could make fierce and intemperate love—in the most deliciously unrestrained and licentious expressions of pure carnality he could imagine. . . .

Brim and Claudia dozed and made love until false dawn lightened the stormy horizon out to sea. He was again relaxed in a corner of the couch, wistfully delighting in her unique beauty by firelight, when his ears caught a familiar thunder in the air—*Defiant*. Covering himself with his discarded coat, he stepped quietly to the rain-streaked doors—just in time to recognize a unique shape as it thundered out of the clouds. Clearance lamps glowing brightly in the darkness, the graceful cruiser swept over Grand Harbor in a perfect arc—like a ship a tenth her size. Only Aram would be flying her that way, Brim thought with a grin. As her landing lights split the streaming darkness with three powerful beams of dazzling silver, he could almost hear the litany in the young A'zurnian's mind: one seventy on the airspeed—not a whisker more or less—and four threes on the Verticals; turn crosswind at five-hundred irals, then simultaneously reset the Verticals to exactly one thousand and turn for a tight downwind. . . .

Claudia stirred on the sofa, and he turned to face her. She had opened her eyes to frown at him again, still completely unmindful of her nakedness—as if they had been living together for years. "That was *Defiant*, wasn't it," she asked.

"It was," he said with a smile. "How could you tell?"

"By watching you, Wilf Brim," she said a little proudly. "I think perhaps I have learned to read you."

Brim placed his coat on an end table and sat beside her, still wholly awestruck by the consummate beauty manifested before him. He took her hand and looked into her eyes. "What else do you read?" he asked.

Her face broke into a little smile, and she squeezed his fingers. "Do you really want to know?" she asked with a serious look.

"I really want to know," Brim said, grinning as he gently rubbed the delightful mound of her stomach.

"Hmmm," she said, wiggling pleasurably under his hand, "one thing I read there is a most profound love for deep space —and all the ships that ply it. But then," she declared with a faraway look, "I already told you about that." Suddenly she frowned a moment, smiling a little wistfully. "No woman will ever completely possess you because of it, either."

"I wonder," Brim said thoughtfully, finding himself drawn inexorably across half a galaxy to the Torond, "if that might not be all too true. . . ." Abruptly, he stopped rubbing. "What else do you read in my face?" he asked.

"Well," Claudia declared in a quiet voice, "sometimes your eyes are full of sadness, Wilf. I guess I've always wondered if there was someone already in your life." She smiled wistfully. "I suppose I've always been afraid there was." Suddenly, she frowned and pursed her lips.

Brim shook his head for a moment, gently leaning forward

to place his hands on her shoulders. "I won't lie to you," he said, brushing her lips with his. "There *is* someone whom I think I love, but she is awfully far away and . . ."

An indignant look suddenly crossed Claudia's face. "Someone you *love*?" she asked indignantly, pushing him back to a sitting position. "Great Universe," she said angrily, indicating the surfeit of crumpled tissues littering the floor. "I've lost track of how many times we've made love tonight—what would she think of you now?" She raised her eyebrows and peered down at his hand on her stomach. "What would she think of *me*?" She groaned. "You could at least have told me before we started this, Wilf Brim. I'll admit that I was every bit as horny as you—but even so, I'm not used to spending the night on my back entertaining somebody else's man!" She glared into his face. "Do you have any idea how easy this sort of thing is for a single girl in a port city like Atalanta? If I wanted to get laid, I didn't need to come to *you*."

Brim started to open his mouth, but she held up a silencing hand. "I'm not finished yet, you hypocrite," she said, drawing up her knees. "I could have a different man here every night if I wanted to—but I've got a hell of a lot more pride than that. I don't sleep with just anybody. And let me tell you—I *never* do it with a man that I think belongs to another woman." She shook her head. "She's a long way off, eh? Well, you *poor* baby! Why didn't you take care of yourself at Payless before you came here? . . ."

Brim ground his teeth and remained silent until she seemed to be finished. Then he firmly put his hand on her arm.

She scowled, but let the hand remain.

"You didn't let me finish, Claudia," he said in good time, looking her directly in her eyes.

"All right," she admitted grudgingly. "I suppose I didn't." She glowered. "But is there anything else to say?"

"There is," Brim answered calmly. "I'll admit that my brains *have* been hanging between my legs tonight," he said. "And pretty much everything you've been thinking about me is true. *But*," he added, raising his index finger in front of her face, "when I said 'she is far away,' I didn't mean only far away in distance. She has recently *married* someone else. . . ."

Claudia's carefully plucked eyebrows rose suddenly and she pushed back into the cushions. "Married!" she gasped.

"Married," Brim assured her.

"Oh, Voot!" Claudia muttered in a much subdued voice. "I'm sorry. I guess, then, she wouldn't mind much at all, would she?"

"You can be *quite* sure of that," Brim answered. "In fact," he added, staring off into the room thoughtfully, "I rather suspect that she'd be glad we've gotten together this way." He gently drew her fingers to his lips—they smelled strongly of love. "There," he whispered, "now you know my secret. Can we still at least be friends?"

She looked thoughtfully into his eyes and pursed her lips. "Yes," she said after a time, "we *must* be friends, that's very important to me, I find. But *only* friends, even when we share a bed—or a couch." She smiled. "I have a few other acquaintances in town," she said evenly. "I broke a date with one of them yesterday afternoon."

"No permanent plans with *anybody*?" Brim asked.

"None," Claudia said emphatically. "Otherwise, you and I wouldn't have sullied my couch the way we have. When it comes time for me to settle down, Wilf, then he'll be *the* one."

He nodded. "I think I'm finally beginning to know you a little bit," he said simply.

"Good," she said, "and now, Mr. Brim, there's something I want to know about *you*."

"What's that?" he asked with a raised eyebrow.

"Promise to tell me the truth?"

Brim grinned. "And hope to die," he declared.

"All right," she said, looking him directly in the face. "When you are—" she shrugged "—you know, panting and groaning like you do..."

"Yes?" She had little room to go on about *his* panting and groaning, he thought with a private smile.

"Well...who are you thinking about?" she demanded. "Her or me?"

Brim laughed. "You," he assured, "every time."

She smiled broadly again with her teeth on her lower lip. "I actually think that you might be telling the truth," she said.

"Thanks," Brim said. "I am—but I guess there's no way I can prove it."

"Well," Claudia began, her face coloring for a moment. "If you're really interested, there *is* something you can do to make me feel sure of your words."

"What's that?" Brim asked seriously. "I think I'd do damned near anything. . . ." His voice abruptly trailed off when Claudia drew her knees up again.

"Prove it, Wilf Brim," she demanded in an urgent whisper. "One more time. . . ."

As morning sun began to stream through the windows, Brim shared a badly needed shower with Claudia, then relaxed on her bed—for the first time—to watch her toilette and discuss the relationship they seemed to have defined during the night. "How could I stay angry with you, Wilf?" she asked through a half-dozen hair pins held in her teeth. Frowning, she inspected her coiffure in a large mirror behind her cluttered bureau. "I wanted you as much as you seemed to want me." She brushed a few last strokes, then carefully inserted the pins one by one. "And," she added at length, "whether or not you know it—or even particularly care—you gave me the most wonderfully scandalous night I have *ever* spent. I could forgive nearly anything for that." Grinning in spite of a sudden blush, she bent slightly to peer down at her crotch. "I shall be quite tender there, I suspect. . . ."

Within the metacycle—in ample time to report for morning watch—Brim returned to *Defiant* with a light heart, the sure knowledge that he had made a lifelong friend, and a moderately strained back. The latter, he realized, was part and parcel of this most delightful and intimate new relationship. He wouldn't have changed things if he could!

Late in the week, Collingswood invited Claudia and a number of her civilian associates on the Payless Affair—as Project Campbell had come to be known—to a top-secret awards ceremony in *Defiant*'s secured wardroom. There, amid rousing cheers and applause, she presented Calhoun, Ursis, and Barbousse with Imperial Comets for their work against the "latest threat from the League," as their engraved citations read. Following this, she summoned a thoroughly surprised Wilf Brim to the forward end of the room and handed him a shining golden envelope embossed with the Great Seal of the Empire.

Embarrassed and a little flustered by the unexpected attention, Brim concentrated on opening the splendid envelope instead of listening carefully to what she had to say. Only the words "Emperor's Cross" and a thunderous round of applause registered before he removed the presentation material—a personal note from Greyffin IV, summoning him to Avalon "as soon as events permit" to personally receive the medal itself.

Shaking his head in disbelief, Brim was quick to discount his part of the mission, but Collingswood only laughed and would hear none of his protestations. "Sorry, Lieutenant Brim," she said with a grin. "You will have to take *that* up with the Emperor himself when you get to Avalon. . . ."

That evening Brim—once again dressed in mufti—escorted Claudia to the Payless warehouse where old *Prize* was commissioned an official Imperial vessel and delivered to the Admiralty Intelligence Operations Division. Subsequently, she would continue in the extraordinarily hazardous D-ship role to which she had been modified—manned exclusively by volunteers from the covert side of "The Firm," as COMINTEL was known, and operated from a secret location. At the —unspecified—conclusion of these duties, ownership would automatically transfer to the sprawling Imperial War Museum in Avalon, where she would go on permanent display as an important historical artifact.

Following the ceremonies, Brim stood on the Payless wharf, sheltering Claudia from the bitter wind and flying spray with his coat. Out on the canal, *Prize* was just beginning to gain way over the racing white caps, her old Laterals thundering defiance at the darkness. Just before she vanished in cascades of spray behind the corner warehouses, Claudia's arm clasped his waist tightly, and he turned to find tears streaking her cheeks.

"Those 'volunteers' at The Firm," she said over the diminishing tumult, "I've heard what kind of missions they fly. "We'll never see her again, will we?"

Brim bit his lip. His mind had been following a dismally

similar path. "Probably not," he said as the last breakers from the starship's wake cascaded under the wharf and broke on the stone seawall beyond. "Nor will we see the likes of her again, either. Old *Prize* was special, somehow."

"Strange," Claudia remarked as they turned back to the warehouse, leaning into the teeth of the wind, "but I think it might be better that way. I can't see her ending up in a stuffy museum. . . . She wouldn't fit there. She'd be . . . *bored*, Wilf."

Later that night, with Claudia asleep in his arms, Brim smiled wistfully, reflecting on her words. She was right, of course. Every starship he'd ever come to know had her own unique personality—like proud *Defiant*, and tough old *Truculent* before her. Even the treacherous Carescrian ore barges. . . . *Prize* would likely spend the remainder of her days in one last, great adventure—the kind she had known since the moment she first soared out from the ancient Cloverfield yards more than two hundred years in the past. And then she would vanish forever in a blaze of glory.

He nodded his head and closed his eyes, sinking dreamily into the warmth of Claudia's perfumed fragrance. Not a bad way to go, he thought as sleep began to overtake him. Not a bad way to go at all. . . .

# Chapter 8

# ANTIQUARIES

Shortly following *Prize*'s departure and the subsequent closing of Payless Starmotive Salvage—"Just when we were starting to get a couple of calls," Barbousse complained with a chuckle—the pace of the war suddenly—and ominously—slackened. Clearly, Kabul Anak was concentrating his forces in preparation for the coming assault. Simultaneously, reports from Imperial spies indicated that small squadrons of Triannic's heavy warships continued to sortie—in support of Liat-Modal's troop transports, it was assumed. But the League's main battle fleet remained stubbornly in harbor near Tarott.

During a rare morning of inactivity—*Defiant* was not due out until the subsequent daybreak—a note from Claudia informed Brim that she would be late meeting him after work. He frowned in disappointment; nearly all her evenings had been spoken for since *Defiant*'s latest planetfall, and he was eager for her company. Now at odds and ends until well into the evening watch, he was idling outside the main hatch when Wellington and Ursis suddenly appeared on the brow.

"What's going on?" he asked, gazing indolently over the surrounding expanse of jam-packed gravity pools. Rumor had it that nearly one hundred fifty fleet units had been temporarily relocated to the big base, and even the skies teemed with ships.

"Until tomorrow morning's takeoff, friend Wilf, very little," Ursis declared over the reverberations of a battleship and three heavy cruisers thundering up from the bay in lofty cascades of spray.

"Actually," Wellington interjected, "Nik and I just now stopped by your cabin and found you were gone. We've signed out to tour the Gradygroat monastery. Would you like to go along? You could be our guide."

Brim shrugged—he certainly had enough time to kill. "Why not?" he said with a grin. "It's a pretty fascinating place. I'll sign the Good Book and be right with you." Moments later, the three Blue Capes were on their way along the brow toward the swarming public tram stop. . . .

"Voof!" Ursis exclaimed, stepping hesitantly onto the vast circular expanse of the Commons Room. "I have *never* seen the counterpart of this—not even in the Great Winter Palace at Gromcow."

"I've never even seen Gromcow," Wellington quipped in an awestruck voice. "Great Voot, Wilf, you weren't exaggerating about this place."

Brim only smiled. "There's a lot to look at," he said.

"Indeed," Ursis said, pointing to the Great Dome of the Sky above them. "The light source up there—a Kaptnor G-seed, isn't it?"

"My stars," Wellington gasped, peering up over her glasses, "I believe it is. I've only read about them, of course —miniature accretion disks that emit a luminous beam of energy. They've focused this one through that funny lens up there—the one that says 'Power.'"

"Apparently so," the Bear said with a look of fascination. "I last saw one during my days at the Dityasburg Institute on Zhiv'ot—where we trapped one for a few days in a special plasma retort." He shook his great furry head and laughed. "And from what I learned there, I would wager that enough energy exists in that one little beam to snuff out an entire planet—or cause a major flareup in the surface of a star."

"Are you serious?" Wellington asked with a frown.

"Completely serious, my dear Dora," Ursis replied. "Properly positioned, the beam from that little G-seed could probably lift this whole monastery off its foundations. In fact," he added, "the golden cone over there—the one with the word

'Truth' carved around its base—is probably the only reason that it doesn't." He nodded his head with an approving smile. "The old Gradgroat-Norchelites provided quite an energy source for their display here—one with enough power to *last*. I like that kind of engineering!"

"Wait just a cycle, Nik," Wellington demanded, eyeing the reflecting cone and scratching her head. "You say that beam of light could launch this monastery into space? Forget you're a theoretical engineer and explain this to me in terms I can understand."

Ursis smiled—he was quite into his element now. "Clearly, the way our Gradygroats have things set up here, Dora, the cone serves to shatter the main beam into thousands of little ones—which it then reflects harmlessly back to the ceiling as lighted 'stars' for the display of the heavens. But if something were to *move* that cone," he continued, "the beam would have nothing to defuse its energy, and—this close to its source— would continue right through the floor with enough thrust to lift everything out into space." He laughed. "Such an event would make things dreadfully difficult for the Friars. . . ."

"It would serve the idiots right," Wellington grumped. "The very idea, wasting all that energy to power a preposterous display." She shook her head.

"'Preposterous' is only a relative term," Ursis pronounced sagely, "especially when one deals in religious matters."

"I suppose you're right," Wellington admitted, "but I still think the whole setup's nothing more than a wild flea in Voot's beard. The very idea. . . ."

In the next half metacycle, Brim and Ursis strolled on around the room, taking in all the displays on the ground floor while Wellington lost herself scrutinizing gloriously detailed holomodels of the Gradygroat space cannon. When they'd completed their circuit of the vast circular floor, she was still deep in reflection. "Fascinating," she said as her two comrades approached, "but primitive. It's a classic study in ideal Rycantean design. Weapons makers were wonderfully hardheaded and practical in those days. Little wonder the Admiralty boffins haven't studied it for centuries."

"Did they build cannon that could live up to the legend?"

Ursis inquired with a smile. "It is said that the ones in orbit here could vaporize large asteroids with a single round."

Wellington thought for a moment, then nodded accord. "Given enough power, Nik," she declared, "artillery systems like this probably *could*. They're certainly designed to handle a lot more energy than anything I've ever encountered."

"But would they fire?" Brim asked. "I remember from your classes that nobody was ever sure they'd go off."

"Oh, I think there's little question that they would fire," she declared. "It's simply that no one has discovered how to pump that kind of energy up there to them." She smiled and raised her eyebrows. "You probably also remember from those classes that the forts are solely powered by one, old-fashioned EverGEN unit—and that's barely enough to maintain the environment and keep them oriented toward Hador for warmth." She shrugged and grinned. "But if they did have a big power plant—something like a large solar flare," she added with a chuckle, "the Gradygroat cannon would undoubtedly be the most powerful weapons in the known universe—by an order of magnitude. . . ." Then she frowned. "Nik," she said, pointing to the ceiling, "do you suppose they somehow ran the space forts from this G-seed, too?"

"Like beaming energy up to the cannon?"

"What do you think?"

The Bear shook his head. "You said it yourself, Dora," he said. "Those big disruptors need something on the order of a solar flare to power them up—and a *big* one if you wanted to fire from all thirteen forts in a salvo. Beamed energy falls off rapidly. The G-seed here probably couldn't even move anything bigger than a pebble if it were fifty c'lenyts or so distant."

Wellington snapped her finger and grimaced. "I should have guessed that myself," she said, chuckling good-naturedly and turning to Brim. "I suppose we'll have to fight old Triannic with ships after all, won't we, Wilf?"

Brim put his arm around Wellington's broad shoulders and grinned. "Looks that way," he said. "But with you handling the disruptors, we won't need all that power, anyway."

"Is true," Ursis pronounced with mock sagacity as they

moved off toward the monastery gardens. "In this day and age, it is *accuracy* that counts! Not power."

Later, seated around a diminutive table at one of the outdoor vcee' shops, the three had just finished a round of steaming, sticky-sweet cvcesse' when a fragile-looking Zuzzuou swooped down from the afternoon sky and side-slipped toward the landing area. "I want to watch that landing from close quarters," Brim said, jumping up from the table. "I'll owe you for the cvcesse'!" Vaulting a hedge and a balustrade, he covered the short distance in good time to watch the cheerfully painted little spaceship settle into place on its gravity pool—savoring the singular sort of design philosophy that could place a high control bridge at the stern of such an angular, top-hampered hull. Smiling, he took in the arched windows—much like the ones on the big tram he'd ridden to the monastery—old-fashioned handrails, exposed docking windlasses, built-up skylights on the cabin roof, and canvas dodgers rigged over the short companionways to the brow. Its Helmsman, a huge brute of a man, was no more mundane than the vehicle he flew. Stationed presently on the cabin roof near the bows, he was vigorously turning a huge crank jutting upward abaft the starboard landing beacon. Like all Zuzzuou drivers, he wore a great silken turban wound in swirls around a tall scarlet cap that protruded through the top like a mountain through a cloud. His black-and-white striped space suit looked almost drab in comparison.

It was wonderful. . . .

When at some length Brim looked around for his companions, he found them near the passenger gate in rapt conversation with one of the returning Friars. He wasn't surprised—at the vcee', Wellington had vowed to remain at the monastery until she at least talked to one of the monks. Brim chuckled, judging that she'd probably seduce one if she thought it would help. When he neared, it was clear that she'd started by asking about the monastery's strange motto.

"As a simple gunlayer, I have no fixed idea what the motto means, m'lady," the Friar responded politely. He was probably tall and powerfully built, but now his shoulders were bowed with fatigue. His face was lined not so much by age as by deep, habitual concentration, and his eyes were those of a professional sniper—though there was an air of gentleness in every line and feature of his being. "In our faith," he continued, "we are taught to believe that the motto will manifest itself when such becomes necessary."

"And what, Gunner Maas, do you perceive as 'necessary'?" Wellington asked, almost nose to nose with the tired-looking Friar.

"Why...a threat to the existence of our Order, m'lady. What else?"

Wellington smiled wryly and stepped back. "I don't suppose I can think of anything more important than that," she agreed. Then she raised her eyebrows. "And you say the cannon were created for the first occasion that The Order felt threatened from space?"

"Aye m'lady," Maas replied, setting his battered knapsack beside him on the grass in resignation—clearly, the man recognized that no respite would come until he satisfied this most persistent group of tourists. "As The Faith teaches," he said patiently, "when rumors of invasion reached the ancient Gradgroat and Norchelite Templars, they combined forces to build thirteen orbital bulwarks and fortify them with the ultimate space cannon."

Brim nodded to himself—it squared with what Claudia said.

"When *was* that?" Wellington asked. "I understand it was during the First Age of spaceflight."

Maas raised his eyebrows and smiled. "M'lady knows her history," he said. "We are taught that the last fort was completed in Standard year twelve thirty-five minus."

"Twelve thirty-five minus," Wellington repeated thoughtfully, nodding her head. She shook her head in amazement. "More than a thousand years before the founding of today's Empire."

Ursis nodded, returning his gaze to the Friar. "Ancient, to say the least," he commented, rubbing his furry chin. "Nevertheless, it is my understanding that a mere thirteen of these primitive weapons once destroyed an entire invasion fleet. Are they the same thirteen that orbit Haelic even today, Gunner Maas?"

"So teaches The Faith," Maas answered proudly.

"Where did they get such prodigious amounts of energy?" Wellington asked. "I could find only small, auxiliary power plants in the monastery holomodels. And those were barely adequate to meet the demands of the forts themselves—certainly not the cannon."

Maas raised his eyebrows for a moment and nodded agreement. "Your perusal of the holomodels was entirely correct, m'lady. Only rudimentary power is supplied at the forts, and it is barely adequate to satisfy day-to-day survival." He nodded his head. "Unless one is a firm believer in The Faith, it is sometimes difficult to accept the knowledge that all required energy will be supplied when the time of need arrives."

"Of that I am certain," Ursis agreed sympathetically.

"However, if one *does* believe in The Faith," Maas continued, raising a tutorial index finger, "our Gradgroat-Norchelite Fifth Article of Religion states 'The Space Cannon, that were created for the protection of Civilization, will receive power from Truth when they are again vital to the needs of Civilization—but not before.'"

"And that's enough for you, Gunner, eh?" Ursis asked deferentially.

"It is," Maas assured him. "It *has* to be."

"So you everlastingly preserve these huge weapons in preparation for a day on which they may once more be needed," Wellington stated.

"That is true, ma'am," Maas declared solemnly. "We maintain them according to the Holy Metal Book of Specifications."

"And I assume that should both the power and the need appear simultaneously, someone will know how to use the cannon themselves," Ursis declared with a great frown.

"Oh yes, sir," Maas answered emphatically. "Excellent simulators have been in constant use for centuries. Holy Laws require that the forts are always manned by at least two firing crews, each with a minimum of five years' training."

"Even when there's no power to fire the real things?" Wellington asked.

"As I have stated a number of times, m'lady," Maas repeated emphatically, "The Faith assures us that when power is needed, power will be supplied." Then, replacing his backpack on his shoulder, he bowed. "Kind visitors," he said, "I must now take my leave. I have endured life in orbit for two solid months, and I am not yet accustomed to gravity here at the monastery."

"Wait," Wellington said persistently, "I'm sorry I made such an issue of the power." She placed her hand on the Friar's arm. "One more question, Gunner Maas—please. Hador rides low in the afternoon sky, and we ourselves must soon return to our ship."

"Very well, m'lady," Maas replied good-naturedly. "One more question, then."

"How might one see the space forts?" Wellington asked breathlessly.

"By Zuzzuous, m'lady," Maas replied with a quizzical frown. "Or have I missed your question?"

"Only a little," Wellington said with a smile. "How should I—*personally*—go about getting up there? Could I ride in one of these Zuzzuous?"

Maas shrugged. "I should never state that such was possible only for members of The Order, m'lady," he said. "But I believe that to do so would require special intercession by the Abbot." He then saluted from the center of his forehead, bowed once more, and determinedly shuffled off toward the monastery.

Brim raised his eyebrows. "Would you actually take your time to go up there, Dora?" he asked.

"Well, antique weapons *are* my stock in trade, after all," Wellington reminded him. "And once this war's over, I expect to continue teaching people about them—that's of course if Greyffin wins and I don't get myself permanently zapped in the process." She shrugged. "So maybe there *isn't* any way now of getting power to those old space cannon. I am still convinced that they did fire at one time, and because of that they're worth looking into." She giggled mischievously. "Especially worthwhile now when the History Faculty budget doesn't have to pay for a trip to Haelic. . . ."

Much later that evening, Brim discussed his day's tour with Claudia—including Wellington's interest in the Gradygroat space cannon.

"She really got herself caught up in the old Gradygroat forts, did she?" Claudia chuckled as she bustled about in the savory aromas of her kitchen. "Well, Wilf, she's not the first to be fascinated—nor likely to be the last. Sometimes I think it's a national pastime."

"She *is* a recognized expert on antique weapons systems," Brim contended.

"Mmm," Claudia murmured, lifting the lid of a steaming pot, "and I'm—at least—a recognized expert on the preparation of torgo puddings, Wilf Brim. What do you say to that?"

"You are a recognized expert on a lot more than puddings, Claudia Valemont," Brim remarked as he got up from his chair. "But right now, I have very little interest in starship maintenance or anything else along those lines. Moments later, she was in his arms, giggling while he unbuttoned her blouse. As usual, she had neglected to wear anything under it. . . .

After supper, they again relaxed to share liqueurs before her fireplace. "*Defiant*'s due out tomorrow, isn't she?" she asked, nestled in the crook of his arm.

"She is," Brim asserted.

Claudia turned her head to look up at him. "Just in case I forget tonight," she told him, "tell Dora Wellington that I'll have the Abbot's permission for her space-fort visit when you get back." She grinned. "It's the least I can do for her part in making you an Imperial Helmsman—and bringing that talented body of yours here to Atalanta. . . ."

Shortly after *Defiant* passed through LightSpeed the next morning, Brim received an extraordinary personal KA'PPA message from Avalon—delivered by the hand of the COMM operator who had received it.

K321681SANBVA

[UNCLASSIFIED]

FM:IMPERIAL PALACE

TO:W.A.BRIM@ CL.921:U/W

INFO:COMFLEETOPS, COLLINGSWOOD@CL.921:U/W/

<<1298DNXCGIUCRT783Q-4ASKJ-S-FSDMSLKJ>>

1. LT. BRIM: IT IS OUR PLEASURE TO PERSONALLY
SUMMON YOU TO OUR ROYAL PRESENCE AT THE
IMPERIAL PALACE IN AVALON FOR THE PURPOSE OF
TENDERING AN EMPEROR'S CROSS INTO YOUR HANDS
IN ACCORDANCE WITH TRADITIONS OF THE FLEET:
AT MORNING WATCH PLUS THREE, 23/51996. YOUR
SPONSOR WILL BE DR. A. A. BORODOV.

2. DUE TO THE EXIGENCIES OF WAR, REGULATION
UNIFORM IS REQUIRED.

[END UNCLASSIFIED]
PERSONAL REGARDS
GREYFFIN IV SENDS
Q07WFO-9

A second KA'PPA message arrived on its heels, also personally delivered from the COMM section. This one was marked "Secret" and transmitted by one L.K.G. gNoord, personal secretary to Greyffin IV. It provided coordinates and times at which a courier ship would rendezvous with *Defiant* to pick up Brim on his way past Avalon—as well as drop him off when *Defiant* passed on her return trip with the latest convoy. Once he finished reading this message, he actually started to believe he might really be going to Avalon again.

Before the watch was over, everyone, it seemed, felt obliged to traipse through the control bridge, personally congratulating Brim by slapping him on the back or shaking his hand. Both became remarkably tender before he finally turned the controls over to Waldo and escaped to his cabin. There, behind a locked door, he struggled for two solid metacycles to discover some way of letting Margot know he was on his way, but none of his schemes made any sense at all. Unfortunately, the new Baroness of the Torond had been quite specific that *she* would contact *him* when the time came to do so.

Finally devoid of fresh ideas, he relaxed by browsing idly

through his mail. Much was the usual junk, but midway through the list a message from A. A. Borodov caught his eye and he enabled it immediately. In his display, the elderly Sodeskayan's muzzle had become significantly whiter in the year that had passed since he and Brim served on the same ship, but the Bear himself was not changed at all. His message of congratulations was so warm and sincere that Brim could almost feel it. Later, as he continued to scroll through his message list, Brim considered the singular honor old Borodov had accorded him. The elder Sodeskayan was now considered by many to be the most brilliant researcher of the Empire in his field of propulsion physics.

Abruptly, he caught sight of an entry sourced: EMBASSY: THE TOROND. Heart pounding in sudden anticipation, he touched ACTIVATE, then held his breath waiting for Margot's golden curls to appear in his globular display. . . .

They did not. Instead, the display filled with standard symbols that spelled out an invitation—and not the kind he had expected at all:

TO:     Wilf A. Brim, Lt., I.F. @CL. 921
FROM: Rogan LaKarn, Baron, the Torond
       @ Embassy of the Torond/Avalon

Your attendance is requested at a ball saluting the Honorable Yossobb Lotord, Emissary to the Court of Mogrund XXIV. In keeping with wartime protocols, regulation uniform dress is requested.

Evening Watch: 25/51996
Embassy of the Torond
Avenue of the Patrons
Avalon

Frowning, Brim immediately understood that Borodov had already notified Margot of his impending arrival. Bears always seemed to know how to handle such affairs. The invitation—on the evening of his audience with Greyffin IV—

was clearly her answer, and it contained more than one meaning for Brim. The message itself was mere "boilerplate," written for impartial—and impersonal—transmission to a standard guest list by unseen embassy secretaries. The fact that *his* had been sent separately—a mere Lieutenant's name would never appear on such a list—was sure sign of Margot's hand. However, since no personal touch accompanied it, Brim was also led to the inescapable conclusion that this would finally be the first of their encounters when they would not be able to "touch." Glancing at her tiny holoportrait—one he had torn from a magazine—he wondered how well he would manage the situation. Ominously, he failed to conjure even a single positive speculation.

Three days later, Brim found himself in the jump seat of another speedy little LK-91 as it rumbled in for a flawless, predawn landing on Avalon's Lake Mersin, then taxied smoothly onto a tree-lined gravity pool. He felt a momentary sadness sweep over him as he thought of the last time he'd seen Avalon's military complex—Margot had met him beside one of these pools. . . .

As he carried his lightweight softpack through the packet's main hatch, he spied a massive black limousine at the bottom of the brow reflecting the first rays of a dawning Asterious triad. Easily the most elegant nonflying machine he had ever encountered, it was manned by two tall and athletic drivers who sprang from the front seat and snapped to attention when he reached the foot of the brow. Dressed in formal red coats, and black jodhpurs of Imperial Guardsman, they had the short haircuts, small mean eyes, and arrogant chins that wordlessly suggested the breed of superpatriots who remorselessly followed *all* orders, under *all* circumstances. Every drop of Brim's Carescrian blood distrusted both men immediately.

"Lieutenant Brim?" one of them asked politely. He had a long scar across his chin.

Brim nodded, wondering if the man ever smiled.

"May we see your identification, please?" The quiet words were no request.

Wordlessly, Brim proffered the HoloID from his tunic.

Both drivers spent considerable time comparing it to his

face before they finally handed it back. "Thank you, Lieutenant," the scarred one said at length, clicking his heels crisply and climbing into the port-side driver's console. The other Guardsman held the back door open while Brim entered a spacious ophet-leather passenger compartment. Moments later, the skimmer departed at high speed in a shower of layla blossoms—spring was glorious in Avalon!—with Brim wryly considering that were it not for the ophet-leather interior, the whole affair would seem rather more like an *arrest* than anything else.

In little time at all, the big limousine was speeding effortlessly through the early-morning traffic on tree-lined Vereker Boulevard as it followed the shore into downtown Avalon. Brim shook his head, recalling that his last two rides on the Vereker had also been in limousines, but neither belonged to the Emperor himself—nor one that had made such rapid progress through traffic. The prominent Imperial flags fluttering on either side of its windscreen appeared to be at least as effective as a siren. When people saw those looming up from the rear, they moved over! Soon the Desterro Monument flashed by on the right and then the gleaming ruby arch over the Grand Achtite Canal. In a few cycles more, the Marva tower had passed into their wake. Following that, congestion on the Vereker increased exponentially as they began to traverse inner districts of the sprawling city, but they were deep into the Beardmore Section before traffic slowed to Avalon's usual morning commuter crush. Brim chuckled as they crawled past row after row of historic buildings. At least every third one appeared to be propped up by some sort of scaffolding. A wonderful place to live, Margot used to say—if they ever finished it. . . .

Then the bottleneck was behind them, and they were gliding through Courtland Plaza, slowing for the perilous traffic circle around Savoin fountain and easing toward a curb lane for the sharp turn through the Huntingdon Gate and into the grounds of the Imperial Palace.

At the precise moment they slowed for the guard station, Brim began to comprehend that this was not merely a short leave he had finessed to Avalon. He actually *was* going to see the Emperor—and soon! He swallowed hard as the awful reality began to sink in—a thousand Gorn-Hoffs were preferable! Taking a deep breath, he forced his hand away from the latching mechanism—too late to jump ship now, anyway. But what in the name of Voot's big toenail was *he*—a poor Carescrian—doing at an audience with Greyffin IV, Grand Galactic Emperor, Prince of the Reggio Star Cluster, and Rightful Protector of the Heavens? He shook his head in sudden panic. He ought to be getting back to the ship—surely there was some mistake. . . . Then, just as he was about to open his mouth, his alternatives evaporated when the limousine pulled smoothly out of the guard station, coasted across a vast goldbrick plaza, and came to rest at an enormously wide staircase. Like it or not, he had *arrived*!

An instant later, the door was pulled open by a slight, grayhaired individual with a narrow face, prominent nose, and the nearsighted eyes of a secretary. "Lieutenant Brim," the man said, extending his hand, "welcome to the Imperial Residence —I am called Lorgan, and while you are here, I shall render any assistance that I can." Despite his peculiar looks, his handshake was firm and masculine. Opening his tabulator board, he inserted a few quick marks, then led the way up the staircase, through an ornate colonnade, and into a great mirrored lobby whose vividly colored ceiling was painted with allegorical scenes from Empires long past.

While Lorgan busied himself with a brace of efficient-looking aides at an ornate desk, Brim studied heroic images of ancient starships behind men and women dressed in vintage spacesuits. He recognized some of them from his early school studies. Most appeared to be planting archaic versions of the Imperial flag on wild-looking landscapes that—by now—had surely become some of the great cities in the Galaxy.

After a few moments, Lorgan provided Brim with a tracking lozenge and a tumbler of sparkling water, then put his hands on his hips and shook his head. "Far be it from me to criticize the perfection we have fairly swirling around us today, Lieutenant," he declared, "but we seem to have reached a snag already. His Most Gracious Majesty, Greyffin IV, already finds himself behind schedule—and it is my bet that he will continue to fall behind as the metacycles pass. Were I you, I should prepare myself for a long day of cooling my heels." With that, he shouldered Brim's softpack, showed him to a comfortable waiting room whose exits were controlled by more patriotic-looking Guardsmen, then excused himself and vanished around a corner. Shrugging, Brim found himself a comfortable divan and began to leaf through a news display. He was still twenty-five cycles early for his audience when Lorgan ushered an elderly Bear through the door. "I understand you two know each other," he said with a wide grin.

"Anastas Alexyi!" Brim exclaimed, springing to his feet to hug his old friend in the Sodeskayan fashion. "Thank you for coming here!"

"But how could I be anywhere else, Wyilf Ansor?" Borodov asked in his accented Avalonian. "You are like a son to this old Bear—and I am much pleased!" Like Ursis, he had a huge furry head with rounded ears, long aristocratic muzzle, large wet nose, and sagacious eyes set in whorls of the reddish-brown fur that marked Bears of truly patrician breeding. Many silver strands had been finding their way into the old gentleman's tonsure of late, however, and—to Brim's way of thinking—the total lack of artificial coloring spoke volumes about his outlook on life. As usual, his uniform was perfectly tailored—*and* he was wearing the insignia of a full captain.

"Voot's wig," Brim blurted. "You've been promoted. Congratulations!"

"Even the Admiralty makes mistakes," Borodov said with a grin. "But I decided I would not tattle on them this time. Research money comes much easier to those with rank, I find in my dotage. . . ."

While they reminisced, Lorgan excused himself only to reappear a few cycles later carrying a tray of delicious patisseries: tarts, turnovers, pies, trifles, strudels, cream puffs, eclairs, and a graceful silver pot of steaming, delicious cvcesse'. "As I told Lieutenant Brim," the secretary said, "it may take a while today."

"It is not to fuss about matters out of your authority," Borodov said, gesturing with both hands. "'No matter how cold the wind blows, Bear cubs and crag wolves find warm caves 'til spring,' eh?"

"Absolutely, Doctor," Lorgan replied without batting an

eye. Clearly, he was quite used to high-level visitors from Sodeskaya. . . .

During the next metacycles, it certainly wasn't as if they suffered from poor treatment. While the morning watch wore on, Lorgan escorted the Blue Capes to an exquisite private dining room, where they snacked on rare Bries, Bel Paeses, Camemberts, Munsters, and Tilsters with delicate crackers and fruit wedges. Then, after a lengthy tour of the palace—afterward, Brim swore he and Borodov had seen more than Greyffin himself!—they repaired to another private dining room for a lunch of oysters, prawns, and lobsters from all over the Empire, served with rich, crusty breads and green salad, everything washed down with a rare bubbling Logish Meem. Their formally dressed waiter topped off the meal with frozen creams and sweet liqueurs.

And still no sign of Greyffin IV. . . .

Midway through the afternoon watch, the two friends were still a million c'lenyts from running out of interesting subjects to discuss, but Brim was now moderately embarrassed about squandering Borodov's afternoon. It had become clear that the Bear was now an important factor in the overall Imperial research effort. At length, Lorgan appeared again in the doorway—and shook his head.

Brim smiled wryly and glanced at his timepiece. "Still busy, eh?"

"Still busy," Lorgan affirmed. "Looks as if it'll be a little while yet before we get another shot at His Nibs." He turned to Borodov. "Doctor," he said, "your office has been on the line almost constantly for the last metacycle—and . . ."

"Maybe you ought to go, Doctor," Brim said quickly. "I'll see you again tonight, won't I?"

"But of course," Borodov said. "I shall be here at the beginning of Evening watch." Then he frowned and shook his head solemnly. "Much as I dislike stranding you here, Wyilf, I suppose I really should go. Some discoveries are born with much difficulty."

The secretary nodded emphatically. "I think it would be a good idea, Dr. Borodov."

The Sodeskayan shrugged phlegmatically. "I shall then take my leave. But I shall return in plenty time for the ball—Lorgan will make sure I find you." With that, he lumbered out of the door and down the hall.

"I know of your plans for tonight, Lieutenant," Lorgan added, "and I am personally sorry for these delays."

Brim shrugged. "First things first," he said pragmatically. "It clearly isn't any fault of *yours*."

After a sumptuous supper in still another private dining room, this in a high tower with a splendid view of the city, Lorgan excused himself after fresh table linens were spread for dessert.

Brim had stepped to the window and was peering out over the city—wondering idly where the Embassy of the Torond might be in the maze of lighted streets—when he heard the door open behind him. "I take it His Nibs is still busy," he said without turning. Borodov was due within the metacycle, and he didn't want to miss him—or the chance to see Margot.

"No, my boy," a deep voice chuckled quietly. "His Nibs has finally escaped."

Brim stiffened. It was not the voice of Lorgan the secretary —but one he had often heard on broadcasts. Taking a deep breath, he slowly turned from the window . . . he was correct. "Your Royal Highness," he whispered, snapping to attention.

"Do relax, Lieutenant," the Emperor said, offering his hand with a smile. "I am delighted to make your acquaintance . . . for a number of reasons." He was a spare man of medium height—neither young nor old—who looked surprisingly like the pictures that hung in every Fleet starship large enough to have a wardroom. Dressed in a magnificently tailored Fleet uniform—with the insignia of a full Admiral—he wore his gray hair short, parted on the left, and combed straight back from a narrow face. He had close-set gray eyes on either side of a prominent, squarish sort of nose, a striking moustache, and a diminutive, pointed beard. In his free hand, he carried a small wooden box.

Brim smiled to himself as he gripped the Emperor's soft, dry hand. He'd been so sure he *wasn't* going to meet this man that he'd had no chance to become nervous! All in all, Greyffin IV was a rather ordinary-looking person—except for that particular bearing of total imperturbability that seems to define everyone who is both rich and powerful.

"I say, Brim," the Emperor muttered, setting the box on the table and lifting its lid, "you certainly have come a long way for this." Inside was an eight-pointed starburst in silver and dark blue enamel with a single word engraved in its center: VALOR. It was attached to an ivory sash embroidered in gold with the words GREYFFIN IV, GRAND GALACTIC EMPEROR, PRINCE OF THE REGGIO STAR CLUSTER, AND RIGHTFUL PROTECTOR OF THE HEAVENS. Opening the sash, he deftly placed it around Brim's neck, then stepped back and frowned. "Looks quite first-rate," he observed presently, pursing his lips and nodding his head.

"Thank you, Your Majesty."

Greyffin laughed a little. "You are most welcome, Lieutenant," he acknowledged, "but I'm dashed if I'll believe you are very thankful for having been put off so much today. I am quite aware that I was *supposed* to meet with you during the Morning watch." Then he sighed. "I am also aware that I am on the verge of keeping you from your assignation with my niece tonight at the Embassy of the Torond. Wilf Brim," he said with a little smile, "you are a most persistent young man."

Brim's insides suddenly turned to ice. "Your Highness?" he asked.

"My niece," Greyffin prompted, "Her Serene Majesty, Princess Margot of the Effer'wyck dominions and Baroness of the Torond." Then he smiled a little sadly. "The lady who would probably be your wife right now were it not for my interference."

"I . . . I," Brim stammered.

Greyffin held up a hand and smiled sympathetically. "Oh I know that you won't discuss this matter, Brim—a trait that I find most commendable. It tells me a great deal about you as a person, and about my niece as well." He smiled musingly again. "I should have known to trust her judgment. She's too discerning to be taken in by a mere social climber."

Brim opened his mouth, but Greyffin held up his hand again.

"Wait, Brim," he said. "Since nothing can change the circumstances that you and Margot find yourselves in, let me at least make sure you know that you have my understanding, and sympathy—if not my approval." He frowned, then smiled a little wistfully and stroked his beard. "I should be a fool if I thought I could talk either one of you into calling off your affair. I suspect it *is* the real thing, as they say. My beautiful and *wonderfully* disrespectful niece has already laughed scornfully at that suggestion, and I cannot imagine anyone with your service record being discouraged by a mere Emperor." He chuckled quietly and nodded, looking Brim directly in the eye. "Yes, right-ho. She *is* beautiful, you young scalawag. Very beautiful—I can't blame you at all."

Stunned, Brim shook his head and raised his hands to his chest, palms up. "I don't know what to say, Your Highness . . ." he stammered.

"Don't say anything, Brim," the Emperor responded with a warm smile. "I shall have to dash off in a moment—more meetings, you know. That's how we Emperors earn our modest livings, if you haven't guessed by now." He glanced off through the window for a moment. "Regrettably, Brim, LaKarn's in town tonight, so I doubt if you and Margot will be able to do much more than look longingly at each other. But there will be a future—unless you get yourself killed in this bloody awful war. And it's that future that concerns me now." He frowned for a moment, then pointed a most Imperial finger at Brim's middle. "Young man," he said, "as your Emperor, I make only one demand concerning this matter: that you are . . . *careful* in your relationship with my niece—very careful. Her marriage is of profound importance—to the Empire, at least. And, as I believe she has already conveyed to you, it is therefore considerably more significant than either of you as individuals." A large warship thundering out of the distant base at Lake Mersin rattled the windows and momentarily claimed the Emperor's gaze before he turned his attention again to Brim. "Quite sorry to be so indelicate," he continued, "but I am really not terribly particular about with whom she sleeps, just so long as she is reasonably discreet about her affairs—and, of course, the first child doesn't look like Wilf Brim. After that, if any of them grows up with extremely black hair, a dimpled chin, and fancies of driving those bloody star buses you love, that's precious little of my business." With that, he extended his hand. "Once again, Lieutenant," he said, "my personal thanks for your extraordinary bravery and commitment to my Empire—jolly decent in the light of your Carescrian background. . . ."

Brim felt his eyebrows rise as he shook the Emperor's hand again. He never expected anything like *that*.

"I don't rule well in Carescria," the Emperor continued, looking him directly in the eye, "as I am sure you know all too well. Perhaps we shall discuss that another day. Meanwhile, keep up your efforts against the League. I doubt if Nergol Triannic would do much more to improve things—and at least I am now painfully aware of my omissions in that part of my dominion."

Then he was gone. . . .

Brim stood for long moments in shock, staring at the empty doorway—which momentarily filled with the ever-present Lorgan.

"Doctor Borodov is at the spinward portico, Lieutenant," he said. "I trust you had a favorable audience with His Nibs." Just as if it were an everyday occurrence. . . .

Brim had rarely seen Margot in the presence of LaKarn—and never since their wedding. He was stunned at the difference it made. Their eyes met for the first time in the reception line at the Embassy of the Torond; she was perhaps five persons away. In her peach-colored gown and long white gloves, she was more beautiful than ever. She recognized him, clearly—but with what a difference. Here—tonight—they were no longer lovers, only good friends, almost as if she had somehow donned a mask that only he could see.

Totally absorbed in a discord of conflicting emotions, Brim followed Borodov blindly toward the noisy ballroom through clouds of perfume and scented smoke until a detached voice from somewhere announced, "Wilf Ansor Brim, Lieutenant, Imperial Fleet," and abruptly he was shaking hands with Rogan LaKarn himself.

"Ah, hello Brim," the man said with a—forced?—nonchalance. He was tall and handsome, dressed in the luxurious black military uniform of a Colonel in the elite Hoffretz' Guards. His severe features were custom-made for the wisps of moustache that decorated a slightly curling upper lip, and his cold blue eyes fairly radiated power and affluence. Brim had to admit, he was quite a package. "So happy you could be with us tonight," he was saying. "Old Borodov tells me you've just come from the Palace. Congratulations, for the Emperor's Cross, old man. Quite an honor, and all that."

"Thank you, Baron," Brim mumbled, finding himself at a complete loss for words. "I do feel honored indeed."

"Yes, I can imagine," LaKarn asserted, turning to Margot. "M'dear, I'm certain you will be... *pleased* to welcome this highly decorated Carescrian into our home. I believe you two were close friends at one time."

"Wilf," she said, giving him a quick little hug, "I'm so proud of you!" For one heart-wrenching moment, her small breasts were pressing his chest, her special perfume strong in his nostrils.

"You are beautiful," he whispered in a torment of emotion. Then her lips brushed his—dry and closed, almost impersonally.

Every atom of his being ached desperately to take her in his arms and... except he couldn't do that. Her *husband* was standing right there beside her.... The whole thing was like some crazy, troubled dream. Universe knew he was desperately thankful just to see her face again—but it wasn't enough. He *loved* her. And he couldn't do a xaxtdamned thing but look!...

Then suddenly, she was introducing him to a fat little gnome of a man with beady eyes, huge turned-up moustaches, a grin that seemed to stretch from ear to ear, and a great wart on the side of his nose. Brim completely missed the name— which seemed to be all right anyway because the grinning dwarf spoke with such a heavy accent that there was no communication possible in the first place.

After an eternity of confusion, he completed the reception line. Then Borodov was beside him in the crowded, noisy ballroom, placing a generous goblet of meem into his hand. "Maybe this will help a lyittle, my friend," he said.

It did.

Throughout the evening, Brim and Margot found precious little time to themselves, and on those few hurried occasions when they did, they had no privacy. But their eyes met often, and *they* spoke volumes, at least. In the end, however, there was really no effective means to communicate. Brim was completely helpless to speak the words he so urgently wanted to convey. In desperation, he once even asked her to dance, but he was so grievously inept that he soon found himself driven from the floor, stammering apologies, his face burning from embarrassment in spite of her protests.

After that, he would gladly have bolted, were he able. Unfortunately, as Borodov explained with a great deal of understanding, such an exit was largely impossible—at least not before the guest of honor departed. Subsequently, every passing moment tore a little more from his flagging composure.

Late in the evening, as he politely attempted to follow a profoundly scientific conversation among Borodov and a small circle of clearly high-level researchers, Brim felt a hand on his shoulder. Swiveling, he encountered the square-jawed, athletic countenance of Crown Prince Onrad, Greyffin's only son and Margot's second cousin. "Your Highness," he said, turning carefully—he'd sipped considerable meem by this time and he knew it—"I had no idea you would be here. It's good to see you."

Onrad gripped his elbow and led him away from the Borodov gathering. "Brim," he said, with a sympathetic smile, "for a man who has just received the Emperor's Cross, you look almost happy enough to be a professional pallbearer." He shook his head slowly. "But then, so does my blond cousin. I warned you both back on Gimmas Haefdon that you'd pay a high price for your love."

Brim looked Onrad directly in the eye and returned the man's smile. "Your Highness," he said, very slowly so as to avoid slurring his speech, "once again, I have no idea what you are talking about. . . ." He steadied himself while the room tilted slightly. "Princess Effer'wyck-LaKarn and I share only casual friendship." Then he raised a tutorial index finger. "But," he continued with great concentration, "it seems to me that the affection of a woman like your most alluring blond cousin would be worth *any* price—whatsoever."

Onrad shook his head slowly as he continued to grip Brim's elbow. "She must really be something else," he muttered. "I greatly admire you, Brim," he said with look of esteem. Then his eyes glimmered with sudden whimsy. "Consider it's only because of the medal," he said.

Brim bowed slightly. "I humbly thank you, Your Highness," he said.

Onrad bowed in return. "Keep up the bloody good work you do in the war," he said. Then he pressed Brim's elbow and vanished into the crowd.

During the remainder of the evening, Brim and Margot managed to touch hands only twice before—at long last—the guest of honor departed. Shortly afterward, a svelte gathering of Torond nobility occupied LaKarn at the exit, and suddenly Margot appeared beside him, took his arm, and—as if *he* were leading—directed his steps to a tiny, curtained alcove. Moments later, she was at last in his arms, her kisses warm and moist—and her lips excitingly parted. "Sweet Universe, Wilf," she sighed, "it's been a lot rougher tonight than I thought it was going to be."

Brim nodded in silence, then pressed her torso closer to his, totally consumed by a thousand delightful sensations her body sent pulsing through his. "A lot rougher," he mumbled.

"But at least we got to speak and see—and *this*," she said, her breath suddenly short and labored, "even these few stolen moments together is better than none at all."

"Yes—Universe yes . . ." Brim agreed just before she smothered his lips in kisses. His heart thundering in his ears, he was just beginning to lose himself when a female whisper on the far side of the curtain warned, "Your Highness, he's asking for you!"

Margot suddenly froze, gasping as if she had run five miles. She forced her eyes closed for a moment, then took a deep breath and pushed herself from his embrace. "Until the next time, my love," she said, placing a lace handkerchief in his hand and frowning. "Take care of your face—I am all over you." With that she dodged through the curtain, and Brim found himself alone in the alcove with only the ghost of her perfume—and a terrible feeling of emptiness. Shaking his head, he carefully swabbed his face to remove her makeup, pocketed the handkerchief, and returned to the ballroom floor. Moments later, Margot emerged from a nearby anteroom as fresh-looking as if she had just arrived at the ball. Their eyes

met one last time—she made a sad little wink—then she
joined LaKarn with a dashing group of black-uniformed officers off at the far end of the ballroom. It was finally time to
leave.

Collecting Borodov from still another crowd of admiring
intellectuals, Brim retrieved his cape and followed the old
Bear to their limousine. Ahead lay continued revelry, and
eventually a Bear-sized bed, at the formidable Sodeskayan
Embassy across town where he spent the remainder of the
night.

Next morning, beneath the towering Colonnade of Winter,
Brim bid affectionate farewell to Borodov and a number of
other Sodeskayan hosts. By this time, he was furtively curious
about Sodeskayan sleeping habits—or, more properly, the
*lack* of such habits. Every Bear he'd ever encountered appeared to be either working strenuously or playing strenuously—day and night—with nothing in between.

Along Vereker Boulevard, he found himself contentedly
dozing on and off as two burly Sodeskayan Guardsmen
smoothly piloted their massive Rill-15 limousine through the
heavy traffic as if it were a child's toy. All in all, he considered sleepily, it had been as good a trip as possible. Certainly
his personal audience with Greyffin IV turned out to be an
exciting occurrence in his life—and the Emperor's Cross was
nothing to sneeze at, either. He buried his nose in Margot's
perfumed handkerchief. He'd been assured that she still loved
him, too, though he'd since begun to have distressing anxieties about their whole relationship—and what he suspected it
cost Margot to sustain it.

As the big skimmer drew smoothly to a halt beside his
waiting packet, Brim noticed another limousine already
parked in the gravity-pool lot. He shrugged—no telling
whom one might encounter on these special Imperial flights.
He thanked the grinning Sodeskayans as they opened the
heavy door for him and handed him his softpack. Then, as
they deftly swiveled the big skimmer around in its own
length, he was stopped on his way to the brow by a now-familiar voice from the other vehicle's window.

"Brim: suffer my presence for a few moments more this morning—I shan't keep you long." It was Rogan LaKarn.

Frowning, Brim set his softpack on the brow platform and strode warily toward the limousine, every sense alert for the slightest ambiguous movement. At the other end of the brick expanse, LaKarn opened his own door and set out in an opposite direction. They met in the middle; neither extended a hand.

"Hear me out," LaKarn entreated with a serious look. "This won't take long because—frankly—I don't like your company any more than you like mine."

"It's your party," Brim replied evenly. "What is it you want to say?"

"Simply this," LaKarn said after a moment of uncomfortable silence. "I cannot permit you to leave here with the mistaken impression that I am insensitive to the pain I caused you last evening. On the contrary, I understand, and even countenance, your hostility toward me, Carescrian. Were our situations reversed, I should probably feel the same enmity toward you." He grimaced in the cool shadows of the early-spring morning, then touched Brim's arm and looked him directly in the eye. "I can give you no hope in your quest for my wife," he continued, "but at least credit me with knowing full well the grounds on which she agreed to our marriage—as well as why *you* will not relinquish her love."

"I have no idea what you are talking about, Baron," Brim said with an expressionless face—inside, however, he was churning like a gravity storm.

LaKarn smiled wryly and continued as if Brim had never opened his mouth. "It is also a fact that I cannot blame you in the slightest for how you feel—she is a *splendid* woman, by the Universe. There are times when I think I could even love her myself, were *you* out of the picture. . . ." He shut his eyes for a moment, then shrugged with his hands turned up at his sides. "That's it, Lieutenant Wilf Ansor Brim—and lover to my wife. It's off my conscience now." He turned to leave, then stopped for a moment to point a finger in the center of Brim's chest. "You may not always think so in the years ahead, but you are a fortunate man indeed."

"And you, Baron," Brim answered quietly, "are a gallant man." No other words seemed appropriate.

Long after LaKarn's limousine departed, Brim stood at the boarding hatch staring sightlessly along the empty road, moved to the very core of his existence. Shortly after takeoff, he withdrew to his cabin and seldom emerged until the rendezvous with *Defiant* two days later. During that period of nearly total isolation, his rival's hopeless words echoed constantly in his mind: ". . . I think I could actually love her myself, were *you* out of the picture. . . ."

Brim's guilt festered rapidly in the loneliness of his tiny cubicle—especially when he came to realize that Margot must often find herself as despondent and lonesome as he did. He remembered the frantic ending to their lovemaking in the back of the limousine—when they were forced to squander their precious moments with the fool Hagbut. And later: the few stolen metacylces in her suite when they had to fight back sleep even while they tried to make love. And that was all they had to show for nearly a year of their lives—except for a few sweet stolen kisses in an empty cloakroom. He shook his head. If it was bad for him, it had to be at least as bad for her. Was that really what he wanted to achieve for this magnificent woman who loved him: a life of embarrassment and frustration? Suddenly he held his ears and shook his head violently. What in the bloody Universe was he trying to do?

Long before the great turning wheels of *Defiant*'s convoy filled the little packet's Hyperscreens, Brim had resolved to remove himself from the love triangle that he knew he had created. . . .

Back aboard *Defiant*, Brim soon learned that more of Anak's support squadrons had sortied from various starports throughout the League, but his main fleets stubbornly remained in harbor at Tarrott. During the subsequent run to Haelic, it became amply clear that the Leaguers were busy marshaling every warship they could locate for the assault. Over its entire route, the convoy was troubled by only three attacks, and these were mere tokens of their former ferocity.

Interestingly enough, top secret situation reports posted in the COMM room additionally revealed that no benders had yet been observed in direct attacks against Imperial Fleet units. Yet the Leaguers by now were obviously finished with the bulk of their training operations. So far, five had attacked *Prize*—and she had methodically destroyed each of them in turn. Change was clearly in the wind, as an earlier generation of Helmsmen once put things. Brim knew in his bones that another phase of his life was rapidly drawing to a close.

*Defiant* was on final into Atalanta when the crew was informed that the base had been officially placed on ALERT-1 status. After this, circumstances began to evolve with mercuric suddenness. By the time Brim taxied to a gravity pool and secured his console, the ship had been transferred from COM-CONVOY to COMFLEETOPS and reassigned to the Task Group/16-Haelic that had been forming in zones H1 and K24-29 for the past two weeks. The move was not surprising. Along with Leaguer attacks, the convoys themselves were also beginning to wind down. Atalanta was now using its hard-won provisions to ready the hosts of Fleet units that had been arriving in a steady stream to swell the ranks of the defenders.

That afternoon, when Brim collected his mail, a note from Claudia explained that she had been summoned to chair a conference in the university city of Pelleas halfway around the planet and would not return for the next two days. "However," she wrote, "I shall need a lift home from the Civilian Terminal, gate 31A, Evening watch plus three. My ticket indicates coach 91. If you find yourself otherwise unoccupied, you can pick up the code key to my skimmer—parked in its usual place at Headquarters—from Rabelais Gastongay in my office. Don't worry if you can't make it—he will. Claudia."

Brim smiled wryly. He'd make it, all right. By that time, he figured he'd need her company badly. Especially after he accomplished his personal plans for the next Dawn watch. . . .

Early the next morning, with *Defiant* temporarily laid up for refitting, Brim grimly put his personal resolution into effect. In the Drive Room, he destroyed the few physical mementoes of his relationship with Margot, then carefully wrapped the ring she had given him in her stained handkerchief and mailed it by way of Borodov. Inside the package, he sealed a short note:

Dearest Margot,

Even though it grieves me more than words can express, I must cease my interference with your marriage and the happiness you might otherwise obtain were I absent from your life. I have hopes that, given proper encouragement, Rogan will one day become the loving husband you must have before your life is complete. After much reflection concerning our latest evening together, it is clear to me that my relationship with you has more potential for bringing pain than happiness. And happiness, after all, is what life is all about; I wish you a surfeit of both. Please know that I have loved you truly and well since the day we met.

> Maid of Av'lon! I am gone:
> Think of me, sweet! when alone.
> Though I range the Galaxy,
> Av'lon's where my heart shall be:
> Can I cease to love thee? No!

Eternally,

Wilf

For the next two days, everyone in *Defiant*'s crew participated in a personal inspection of the Atalanta Fleet Base by Star Admiral Sir Gregor Penda. Fundamentally, this consisted of polishing everything visible inside or outside the ship—including the ship itself—then waiting all day until the Admiral passed their gravity pool at high speed in his limousine. For Brim, it served as a welcome diversion, in a way. Sending the package to Margot was one of the most unpleasant episodes of his life—and he couldn't get her off his mind.

He joined the throng waiting at gate 31A in the Civilian

Terminal at plus 2.70 of the Evening watch—a few cycles before Claudia's passenger express thundered up from one of the long-distance tunnels, its bullet-shaped traction engine still glowing from the heat of its passage. Turning onto an amber track-tube siding, the serpentine chain of metal cylinders slowed, then floated smoothly to a stop alongside the platform. Brim found coach 91 third from the rear, and made his way through the noisy throng just in time to see Claudia descend the steps. Her face lit up as their eyes met; then she stepped to the platform and was swallowed up in the press of departing passengers.

Brim marveled as he pushed through the crowd. Claudia Valemont was so remarkably beautiful that each time she appeared in his life he had to reaccommodate himself to her loveliness all over again. Moments later, her quick public embrace and kiss left his lips moist with a promise of delights to come. Her sparkling brown eyes also said that she was glad to be with him for all the other considerations that encompassed a true—intimate—friendship.

As usual, they found whole Universes of provocative topics to chatter about while they toasted and dined in one of the Rocotzio Section's elegant little bistros. Then—a little tipsily—they retired to her hearth and couch to celebrate those deliciously carnal elements that perfected their relationship.

Early in the Dawn watch—long before Hador had begun to lighten the horizon—Brim found himself once again relaxed at the end of the couch, contemplating her radiance by the glow of embers in the fireplace. No royalty here: this was a beautiful, intelligent—fascinating—woman who made her honest way in the Universe by being excellent. Her long hair had become a tangled brown halo around the soft features of her face. She was partially covered by a light quilt, but her shoulders were bare and one exquisitely dark nipple peeked out from beneath the coverlet.

An ember snapped in the fireplace, and her eyes opened. She smiled sleepily at him for a long time in the stillness of the dimly lit room; then she frowned. "Wilf Brim," she said softly, "we aren't going about this very well, are we?"

"What do you mean?" Brim asked, raising an eyebrow.

She sighed. "What I mean is that I could think of very little else during the conference except tonight—and you. I'm afraid I could become *very* attached to you."

Brim rubbed her foot. "I think I'm already that way about you."

She shut her eyes for a moment. "Wilf," she said seriously, "come to your senses. I know that you are on the rebound. And frankly, if you care for this 'distant' lover of yours as much as I *think* you do, then it's my bet that she must once have loved you an awful lot in return—probably, she still does."

"It's all over between us," Brim said unemotionally.

She looked him in the eye. "I've been in love once or twice myself," she said with a wry smile, "and I know the truth about *that*. It takes a long time for love to really stop. Down deep, Wilf, I think you know it, too." Pushing aside the comforter, she sat up on the couch and crossed her legs on the cushions. "Let's suppose I *did* let myself go all the way in love with you," she said, "it would be very easy for me to do that right now—and then that distant lover of yours suddenly decided to leave her husband and return to your arms." She took both his hands and stared into his eyes. "You'd either leave me right then or—worse—you'd stick it out and learn to hate me." She raised an eyebrow. "Either way, I'd lose, right?"

Brim could only shrug. For all he knew, she might be correct.

"On the other hand," she continued, "what if—right out of the blue—*I* met somebody who simply swept me off my feet? And this great, hulking stud had the same feelings about me?" She chuckled and shook her head. "Wilf, dearest lover—let's the two of us enjoy what we have right *now*: great sex and a wonderful, wonderful friendship. It's more than most people get from the best marriages. And—what the hell—maybe someday we *will* get together. But for now. . ."

Brim smiled with relief. "For now?" he asked.

Claudia settled back against the pillows. "We've got a whole box of tissues we haven't used yet, Wilf Brim," she said, wiggling her bottom. "Let's get busy. . . ."

* * *

Three mornings later, Brim stood on *Defiant*'s sunlit bridge checking a number of retrofits that had been made to his Helmsman's console when Wellington came bustling up with Ursis in tow. "Wilf," she said, a great smile on her face, "that pretty friend of yours, Claudia Valemont, actually arranged a tour of the Gradygroat orbital forts! I got an invitation from Abbot Piety at the monastery just a metacycle ago. Regula Collingswood was with me when the messenger arrived—and said I should take Nik and you with me. Isn't that wonderful?"

Behind her, Ursis raised his eyes to the heavens and nodded his head in resignation. "'All snow melts when needed,'" he quoted stoically.

"Indeed," Brim said, looking at both with a grin. "Did the Captain indicate how we are supposed to get there?" he asked.

"Of course," Wellington said. "We're to take launch number four—the little one. She says that way she'll be sure we're back quickly if we're needed."

Brim nodded. "She's certainly thought of everything," he said.

"You bet!" Wellington gushed. "Come on, Wilf," she urged, "let's get going before somebody starts a major war around here and interferes with the really *important* work."

Brim met Ursis's laughing eyes. "I'll need about fifteen cycles to get ready," he said, grinning now in spite of himself. "Let me throw a clean battle suit in my softpack and . . . ah . . . call off a couple of engagements. I'll meet you on the boat deck. All right?"

"Fifteen cycles," Wellington said excitedly. "We'll be waiting, won't we, Nikolas?"

"Indeed," Ursis said impassively. "We shall *definitely* be waiting. . . ."

By the following morning, they had inspected eight of the thirteen orbital forts: enormous, massively armored contraptions—perhaps three or four times the size of a battleship—that looked like an egg embedded at the large end in a thick, disk-shaped structure perhaps half again its diameter. Four angular turrets were mounted equidistantly around the disk's rim, each equipped with a pair of colossal disruptors: striated and finned monsters nearly six hundred irals long that were more than twice *Defiant*'s entire length.

Inside the egg-shaped portion of each fort they discovered a scale model of the monastery stop City Mount Hill in Atalanta, each complete with a Power window at the apex of the ceiling and a floor with concentric Destruction and Resurrection rings surrounding a central cone of Truth. The only difference that Brim could see was that Hador itself provided the illuminating beam through the Power windows instead of the monastery's G-seed. He shook his head. The outrageous Gradygroats had even gone to all the trouble of building in automatic attitude controls so that the big forts were always aligned to that light. There had to be *something* in their teachings that was worth going to all that engineering. Smiling, he promised himself that if he could ever find the time, he would go back to the monastery library for serious study.

The disk structures—with their four great turrets and prodigious disruptors—were clearly the most fascinating elements to both Ursis and Wellington. After minute inspections of the firing rooms and the disruptors themselves, both had become convinced that the tremendous mechanisms were simple enough to be quite workable, and—insane as it seemed—perfectly maintained, at least according to the metal pages of huge maintenance compendiums the priests gave them to read.

The only factor that didn't make sense at all was the age-old issue of supplying adequate energy to fire such phenomenal artifacts. Toward the middle of their visit to the seventh fort, Ursis had used The Manuals to trace energy channels within one of the disruptors back from its discharge tube. Inexplicably, it seemed to end in a singularly angled breech fitting—perhaps six irals wide—that faced a darkened crystal window of the same size and angle in the floor of the turret. Both Wellington and Ursis immediately agreed that this must constitute the power input. But what kind of energy came through that window—and from what?

Unfortunately, beneath the turrets, the colossal disk structures were hollow for the most part—and virtually empty.

The vast expanse of wall directly beneath the chapel floor was nearly featureless, except where it was pierced by a large crystal lens. Whatever function the lens had once served was now apparently gone. It was covered on the chapel side by the Truth cone and, clearly, retained only a vestigial existence—like a similar device mounted at the center of the opposite wall. Aside from these artifacts, and the eight crystal windows opening into the rim turrets, there was little to see. As Brim tucked himself into the simple bunk provided by the Friars—a far cry from Claudia's couch!—he grinned. So far, the trip had been utterly fascinating—and utterly useless.

In the morning, at the ninth fort, they concentrated their efforts on the simulation rooms to see if they could pick up any clues from the theoretical operations. For two solid metacycles, the three Blue Capes watched Gradygroat gunners struggling with outlandish target environments—literally hundreds of simultaneous targets moving at wildly disparate speeds all the way from a few hundred c'lenyts per metacycle to just below LightSpeed. They got no clues to providing the disruptors with energy, but were at least rewarded with the Gradygroat's unique overall strategy. As the simulator room was subjected to "attacks," it soon became clear that none of the thirteen forts operated independently. Instead, each was a node in a closely linked network that relied on group fire-power—it explained why each great space fort was actually four independently targeted *sets* of cannon. Taken as an entire system, they formed a nearly impervious shield around Hae-lic, and the one clear invasion path to Avalon.

*If only the xaxtdamned Friars could fire them!* But then, that was at least part of the reason why Gradgroat-Norchelites had been sniggeringly referred to as "Gradygroats" all those years. They simply *couldn't*. . . .

Later, in the bustle of the last four forts—while Wellington searched for anything they might have missed—Ursis concentrated his studies in the chapels. "Would it not be bizarre," he commented to Brim, "if the answer were actually in their bewildering motto—virtually staring us in the face—and we lacked the insight to see it? 'In destruction is resurrection; the path of power leads through truth.'" He shook his great furry head in frustration. "I cannot comprehend. Voof!

'Chilled claws make welcome bedfellows with roaring fireplaces,' if you get my gist, Wilf."

Brim smiled. "Absolutely, Nik," he equivocated. "I think. . . ."

The three Blue Capes returned to *Defiant* late in the Afternoon watch of the same day with almost unshakable faith that the cannon *could* be fired, and probably had been fired at one time. But whatever mechanisms powered them during those long-gone days had been lost before time began, and it was doubtful if the huge batteries would ever again find any practical use.

That night, when Claudia picked him up after work, Brim could tell from her face that something serious had transpired while he was gone. "Want to tell me about it?" he asked while she piloted her little skimmer off into the evening.

"I guess I always *have* worn my emotions on my face," she sniffed as a tear rolled down her cheek. Abruptly, she pulled into an empty parking place and switched off the traction. "Hold me, Wilf," she said in a tight little voice. "Old *Prize* was lost yesterday, with all hands. I got word when I was leaving the office. . . ."

Brim completed her drive home.

In the early-morning darkness, they awakened to a special alert from Claudia's office: after many speeches and much fanfare, Triannic's Battle Fleet had finally sortied from the great League base at Tarrott—almost as if he wanted to announce his intentions to the Universe. The long-awaited attack was finally underway. . . .

# Chapter 9

# LEGACY

Hador was little more than a glow on the seaward horizon when Claudia brought her skimmer to a halt at *Defiant*'s gravity pool. Dressed in a one-piece jumpsuit with no makeup, she had been uncharacteristically quiet while she navigated the already busy streets. Now she peered at Brim's face as if there were something important she needed to say but couldn't find the words.

"Wish me luck," Brim enjoined quietly, taking her dainty hand and returning her gaze. "Before this one's over, I'll most likely need every scrap and shred I can get."

Claudia nodded and pursed her lips. "You know you have all my best wishes for that," she said with a frown. "But strangely enough, I don't have even the slightest doubt about your coming back—all in one piece, too." She shook her head. "What bothers me is *whom* you'll be coming back to. . . ."

Brim raised his eyebrows. "I don't understand," he said.

Claudia smiled a little. "Maybe I don't either," she said. "Kiss me now, Wilf; all things will be revealed with time."

Brim kissed her easily, holding her shoulders for a moment. Then he opened his eyes and continued to peer into her face. Something was going on in that gorgeous head, and he couldn't fathom what it was.

Without warning she embraced him fiercely, crushing her lips into his for a long, impassioned moment. When she finally released him, they were both a bit breathless. "There,

Lieutenant Brim," she whispered with a half-smile. "That may just have to tide us over some critical moments in our friendship. I wanted to make sure that you understand which direction *I'm* coming from, if I'm correct."

Brim raised an eyebrow.

Claudia smiled. "Call it a premonition," she said. Then she peered solemnly into his eyes. "I'll be waiting at the gravity pool when *Defiant* returns," she said, gripping his hand until it hurt. "Make sure that I'm right: that you're on her, and all in one piece. . . ."

"You'll not be rid of me so easily," Brim said, pressing the latch and stepping to the pavement.

"I shall count on that," Claudia said. She blew him a kiss. "Now we must both hurry." Her skimmer was moving the moment Brim closed her door, and was out of sight before he could stride halfway across the brow.

He arrived at *Defiant*'s main entry hatch just in time to catch Collingswood's summons to an emergency briefing in the wardroom. He rushed along the corridor, taking a seat only moments before she finished a chart on the forward marker board.

| Imperial | TYPE | League |
|---|---|---|
| 81 | DESTROYERS | 119 |
| 23 | LIGHT CRUISERS | 37 |
| 8 | HEAVY CRUISERS | 4 |
| 9 | BATTLECRUISERS | 12 |
| 24 | BATTLESHIPS | 36 |
| 4 | FAST BATTLESHIPS | 0 |
| 0 | &lt;classified&gt; | (est) 48 |
| 20 | MISC. SUPPORT | (est) 60 |
| 169 | Total Ships | 316 |

While the last few stragglers took their seats, Collingswood finished her mug of cvcesse', traded it to Grimsby for a full one, then motioned for the doors to be closed. "Well," she started, pointing to the board, "as if most of you haven't guessed, Kabul Anak's Attack Groups have finally embarked from Tarrott, and what you see here are his numbers relative to ours. Overall, the two lists are nearly meaningless—but certain details are worth some consideration." She pointed to the next-to-last entry. "Here's a good example: the Leaguers have forty more support ships than we have, a considerable delta for them—if statistics are your game. In reality, however, that's bad for them. Atalanta's really the only support 'ship' we need. Remember, Anak and his hoodlums are coming to us, so, all things being equal, those sixty support ships probably aren't enough—they're counting on the use of this base as much as we are." She stopped for a sip of cvcesse' and peered at her notes for a moment. "Now, if we forget those support ships," she continued, "the odds drop to 149 for us and 256 for them—still awfully one-sided for the Leaguers since now we're counting actual warships. But a closer look shows that eighty-six of that 107-ship delta is in destroyers and a classified type of ship called a 'bender' that many of you will see in a briefing for the first time this afternoon— once *Defiant* is secured. Both carry a certain sting, to be sure," she added with a smile, "but they don't in any way compare to the remaining classes—and in those, we're *much* closer to parity. For example," she said, pointing to "Light Cruisers," "they have only fourteen more than we do, and two of *ours* are Defiant-class—I.F.S. *Deadly*, our first sister ship, is due in momentarily." She waited while a rustle of excitement swept the room. "Since we all know that one Defiant is worth at least ten of any other class, that lowers the odds considerably." After these words, she was able to sip her cvcesse' for a significant interval.

When the cheering and whistling at last subsided, Collingswood proceeded to describe Anak's two major fleet components; both had sortied in the first metacycles of the Night watch. "Anak means business," she warned, "make no mistake about that. His primary cluster combines an Advance Attack Group under Rear Admiral Dargal Zark with a Main Group that he personally commands. The Advance Group alone is huge: forty destroyers, seventeen light cruisers, and eight battlecruisers. Add to that the Main Group, and you're looking at a real threat: twenty-nine destroyers, ten light cruisers, and twenty-seven battleships—including the three big ones they just launched: *Rengas*, *Parnas*, and *Nazir*. For those of you who haven't yet noticed," she warned, "we've got a *serious* fight on our hands. . . ." The mighty armada was scheduled to arrive in no more than seven days' time.

Anak's second attack component was Vice Admiral Liat-Modal's transport fleet—the Surface Occupation Group—that had spent the last twenty-eight days at a staging base on maneuvers. Although these vessels also sortied from their staging area in the early metacycles of the Night watch, they were not expected at Haelic until at least a day following Anak's initial attacks. "These transports," Collingswood continued, "are escorted by about fifty Gorn-Hoff and Castoldi destroyers, ten light Gantheisser cruisers, four ancient 200/300-class heavy cruisers, the five small battlecruisers of Anak's Third Scouting Group, and their Fourth Battle Squadron—nine old battleships in the *Lempat* and *Parang* classes. Not exactly the stiffest competition, but the transports are well protected nonetheless—and the way Nergol Triannic sees things, Liat-Modal won't need much protection by the time his ships come into play."

Facing this, Admiral Penda had organized his Atalantan defense force into three defensive squadrons. The first, Task Group 16 (TG 16)—under overall command of His Royal Highness, Prince Onrad—would depart almost immediately to travel at the best speed possible in an attempt to drive around Anak's flank and attack from the rear. This force had been selected from the swiftest ships available: thirty-six T- and K-class destroyers, a group of light cruisers including *Defiant* and *Deadly*, six of the newest and speediest battlecruisers under the flag of Rear Admiral (the Hon.) Zorn Hober, Vice Admiral Erat Plutron's four fast battleships, and the heavy disruptors of eight battleships commanded by Rear Admiral Le'o Argante. TG 16 was also ordered to intercept and engage Liat-Modal's transports on the way—if they could be located.

The second defensive squadron, Task Group 17, was Atalanta's main line of defense. It was scheduled to depart a day or so after Onrad to confront Anak's battle fleet head-on. This powerful armada comprised fifty-four destroyers, eighteen light cruisers, and fifteen of the Empire's newest battleships. Unfortunately, six of the latter were even now undergoing urgent repairs from recent—and severe—battle damage.

A third defensive force, Task Group 18 under the pennant of Vice Admiral Congor Folkrum, comprised Penda's last line of defense—his reserves, such as they were. The small armada combined eighteen powerful P-class destroyers with eight heavy cruisers and four old battleships—grizzled veterans of more than thirty years' duty each. These outmatched ships were to sortie as a last-ditch defense line—but everyone understood that unless Anak's forces had been significantly weakened by that time, the Task Group could have only limited effect before it was destroyed.

The briefing continued for nearly a metacycle more, providing details the crew would need for their departure during the second Night-watch metacycle. Collingswood saved one final announcement for the end. *She* had been named commander of Task Group 16's light cruisers, and *Defiant* would carry the designation COM/LC-16 under command of acting Captain Baxter Oglethorp Calhoun.

Brim grinned to himself as he made his way through the excited throng toward the bridge. No doubt about it, Carescrians were on their way up in the Fleet—at least one tiny segment of it, anyway. . . .

During the last few moments of Dusk watch, Brim relaxed at his glowing console while noises of imminent departure swept the bridge. Somewhere behind him, a Reynolds wavetuner muttered in its casing as it cycled frequencies. He could feel the steering gear running through its spherical pattern, and deep in the bowels of the ship a gentle pulsing indicated that Ursis had the gravity generators idling in preparation for takeoff.

Outside, rain spit occasionally from a low ceiling, but underneath the air was clear. Below *Defiant*'s bridge, mooring squads moved along the wet hullmetal securing dockside gear, pulling covers from the optical mooring system, and dogging down inspection hatches. On an adjoining gravity pool to port, I.F.S. *Deadly* moved restlessly to the shifting winds, her bridge Hyperscreens aglow like scowling, hooded eyes. Brim smiled in spite of the grim circumstances—the new cruiser certainly *looked* as if she were aptly named, at any rate. Far out to sea, the green light from a navigational buoy blinked in the darkness as it rode to the swells, and the old Gradygroat hymn abruptly surfaced from some recess of his mind:

> Oh Universal Force of Truth,
> That guards the homeland of our youth,
> That bidd'st the mighty cosmos keep
> Thine own appointed limits deep:
> > Oh hear us when we ask your grace
> > For those at peril far in space. . . .

Somehow, the venerable anthem seemed terribly appropriate. He wondered what the Gradygroat gunners might be thinking in their useless space forts. They'd certainly know that something was up on the surface. They could probably *see* it. . . .

At approximately Twilight watch plus three cycles, Onrad's Task Force 16 began to loose for space. By Night:0:50 all canals were cleared of traffic, and the high-speed Drive tender I.F.S. *Nimrod* got underway, standing out toward takeoff vector 91E in the harbor. Less than fifty cycles later, the last of the support ships—I.F.S. *Gregory Steele*—cast off from its gravity pool and nosed up the grand canal with a load of spare gravity generators. Next, while larger warships continued to test their navigational gear and generators, destroyer flotillas began to move along the canals toward the harbor, then thunder up from the bay every few moments in groups of four. The cruisers were scheduled to follow close on their tracks. As Brim made his last checks of *Defiant's* steering systems, a communications yeoman appeared beside his recliner. "Message for you," she said quietly.

He frowned. "Why didn't it come through my COMM window?" he asked.

"All the normal COMM links have been shut down for more than a metacycle, Lieutenant," she asserted. "*This* message came through the maintenance channels and—well," she laughed soundlessly, "I thought you might want this one delivered a little differently...." At that moment, alarms chimed on the bridge while Calhoun called all hands to stations for departure, and as quietly as she appeared, the woman was gone.

Maintenance channels? Puzzled, Brim hastily unfolded the small scrap of message plastic from its envelope, then suddenly grinned when it all came clear. "Good luck and universe speed you, lover," the note read in old-fashioned symbols. "Expect all equipment back in one gorgeous hunk. Claudia." Cheeks burning, he tucked the plastic into the arm pocket of his battle suit.

At approximately Night:2:40, Ursis cut generator number four onto the main energy bus; all mooring beams were shut off to the gravity pool; and Brim eased *Defiant* onto the canal, followed immediately by I.F.S. *Deadly*, and the four highspeed P-class cruisers *Perilous*, *Perdition*, *Perisher*, and *Poison*. Out on the open waters of Grand Harbor, the ships went immediately into Readiness Condition One. At Night:2:58, with the ruby eye of vector 91E centered in his Hyperscreens, Brim began his takeoff run, lifting from the water a few clicks afterward and standing out to space on course 6145H at maximum takeoff velocity. Only cycles later, he cleared the Northforty-five-J synchronous buoy while Ursis started the four DDB-19A7 Drive crystals, and within moments the LightSpeed indicator was on its way past 1.1—Haelic suddenly ebbing into the starry blackness astern as if it had never existed....

Within a metacycle, Onrad's six battlecruisers and five fast battleships were also reported spaceborne; by Night:4:19 the Prince, himself, with his eight battleships took departure as well, all ships setting course 6145H across the galaxy. These thirteen capital warships—with their ancient, traditionbound names—were the vital heart of Task Force 16. I.F.S. *Resolve*, Onrad's flagship, was the scarred victor of a dozen deadly jousts against Anak's power. She was followed by I.F.S. *Intractable*, I.F.S. *Spiteful*, and the just-commissioned I.F.S. *Ateb Credu*. A second division under Vice Admiral Jacob Sturdee comprised I.F.S. *Conqueror*, I.F.S. *Canodd*, I.F.S. *Morwir*, and I.F.S. *Thunderer*—the last had the largest number of high-amplitude disruptors and turrets in known space. Ahead of these cruised the four fast battleships of Vice Admiral Erat Plutron: I.F.S. *Queen Elidean*, I.F.S. *Ganriel*, I.F.S. *Daithom*, and I.F.S. *Barreg*. Many considered these the finest warships in the known universe: all had been designed with a nearly perfect balance of stout armor, powerful armament, and extremely high speed. They were considerably smaller than Kabul Anak's three massive Rengas-class battleships, but with proper leadership—in the person of the wily old Plutron—it was widely accepted that the powerful squadron would make more than a match for anything it might encounter. Anywhere.

In the van, Onrad's battlecruiser squadron pushed through space under the broad pennant of Vice Admiral Zorn Hober in I.F.S. *Benwell*. Astern *Greyffin IV*, *Princess Sherraine*, *Gwir Neithwr*, *Oedden*, and *Iaith Galad* followed in her wake. Three of the sleek battlecruisers were veterans of Anak's earliest raids. Many on board those ships still had deep grudges to settle.

Brim knew that Onrad needed to destroy as many of the Leaguer ships as possible—especially the Surface Occupation Group with its nearly one hundred thousand ground troops. As Collingswood had put it during her briefing, "We want to rid ourselves of this garbage out in space, not anywhere *near* an inhabited surface. . . ." However, Onrad was also painfully aware of the League's numerical superiority in ships—and Anak's secondary goal of destroying the Imperial Fleet. So it was his added responsibility to preserve every fighting ship he possibly could. The Prince's handling of the dilemma would prove his mettle as a future Emperor one way or another. And if he lost, he might as well not bother coming home.

Two days later, Brim dozed in a jump seat listening to KA'PPA reports of Task Force 17's departure—during what should have been Haelic's ancient Festival of Lights. This year, Atalanta had shelved tradition in hope of happier tomorrows and a more secure future, but he recalled illustrations from previous observances: children with colorful flags, speeches, festive bunting, parades. Today, the city's streets would echo to the mighty thunder of great warships lifting from the harbor. He wondered how Claudia was spending her time, then chuckled to himself. He knew how she'd spend at least part of it were *he* in town . . .

Four powerful star fleets—the accumulated might of Greyffin IV's galactic Empire and Nergol Triannic's League of Dark Stars—were blindly racing toward one another and a head-on collision with fate. With them traveled issues infinitely greater than the aggregate, weights of their hullmetal or manpower. Only one fleet could emerge victorious from their combat. Immediate objectives were defense—or invasion— of a small planet circling a third-class star. Secondary goals, however, would decide the fate of Avalon and a number of neighboring planets. And even these were small compared to the *real* issues hanging in the balance. The upcoming battles would ultimately decide the whole warp and woof of civilization—for generations to come. . . .

As Task Force 16 continued across the galaxy, its crews settled back into traditional, workaday routines. Every six metacycles, each ship conducted rigorous disruptor practice —and for lack of anything else to do, there were countless inspections of everything—including brasswork and silver-service polish. Aboard I.F.S. *Invincible*, Captain (the Hon.) Katherine Lorant convened a special mast and clapped two junior navigating officers in the brig for three days each, a woman for "unauthorized partial nudity on the bridge," and a man for "gross misuse of navigational tables."

The initial clash with Leaguer ships occurred on the fourth day out. At approximately Dawn:1:03 Atalanta standard time near BD*2/31:0, I.F.S. *Kracken*, a K-class destroyer on remote patrol, KA'PPAed sighting two benders at Red, Red-Orange and slightly to nadir, bearing Green, Green-Blue. A few cycles later, *Kracken* again KA'PPAed—this time to report that she was under attack. Thereafter, nothing more was heard until the reconnaissance craft called back with the words, SCRATCH TWO BENDERS. Following this, however, no further sightings occurred for nearly two more days.

At last, on the sixth day out, a destroyer on the far yellow wing of Task Group 16's van KA'PPAed three electrifying words: ENEMY IN SIGHT. Brim watched the words flash across his situation display at Morning:2:20. Moments later, the de-

stroyer flashed a second signal: TRANSPORT SQUADRON IDEN-
TIFICATION DEFINITE. SMALL BATTLE CRUISERS AT
YELLOW-YELLOW. BEARING GREEN, YELLOW-GREEN AT FIF-
TEEN THOUSAND LIGHTSPEED. DISTANCE 99188. MY POSITION
GV*21/-78:98. I AM ATTACKING WITH... The transmission ended
abruptly at Morning:2:23. After five more cycles, it was generally conceded that Liat-Modal had apparently drawn first
blood—but his small victory was nearly a cycle too late. Behind him, Brim could hear Collingswood wrapping up her
first report to Onrad that the game had been flushed.

"Well, my friends," she announced straightaway on the
bridge intercom, "it seems that Prince Onrad requires us to
have an early look at the Leaguers." She grinned. "Commander Calhoun, you may call the ship to action stations.
Wilf, bring us onto an intersecting course with those battlecruisers.

"Aye, Captain," Brim said. "Mr. Chairman, I shall need a
course alteration to GV*21/-78:98—updated by fifteen thousand LightSpeed at bearing green, yellow-green."

"A moment, Lieutenant," the voice of the Chairman said.
Presently, it returned with, "Updated course alteration will be
48.1 at −10 Nadir in thirty clicks, Lieutenant."

"Very well," Brim acknowledged. "Make to the other ships:
'Alter course in succession: 48.1 at minus 10 nadir.' Then
give me a countdown from five for the turn."

"Aye, Lieutenant," the Chairman intoned, "countdown
from five."

KA'PPA rings flashed out past the Hyperscreens as Brim
checked his controls. "Stand by to change course," he
warned.

"Five..." counted the Chairman, "four...three...two
...one...*now.*"

*Defiant* careened sharply to starboard as Brim turned onto
the new course. Whirling in his seat, he watched the other
ships follow, one after the other, in perfect formation. "We'll
need combat speed, soon, Nik," he warned Ursis's visage in a
nearby display.

The Sodeskayan nodded grimly, then turned to his control
panel and went to work. "Fusion rates for all Power Chambers
are now at maximum ratings, Wilf," he reported presently.

Brim nodded. Fresh shades of colors were already spilling across his power panel as *Defiant*'s eight big cascade accelerators pumped tremendous power into the waveguides. A thrill tingled along his spine. Was it the coming danger that excited him—or was it simply the majesty of a big warship powering up for combat? He shrugged. It was hard to tell the difference.

He switched his intraship to the odd-shaped sick bay where Flynn and his medical crew were hurriedly setting out instruments and dressings. Behind them, the two long rows of healing machines appeared to be empty—for the moment. He shuddered: he would be lucky indeed to avoid one of those slowly pulsing boxes himself in the next few metacycles, and he knew it. Far below in the scorching heat of "Drive Alley," he watched Gamble and Provodnik scurry among rows of gleaming feed tubes, shouting orders and encouragement to the hard-pressed power stokers, and checking readouts on the howling Admiralty N(112-B) power chambers that lined both sides of the Gallery. He shook his head; scenes like that made him doubly glad he was a Helmsman.

Inside the bridge, Grimsby was busy passing out high-energy snacks and hot cups of cvcesse'. "Ye'll need more than armor and disruptors to fight this battle, young Brim," Collingswood's elderly steward predicted as he passed the Helmsman's stations balancing a huge tray on one hand.

"I'll take your word for that, Mr. Grimsby," Brim answered grimly, grabbing a sandwich and a steaming cup. The cvcesse' seared his tongue, but blazed down his throat delectably. He grinned as he glanced at the right-hand seat, where Aram was fanning his mouth.

"Maybe we can make it that hot for brother Liat-Modal," the young A'zurnian quipped over the thunder of the Drive.

"We'll do our best, young man," Wellington piped in from Brim's left. "Believe me."

"Securing internal space-tight doors," Calhoun warned through the intercom.

Brim shuddered in spite of himself. If *Defiant* took significant damage in battle, that order could mean life for some—and certain death for others who might find themselves trapped in a melting portion of the ship or doomed to the hideous agony of runaway radiation.

Everywhere he focused the intraship, companionways and corridors were empty and still except for a few carelessly closed hatches swinging irregularly here and there as the ship worked. "*Defiant* is at action stations, Captain Calhoun," Barbousse reported behind him. "We've got all three N-ray searchlights sweepin' a forward cone around us."

"Very well," Calhoun said calmly. "Carry on, Chief."

Brim grinned. Calhoun spoke like a man who'd commanded a ship for years—as he probably *had* in his presalvage days.

Outside on the decks, Wellington's big disruptor turrets indexed through their arcs of fire as firing crews tested their mechanisms for the thousandth time. The long-barreled 155s gleamed dully in the light of the passing stars.

Abruptly, symbols for "The Captain" flashed across Brim's intraship followed by Collingswood's very serious face. "Good afternoon, Defiants," she began presently. "It seems that the tables are to be turned shortly. Within the metacycle, it is *we* who shall be the hunters—and the Leaguers will be faced with the task of defending slow, helpless transports." She frowned for a moment, then nodded to herself. "I am taking this opportunity to make each of you aware that we shall soon encounter what we believe to be a strong force of Leaguer warships escorting some thirty troop transports. If we're right, the transports belong to Admiral Liat-Modal, and they *must* be destroyed."

Brim visualized nearly five hundred fifty Blue Capes at monitors throughout the ship, hanging on her every word. Like most vessels of war, *Defiant* had few Hyperscreens away from the bridge area—most of her crew were blind to events outside the hull, reacting only to streams of orders from the eyes of the ship on the bridge. Collingswood's willingness to keep them informed was only one of the many reasons why many crews considered her the finest commander in the fleet.

"I don't need to tell you the critical importance of our next few metacycles," she continued, "or the risks we shall take during them. Numerically, the odds are in our favor, at least for this particular battle. However, since *we* are going in first, we shall face the bulk of their defenses alone—at least until the more powerful warships catch up. But we've got a good turn of speed, and we're an experienced crew. That's probably enough to see us through—so long as each of us does his and her duty for the Empire. That's no small order, especially with the odds we shall face in the next few cycles, but it's all anyone will ask from you—Prince Onrad, Admiral Penda, Greyffin IV, and myself included." She paused and closed her eyes for a moment, then pursed her lips. "That's about it," she said. "Good luck to each of you. And may the Universe watch over us and our ship." The display faded and returned to its previous view. Brim turned in his seat and watched Collingswood settle back in her recliner, clearly drained of emotion.

"Good words, Regula," Calhoun said quietly. "Not easy, those.. . . . "

"We're picking up something at the extreme range of our directors," Wellington announced tensely a few moments later. "From the size and the bearing, I'll guess it's our first contingent from the League."

Brim pegged her report at precisely Brightness:1:03. Not long afterward, he spotted the ships himself through the Hyperscreens, a constant pattern of long, green Drive plumes standing out in cold relief from the random starry background.

"Bloody good o' the misbegotten zukeeds to stumble in at all!" a wag exclaimed from the rear of the bridge. "Be just like 'em to say they're comin' an' then fail to show."

Brim chuckled as he slowed *Defiant*'s headlong flight—Collingswood's job was to report on the enemy fleet after all, not to race it home.

"By the very Universe," Wellington commented as they drew steadily closer. "They haven't even formed their transports into wheels!"

"You're . . . right," Calhoun declared as *Defiant* began to pull abreast of the rearmost Leaguer ships. "Liat-Modal must be suffering from mental saddle sores."

"Perhaps not," Calhoun warned quietly while Collingswood made her report to Onrad in the background. "Those are slow ships over there, noo," he said, indicating the transports off to starboard, "an' a perfect opportunity for the Leaguers to use their benders. We may e'en now find ourselves lookin' down the bore of a hidden torpedo tube."

"Aye, Cal," Wellington acknowledged, busying herself at

the COMM sectors of her console. "I've got extra lookouts everywhere," she asserted presently, "especially below in the ventral observation stations."

"Well done, Dora," Calhoun responded with a grin.

Off to starboard, a number of Drive plumes were now arcing away from the convoy toward them. NF-110s, Brim guessed from the throbbing shade of green.

"Stand by to engage," Calhoun warned in an eager voice.

Brim stole a glance aft at *Defiant*'s great wide Drive plume curving gracefully away into the distance. She could match speed and firepower with any NF-110 *or* Gorn-Hoff. For a moment, he thought of Collingswood's remarks and wondered how the Leaguers felt now that *they* were on the defensive end of things.

"All crews, energize your disruptors."

"What do you reckon they'll do with those battleships?" Aram asked, nodding through the forward Hyperscreens toward the huge outlines of capital ships now clearly discernible against the Drive plumes of the transports. Their ponderous main batteries were still parked in the fore-and-aft positions.

*Defiant* bumped around a space hole, and Brim found himself busy with the controls for a moment. Then he frowned, watching the forward turret index off toward the incoming escorts. "My guess is that the big boys are watching Onrad's battlecruisers coming in from astern," he said presently. "They'll expect the Gorn-Hoffs to take care of smaller fish like ourselves and the destroyers." He grinned and glanced across at the young A'zurnian. "At least, that's what I *hope* they'll do," he added with a chuckle. "Those rustbuckets may be old, but they do have *big* disruptors!"

"Light cruisers: take independent action against escorts," Brim heard Collingswood order. "That frees *Defiant*, too, Cal," she added. "I'm finished with my reporting."

"Did you hear that, young Brim?" Calhoun asked.

"Aye, sir," Brim answered, "independent action." With that, he eased *Defiant*'s helm to port apex and skewed course toward the approaching escorts.

Suddenly, a tense voice shouted from his situation display. "Look out! Torpedoes—bearing yellow!"

Brim put the helm hard over and shoved *Defiant*'s nose to

nadir just as a spread of three torpedoes flashed overhead, missing the bridge by no more than thirty irals before they disappeared off to starboard. "Where in thraggling xaxt?..." he started, but he was cut off by a second warning, shouted this time from directly behind him on the bridge.

"Bender at Purple plus ten!"

Brim spotted the ugly little ship at the same time, closing in slowly from port. Evidently, she had just now entered *Defiant*'s N-ray coverage zone. In the background, he could hear the calm voices of Wellington's disruptor crews calling out a litany of bearings. Even as they spoke, the single forward 152 indexed around, dipped, then slowly elevated and steadied. A cycle later, it hurled out a stunning bolt of green brilliance that shattered the darkness and blanked the stars themselves, jerking the deck and filling him with a wild exultation.

"Great Universe!" someone gasped. Wellington's crew had scored a direct hit with a single shot. Instantly, the bender disappeared in a shattering burst of wild flame and energy, literally dissolving from 'midships outward until she was totally engulfed in a bright, roiling puffball that altogether consumed itself in a few cycles—except for two sparkling comets that receded quickly into the distance: the heavy structures of her power chambers.

Brim glanced down at his hands. Surprisingly, they weren't even shaking.

"Bearing Blue and up 200," one of the disruptor chiefs ordered, "distance 4100...." The forward disruptor indexed back to starboard and began to line up on the incoming escorts. "Shoot!" This time, it fired in concert with the main batteries aft for a full salvo. The bridge deck kicked violently under Brim's feet and cvcesse' containers rattled from consoles all over the bridge. When the clouds of sparkling radiation dissipated outside, Brim altered course a little to make the shooting easier, then cleared space around him. Nothing. At least nothing he could *see*....

*Defiant* thudded past the well of another space hole, then steadied again on course.

"Shoot!"

Brim swiveled to visually clear the space around them.

"Hey, look!" a woman's voice squealed. "We hit another one of the bastards! Good show, Dora!"

"That'll do for 'im!"

"Yeah. Good shooting, Dora!"

Brim glanced over at the ravaged Gorn-Hoff, afire in three places 'midships and beginning to fall off to starboard nadir, clearly out of control. The curved armor coating over her deckhouse had been peeled back like a cheap food container exposing most of the ship's interior to space. He could almost *feel* the enemy Helmsman's desperation as one by one his controls failed.

"That fixed the bloody zukeed!" someone shouted exuberantly. The enemy ship continued steadily on a straight course for a few more cycles, then began to roll to the right until its decks were nearly vertical to *Defiant*'s. Suddenly, its back broke in a cloud of sparks and debris; moments later, the blasted wreck separated into two fragments and fell rapidly away aft.

"Benders again, for the love of Voot—LOOK OUT!" someone else yelled out in a voice shrill from stark terror.

Brim whirled in his seat in time to spy two of the ugly little ships as they slipped inside N-ray range. His eyes focused only clicks before *Defiant*'s bridge jumped violently with incredible concussion and noise. Gravity pulsed from a massive energy release, throwing him violently against his restraining harness. At the same instant, the aft Hyperscreens shattered and cabin pressure dropped with the force of a powerful explosion. Suddenly, a white-hot hullmetal splinter whirled through the back of his seat and melted a large area in the upper arm of his battle suit. Caught off guard, he bellowed in pain as the shard burned through his flesh, then smashed against an instrument panel in a shower of sparks and fell smoking to the deck at his feet. For a moment, he caught sight of blood streaming from the blackened, smoking rip in his suit. Then his battle suit sealed itself—and his arm—in a second avalanche of pain and torment. Grinding his teeth, he forced himself to focus on the controls again. Somebody was screaming in the background—more like a wild animal than anything else. He forced that from his mind as he struggled with the controls.

"Damage Control . . ." he heard Calhoun demand, "report!"

"Disruptor hit just abaft the bridge," someone answered above a cacophony of pleas for medical teams on the voice circuits—and the wild-animal screaming that continued as an insane background. "Radiation fires in electrical compartments five and sixteen. Companionway nineteen from COMM house blocked. . . ."

*Defiant*'s 155s lashed out twice as she passed the bender—both times they missed by a c'lenyt. Grimly, Brim banked around to close the range, but the little ship was more maneuverable, easily turning inside him and out of N-ray range. He was still trying to ignore the screaming when it stopped abruptly, abandoning the voice band to absolute silence for a few moments until the confusion began again. In the next moments, he checked on Aram—who was clearly unscathed—then glanced around the bridge. Aft, everything was covered by glittering Hyperscreen shards. The whole rear of the bridge was now open to space and a confused Hyperlight starscape beyond. Loose equipment rolled free in the aisles, and two massive canopy supports had smashed across a number of consoles. Here and there, stretcher bearers and damage-control teams picked their way through the glowing wreckage. Yet *Defiant*'s controls appeared to be unaffected—and no change registered on her LightSpeed meters. He switched his intraship display to Ursis.

The Bear looked up grimly, then nodded and touched his forefinger to his thumb in the universal sign of satisfaction.

"Casualty report!" Calhoun ordered behind him.

"One moment, Commander," a voice answered. Then presently: "Fifteen starmen trapped in COMM compartment seventeen and destroyed by radiation . . ."

Brim shuddered at the thought of the trapped men dying by inches in the most excruciating pain known in the galaxy. He gritted his teeth as the report went on.

". . . One officer located under wreckage in companionway nineteen—moved to sick bay, all countermeasures personnel on bridge duty killed by flying Hyperscreen shards . . ."

Brim forced his mind from the horrible disclosures, visually cleared space again—for whatever little *that* seemed to be worth anymore—then looked up as Collingswood tapped him on the shoulder and pointed out through the Hyperscreens.

"Dora, Wilf," she exclaimed breathlessly, "look—the Leaguer battlecruisers are moving out wide. They're getting ready for Onrad and leaving the old battleships to protect the transports. Now's the chance for a torpedo run!"

Brim understood immediately. With *Defiant*'s tremendous speed, they could be in and out of the formation before the lumbering old warships could fly into range. Liat-Modal had committed a disastrous mistake—one the Imperials had learned to avoid by their own costly process of trial and error. "Aye, Captain," he responded, completely forgetting the dull throbbing in his arm as he eased the helm over to starboard nadir.

"Chief Barbousse!" Wellington ordered over the intraship. "We'll have the torpedoes, if you please."

"Aye, Commander," Barbousse's voice answered from Wellington's console. "All tubes are loaded and primed."

Wellington glanced over at Brim and pointed into the Leaguer formation. "I'm going after *that* one, Wilf," she said, "the transport second from port in the top echelon—I think it's the biggest. We've got it locked in on the directors."

"I see it, Dora," Brim said grimly, skidding the ship slightly to provide a better angle of fire. She'd picked the biggest one, all right, but one of the old battleships was still cruising nearby, her massive turrets even now swinging *Defiant*'s way. The disruptors looked to be at least ten c'lenyts in length! He shuddered, but held his course. Ahead and to starboard, the transport was growing steadily in the Hyperscreens, but at best Barbousse faced a terrible deflection shot.

"We'll use a spread of all four torpedoes, Chief," Wellington ordered.

"Aye, Commander," Barbousse's voice answered tensely from Wellington's console. "Spread of four." Then the big rating's visage appeared on Brim's intraship. "Steady, sir," he said.

"Steady..." Brim started to answer, but he was interrupted by a tremendous explosion outside as the old battleship fired off a ranging salvo at them. It missed, but the energy concussion nearly knocked *Defiant* on her beam ends. Loose equipment and debris cascaded along the deck again while startled crew members stifled screams on the voice circuits. No sooner had Brim fought the cruiser back on an even keel than the battleship's old K-149A disruptors began glowing as they built up their next charge. Grinding his teeth, Brim steered closer to the transport. It would be hard for the battleship to fire without risking damage to its ward. "How're you doing, Chief?" he asked.

"We're awfully close, Lieutenant," Barbousse answered through clenched teeth. "I can't miss at this distance, but you'll have to get out of here fast when I let 'em go, or we'll get caught in our own blast."

"I'm ready," Brim said tightly. "Let 'em go."

"Aye, sir," Barbousse said. Presently four torpedoes streaked past the starboard Hyperscreens, hurtling toward the transport from point-blank range.

"Nik!" Brim bellowed, "lemme have full EVERYTHING!"

"Full everything coming up, Wyilf!" Ursis said in an excited voice. "Now!"

A split instant later, all four torpedoes hit the speeding transport in a tightly spaced pattern just abaft the bridge. In the scant clicks Brim could watch, the big starship's hull erupted first in a glowing pulse of flame and debris that was rapidly followed by a huge, expanding puffball of atmospheric vapor as the hull ruptured, then split lengthwise like some gigantic rotten fruit. Brim squeezed his eyes shut for a moment—he'd never seen ten thousand beings perish before—at least not all at one time. He felt the gorge rise in his throat.

"Voot's beard, you two!" Wellington exclaimed happily over the thunder of the straining Drive crystals, "nobody told me you two practiced using cannon. Where'd you get the powder?"

"Thought *you'd* brought it aboard!" Brim bellowed as he headed straight for the rear deckhouse of the battleship. The aft turrets were indexing around at him, but not nearly fast enough to track his speeding cruiser. Suddenly, he had an idea. "Chief!" he exclaimed through the intraship, "you got a couple of space mines on the tracks back there?" In the display, he watched Barbousse glance down at his consoles.

"Four, Lieutenant," the big rating answered. "Like the regulations say." He touched a bank of sensors. "They're armed now. . . ."

"Let 'em *all* go on my count of three," Brim said through clenched teeth. "One . . ." The angular battleship was huge in *Defiant*'s Hyperscreens now—and so were the disruptors as they continued to index. "Two . . ." He clenched his teeth and headed for a point only a few irals from the top of the battleship's bridge. "Three!" A milli-instant later, the massive stern and huge aft turrets passed under *Defiant*'s sharp bow, and in a trice he cleared the bridge, hauling the controls back into an almost vertical climb away from the battleship's deck. Almost spasmodically, the forward turrets erupted in full salvos, but the great energy beams passed far beneath *Defiant*'s soaring hull. Then a great pulsing glare flooded the bridge from aft as the powerful space mines exploded—with no Hyperscreens to filter the blinding flash. Brim swiveled in his seat in time to watch the massive old ship swerve sharply off course, her entire stern a mass of seething radiation flame. An instant later, she was rammed by a transport coming up at full speed from aft. The latter scraped along the massive armored flank of the battleship in a bright shower of sparks, then rose up at the bow as if in pain as the battleship slid beneath its hull in a secondary discharge of flame and shimmering ice crystals.

Brim had just turned back to his controls when *Defiant* seemed to stop in midspace as if she had struck some preposterously invisible wall. The bridge lurched violently upward, and he was again thrown against his restraining harness so brutally that his neck nearly snapped. Whole consoles broke loose in the absense of cabin gravity, smashing through the side Hyperscreens in cascades of flying debris. A bright glow pulsed from beneath the hull, then died suddenly—along with the thunder of the Drive. Without Alpern or his crew to man the countermeasures gear, they'd been torpedoed themselves. He knew it! Abruptly, the big ship rolled on her side and veered off to nadir—only moments before a second swarm of torpedoes blazed overhead. They'd never had time to launch a decoy pseudopod.

"We've lost E turret!" Wellington exclaimed over the intraship.

"Both crystals are fractured, Wilf!" Ursis roared a moment later. "And something terrible's happened in the Drive chamber."

Suddenly, Provodnik's helmeted face appeared in the intraship. Behind him, the Drive chamber was a blazing arena of destruction. Bodies lay everywhere, and great bolts of energy probed here and there through the thick smoke from fractures in the feed tubes. The young Bear's eyes were opened wide, almost as if he couldn't believe what had happened. He slowly dropped his jaw as if he wanted to speak; instead, he vomited a crimson spray of blood against the faceplate of his helmet. When this cleared, his eyes had turned up in his head, and he soon slid from the intraship's view.

Brim almost threw up himself as the remainder of the transport fleet boiled around the cruiser's faltering path. One big vessel passed so close she scraped her KA'PPA tower along *Defiant*'s keel plates, filling the hull with an ear-splitting, clanging rasp and shaking the bridge so violently that Brim momentarily lost his touch on the helm. Before he could recover, *Defiant* veered off to starboard, narrowly missing another transport—but inadvertently saving herself from an onrushing battleship whose field of fire was suddenly obscured. Biting his lip, Brim hauled the ship over into a tight bank and charged around into the very teeth of the convoy— which immediately disappeared in streaks of shimmering light as they swarmed past at double *Defiant*'s present speed.

And suddenly there were no more Leaguers. It was only Brightness:1:43, forty cycles to the click since Wellington's first sighting—and they were out of the war! In the few cycles since his first reversing turn, the Leaguers had once more become a distant pattern of bright sparks against the starry blackness. Aft through the shattered Hyperscreen frames, he could now see the ghostly, HyperSpeed images of Onrad's task force bearing down at high velocity with Admiral Plutron's quartet of fast battleships in the van. Liat-Modal was about to lose much of his fleet—and a hundred thousand Leaguer troops had just been placed under an irrevocable death sentence.

"KA'PPA signal from Admiral Plutron in *Queen Elidean* to you personally," a COMM rating announced to Collingswood, her voice muffled by the emergency battle circuits. "I thought perhaps you might want it delivered by hand."

"Thank you," Collingswood answered—as if she expected the message. Presently, Brim heard her chuckle. "Return this to the Admiral, please," she ordered. "'Eyebrows somewhat singed, but essential parts intact. Will demonstrate in port.' I believe that will do for an answer."

"Aye, Captain. . . ."

In the background, Brim could hear a struggling rescue officer. "Over here, lads," she puffed. "Lively now—there's two blokes trapped under this lot of rubbish."

Brim swiveled his seat while *Queen Elidian* blazed majestically past, followed closely by *Ganriel*, *Daithom*, and *Barreg*. Aft, in the hardest-hit portion of the bridge, rescue teams were chopping away with laser axes at the twisted remains of a heavy overhead Hyperscreen support. Beneath, half buried in blood-soaked debris, two obscene chunks of flesh protruded from a flame-blackened battle suit. He shivered in spite of himself as the horrible spectacle was obscured by two ratings carrying a dripping, blood-drenched stretcher piled with the remains of three shattered bodies—not one of them was more than two-thirds complete. He turned back to his console and waited for the damage report while he shook his head. The horror remained fixed in his mind's eye. War could be romantic only to those who had never experienced the realities of combat.

Suddenly, Ursis's brooding visage appeared in his intraship; behind him, the ruins of the Drive chamber continued to spark and flicker in scintillating clouds of free ions. Brim glanced over to the Bear's duty station on the bridge. It was now filled by the clearly human form of Gamble. He nodded to himself. Provodnik's loss would be appalling to his Sodeskayan friend. Bears tended to stick together. "Except for loss of lives here, Wilf Ansor," the Bear reported, "things are not so bad as they look." He motioned with a bloodstained arm to animated groups of ratings swarming over the feed tubes with bubbling dispensers of radiation sealant. "*Defiant* is probably finished with battle now, but we should be able to maintain almost half speed within the metacycle—and that will get us home."

"What about Provodnik?" Brim asked gently, but he already knew the answer.

Ursis raised his eyes and bit his lip. "My countryman Provodnik has departed to join his eternal ancestors," he said in a melancholy voice. Then he shrugged phlegmatically. "One always expects that the cost of war will be exorbitant, Wyilf Ansor—and one is seldom disappointed."

During the next metacycle, Prince Onrad himself ordered *Defiant* to set course back to Atalanta. WORST CASE, REGULA, he KA'PPAed just before his attack, WE SHALL NEED YOUR DISRUPTORS WHEN YOU ARRIVE—OTHERWISE WE SHALL NEED YOUR HELP CELEBRATING. Shortly after that, at Brightness:2:71 by Brim's watch, a series of tremendous flashes pulsed among the stars ahead, rapidly increasing in frequency and number until the entire starscape was blanked by a violent—constant—strobing that was punctuated here and there by glittering blossoms of pure color that marked a hit on some unlucky starship.

As the heavy firing continued—receding farther and farther into the distance ahead—incoming KA'PPA reports served as clear indication that Onrad was successfully pressing home his attack and the Imperials were winning the day.

In due time, *Defiant*'s lookouts began to point out clumps of debris and glowing, burned-out wrecks along their path. Most were the remains of transports—still coasting along their last controlled flight path on momentum alone as they inexorably decelerated toward LightSpeed. Some were surrounded by pitiful clouds of glimmering lifeglobes, but many had none. Brim supposed it mattered very little either way. By the time League salvage vessels could fly to the rescue, the 'globes would long ago have exhausted their life-support systems. One of the hulks they passed at close range was surrounded by no more than five 'globes, but appeared to be covered by thousands of tiny insects—each the shape of a human being—Collingswood's space garbage. . . .

Among the Leaguer warships they passed, most were Garn-Hoff attack cruisers and a few NF-110s. Those that could still move under their own power occasionally fired off a salvo or two, but most of these were efficiently dealt with by Wellington and *Defiant*'s intact complement of 155s. The only benders they encountered were also total wrecks. Messages beamed back from Onrad indicated that the fragile starships were relatively helpless in major fleet actions when they could be spotted before they fired their torpedoes. Collingswood and Calhoun gave wide berth to the three disabled Leaguer battleships they passed—one was the group flagship, *Lempat*, veteran of nearly all the war's early engagements. Colossal radiation fires were burning at three points along her corpulent hull, and she was clearly coasting down toward LightSpeed. Nothing remained of her massive tower bridge save a burnedout stump that emerged from the blackened skeleton of a forward deckhouse. If Liat-Modal had been anywhere near his duty station when that blow came, he had been reduced to atomic particles along with most of his staff.

Now and again, they slowed to pick up survivors of Imperial warships who had taken to their 'globes, but they bypassed those that—like themselves—were still underway or had deployed no 'globes for one reason or another. Support ships like *Nimrod* and *Steele* would eventually take care of them, along with their crews.

By Brightness:3:77, the flashes—now far in the distance ahead—began to peter out, and during the next metacycle subsided completely. From the stream of KA'PPA traffic recorded in the COMM station, Brim learned that the last of the transports had been destroyed—nearly forty cycles after the last Leaguer defenders fled from their charges at top speed. At Evening:00:05, Onrad himself KA'PPAed, ALL TASK FORCE 17 SHIPS RETURN TO CRUISING STATIONS NOW, then he set a diagonal course that would eventually bring his task force into contact with Penda's Task Force 16—if neither had spotted Anak's main battle groups first. Clearly, the opening stage of the battle had been resolved by the Imperials. When the next stage would come, however, was anybody's guess. . . .

It began a lot sooner than anyone suspected. During the very next watch, at Evening:1:10, reconnaissance scouts from Task Group 17 finally located Anak's battlecruiser fleet at long range. Both scouts were eventually destroyed, but not before they broadcast significant position information concerning the invasion fleet. Miraculously, Penda had placed his fleet directly in Anak's path. The Leaguer Admiral was now without the veil of secrecy that had protected him up until then. Onrad issued immediate orders setting Task Group 16 onto a converging course, but it was clear from the beginning that he could never hope to cover such a distance in time to coordinate his efforts with Admiral Penda's attack. Task Force 17 would have to go it alone. . . .

With the Drive stabilized at just below half speed and a course set directly for Atalanta, little remained for *Defiant*'s crew except to wait fretfully for battle reports on the KA'PPA. They had already made their contribution to the battle; their fate would now be settled by others—at a distance.

Brim was in the wardroom during Night watch, huddled around a KA'PPA display with Ursis and most of the other off-duty officers when the critical message arrived from Penda's forward scouts: ENEMY IN SIGHT. WE ARE ATTACKING.

"Voof," the Bear said imperturbably between puffs of his Zempa pipe, "now it continues, eh?"

"Continues and ends, perhaps," Wellington offered.

"Ends?" Ursis laughed grimly, looking the gunnery officer in her face. "You are a student of history, Dora. Have you uncovered a time when there was no war anywhere among the civilized domains?" He blew a long puff of Hogge'poa toward the ceiling. "So long as the old are willing to send their young off to kill and die for them, there will be war."

"One always hopes that things will change for the better, Nik," Wellington said, staring into her goblet of meem.

"Indeed, one always hopes," Ursis sighed wistfully. "Unfortunately, one is usually disappointed." Just then a series of messages began to flash across the KA'PPA display. . . .

In the opening clashes, Penda's Imperial ships appeared to give good account of themselves, inflicting grievous damage on the invading fleet, in spite of the tremendous firepower of Anak's new super battleships. During the first turbulent moments alone, thirteen of the League's seventeen light cruisers were destroyed by accurate fire from their Imperial peers. And six of Anak's eight powerful battlecruisers were annihilated by the Empire's crack 1st Battle Squadron—quickly proving the folly of too much armor sacrificed for maneuverability. Throughout this phase of the battle, the benders proved to be little more than an annoyance, although at least two Imperial destroyers and a light cruiser were lost to their torpedoes. Nevertheless, during the metacycles that followed, the Leaguers' overwhelming numerical superiority made its presence felt, and the tide inexorably began to change against the outnumbered Imperials.

One by one, foreboding messages began to arrive at *Defiant*'s communications center, each with grimmer news than the last. In a single blow, the three old battlecruisers under Vice Admiral Theobald Corinth, *Dilaf*, *Llongwr*, and *Ennil*, were destroyed with no survivors. Grizzled old Corinth had exacted a high price for his ships, however: he'd taken the League's giant new battleship *Nazir* with him, along with the Second-Division flagship *Karmat* and three heavy cruisers. Not long afterward, proud *Ganeth*, scarred veteran of a dozen clashes with the forces of Nergol Triannic blew up with all hands, after devastating Anak's giant *Parnas* and crippling two of her escorts, the First Squadron battleships *Samrad* and *Posen*. Then in quick succession, *Vanguard* and *Calid Isel* withdrew from the battle with severe hull and Drive damage after disabling or destroying six of the nine battleships from Anak's Second Squadron. Within the megacycle, *Triumph* and *Superb* were also put out of action after wreaking havoc in Anak's Third Squadron, and it was soon clear that only a miracle could save the day for the Imperials.

In *Defiant*'s wardroom, the news was received at first with tears of sorrow, then with utter horror. Nergol Triannic's invading armies may well have been destroyed in the early phases of the battle—along with all his plans of occupation. But in the absence of effective opposition by Imperial ships, his powerful fleets would soon be able to utterly destroy the base at Atalanta. "And from there," as Aram put it, studying a map of galactic approaches, "Avalon will be an easy step, indeed."

Brim visualized the coming terror that would soon be unleashed over the streets of the ancient city. He ground his teeth helplessly, thinking of the brightly dressed natives—especially Claudia. They'd all suffered enough of Triannic's evil already—and the worst was clearly to come. . . .

News of *Dinas Pont*'s near destruction and the critical wounding of Admiral Witan Penda brought tears to many eyes—including Brim's. He had been recording a rough tally on his napkin during the preceding metacycles. According to his figures, Rear Admiral Klaus Fischer—who had taken temporary command when Penda was wounded—faced sixteen capital ships with only two surviving battleships, *Invincible* and *Sterling*. The latter were powerful warships, to be sure, but in her combat, even the mighty *Dinas Pont* had been able to destroy only four enemy battleships before she was overwhelmed by sheer numbers. By Morning:3:30 Atalanta time, Task Force 17 had been reduced to hit-and-run raids against Anak's still-powerful fleet as it sped on its way toward Atalanta, now only a single day's travel in the distance.

At Morning:3:61, Folkrum Congor and Task Force 18 sortied from Atalanta on direct orders from the Admiralty. Approximately 12 metacycles later, they joined the remnants of Task Force 17 in a last desperate attempt to stop Anak's fleet. As predicted, the old ships were no more than a foolish sop to Admiralty pride. The leaguers swept past Congor's battleships as if they had no existence. Fortunately, Congor himself was nobody's fool, and after making what appeared to be a last-ditch stand, he quickly withdrew his ships and then joined with the remnants of Task Force 17 to harass the enemy's flanks until Onrad's powerful reinforcements could arrive.

The next morning, with Prince Onrad still nearly a day distant, Atalanta reported its first attacks by Leaguer capital ships. From this first dispatch, it was obvious that Admiral Anak intended to inflict maximum punishment for the part the city and its base had played in building up the Imperial fleet. Brim was at *Defiant*'s controls when he read the first KA'PPAed message, and he felt himself tense at the grisly descriptions.

Clearly, he was not the only one on the *Defiant*'s airless bridge who was reading the messages that morning.

"Great Universe," Collingswood swore in an unhappy whisper, her voice muffled inside her battle helmet. "Such horrible destruction and suffering—I feel so powerless." She shook her head despondently.

"Indeed," Ursis answered. "One wishes he could do something—anything—to help."

"Speaking of 'powerless,'" Wellington grumped, "I surely hope our dim-witted friends the Gradygroat gunners are enjoying themselves this morning in their xaxtdamned useless space forts." She laughed grimly. "I guess they probably never *will* figure out how to get power through truth. . . ."

"GREAT *THUNDERING* UNIVERSE, Dora!" Ursis's bass voice erupted over the voice circuits. "That's *IT!*"

"What's 'it,' Nik?" Brim asked, tearing his eyes from another dismal message passing through his display.

"'Power through truth,'" Ursis repeated in an urgent voice. "I know how the ancient Gradygroats powered their space cannon."

"You *what*?" Wellington gasped.

"I understand the old Gradygroat space cannon," Ursis reiterated. "The secret's been right in front of us all along. We simply never looked at what lay directly beneath our noses. Their motto! Think of the second line first: 'The path of power lies through truth.' It's the key to everything."

"A key to *you*, maybe," Wellington stated flatly. "It's still gibberish to *me*."

"Visualize the main floor of the monastery," Ursis said, ignoring her sarcasm. "That gold cone of Truth that reflects the energy beam from the G-seed. If somebody removed it from the center of the floor, what would happen?"

"I . . . I think I remember *you* claiming something crazy like lifting the whole monastery into space at escape velocity, or something." Brim interjected.

"It's *exactly* what I said, Wilf," Ursis said evenly. "Take that reflecting cone away and the energy from the Kaptnor G-seed would flow directly from the Power lens into the floor. It would lift the monastery. I know it."

"But *then* what?" Wellington interjected. "How does that get power to the old space cannon?"

"Patience, Dora, my friend," Ursis said excitedly. "That is the one part of which I have no proof. But do any of you remember the egg-shaped chapels built into each of the space forts—and how each of them is always oriented toward Hador?"

Brim nodded. "Yeah," he said with a grin. "I can still remember thinking that if the Gradygroats went to all that trouble, there *had* to be something worthwhile about their teachings. I actually thought of going back to the library someday to read about them. And maybe I still will—provided the xaxtdamned Leaguers don't blow it up first."

"If I am correct, Wyilf Ansor," Ursis declared, "you probably will never get the chance." He held up a slender finger. "That is where the first line of the Gradygroat motto comes into play: 'In destruction is resurrection.' Because when that monastery lifts off from City Mount Hill, it will be programmed to fly directly into the surface of Hador."

"Into the surface of Hador?" Wellington interjected suddenly. "Nikolai Yanuarievich Ursis, what have you been smoking in that foul Zempa pipe of yours?"

Ursis grinned and turned in his seat. "Dora, my dear," he implored. "Listen for a moment. We have very little time to act. I believe it was you who once said that it would take a power source the magnitude of a solar flare to run those cannon. Well, when the monastery—and its G-seed—crashes into the photosphere of Hador, a solar flare is *precisely* what you will have. And, as the Gradygroats say, 'The path of power lies through truth.'"

"Great thundering Universe," Wellington exclaimed suddenly. "Of course. The energy from the flare will flow into the space forts through Power windows that *always* face Hador. . . . But then what? How will it get to the cannon?"

Ursis grinned. "The Gradygroat gunners will first remove the Truth cones from the floors of their chapels. This will in turn uncover the crystal lens in the floor that opens into the fort's disk structure. The flare's energy will actually be distributed by those *inner* cones—the ones whose use we could not fathom when we inspected the disk structures. They work in the same manner as the central cone in the monastery. Where *that* one reflected the G-seed's energy to specific 'star' locations in the ceiling, these are shaped to direct individual beams through the windows under each cannon—and finally into the angled breech fittings on the weapons themselves."

Wellington only shook her head. "Universe, Nik," she whispered. "I think you're right—you've *got* to be right. We've seen everything but the guidance system in the monastery with our very eyes. And, right now, I'm willing to take that on faith." Then she put a hand to her helmet. "But how do we get all those Truth cones removed from way out *here*?"

"That *is* a problem," Ursis asserted with a frown. "Captain," he said, swiveling toward Collingswood, "you've been listening. Where would *you* start? We must at least get the monastery off the ground before it is damaged beyond its ability to fly—or the G-seed is released and *by itself* destroys Atalanta."

"I've been trying to think of something while you talked," Collingswood answered. "The Gradygroats ordered everybody out of the monastery early in the attack, so there's no one *there* to help." She shook her head. "I suppose we might try Operations in Atalanta. Perhaps they could send someone up the hill. . . ." She called up the COMM center. "See if you can raise anybody in the OPS room back at the Fleet base."

Long cycles passed silently until a rating's voice reported that she had been unable to contact anyone. With the base under direct space attack, only immediate operational messages were getting through.

"Try again with a 'Captain's Priority Immediate,'" Collingswood suggested.

"Beggin' the Captain's pardon," the COMM room answered, "but that's the priority we had to use to get 'em to talk long enough so they'd turn us down."

"Pretty busy there, then, eh?" Collingswood asked.

"Aye, Captain. They sound *very* busy."

"Thank you, COMM," Collingswood said. "Any other ideas here on the bridge?"

After an interminable moment, Brim broke the silence. "How about that Intelligence unit on Atalanta that helped run the Payless operation? I'll bet they'd have someone to send."

"You're right," Collingswood said, nodding her head, "but I wouldn't have any idea how to get in touch with them. They always called *us*, if you remember." Then she paused. "Even if we *could* raise them," she continued after a few moments, "is there any reason to think that they would even *believe* us?"

"Borodov would believe us," Ursis interrupted quietly. "One finds it easy to forget that he is in the Intelligence Command, but he will also know how to contact the unit at Atalanta."

"Try it, Nik," Collingswood said tensely. "COMM room— see if you can get set up a scrambled two-way KA'PPA to Captain A.A. Borodov. Try the central research center in Avalon."

Only a few cycles passed until the COMM center announced, "We have him, Captain." Moments later, the characters BORODOV HERE. BEST REGARDS AND GLAD YOU ARE ALIVE, flashed across Brim's COMM console.

"You'd better explain it to him, Nik," Collingswood said.

"Aye, Captain," Ursis replied. "I am ready." He touched his console. "COMM center, please send the following: 'Regards from Collingswood, Wellington, Brim, and Ursis. Ursis sends presently. Situation follows:...'" With that, he summarized their discoveries concerning the Gradgroat-Norchelite monastery, its orbital forts, and Collingswood's inability to contact Atalanta. "'Can you put us in touch with anybody at the base who might help?'" he asked in conclusion.

Clearly, he had caught the older Bear flat-footed. Long moments passed before an answer passed across Brim's display. VOOF! Borodov began, then followed with a KA'PPA socket address. THESE PEOPLE WILL HELP, he concluded. DELAY TEN CYCLES BEFORE CONTACTING. I SHALL PERSONALLY TRANSMIT YOUR AUTHENTICATION.

The short interval passed like ten years. Then KA'PPA rings glimmered out from *Defiant*'s mast. Almost immediately, a reply flashed across Brim's display. REGARDS TO PAYLESS COLLEAGUES. ATALANTA UNDER EXTREME HEAVY ATTACK. DISPATCHING TWO TEAMS BY SEPARATE ROUTES TO MONASTERY WITH PORTABLE KA'PPAS. WILL CONTACT DEFIANT ON ARRIVAL. EXPECT HEAVY BOMBARDMENT WILL HAMPER SPEED. WHERE DO YOU BERSERKERS COME UP WITH ASSIGNMENTS LIKE THESE?

Collingswood smiled sympathetically. "COMM room," she

ordered, "you will please transmit the following: 'Idle fingers are the evil playthings of Voot—we have only your best interests at heart.'" Then she nodded. "Follow that with 'Good luck and Universe speed your steps, brave friends.'" Afterward, she looked around the bridge. "My colleagues," she said, "I believe we may just have a miracle on our hands."

# Chapter 10

# THE MIRACLE

Morning watch changed to Brightness watch and still no word arrived from either monastery team, although Atalanta's Intelligence Unit was in almost constant contact with *Defiant's* COMM room. Brim had long since turned the controls over to Aram and was relaxing at his console reading every message that came through. During that time, the savage battle for Haelic continued apace—and from eyewitness reports, it was now quite doubtful that the Imperials could hold out until Onrad arrived. Much of Atalanta city was already in flames and the Fleet Base was under almost constant attack. Antispace batteries ringing the area were making Anak's task as difficult as possible, but inexorably these fortified emplacements were being demolished one by one. When the Evening watch began and still neither team had been heard from, Collingswood appeared on the bridge. Brim watched her slump dejectedly into her console.

"Things look bad for the monastery teams," she said after a few moments. "Neither has called Joel for three metacycles now, and from the reports, I gather that many of the city streets are little more than long ravines of fire—although the Leaguers at least seem to be ignoring the monastery. Atalanta's latest bulletin describes the air as so full of smoke and dust that visibility is no more than a quarter of a c'lenyt." She shook her head. "The Center is sending two more teams out into that inferno, and I am of a mind to stop them. I realize that the issue is of historic importance, but risk is one thing—predestined suicide is quite another."

Brim nodded as he scanned the starscape for the ten millionth time that watch, then checked his proximity indicators. All clear. He was listening for Collingswood's decision when his COMM console suddenly came alive with KA'PPA text: TEAM B REPORTING FROM MAIN ENTRANCE G-N MONASTERY. NO ONE IN SIGHT. CAMPUS ABANDONED. REQUEST INSTRUCTIONS TO COMPLETE MISSION. REGRET DELAY. NECESSARY TO PROCEED ON FOOT—ALL APPROACH BRIDGES/ROADS DESTROYED. MANY OF TEAM B WOUNDED. TEAM A APPARENTLY WIPED OUT IN BOMBARDMENT LAST METACYCLE. MONASTERY ONLY SLIGHTLY DAMAGED. MEL SENDS.

"One of the teams got through," Collingswood uttered excitedly. "Nik, it's your show now."

Ursis dictated a string of instructions that described and located the gold cone, then recommended its removal by destruction of its base—in spite of the room's spectacular beauty. Incidental damage was of little consequence. He ended with a warning: "At all times," he admonished, "avoid personal contact with the high-energy beam from the ceiling. Also, the cone should be removed by remote control if possible. Consequences of these actions are unpredictable, but suggest you find solid cover at considerable distance from the main campus before accomplishing actual removal operations. May the Lady Fate look after you and your party, Mel. Ursis sends."

Within cycles, the team began a monologue of its progress: CONE LOCATED. USING M-87 BLAST PIKE WITH REMOTE TRIGGER FOR REMOVAL. LADY FATE NOWHERE ABOUT—TOO DANGEROUS DURING RAID. THANKS ANYWAY.... MEL.

"Yea gods," Wellington quipped nervously. "No wonder it took them so long to get there on foot; M-87s are big—and heavy."

"They *did* go prepared, though," Collingswood said in an awe-filled voice. She shook her head. "It must have been like walking through one long, continuous explosion."

M-87 IN PLACE WITH REMOTE FIRING UNIT. LEAVING NOW TO TAKE COVER. ANY FURTHER INSTRUCTIONS? MEL.

"No further instructions—from Ursis," the Bear dictated quietly.

The Defiants waited in silence for nearly three quarters of a metacycle before the next message arrived. From his brief experience during the bender raid—and the Carescrian attacks early in the war in which he'd lost his entire family—Brim could easily conjure the sort of vicious inferno Mel and his team had to endure: searing flame, radiation, and absolutely hellish concussion. He shook his head slowly in admiration. If he presumed they were merely office workers instead of trained soldiers, that somehow doubled—tripled—the heroic nature of their mission.

At last, a series of KA'PPA characters began to flow across his screen. TEAM B REPORTING FROM SHELTERED LOCATION APPROXIMATELY 1.5 C'LENYTS FROM MONASTERY. M-87 ACTIVATED APPROX. 4 CYCLES AGO—CONE REMOVAL DEFINITE. ENERGY BEAM APPEARS TO BE MELTING LARGE HOLE THROUGH CENTER OF FLOOR. NO VISIBLE RESULTS OUTSIDE YET. HAVE WE NEGLECTED SOMETHING? PLEASE ADVISE. MEL SENDS.

Brim froze. Had Ursis and Wellington guessed incorrectly?

"What's wrong?" Collingswood asked in a tense voice.

Ursis hesitated a moment, his head bent in thought. "Nothing—I suspect—has gone wrong, Captain," he said presently. "The monastery is a massive structure that will provide extraordinary inertia to overcome before it finally moves." He glanced at his message display. "We should see a different sort of message in a few . . . Aha!"

Brim glanced into his own display just as a new KA'PPA message flashed into being.

DISREGARD LAST MESSAGE CONCERNING G-N MONASTERY. NEW CIRCUMSTANCES APPLY: VAST CLOUDS OF SMOKE AND DEBRIS NOW RISING AROUND BASE.

"It begins," Ursis growled. "COMM room, please dictate to Mel: 'Request narration as long as possible—Ursis sends.'"

"Aye, Lieutenant," the COMM room answered. Moments later, the COMM panel began to display: RING OF FLAME ERUPTS AROUND BASE OF MONASTERY. DEEP ROLLING THUNDER IN AIR—CAN FEEL MORE THAN HEAR. WOW! MEL SENDS.

Ursis nodded. "That," he said, "is a predictable beginning. We should receive a wealth of information soon—if our friend Mel can send rapidly enough to describe it all."

Brim watched the monitor closely. As Ursis predicted, the next message came on the very heels of the first.

ENTIRE TOP OF MONASTERY CRAG GLOWS RED HOT LIKE CRUSTING LAVA. CAMPUS BURNS EVERYWHERE. TOWERING SMOKE AND FLAMES COVER MAIN BUILDING COMPLETELY. NOISE INCREDIBLE! SKY FILLED WITH CRAZED BIRDS, BLOWING LEAVES, AND DUST. OAK TREES SHAKE LIKE WILLOWS—MEL.

By now, everyone on the bridge had clearly tuned into the message socket, for the voice circuits quickly picked up with a murmur of voices and whispered exclamations.

"Lord—can you *imagine* that?"

"The *size* of that thing. Is it blowing up?"

"More like 'lifting off,' I think."

"Great Farkel's eyelash—who'd ever think the Gradygroats could . . ."

"*Silence!*" Collingswood rebuked, "all of you. This is a ship of war, not a theater."

"Aye, Captain."

"Aye, sorry."

"The messages from Mel continued to arrive at short intervals: MAJOR EARTHQUAKE BEGINS. CANNOT STAND UPRIGHT. BUILDINGS COLLAPSE WHILE LAVA FLOWS FROM HILLTOP CRAG LIKE CANDLE WAX. COLUMN OF SMOKE AND DEBRIS TOPS 10 THOUSAND IRALS. LEAGUER SHIPS INVESTIGATE, BUT KEEP PRUDENT DISTANCE. NOISE UNBEARABLE—MEL.

TOP OF CRAG JUST DETONATED. TREMENDOUS CONCUSSION. SUDDEN WAVE OF HEAT HITS WITH PHYSICAL FORCE. EARTHQUAKE AND INCREDIBLE NOISE CONTINUE. CONDITION OF MONASTERY UNKNOWN: MUST ASSUME TOTAL DESTRUCTION—MEL.

BELAY LAST MESSAGE E@TIRE MONASTERY RISING VERTICALLY THROUGH(&(&∧ SMOKE LIKE OLDD CHEMICAL ROCKET. LOW-FREQ. VIBRATION FROM EARTHQUAKE ∧∧%PREVENTS CONCE*NTRATION. NOISE TERRRRIBL. +++SHELTER CAVED IN—GONE. BATTLE SUIT MEEEELTING. HEAT IS . . .

"COMM Room," Collingswood complained tensely, "the last message was garbled—and we didn't get all of it."

"The last message was received in a garbled condition," COMM replied, "and the last characters received were: 'Heat is.' I'm afraid that's all there is."

"I see," Collingswood said over the now-quiet voice circuits. "Thank you, COMM. I was afraid of that."

Brim knew in his heart that it was the last communication from Mel. He checked his instruments idly, Aram continued at the helm. What next? Even while the KA'PPA dialogue had taken place, messages about Haelic's worsening situation continued to pour across another portion of his COMM display. He shook his head and brooded about Claudia in the middle of the perfect hell that Atalanta base must have become. *If* she were even alive still. Grinding his teeth in angry frustration, he absently glanced through the Hyperscreens into the vast starscape ahead. Would there even *be* an Atalanta when they arrived at Hador? And if there was, whose flag would it fly? While he ruminated despondently, a new message filled his COMM panel: ALL CONTACT LOST WITH TEAM B. ONE TEAM-A SURVIVOR LOCATED: MAY LIVE. MONASTERY LAUNCH APPARENTLY SUCCESSFUL IN ALL RESPECTS. LOCAL TRACKING STATIONS PREDICT IMPACT ON HADOR IN 3.5 METACYCLES. LEAGUERS AVOIDING IT. CAN WE BE OF FURTHER HELP? JOEL SENDS.

In spite of the sacrifice, Brim felt his spirits rise a little. Any chance against the Leaguers was better than none at all.

"Great *thundering* Universe," Wellington suddenly exclaimed through the muted uproar that had started up on the voice channel again. "Now that the thing really *is* on its way toward Hador, we've got to do something about contacting the Gradygroat *gunners*. They'll need to remove the cones in their orbital chapels *before* the flare begins. Otherwise . . ."

"I wonder if this Joel person at the Intelligence office might know," Collingswood speculated. "They're supposed to keep track of that sort of minutiae, aren't they?"

"Doesn't cost anything to ask," Wellington answered. "And I seriously doubt if their circuits are overloaded with intelligence-data requests right now."

"Nik, you'll be the one who explains it to the Gradygroats, if we get through," Collingswood asserted.

Ursis took a deep breath. "I think I am ready, Captain," he said stoically, "even for Gradygroat gunners."

"COMM," Collingswood ordered, "send this to the Intelligence people: 'Can you help us contact the Gradgroat--Norchelite orbital forts?'"

Only after considerable delay did an affirmative answer arrive. To Brim's surprise, he discovered that none of the orbital forts was equipped with KA'PPA gear—The Order no longer operated its own deep-space starships, so they communicated by ordinary LightSpeed radio link. Ultimately, the situation resulted in long and very cumbersome, two-legged communications. One leg—via KA'PPA—was between Collingswood and Joel in the Intelligence office. The other, between Joel and the Gradgroat-Norchelites, was via radio—and just setting it up required considerably more than a metacycle of careful haggling among Gradygroat Administrators. Barely two more remained before the monastery's impact when contact was finally made with the Chief Gunner of orbital fort number one.

At this point, a weary Nikolas Ursis took over again—demonstrating beyond a doubt why he had been so singularly successful as a professor at Zhiv'ot's Dityasburg Institute on Sodeskaya. When necessary, he could draw on an infinite supply of patience, and the Chief Friar required nearly a metacycle of delicate persuasion before he reluctantly agreed to "desecrate" the chapel of his fort. "Knowledge may have its limits," the Bear observed afterward, shaking his great furry head, "but not so with ignorance."

The second fort, however, was far easier to deal with. Fortunately, Ursis had the presence of mind to enlist the first Chief Friar when he began his talks with the next. In turn, these two helped convince the Chief Friar of fort number three. By the time Ursis and his four Chief Friars completed negotiations with fort number five, the Gradygroats decided —in the interests of a highly volatile time frame—to contact the remainder of the forts themselves. Following that, no more was heard from the Friars for nearly three-quarters of a metacycle—at least according to Brim's timepiece. By his own reckoning, he had personally watched every click and cycle that passed. Slowly....

At last, however, the critical message arrived—scant cycles before the monastery's calculated plunge into Hador: GRADYGROATS F-I-N-A-L-L-Y REPORT ALL ORBITAL FORTS READY TO FIRE WHEN POWER AVAILABLE. LITTLE WONDER THE XAXTDAMNED FOOLS FORGOT HOW TO WORK THEIR RIDICULOUS CANNON! JOEL SENDS.

At approximately Morning:3:50 on *Defiant*'s ninth day out from Atalanta, the colossal Gradgroat-Norchelite monastery —more than 1700 irals long with an estimated weight of three hundred ninety thousand millstons—impacted the star Hador at a velocity of nearly 0.46 LightSpeed. In the last nanoclicks of its existence, the whole prodigious energy charge of its Kaptnor G-seed was released in a single, monumental explosion. On the instant, a gigantic prominence of pure, glowing energy looped violently upward from the star's surface in a writhing fabric of crimson and yellow brilliance that extended merely half a million c'lenyts out into space—toward Haelic and its waiting orbital forts. The rolling waves of particles it released began to wash over the orbital forts a little more than a metacycle later, and at Brightness:0:26 the Norchelite space cannon spoke for the first time in nearly a millennium....

GREAT GODS OF PELLETIER! Joel reported in a long message from Atalanta, THE GRADYGROATS ARE FIRING EVEN AS I TRANSMIT. FLASHES BURN THROUGH THE PALL OF DRIFTING SMOKE LIKE GREAT WHITE FLARES. AMAZING! ONE HOPES THE CRAZY FRIARS DO SOME GOOD AFTER ALL THIS. BY THE BYE, A RESCUE PARTY HAS LOCATED TEAM A ABOUT 1.3 C'LENYTS FROM THE RUINED MONASTERY GROUNDS. ALL DEAD—JOEL SENDS.

Brim shook his head silently. With *Defiant* running on autohelm, his mind quickly reverted to thoughts of Claudia. Was she still alive? Dead? Worse—was she injured somewhere beyond the reach of rescuers? He shuddered, powerless to satisfy any of his anxieties—or forget them.

Not long afterward, reports began to arrive concerning an abrupt swing in the tide of battle. Even a near miss by one of the Gradygroat cannon was enough to severely cripple a battle ship—and after literal centuries perfecting their tactics, the Gradygroat gunners were superlative. Within a metacycle, the Leaguers found themselves falling back to regroup, and for the first time in two days, Brim began to receive bulletins describing Atalanta's skies as CLEAR OF ENEMY STARSHIPS.

During the next half-day, Kabul Anak sacrificed a major portion of his fleet in a vain attempt to overpower the Gradygroat forts. He ordered ship after ship—then squadron after squadron—against the deadly gunners and their prodigious space cannon. All forms of attack failed—even benders. The network of space forts was virtually impregnable. Attempts to saturate any single node invited instant devastation from at least three others—and the Leaguers had lost far too many of their powerful ships to even hope that they might saturate as many as four.

During the Evening watch—precisely at Evening:1:21—the van of Prince Onrad's onrushing Task Force 16 encountered the first of Anak's disorganized squadrons, disabling two battleships, *Posen* and *Ikat*, while destroying the last of Anak's light cruisers. By Evening:2:0, the two fleets were joined in pitched battle, but this time, Anak fought at considerable disadvantage. His starships had been in ceaseless mayhem for nearly three days while Onrad's were relatively fresh after their headlong—and unopposed—dash across space. Soon, reports began to arrive in *Defiant*'s COMM room regarding destruction of the League battleships *Parang*, *Padom-Ta*, and *Debusin*—all to the powerful disruptors of Erat Plutron's fast battleships. Then *Indang* fell to the superior firepower of Vice Admiral (the Hon.) Jacob Sturdee's old *Conqueror*. Kabul Anak found himself temporarily out of the battle when his great *Rengas* was crippled by three direct torpedo strikes in her steering units. He transferred his flag by destroyer to the smaller battleship *Mondor*, but his messages of command dwindled sharply after the incident—Collingswood guessed that the Leaguer Admiral was either gravely wounded or perhaps dead. Clearly, he was no longer in effective command, for the overall performance of the League Fleet rapidly deteriorated from that juncture.

The carnage continued through the Night watch with many more of the League's greatest ships destroyed or sufficiently damaged to put them out of action permanently. Then, toward morning, a second major change in the battle became apparent—as if the enemy ships had given up and were now maneuvering primarily for the purpose of safety. At the beginning of the Morning watch, every Leaguer ship suddenly—and simultaneously—broke off action and headed back at high speed across the galaxy toward Tarrott, each on a different trajectory. Before the victorious Imperials could regroup for a chase, Onrad wisely broadcast orders terminating all efforts to chase the fleeing Leaguers. OUR MISSION HAS BEEN ACCOMPLISHED BEYOND OUR WILDEST DREAMS, IMPERIALS, he Ka'PPAed. PAST THIS POINT, COURAGE BECOMES FOLLY. DO NOT PURSUE THESE LEAGUERS ANY FARTHER! . . .

The battle for Haelic was over.

Two mornings later, Hador had grown to a huge—still lopsided—ball off to starboard and Haelic's disk now filled *Defiant*'s forward Hyperscreens as Brim set up the ship for landing—a difficult task with as much drifting wreckage as presently fouled the orbits above the planet. It was no time to be careless with approach procedures.

For the last nine watches or so, the message channels had carried little else but congratulatory messages for Wellington and Ursis from all over the empire—including long, personal notes from Greyffin IV himself. It was clear that the two Blue Cape officers had become heroes of the day—perhaps the century—for their discoveries leading to activation of the Gradygroat space cannon.

Shortly after the cruiser slowed through approach velocity, a grinning Calhoun leaned over Brim's recliner. "We're aboot to pick up an escort soon, laddie," he said with a smile. "I thought I'd let you know so it wouldn't be so much of a surprise."

Brim arced an eyebrow.

Calhoun chuckled. "Wellington and Ursis have been elevated to the status of gods ahead on Haelic," he said. "The two of them *did* sort of save the Empire, when you get right down to it. At any rate, the Admiralty's thrown open a big part of the base at Atalanta to the public, and it sounds to me as if most of the city is already there waiting for *Defiant* to land—or more correctly, waiting for our two colleagues. So they've laid on an honor guard to escort us down. I think you'll see some interesting ships when they arrive." He clapped Brim on the shoulder and was off, back through the bridge toward the companionway.

Brim shrugged. What did all *that* mean? He queried Haelic's Planetary Center and got the weather report for Atalanta—marginal: a light breeze off the bay, smoke and haze to ten thousand feet, and limited visibility. Then, following check-in for a landing at the base, he had just started his descent to a synchronous marker buoy when Waldo suddenly reached across the consoles and touched his forearm.

"Wilf," she said, pointing through the Hyperscreens, "I think I've spotted our honor guard—*Universe*!"

Brim followed her finger, then made a rapid intake of air. Ahead and slightly to nadir—silhouetted in stark relief against the bright surface of the planet—were two pairs of stately capital ships, in perfect finger-four formation and on the same general bearing as *Defiant*. The mammoth vessels looked as if they were practicing for an old-fashioned Fleet review around Avalon. Brim's present rate of descent would soon carry him forward of the lead ship in the center formation.

"Fleet CL.921, here, Haelic Center," he said, "descending through approach level two two three zero at two nine zero zero velocity; heading zero one zero spinward. Present vector will intersect with four large warships that appear to be—" he squinted into the distance—"the four *Queens*," he reported a little breathlessly. "Please advise."

"Planetary Control here," a voice drawled in a strong Vogordion accent. "Maintain present flight parameters and contact *Queen Elidean*, on two one nine five five."

Frowning, Brim shrugged to Waldo—who shrugged back and scratched her head. "Maintaining present flight parameters. Will contact *Queen Elidean*, two one nine five five." He paused and brought the *Queen's* identifier to his display while the Chairman changed frequencies. "CL.921 to BB.119: descending through approach level two two one five at two nine zero zero velocity; heading zero one zero spinward. Have been adviced to maintain flight parameters that will intersect close ahead of your bow."

"CL.921," a soft female voice aboard *Queen Elidean* answered presently, "those orders are correct." As she spoke, the second pair of battleships moved abreast of the first two, forming a chevron with its center missing. "Admiral Plutron requests you bring *Defiant* into point position. We note that you have significant damage to your starboard underpan. Does that pose any particular problems?"

"BB.119," Brim responded, "all control systems appear to be intact—we have checked as closely as possible. No problems anticipated. Will appreciate notification if you see anything when we pass."

"CL.921: Will notify," the voice of the *Queen* promised. "When you are in position, continue normal landing procedures. The tower will vector you over the city, into a shallow turn to port around City Mount Hill, and then a long, straight-in final approach. We will follow."

"CL.921," Brim responded, "we thank you, *Queen*." Then he swung around in his seat to Calhoun, who had just seated himself at his console. "Voot's been busy again," he said, shaking his head.

"Bastard never sleeps." Calhoun chuckled, his face green with reflected light while he adjusted a display.

"You'd better get the people in their seats early," Brim warned. "We really *don't* know what she'll be like without E turret under the starboard belly pan."

"Good idea, laddie," the elder Carescrian agreed, taking his silver whistle from his breast pocket.

Scant cycles afterward—with alarms ringing in his ears—Brim sent *Defiant* charging between the two pairs of immense battleships: collections of massive armored casemates, fearful disruptors, stacked bridges, and lofty KA'PPA towers. "Half speed, all generators, Nik," he ordered, "it looks a little close from here."

"Half speed," Ursis acknowledged.

It was a ticklish time for Brim: too little speed and he'd make an utter fool of himself—the Fleet placed a high value on risk-taking. Too fast, however, and he ran the chance of collision—plus a ruinous court-martial. He grinned. If he could come alongside a transfer ship in a Carescrian ore barge at 0.87 LightSpeed—often during severe gravity disturbances in areas full of space holes—then he presently had little to worry about.

All four battleships had clearly been involved in *serious* action. Their disruptors were mottled from the the terrific heat of repeated firing, and extensive areas of radiation burn discolored their dented and patched hulls. *Ganriel* was minus her entire C turret while *Queen Elidean's* bridge had lost all its Hyperscreens. Nevertheless, the fierce-looking ships were clearly operational: every bit as dangerous as they looked. Brim felt his chest swell as he pulled into position and continued his original descent. *He* was part of their fleet, too—and proud of it.

As they drew near Atalanta, the atmosphere became charged with ragged layers of thick smoke and haze at many different levels—like some fantastic system of floating islands, Brim thought. By the time they reached approach altitude, Hador was lost in a thick overcast above, and the remaining Universe had turned to a uniform gray.

"Fleet CL.921," the tower commanded, "turn port around City Mount Hill to heading zero five three and reduce speed one nine zero."

"Fleet CL.921 turning City Mount to zero five three at one nine zero," Brim repeated. Behind him, the four massive battleships followed his gentle turn in perfect formation—completely unperturbed by any crosswinds. Bow on, they presented squared-off silhouettes with pairs of super-firing turrets centered on each of four surfaces and the top deck surmounted by a frowning bridge and KA'PPA tower.

Below on the ground, damage to Atalanta begged description. The great Norchelite crag atop City Mount Hill was now a shallow crater lined with obsidian glass that had dribbled and crystalized along the outside like an overfilled bowl. Brim shook his head sadly as the Gradgroat-Norchelite words echoed in his mind: "In destruction is resurrection . . ." Resurrection from this kind of destruction was going to take a long, *long* time.

Downhill from this area of total destruction, the once-beautiful city was now a patchwork of burned-out, cratered deserts amid portions that appeared to be relatively untouched—although Brim was hard-pressed to locate any section of town that had been spared at least some devastation. Great fires still burned in many places, sending towering columns of sooty smoke into the sky. He shuddered. The landscape was literally strewn with wrecks. One monstrous hulk—probably a battleship from the size of its burned-out skeleton—had crashed into a neighborhood of large estates taking at least a thousand dwellings in its final detonation. Another starship—this one clearly a Gorn-Hoff cruiser—perched almost vertically in the center of the city's huge J.C. West Memorial Coliseum. Still another had attempted a crash landing along a wide avenue, replacing the pavement by a deep trench that continued nearly a c'lenyt to a huge depression ringed by an area in which no one stone appeared to remain upon another. He took a deep breath and tried to purge Claudia's lovely face from his mind's eye. How *anyone* could have survived such a searing, radiating holocaust . . .

At last on her assigned heading of one two five, *Defiant* started out over the austral end of the base toward the bay. Destruction appeared to be even worse here—if that was possible. The great seawall had been breached in a dozen places, and much of the gravity-pool area lay beneath the waters of the bay. Masts and half-submerged hulls rose from the shallows like beached sea monsters from some child's story, although the flooding had at least extinguished the tremendous fires that must have started from the wrecked ships.

"Fleet CL.921 is five c'lenyts from the outer marker," the tower reported. "Turn port heading zero zero five—localizer is at or above one thousand five hundred; you are cleared for landing vector three seven one."

"CL.921 turning zero zero five to localizer at fifteen hundred, cleared for vector three seven one—thank you, ma'am," Brim answered. The battleships were keeping formation behind him as if they were attached to *Defiant*'s stern by cables.

Little more than a cycle later, Waldo reported capture of the localizer and glideslope beams. Then Brim began his final letdown. Far ahead and to port, two long piers jutted out into the bay from the mouth of the Grand Canal. He frowned. He didn't remember anything like those when he'd taken off—and they certainly hadn't been constructed during the battle! He squinted as he peered into the distance—they were two lines of *starships*! Then, he was at the outer marker beacon, and there was little time to consider anything but the helm until *Defiant* was down and taxiing on her gravity gradient.

"CL.921: use port taxiway channel three one and proceed directly to escort at Grand Canal entrance," the tower instructed.

Another escort? Clearly, Brim considered, this was serious business! "CL.921 to port three one and Grand canal escort," he repeated, swiveling in his recliner to check the battleships —they had stopped.

Behind him, Collingswood ordered Wellington and Ursis to the main hatch. "You may want to freshen up a bit on the way," she cautioned. "I think you are both in for a hero's welcome you won't soon forget."

"Go to it, Dora," Brim whispered as Wellington slipped out of her recliner.

"I think I'd rather face Triannic's whole fleet," the weapons expert replied with a grimace, "except I guess there's not much of it left, now, is there?"

Brim kissed his clustered fingertips when Ursis glanced his way.

The Bear raised his eyes to the heavens. As a rule, he avoided large gatherings—and from the descriptions of the one waiting to start in Atalanta, "large" was not an adequate term.

Brim turned off the landing vector between two orange buoys painted with the numerals "31," then lined up on a progression of similar markers that extended...He could scarcely believe his eyes. Channel 31 led directly into the mouth of the base's main canal, between the two long lines of starships he had seen from the air—all visibly survivors of the battle for Hador-Haelic.

As *Defiant* passed with her great banner snapping in the wind, the decks of each warship were packed with wildly cheering Blue Capes—many of whom were clearly wounded.

Brim had never seen such a collection in his life. Destroyers, cruisers, battlecruisers, battleships—every fighting vessel that had managed to return from the conflict. Many were grievously damaged—missing whole turrets and sections of their superstructures. Others seemed hardly touched by the battle except for their mottled disruptors. But no matter how grim the damage, their crews were on deck to cheer for Wellington and Ursis—and some to weep.

When they came to the mouth of the canal, the ancient stone seawalls on both sides were similarly crowded by literally thousands of civilians who cheered and waved wildly when the cruiser passed. Many ended up falling into the water. Brim found himself wondering about Claudia for the millionth time that morning while docking parties wearing huge protective mittens spread out over *Defiant*'s decks uncovering optical cleats and opening hatches where additional mooring gear was stowed. He'd soon know if his beautiful Atalantian friend had survived the battle for her beloved city —or if she had *not*. . . .

*Defiant*'s assigned gravity pool was in a special compound adjacent to the headquarters complex. He'd suspected they'd use it when he first saw the waiting throngs. Otherwise, Wellington and Ursis faced the eminently real peril of being trampled by the very people who had come to cheer them. While he eased the cruiser through a set of canal gates and onto the pool, he could see a great expanse of faces and waving arms outside the compound's stout fence. He scanned the nearer crowd of dignitaries—all holding their ears against the noise —as he braked the starship to a final halt in a cloud of dust and blowing soot. No sign of Claudia. But then, she *wasn't* all that tall, he remembered—she'd easily been swallowed by the crowd when he'd met her train. "Finished with generators," he called to Gamble at the systems console.

"Aye, Lieutenant Brim," Gamble answered, "finished with generators." He passed his hands over a sequence of tiny colored lights on his overhead panel and the rumble of the generators immediately abated—to the clear relief of the welcoming committee. As a brow extended from the lip of the pool to connect with *Defiant*'s main hatch, the throng pushed immediately to the entrance—except for the diminutive figure of a woman with long, brown hair who remained in place and continued to wave toward the bridge.

Brim's spirit soared like a rocket. Claudia! And not a single bandage. He waved back through the Hyperscreens, and she blew him a kiss. He felt his heart thumping in his chest as the wind lifted her skirts. Universe! She was beautiful even at a distance. Then the changeover from local gravity—and his extreme nausea—brought him back to reality as if he'd been smacked by a brick.

In due time, he watched Wellington and Ursis make their way across the brow while he powered off *Defiant*'s flight systems. The two Blue Capes were met at the landward end by Prince Onrad, Lord Beorn Wyrood, a still-limping Admiral Penda, and whole collections of officers whose least rank still read "Admiral." Then, while the high-echelon assemblage crowded into a veritable parade of limousine skimmers, he secured his helm and prepared to exit the bridge. Before he could leave his console, however, Claudia was at his side with a concerned look on her face.

After they shared a long kiss, she drew back for a moment and looked him directly in the eye. "Someone in the base infirmary was calling your name when they brought her in," she said, "the lone survivor of the monastery teams. She's one brave lady, Wilf."

"Calling *my* name?"

"Are there other Wilf Brims around here?" Claudia asked with a little laugh. "I certainly haven't met them."

Brim frowned. "Must be somebody I met during Payless," he conjectured. "I don't know many people in the Intelligence office here."

Claudia smiled gently. "Her name's LaKarn, Wilf—*Princess* Margot Effer'wyck-LaKarn. I don't think she wants anybody to know who she really is, but I recognized her face as soon as they cleaned her up. Her wedding was broadcast not so long ago." She tilted her head slightly and smiled a little sadly. "I have the feeling that maybe you two were, shall we say, 'good friends' at one time." She closed her eyes for a moment. "She's beautiful, Wilf," she said. "No wonder you . . ."

Wilf took her hands—somehow it all made a sort of preposterous sense. "Can you take me to her?" he asked.

"That's why I'm here," Claudia said, placing a kiss on his cheek. "What are friends for, after all?"

Inside the crowded infirmary, Claudia led Brim through a maze of antiseptic-drenched halls to a rare private room in a small wing. She stopped at the door and took his arm. "You won't need me in there," she said.

Brim looked into her eyes for a long moment. "How can I thank you?" he asked.

Claudia smiled with her eyes. "I'll find a way," she said quietly. Then she kissed him and started down the corridor. "We'll talk about it sooner than you think," she called over her shoulder. Then she was gone.

Brim took a deep breath of too-clean air and walked hesitantly into the tiny room. The healing machine's hatch was open and . . . his heart suddenly pounded all out of control. There could be no mistaking that gorgeous face—even though much of her lovely body was shrouded by the healing machine's amoebalike apparatus and her hair was covered by a softly glowing cloth.

As he stood over the open hatch, her eyes opened and blinked sleepily. "Wilf . . ." she whispered as her face broke into a smile.

"What in the name of Voot are you doing *here*?" he asked, reaching gently into the machine to touch her cheek. "I thought you were back on Avalon. . . ."

She hesitated a moment as if testing her capacity to speak. "I had to share this time of danger with you, Wilf," she whispered. "Otherwise, I could never look you in the eye."

Half blinded by tears, Brim leaned into the chamber and they kissed—for a long, *long* time. . . .

"But who brought you here?" he asked when his heart returned to something approximating normal.

Margot's eyes twinkled for a moment, and she giggled weakly. "Cousin Onrad smuggled me here on *Resolve*," she explained. "He needed a bit of persuasion, of course—but under all that bluster, he's rather a darling pussycat. And it wasn't as if I couldn't find plenty to do when I arrived."

Brim shook his head. "Like trying to launch a monastery," he said with a feeling of awe, "in the middle of the most devastating bombardment ever—anywhere."

She smiled and frowned. "I suppose it *was* sort of a chancy thing to do," she said quietly, gazing around at the edges of the healing machine. "But then, I didn't make it anyway. . . ."

"Success is no measure of heroism," Brim quoted from a nearly forgotten textbook.

She smiled. "If it makes me a hero to you, I shall be well satisfied, Wilf. Otherwise, no one must know I have even been here."

"B-but . . ."

Margot giggled again. "Greyffin and Rogan both think I am home—in Effer—'indisposed,'" she said with a grin. "Won't they have a fit when they learn I'm *not* preggers."

"That's what you told them?"

"Best excuse I could think of," Margot declared with a little blush. "Lately, Rogan's been doing everything he can to produce that heir Greyffin wants so badly."

"I, ah, see . . ." Brim said. All of a sudden, it was a lot easier to think about Claudia. "Why didn't you get in touch with me?" he asked.

"Well," she said, looking up into his eyes, "after you sent my ring back, I didn't really know if you'd talk to me. And you hadn't answered your mail since the party. . . ."

Brim thought for a moment—took a deep breath—and then related his conversation with LaKarn beside the gravity pool. "Rogan claimed he could love you," he said in conclusion. "And after what I put you through that night, it just seemed to be the best thing I could do for your life."

Margot smiled and shook her head sadly. "I am far too much in love with *you*, Wilf," she said, "for that to make any sense. And I can't hide it from Rogan, try as I might. He quickly tired of the game and went back to his other loves. It's better all the way around. . . ." Then she peered into his face and frowned. "You *do* still love me, don't you?" she asked.

"I never stopped loving you," Brim answered, "not for one moment."

Margot closed her eyes for a moment, then whispered quietly, "'Life might change, but it may fly not; / Hope might vanish, but can die not; / Truth be veiled, but still it burneth; / Love repulsed—but it returneth!'"

After that, they simply gazed into each other's eyes.

Eventually, a medical officer entered the room, nodded absently, then studied the readouts at the foot of Margot's machine. The small, heavyset woman—a Captain—had a round face, a button nose, and thin, serious lips. She was clearly suffering from considerable fatigue, but she was smartly dressed in a a fresh uniform with shined boots. A professional if Brim had ever seen one. When she peered into the healing machine she seemed to brighten. "You are much improved this watch, Your Highness," she said, "and you look it." She laughed grimly. "For a while there, you had us worried." Then she looked up. "I assume you are Wilf Brim, Lieutenant?"

"A-aye, Captain," Brim stammered in surprise.

"Prince Onrad left orders to expect you—he said you would know the Princess's true identity. Evidently, he spoke to a friend of yours from the base here. I think he said her name was 'Claudia'. . . ."

"I wouldn't be surprised," Brim asserted—nothing else seemed appropriate.

"Well," the medical officer continued, "at this juncture, it appears that the Princess will probably recover completely— after *a great deal of rest*." She pronounced the last few words looking emphatically down into Margot's face. "Prince Onrad has ordered her aboard *Resolve* within the next metacycle for the journey to Avalon," she continued to Brim. Then she smiled. "He said that I should expect you to accompany her to the ship's sick bay."

Brim nodded. "Probably that would be easier than trying to talk me out of it, Captain," he said.

Aboard *Resolve*, Brim found a message from Collingswood, summoning him to her cabin, ". . . when you get back to *Defiant*." He chuckled ironically to himself. *Everyone* seemed to know where he was.

Later, the irony returned to haunt him when his conversation with Margot was once more interrupted—this time by a *much* too familiar voice.

"Thought I might find you here, Brim," LaKarn snorted irritably from the doorway, "with my wayward wife." He strode to the opposite side of the healing machine and glared inside. "*Indisposed*, eh, my blond beauty?" he demanded sarcastically. "Well, you may not be pregnant, but you've certainly got yourself indisposed this time—and you damn well deserve it!" He glared over at Brim. "Had you even the *hint* of a brain, Carescrian, you'd understand how xaxtdamned lucky you were that you *didn't* get to marry this one. She is magnificent in bed, as you well know," he grumbled, "but I think she has a secret death wish." He peered angrily back into the chamber. "It's that damned Onrad who brought you here. You've got the man wrapped around your little finger. The meddling *hab'thall*." He spit angrily into her face.

At that, Brim lost control. "For Voot's sake, LaKarn," he said, blindly starting around the end of the chamber, "let her alone. Can't you see what kind of shape she's in?" He grabbed the Baron by his lapels and shook him like a terrier with a rat. "You quivering gratz hen," he thundered to his suddenly—and thoroughly—terrified rival, "if you weren't her husband, I'd cave in your ugly face!"

At that moment, he felt a strong hand on his shoulder. Reflexively, he smashed LaKarn against the wall, then instantly whirled at his new opponent from a crouch—only stopping himself from further mayhem when he saw who it was. "Your Highness," he gasped, looking up into the face of Prince Onrad.

"Let me take care of this, Wilf," the prince growled calmly, shutting the door and striding to where LaKarn slumped against the wall, face crimson with fright and anger. "All right, Baron," he said, "if you have something to say about me, then say it to my face."

Instantly, LaKarn lashed out at Onrad with a stream of invective so foul that it would do justice to a Varnadoan goal. Onrad parried with the words of a gentleman, and soon the two nobles were so completely absorbed that Margot and Brim were nearly forgotten. And, to the latter's astonishment, it rapidly became clear that LaKarn was *not* a strong ally of the Empire by any means. In fact, if anything, it sounded as if the whole Torond officer class might be sympathetic to the cause of Nergol Triannic—against the wishes of their elderly Grand Duchess Honorotha, LaKarn's mother. After a few heated cycles, Onrad suddenly turned from his assailant to frown at Brim and then at the healing machine. He pursed his lips. "You two have more important things to do than listen to this drivel," he said. With that, he opened the door and glared at LaKarn. "Come on, black shirt," he growled, "we can continue this elsewhere."

Wrapping the ebony cloak around him, LaKarn stormed past Brim and stopped at the healing machine. "We shall continue this another time, my beauty," he growled, "have no fear about that." Abruptly he laughed. "Pity you'll have to keep those gorgeous legs together for your friend Brim this time," he added, "because once I get you home, *I* shall keep them spread until you produce." He looked triumphantly at Brim. "And *you*, Carescrian, can dream about that—every lonely night!" With those words, he strode through the door with Onrad close on his heels.

Suddenly, the only sounds in the room were the quiet burbling hum of Margot's healing machine and the all-pervading rumble of the battleship's generators. Brim looked tenderly into Margot's tear-streaked face. "Can you leave him?" he asked.

"No," she answered. "Before any of my own wishes or my happiness comes my duty to the Empire—this marriage keeps Rogan and his resources on Greyffin's side. Otherwise—well, I think you got the gist of their argument."

Brim nodded, fighting back tears of emotion. Perhaps, he thought for a moment, this was really why he loved her so deeply. "We'll work it out," he said presently. Somehow, he would make that happen. . . .

"This Claudia the doctor mentioned," Margot began with a little smile. "During my delirium, I remember vivid flashes of a most exquisite woman with long brown hair. Does that sound like her?"

"Yes," Brim answered softly. "A lot like her."

"Come closer," Margot said.

He bent into the healing machine until his face nearly touched hers.

"Is she good in bed, Wilf?" Margot whispered.

Brim swallowed, "Yes," he answered softly. "She is."

Margot closed her eyes. "Thank the Universe," she breathed. "Then our love may yet survive."

Suddenly, alarms rang in the corridor. "All hands to stations for liftoff! All hand to stations for liftoff! . . ." A knock on the door produced a voice. "Lieutenant Brim, time to go. Prince Onrad has laid on a staff skimmer for your use outside the main brow."

"Thanks," Brim called without opening it. Then he thrust his head inside the healing machine again, this time to share a long good-bye kiss. When they finished, both were a little breathless.

"Would you like my ring back?" she asked as he continued to cradle her cheek in his hand.

"I would gladly *kill* for that ring," he swore in surprise.

"You'll find it in the compartment at the head of the machine," Margot said, pointing with her eyes. "The medic said it was the only thing I had with me that didn't burn."

Brim shuddered while he reached into the little personal-effects compartment. Its only contents were a small, charred box. Inside were the ring and the carbonized remains of her handkerchief. "I shall never part with these again—so long as I live," he promised, fighting back tears that suddenly welled up in his eyes. Then the five-cycle alarm clattered outside the door. He pressed his lips to hers one more time, then ran for the battleship's main hatch.

He just made it.

Mighty thunder from *Resolve*'s departure still echoed through the heavens when Brim stepped from the staff skimmer at *Defiant*'s gravity pool. He immediately hurried to Collingswood's cabin and knocked.

"Come in and take a seat for a moment," Collingswood called over the music wafting through her half-open door.

When Brim entered, she was at a work station in her usual place. This time, however, the oak desk was nearly bare, and she was dressed in her formal uniform. Moreover, as he took his seat, he noticed that the cabin was completely upset, with lockers empty and shelves bare. Off to one side of the room, Grimsby was busily packing space trunks.

Looking up from his work, the elderly steward winked at Brim, smiled mysteriously, then shuffled out of the cabin and closed the door.

With growing concern, Brim waited for Collingswood to speak. Suddenly, his eye caught a new *captain's* insignia on the left collar of her tunic. He grinned. "Congratulations, Captain, er . . . *Captain*," he stammered happily. "Looks like Grimsby's packing you for a celebration leave."

Collingswood looked up from her work station and smiled tiredly. "Thank you, Wilf," she said with a wistful look, "but I'm afraid it's not leave I'm packing for."

Brim frowned and started to speak, but Collingswood held up her hand. "A moment, Wilf," she said. "I shall go into all that soon enough. First, let me talk about you." With that, she handed him a small box she had placed on the corner of her desk. "Congratulations yourself, *First Lieutenant* Brim," she said as he gingerly lifted the lid. Inside was a set of insignia. "Unfortunately, they're brand new," she said. "I've given all my old ones away through the years. But this time at least, I get to make the presentation myself instead of KA'PPAing someone else to do it for me, as I was forced to do for your last promotion." She reached across the desk to shake his hand.

Brim was nearly speechless. "T-thank you, Captain," he stuttered. I'm honored."

"It's not the only news I have for you, I'm afraid," she said, resuming her perch at the work station.

Brim braced himself—somehow, he had a feeling he'd already used up the month's good-news quota. While he watched, vivid colors began to cascade over her screen, then stopped. She frowned for a moment, nodded, then slowly and deliberately removed her glasses and cleaned them with a lacy handkerchief. "I suppose I also ought to let you know," she said at length, "that you are being pushed out of the nest, so to speak."

Brim frowned and raised an eyebrow. "Captain?"

Collingswood lowered her head and pinched the bridge of her nose. "It was a difficult decision for me, Wilf," she said, "but I could no longer in good conscience keep you under my thumb. You are therefore to report in the capacity of First

Lieutenant to I.F.S. *Thunderbolt*, just completing a major re-work at Gimmas Haefdon. You'll do well with her captain, Vern Engerstrom," she said, "and it's clear that you're ready for that sort of job—Number One."

Number One! Brim felt his heart begin to pound—for the thousandth time that day, it seemed. "But Captain . . ." he protested.

"No 'buts,' Wilf," Collingswood said firmly. "You've served *Defiant* well—and everyone concerned with her—but you can't be only a Helmsman all your life. You need to move on now and continue to grow. You leave for Gimmas tomorrow afternoon on S.S. *Kersearge*—while I embark next week for Avalon. You see, Wilf, *I* have a new job too—in the Admiralty."

Brim shook his head in utter shock. "B-but who can possibly take your place running *Defiant*?" he asked.

"The first Carescrian Captain in His Majesty's most Imperial Fleet, that's who," Collingswood answered with a smile. "A friend of yours named Calhoun—I thought you might approve. And he'll have Aram to help him out."

Brim grinned. "I approve," he said quietly.

With glistening eyes, Collingswood got to her feet and moved from behind the desk with her arms open. "I shall miss you, Wilf," she said hugging him tightly. Then, abruptly, she glanced at her timepiece and dismissed him with military brusqueness. "That will be all, Lieutenant," she said crisply. "Your orders are in your message folder."

He bowed. "Thank you, Captain," he said, then turned and made for the door.

"Do well," Collingswood called after him. "Our paths will cross often, so I shall check on your progress with some frequency."

"Aye, Captain," Brim promised, still a little in shock, "I shall do my best."

On his way along the companionway, he met Admiral Plutron headed in the opposite direction. "Good evening, Admiral," he said. Plutron had put on a few pounds since their last encounter long ago on Gimmas Haefdon.

"Good evening, Lieutenant Brim," the gray-haired officer answered. "My congratulations on your promotion."

"Thank you, Admiral," Brim said as they passed, carefully smothering the smile that threatened to form on his face. Old Plutron was carrying two large bottles of Logish Meem. Clearly, he was heading for Collingswood's cabin and the demonstration she promised him days ago in space. . . .

Sounds of reveling Bears drifted up from the wardroom on the next deck below as Brim reached his own cabin: ". . . To ice, to snow, to S-o-d-e-s-k-a-y-a we go! To ice, to snow, to S-o-d-e-s-k-a-y-a we go! . . ."

He grinned in anticipation. He planned to join that party as soon as he could freshen up—he had a great deal to celebrate himself. . . . He was rinsing his face when he heard a polite knock. Grabbing a towel, he opened the door. It was Barbousse.

"Congratulations, Lieutenant Brim," the big rating blurted out, hat in his hand. "I . . . um . . . heard about your new ship, Lieutenant," he said. "I want you to know that I already tried to get a transfer to her, but this time, they turned me down flat."

"Come in," Brim said, opening the door wider. "Sit down and tell me about it."

"Oh, I can't stay, Lieutenant," Barbousse said, handing Brim a small blue envelope. "I just dropped by to give you this message. But I wanted to make sure you knew that I *tried* to be with you on that new ship of yours."

"I'm honored that you even thought about it," Brim said. "But why do you suppose they turned you down?"

Barbousse shrugged. "Well, sir, Captain Collingswood's got me signed up for this new officers' school, an' I can't seem to get out of it."

"Officers' school?" Brim asked with excitement. "That's *wonderful*! Which one?"

"The Helmsman's Academy," Barbousse said, his face reddening. "I don't suppose I'll ever be a Wilf Brim or anything, but I'd sure be proud to serve in the right seat with you someday, Lieutenant."

Brim shook his head—nearly speechless with emotion. Then he put both hands on the man's broad shoulders. "You'll be a *great* helmsman, Utrillo," he said. "And I shall be proud to serve with you—*always*!"

Before Barbousse took his leave, he pointed to the blue envelope. "I suppose you'll want to be readin' that soon as you can," he suggested, "beggin the Lieutenant's pardon. Um . . . it's from Miss Valemont. She left it with me about half a metacycle ago."

Eagerly, Brim tore open the light plastic envelope and extracted a letter in beautifully inked, old-fashioned script:

> My windows here are all boarded up, friend— but the kitchen is still intact, and a victory celebration supper is on the stove. I shall fetch you at the start of the Evening watch, First Lieutenant Wilf Ansor Brim. —regrets only, Claudia.

A metacycle later, Brim watched the lights of a battered little skimmer bear down the road toward the end of the brow. He'd made his apologies to the Bears in the wardroom, and they appeared to understand. Some opportunities were simply too good to miss!

He shrugged. If his previous assignment to a T-class destroyer were any indication, this was likely to be the last peaceful evening he would spend for quite a long time— especially with the challenges he knew he would face as First Lieutenant. He smiled while he shifted the bottles of Logish Meem under his arm. Nobody he might encounter on the frozen planet of Gimmas Haefdon was likely to be *anything* like Claudia Valemont—and he meant to make the most of this last evening with her. For a while. . . .